THE ARBELLA STUART CONSPIRACY

The Marquess House Trilogy
Book Three

Alexandra Walsh

SAPERE
BOOKS

THE ARBELLA STUART CONSPIRACY

Published by Sapere Books.

20 Windermere Drive, Leeds, England, LS17 7UZ,
United Kingdom

saperebooks.com

ISBN: 978-1-913335-85-4

To Kathryn, my almost-twin sister
Love you

PROLOGUE: THE BETHLEM ROYAL HOSPITAL, LONDON, SEPTEMBER 1660

"What have you done to her?"

A shaft of light had illuminated the miserable space as the door was flung open. The single occupant of the cell huddled further against the corner, burrowing deeper into the mean bed of damp, stinking straw, trying to hide in the inadequate camouflage. The greying mess was the only relief in the stone room where the grimy water dripped ceaselessly down the walls, making them slick and icy to the touch. Rats skittered away from the sudden invasion of light and noise, disappearing through gaps in the stones, swallowed into the welcoming darkness.

"And you claim this is one of your better cells?" came the man's voice; cold, derisive, ringing with distaste. "We will discuss this place once my business here has been concluded," he promised. "These people are not animals; they deserve better than the rancid treatment you claim will cure them."

The long shadows of several men flickered in the doorway and the voice of the Warden spoke, his tone nervous. "Is it wise to approach the prisoner — my apologies — the patient?" he asked. "What if you are attacked?"

A mirthless laugh bounced off the stone walls. "It is unlikely any of your so-called patients would have the energy or the strength to attack me, not on the vile grey sludge you feed them," he retorted. "Now, leave us, we have business to complete."

A cold shudder of fear ran down the spine of the woman in the straw. From the moment she had heard his voice, she was unsure whether to feel relief or fear. Had he come to help, or do her harm? Lifting a filthy hand with broken nails and festering sores, she afforded herself a wry smile, aware she presented a vastly different picture from the last time they had been together, dancing in the flickering candlelight of the majestic ballroom.

She heard a gentle thud, a different noise from the usual clangs, and there was no grinding of the key in the lock. A moment later, he was crouching in front of her, his breath warm on her cheek, smelling, as it always did, of cloves and cinnamon. His cologne was sharp, cutting through the stench of her own wasted, ailing body, and his touch, when it came, was gentle.

"My dear," he whispered, "are you able to open your eyes? We must take you home."

"Home? I have no home," she croaked, her voice parched and rusty through lack of use. "You took it."

"You will come to my home, as my guest, and when you are well, I will return you to yours."

Even in her sorry state, she knew this man never did anything without an ulterior motive and she wondered what he would require in payment for saving her from this living hell. "Homes come at a high price," she whispered.

"Everything has a cost," he agreed, "but I will ask nothing of you until you are well, and if you are never recovered enough, then it will be my honour to ensure you are cared for and live in comfort for the rest of your life."

"And how long will that be if I refuse your command?" she asked.

"Your life will, I hope, be long and happy."

"I am old," she replied. "My years are few and this place has shortened them further."

He held her gaze for a moment, before clapping his hands. The door opened, this time to admit three women. The woman in the straw cowered; her instinct was to hide after the months of cruelty that had been inflicted upon her by both the male and female gaolers. Yet when her eyes ran over these women in their well-made dresses of starched cotton, she realised they were strangers.

"Fill this," ordered the man, pointing to the bronze, free-standing bathtub that had materialised in the cell while she had kept her eyes shut.

He walked across the room and made himself comfortable on the padded chair that had also been carried into the cell. "A screen will be brought in to spare your modesty," he continued, "then these especially selected ladies, who will now form part of your staff, will wash and dress you. After this, we will return home, where you will see my physician."

Finally understanding that her ordeal in Bethlem Royal Hospital was over, the woman rose. Many entered this place, known as Bedlam, the notorious and terrifying home for the mentally afflicted, but few left alive. "What do you want of me?" she said, her voice sounding more like her own.

"Nothing," he responded, his tone slippery with insincerity.

"You've never been able to lie to me," she replied. "My body may be frail, but my mind is as sharp as ever. There is a task you need me to perform. I would rather be prepared."

"Prepared for what? Refusal?"

"No," she said, and was pleased to see relief in his eyes. "You are removing me from this vile situation and for that I am grateful, but I need to know why."

"You are to do something which no one else in my realm is capable of."

This was not the reply she had expected and, despite herself, she was intrigued "And what is that?"

"Write."

Her laughter was bitter. "There are many writers in your realm," she said. "Why do you need me?"

"Because I trust you," he said, and for once his words were sincere.

"And you do not trust your many players, playwrights and poets?"

"Not as I trust you."

"What if I refuse?" she asked.

The man threw back his head and laughed. "You won't refuse. You will, of course, be able to decide who will work with you."

"Work with me? Is this task so huge I'll need assistance?"

"I suggest you choose three trustworthy helpers, who will be sworn to secrecy —"

"Before they are murdered when the task is complete," she interrupted. "Don't play me for a fool."

The women returned, carrying steaming pitchers, jug after jug until the linen-lined bath was brimming with fragrant water. Screens were erected and one of the women, a slim blonde with clear green eyes, stripped the tattered dress from the woman's body, handing it to a maid to dispose of, before helping her into the water.

A sigh of happiness escaped the woman's lips as she sank into the water, the filth on her skin beginning to dissolve.

For the next half hour, as she was scrubbed clean, deloused, and dried in crisp linen sheets, she contemplated the strange offer. An outright refusal would earn her a place in a gaol cell again, of this she was in no doubt, and the thought terrified her. She had been lucky to survive this incarceration; another would kill her. This man was ruthless; he might persuade the court he espoused liberal beliefs but when he wanted something, there were no lows to which he would not stoop.

As she was helped from the cooling bath and laced into a simple dark green dress, a plan began to form in her mind. It was not ideal, she knew, but it was better than the alternative of remaining here. Matching shoes were slipped on her stocking feet and her damp hair was wound into a neat style under a simple cap.

"You're ready, madam," said the woman with green eyes.

"Thank you," she replied. "What is your name?"

"It's Anna, my lady."

"You will travel with me, Anna," she said and, taking the woman's hand, led her around the screen.

"You are returned to us, my dear," he said, but his smile did not warm his eyes.

"I accept."

"You do?"

If this man thought he could play games with her, then she would let him believe so, but she knew secrets he did not. A wicked smile flashed across her face as she pondered all the ways she would be able to make him pay. "Because you will pay," she muttered in her mind like a curse, "and you will pay for years and years to come."

With a flourish, he stood, offering her his arm as though they were intending to traverse the pleasure gardens at Hampton Court Palace.

She placed her hand on his and allowed him to lead her from the stinking cell.

PART ONE: MARQUESS HOUSE, 2019

CHAPTER ONE

"Watch out!" shouted Dr Perdita Rivers. A sickening shriek filled the air as the wall above her began to crumble; bricks sheered away from the ceiling, cascading past her in a rush of dust and dirt. Perdita dived out of the way, waiting for the fall to be over. As the tumult ebbed, an uneasy silence emerged and Perdita shook the debris from her long dark hair before calling out, "Is everyone all right?"

Piper Davidson, her twin sister, emerged from the cloud of dust and debris, followed by two more dusty figures.

"Way to go, Perds!" exclaimed Kit Mackensie, the taller of the two. "It's answered your question: is there more basement behind the false wall? Yes, there is!"

"I didn't expect it to collapse when I pushed it though…" Perdita laughed.

"It isn't a supporting wall, is it?" interrupted Piper, a hint of concern in her voice.

"No, it can't be, it doesn't line up with any of the others," interjected Callum Black, the fourth grime-covered shape. "It was probably added later when whatever is in there was no longer being used."

While they were speaking, the dislodged debris of centuries had subsided, and a wide space was opening up before them.

"It's a grotto," said Perdita, a grin unfurling across her face and making her unusual grey-green eyes sparkle with excitement. "The Tudors first popularised them," she explained as she edged forwards, her torch sweeping the floor, watching for obstacles left behind by the collapse. "Then there was a resurgence of interest in them during the Victorian times."

Kit shook pieces of plaster from his dark, curly hair and followed Perdita into the yawning space. "Perds, I've spent a huge part of my life at Marquess House and I had no idea this was here. How did you discover it?"

"I've been studying the plans that were drawn up when Granny Lettice was renovating the house. There were drawings for a grotto and even an ancient photograph of her standing in the entrance, so I knew it had been built. It was mentioned in letters between Lettice and her husband William as well. William was a go-getting Victorian business magnate with his eye on creating a modern future and had been all for flattening what he saw as these old-fashioned Tudor buildings and creating a modern estate in its place, taking in new and fashionable designs."

Piper stared at her sister, wide-eyed, her horror reflecting Perdita's own panic when she had first discovered how the beautiful heart of their home had come close to being destroyed forever.

"From all I've discovered so far about Lettice Hawkland," Perdita continued, "she loved leading fashionable trends, and the Tudors were the height of fashion in the Victorian era. If she had been in possession of a genuine Tudor manor, I bet she was delighted that she could restore the ancient core of the house as it would have been the envy of her fashionable friends. As a compromise, her husband, William Lakeby, our great-great-great grandfather, built the cutting-edge, modern wing where, once it was complete, they lived in aspidistra-adorned luxury.

"William tried to persuade Lettice away from what he saw as her romantic side. Lettice, however, was no fainting Victorian damsel but a woman who knew her own mind, so she stood firm and William crumbled. He even agreed to build her this grotto."

"How do you know all this Perds?" asked Piper.

"It's all in the archives," Perdita replied, "and I've been going through them, compiling a history of Marquess House."

"So why do you think it was boarded up?" asked Piper, climbing over a pile of rubble, her torch illuminating the shell-encrusted walls.

"No idea," replied Perdita. "Perhaps they stopped using it or it went of fashion. Careful, Pipes, there's a slope."

"It's a pool," Piper exclaimed.

"Cal, come with me and let's see if there's an exit or whether it's been blocked up," called Kit, edging his way through the gloom.

Perdita and Piper remained together, and Perdita gently took Piper's hand.

"Are you OK, Perds?" Piper asked.

Her sister nodded. "I'm finding it difficult to believe that it's a year tomorrow since Granny Mary died and our lives changed completely," she replied.

Once again, she thanked every deity she could think of for her sister. It had always been the two of them against the world, especially after their mother, Louisa, had died when they were children.

The previous year, Perdita had been working on an archaeological dig in Pembrokeshire when her then fiancé, Warren Dexter, had arrived with the news that her estranged grandmother, the historian and philanthropist, Mary Fitzroy, had died. The following day she had received a letter from Alistair Mackensie, who had been Mary's solicitor, inviting her to her grandmother's stately home, Marquess House in St Ishmaels, only a few miles from the dig site.

During the interview, Alistair had explained that she and Piper were the main beneficiaries of Mary's will and, apart from a few personal bequests, they had inherited everything — her manor house, an extensive research centre and a vast fortune. They were now worth in excess of £300 million between them.

It had taken the twins a while to come to terms with their inheritance. They could not understand why their grandmother had shunned them in life — abandoning them after their mother's death when they were seven years old — yet had embraced them in death. Determined to unravel this mystery and, with Piper in America accompanying her husband, Jeremy Davidson, Perdita had resigned from her university job and moved into Marquess House.

Once ensconced, she had searched her grandmother's published and unpublished books for clues and, to her astonishment, had discovered a trail of information left by Mary for her to find. It seemed the key to Mary's behaviour lay in her unfinished manuscript *The Catherine Howard Anomaly*, which she had been working on at the time her only child, Louisa, the twins' mother, had died.

With the help of Alistair's son, Kit, Perdita had uncovered more than she had imagined. Not only had she discovered the truth about her mother's death and the real reason Mary had stepped away from them, she also revealed an incredible but provable alternate version of Tudor history concerning Henry VIII and his fifth bride, the teenager Catherine Howard. Struggling to understand why such an incredible historical revelation had been covered up, Perdita was told the real danger she now faced was from a shadowy section of the British Secret Service called MI1 Elite.

This organisation was tasked with retaining the accepted version of history. It worked by clandestinely removing and destroying any historical evidence that emerged which might offer an alternative or more truthful view of events than the one recorded in the history textbooks and accepted as correct. What made matters worse was that Perdita's former fiancé, Warren, had been part of this highly secretive and dangerous section of the British government. It transpired he had been married throughout their relationship and had seduced her in order to discover what she knew about her grandmother's work. While Perdita had dealt with her own emotional upheaval, Piper's marriage to Jeremy had collapsed when he had an affair with a co-worker called Kirstin.

The twins were told they were protected by an ancient document called *The Milford Haven Treaty* that created a sovereign state within Marquess House, making them immune from arrest by the Secret Service while they were living there. However, in order to get around this, the new and ruthless head of MI1, Inigo Westbury, had reintroduced The White List, an assassination register of academics who tried to reveal more than the government was willing to allow. Although Alistair had been able to have the arrest warrants for treason quashed, it nevertheless meant Perdita, Piper and Kit had been in incredible danger and had been forced to flee for their lives to the Mackensie's stronghold in Andorra: Castle Jerusalem.

With their lives still at risk, Perdita and Piper had been stunned to discover more secrets concerning their new lives. The most surprising were the aristocratic titles they were now entitled to use — Perdita, as the eldest twin by ten minutes, held the unusual and ancient title once bestowed upon a wife of Henry VIII, the Marquess of Pembroke, a male title for a woman, while Piper, as her heir, was Viscountess Cleddau.

Yet, there were more revelations. Before their desperate flight from Marquess House, Perdita and Kit, with help from Mary's clues, had found a hidden ruby ring which was one third of a trio of jewels that if reunited were able to prove beyond all doubt the version of events Perdita and Kit had begun to unravel.

This discovery had made Perdita determined to discover the location of the matching ring, especially when Alistair explained there was another family member who was trying to steal Marquess House from them. This man was Randolph Connors, the son of Mary's sister, Cecily. A wealthy businessman with no conscience, he was a dangerous adversary who wanted to claim the mansion for his baby granddaughters.

Despite this new threat, Perdita had ploughed on, even more focussed on discovering the real truth. With help from Kit, Piper, and the research teams at both Marquess House and Castle Jerusalem, they had sifted through a cache of letters bought by her grandmother, which Perdita was convinced were somehow linked to the discoveries they had made about Catherine Howard.

As the letters gave up their secrets, a series of historical events were revealed. At first, Perdita had been hard-pushed to believe them, yet she could not entirely dismiss the new information as their uncanny ring of truth helped to plug the many anomalous gaps concerning the Babington Plot: a labyrinthine trap set by Elizabeth I's spymasters which resulted in the execution of Mary, Queen of Scots.

Piper had managed to track down the second ruby ring, but a subsequent run-in with MI1 Elite had finally returned them to

Marquess House, where Perdita and Piper had insisted they intended to remain.

Now, nearly four months later, with spring unfolding around them, the twins were searching for a clue to the third and final piece of jewellery, a silver locket set with a single diamond, which they hoped would solve the puzzle they had begun to unravel with the two ruby rings. Perdita's latest research had led to her uncovering this grotto, which she hoped would reveal more answers.

Perdita allowed the light from her torch to play over the grotto's walls, and her breath caught in her throat as a shape came into sharp relief; walking nearer to ensure she was seeing the image she had hoped she would find, she called out to her sister. "Piper, there are mermaids."

A moment later, her sister was by her side, grinning. "Of course there are mermaids," she said, her tone matter-of-fact. "There are mermaids everywhere in the house, why would down here be any different?"

Perdita traced the beam of her torch around the image. The delicate features of the mermaid were in profile as she swam across the wall. A long, elegant arm with tapering fingers stretched towards what would once have been the opening of the grotto, which, if Perdita had read the plans correctly, should have led to a garden with a view of the lake, Llyn Cel — a wide body of water that dominated the grounds of the manor house she and Piper had inherited from their grandmother.

"Do you think Granny knew it was here?" asked Piper.

"Probably, but maybe she didn't think restoring it was important," replied Perdita.

"I wonder why?"

Before Perdita could respond, there was an ear-splitting ripping sound and light flooded the grotto.

"Windows," called Kit as Perdita and Piper hurried towards him and Callum. "And the bricked-up space in the middle must have been the door."

With light flooding the cavern, Perdita turned to take it all in and as the vast space was revealed to them, she gasped at its shimmering beauty. The shells that festooned the walls were largely intact, and some of their natural iridescence continued to glimmer through the years of dust.

"My goodness, there are mermaids everywhere," she said.

"And look, underneath the mosaic mermaid, there are the words: *Spe et nereidum*," added Piper.

"Hope and mermaids," translated Perdita as she gazed about her. She swung her torch around the grotto and let it play over a pile of tarpaulins in one corner. Walking over, she lifted the edge, her eyes widening in surprise.

"What have you found?" asked Piper, hurrying over to join her.

"A few old trunks and some paintings, I think," Perdita replied.

Kit and Callum joined the twins, helping them to move the ancient covering. Three trunks were stacked against the wall, battered and dusty, but their quality had ensured they had survived the years of their incarceration in the grotto. The three paintings were wrapped in waxed cloth and leaned against the trunks.

"Wow!" exclaimed Perdita. "I wonder what's inside."

She reached towards the top trunk, but Kit put a restraining hand out.

"We should ask Geraint to check out the structure before we move anything," he suggested.

Geraint Williams was the architect Perdita and Piper had employed to oversee their extensive building plans. With some reluctance, Perdita withdrew her hand.

"You're right," she said, "I'll ask him to have a look before he leaves this evening. If it is structurally sound, I'll arrange to have these things moved somewhere we can examine them properly. Then we'll have to decide when we can fit the renovation into the building schedule."

"You're going to restore it?" asked Callum.

"Why wouldn't we?" said Piper. "It's breath-taking. Perhaps we can reinstate the pool. I've always fancied my own swimming pool."

"In the meantime," said Kit, "we ought to let Dad know we've found the grotto and it hasn't damaged his precious wine cellar."

"Alistair will be relieved," Callum grinned.

CHAPTER TWO

The next morning, Perdita placed her mug on the desk in her office and dumped her computer and handbag on the chair. The large office in the Marquess House Research Centre had once belonged to her grandmother, Mary Fitzroy, but Perdita had taken it over the previous year when she had moved into her new home. There was another, almost identical office, deep within the heart of the building in an area called The Dairy which had state-of-the-art climate control and restricted access in order to protect the many thousands of ancient documents stored within it. There was also a dedicated restoration team who not only worked on documents owned by Marquess House but also liaised closely with the Mackensies and their multi-national business Jerusalem. Perdita used the office in The Dairy when she was examining any delicate original documents, but her main base was in the Research Centre.

"Morning," called Jenny Procter, the Chief Librarian and Archivist, popping her head around the door as she went past. "Wonderful celebration last night."

"It was great fun, wasn't it?"

"Your grandmother would have loved every moment," she said.

Perdita nodded. A large party was not the usual way to celebrate the first anniversary of a person's death, but everyone who had known her grandmother had assured her Mary would have been delighted. The evening had been a huge success, although at one point, Perdita and Piper had stolen away to visit the graves where their family lay, finally scattering their father's ashes on their mother's grave. He had died from cancer six months before their grandmother had been found dead.

"They're together again at last," Perdita had said, as they had laid bluebells by their mother's headstone.

"I bet they're having a ball," Piper had added.

After putting flowers on the graves of their grandmother and their grandfather, whom they had never met, they had returned to the party.

On their stroll to the house through the ornamental lights that gave the gardens a magical glow, Perdita had glanced over at the black waves of Llyn Cel.

"Looking for the mermaid?" Piper had asked, causing Perdita to stop in surprise.

After a moment's consideration, Perdita said in a quiet voice, "I saw her." Until now, Perdita had almost denied it to herself and had not confided what she thought she had witnessed in anyone. "The night Kit and I had to run for our lives," she continued. "It was only a glimpse, but it was definitely her." Perdita had glanced at her sister, who was watching her but did not appear concerned.

"Why haven't you told me before?" asked Piper.

"The time was never right; it isn't the kind of thing you drop into a conversation. Do you think I'm mad? Or that I was seeing things because of the stress I was under?"

Piper had slipped her arm through Perdita's and they had begun to walk back to the party. "I neither think you were seeing things because of the stress nor that you're mad," she had replied before taking a deep breath and finishing, "because I've seen her, too. Only a glimpse, but I know what I saw."

Perdita had stared at Piper in amazement. Of the two of them, it was always Perdita who was given to an overactive imagination and, as their father used to describe it, "flights of fancy"; Piper had always been the more pragmatic.

"Truly?"

Piper had nodded. "When we came home a few months ago and you gave me the letter Granny had left for us to find. Granny was at my wedding; she crept in at the back and watched, then vanished before anyone saw her. It made me understand how much she had loved us and the huge sacrifice she had made when she stepped away from our lives after Mum died. I went for a walk later that evening to try and clear my head, thinking about Granny and how different our lives could have been. As I stared out over the water, I saw a figure. It was fleeting, almost between breaths, but it was her." She paused, then added, "Perhaps we should keep it to ourselves though."

"Probably a good idea — no one would believe us anyway."

Perdita had thought about the conversation for a long time after the party was over. In her heart and her academic brain, she knew there was no such thing as mermaids. It was an evolutionary and biological impossibility, yet, like Piper, she was sure about what she had seen. She wondered whether mermaids only revealed themselves to those who needed to see them, those who needed hope at the moment of impossible danger or despair. It was an idea that had brought a smile to her face as she had fallen asleep.

Now, she was staring at the long wall of her office, where, inspired by the eccentric family tree Kit had created during their time at Castle Jerusalem in Andorra, she had made a visual timeline of her most recent research. At its heart was an image of Catherine Howard, accompanied by a picture of the carved mermaid and the trio of Latin inscriptions Perdita now associated with the teenage queen and the three pieces of jewellery that were connected to her: *Semper Sorores, Iuncta Sanguine* and *Spe et Nereidum* — Sisters Always, Joined in Blood and Hope and Mermaids. These phrases seemed to be intrinsic in Perdita's search and, not for the first time, she wondered whether the mermaid icons that were evident throughout Marquess House were merely a symbol of femininity, a whimsical fancy, or a clue to the mysteries of the past.

Ever since their return to Pembrokeshire a few months earlier, she had been hunting for what she viewed as the final part of the puzzle in the quest her grandmother had set her upon: the missing silver locket that had once belonged to Catherine Howard, the fifth queen of Henry VIII. The locket had been a gift to the young Catherine from her elder half-sister, Lady Isabel Baynton, when she had first arrived at court to serve as a maid to the new queen, Anne of Cleves. These were facts Perdita had learned from the document her grandmother had discovered in the archives of Marquess House that had become known as *The Catherine Howard Codex*.

This document, combined with her grandmother's unpublished manuscript about Catherine Howard, had led Perdita to discover the hiding place of a ruby ring that had been given to the young queen consort by her supposed rival, Anne of Cleves. The documents discovered by Perdita and her grandmother had told a different tale: one of closeness, friendship, and care, with the two women supporting each other during their violent marriages to Henry VIII. The ruby ring was one of an identical pair, designed by Anne to hold a secret cavity which the women used to pass messages to each other.

Yet somehow, these rings, when combined with the silver locket, were supposed to prove beyond all doubt the secrets Perdita had begun to uncover. Despite her best efforts, she had still to ascertain how three separate pieces of jewellery could provide such conclusive evidence. The more she delved into her research, the less Perdita understood about the connection between the three pieces.

Flipping open her laptop, she began dealing with her emails, aware she had a number of meetings that morning. The first was with Geraint Williams, the architect, to discuss the new building works, the discovery of the grotto and the removal of the trunks and paintings they had discovered.

After that, she was getting together with Jenny Procter and her assistant, Izabel Barnes, to discuss the continuing translation and digitising of the Lady Pamela letters. This cache of previously unstudied correspondence had been another part of Mary's legacy and had been bought from one of her old friends, Lady Pamela Johnson. They had formed the basis of the second manuscript which her grandmother had abandoned. This had been entitled *The Ladies of Melusine*, after an ancient water-goddess, who legend claimed was the ancestress to numerous Mediaeval and Renaissance royal families, including the Tudors.

Until recently, these letters had sat, untouched, in a box in the Marquess House archives but through the diligent work of both the library teams in Pembrokeshire and at Castle Jerusalem, headed up by Dr Deborah Black, these letters had given up another staggering secret concerning the previously unknown legitimate Tudor heirs that Catherine Howard had given birth to: a boy and a girl.

While Perdita and the two teams had managed to discover the identity of Catherine's daughter, they were still trying to fathom what had happened to her son and his heirs. During her research, she had concluded that Catherine Howard's son, the baby boy named Nicholas, had survived into adulthood, and had married but under the name of Ralph Fitzalan, duke of Hereford. His wife, the daughter of Katheryn Parr and Sir Thomas Seymour, Lady Mary Seymour, had given birth to their only child, a son. However, despite extensive trawling of all the evidence they had so far uncovered, Perdita did not know his name, only his codename from the letters: Prometheus.

One of the letters suggested that Ralph Fitzalan had died from his injuries at the Siege of Fotheringhay Castle. His son should then have become the rightful king, but for reasons as yet undiscovered by Perdita, this had not transpired. Instead, James VI of Scotland, the son of Mary, Queen of Scots, became James I of England after the death of Queen Elizabeth I in 1603.

Looking up from her computer, she once more gazed at the wallchart, wondering where else to search for information, when another thought interrupted her. For the past week, she had meant to hunt out the photographs she had taken some months earlier of the ceiling bosses in the Marquess House chapel, as she thought they might be useful. Perhaps they would nudge her in the right direction.

Since her return to Marquess House, the faces of the women from the chapel had slipped her mind. Scrolling through her phone, she located the series of images and sent them to the colour printer in the corner of her office. A moment later, Perdita gathered the printouts and spread them on the round table she used for meetings, examining the details of each face before writing the names of the women across the top of the images.

"Anne Boleyn, Catherine Howard, Penelope Fitzalan and Arbella Stuart," she said aloud as she pinned each face to the wall and stood back to examine them. The faces were carved in wood, and now they were blown up to offer more details it showed that the carving was basic while the paintwork was careful, if a little flat. She made a mental note to ask Piper for her opinion. As a talented artist, Piper would no doubt be able to explain them in more detail.

Perdita's eyes went first to Anne Boleyn, a woman who was the subject of numerous paintings. King Henry VIII's love for Anne had caused him to split with the Catholic church and create the Church of England in order to be able to grant himself a divorce from his first wife, Katherine of Aragon. Anne's dark eyes stared out and Perdita considered the narrow face, dark hair, and gently smiling mouth, before moving her gaze to Catherine Howard.

Her face was rounder, smoother without the suggestion of cheekbones that highlighted Anne Boleyn's face. Catherine's youth was apparent, and the hair that showed through her half-hood was auburn. Perdita's eyes moved to the woman whose initials were AS and whom she had deduced was Arbella Stuart, once a potential heir to Elizabeth I's throne, and a woman whose name continued to pepper Perdita's research, though, as yet, she could find no obvious link between Arbella and the two famous queen consorts. Anne Boleyn and Catherine Howard, as well as sharing the dubious pleasure of being wives number two and five for Henry VIII, had also been first cousins. Anne's mother, Elizabeth Boleyn nee Howard, had been the elder sister of Edmund Howard, Catherine's father.

The final face was the one that intrigued Perdita the most. Although she had no corroboration, she believed this was the face of the mysterious Penelope Fitzalan. A woman who seemed to have been obliterated from the pages of history, yet whose name, like Arbella, had cropped up time and again during their investigations. There was also no denying her link to Marquess House because Perdita had seen the book Penelope had written while she had lived here, *The Llyn Cel Mermaid and Other Local Legends*, and from the small amount Perdita had read, her knowledge made it clear Penelope knew the area and was writing from personal experience.

There was also a small collection of letters that had been discovered by Lettice Lakeby in which Penelope had claimed there was a secret hidden at Marquess House that she was prepared to die to protect. It was this that had led Perdita to deduce the secret had been Catherine Howard herself. There had also been clues leading Perdita to discover the first of the missing ruby rings, hidden in a purpose-made jewellery box in the tunnel that linked the house to the island in the middle of Llyn Cel itself.

Beyond this, Perdita had been unable to discover any more. Izabel believed one of the later correspondents in the Lady Pamela letters could have been Penelope Fitzalan, and Perdita hoped this might reveal more information about the mysterious woman.

"Hi Perds," a cheery voice called, "still all right for a quick chat?"

The soft Welsh lilt of Geraint Williams cut through her racing thoughts. In his mid-thirties, he had closely cropped curly blond hair and the build of rugby player, although his vast size belied his gentle nature.

"Hello," she said, "yes, of course."

She ushered Geraint over to the two sofas on one side of the room.

"I won't take up much of your time," he began without preamble, sitting opposite her, pulling out his tablet and flicking through a few pages until he reached his notes.

"Everything is going smoothly over at The Mary Fitzroy Heritage Museum."

Perdita beamed. Her trawl of the archives earlier in the year had revealed some unexpected plans and architects' drawings which her grandmother had commissioned six months before her death. Mary's intention had been to convert an old tumbledown farmhouse and outbuildings that lay on the far edges of the Marquess House land into a purpose-built museum and learning centre. She had felt that the vast amounts of history in the Pembrokeshire area were often neglected by scholars, and she wanted to change what she thought was a huge oversight.

Although the building work had never been started, planning permission had been submitted to the local council and passed. Once she discovered this, Perdita, who with Kit's brother, Stuart, was working with her erstwhile colleague, Dr Olaf Dade, on eventually raising the wreck in the bay, had decided this vast space would, one day, be ideal as a state-of-the-art home for the ship. Three weeks earlier, the building work had begun on The Mary Fitzroy Heritage Museum and both twins felt it was a fitting tribute to their grandmother.

After a few minutes updating her on the work, Geraint then said, "I've also checked the grotto, and I wouldn't be comfortable with you poking around down there at present."

"Is it dangerous?"

"Not as such, but the area has been closed off for years and until my team has had a chance to ensure the walls are secure and repair some of the glass that was broken behind the boards, I'd be nervous about you being down there."

Perdita nodded. It was as she had expected. "Will we need to inform the local council?" she asked. "This is a Grade I listed building, so I imagine there will need to be an inspection of what we've discovered before we can begin repairs."

"I've already contacted them," he said. "Sorry, Perds, your sister said you were hoping to get down there and do some digging but until I'm satisfied it's safe, would you be able to wait for a bit?"

"Of course," she replied. "Although, if you do have people down there, could you ask everyone to keep an eye out for a silver locket? It's unlikely they'll find anything, but it would be worth making your team aware that we're searching for one."

Geraint made a note on his tablet. "Silver locket, OK, will do," he said, standing up. "As for the trunks and the paintings that were down there, I don't see any reason why they shouldn't be moved. Where would you like me to put them?"

"In The Dairy," replied Perdita. "When do you think you'll be able to move them?"

"We could probably get them up there this afternoon. The sooner the better, I think, now they've been exposed. Do me a favour, Perds, wear a protective suit when you first open the trunks — we have no idea what's inside. Well, I won't hold you up anymore; I'm heading back over to the museum site, so I can pop in and see Mark on the way. One last question: will you be wanting to restore the grotto?"

"Oh yes," replied Perdita, "it's so beautiful, I don't understand why it was boarded up in the first place."

"Right, I'll begin putting together a restoration team then and have someone work up some preliminary plans," he said, making a few more notes. "See you later."

Despite all the work she had planned to get through that morning, Perdita was relieved when she heard Kit's voice.

"Knock knock," he called from the doorway. "Are you busy?"

"I probably should be," she admitted, "but I don't seem to be getting anywhere fast. What's up?"

Kit had flopped onto the sofa and was pulling his laptop out of his battered Fred Perry sports bag. "Remember the New Zealand document?" he asked.

Perdita sat beside him. "Yes, you bought it about a year ago when I first moved in. You told me it's an ancient document of ownership of the islands going all the way back to the 1600s and hugely predating Captain Cook, who didn't discover them until April 1769."

"Gold star," he said, grinning.

As part of Jerusalem, Kit rescued and restored important antiquities and documents. If these were of national interest, the company would either lend or donate the items to the government of their country of origin, depending on the political climate at the time. Megan, the eldest of the three Mackensie siblings, ran the organisation from Andorra, covering Africa and Asia, while Kit's brother, Stuart, looked after the Americas, the Caribbean, and a few other places. Kit's responsibility was Europe, Scandinavia, Australia, and New Zealand.

"Has Deborah found something?" continued Perdita. The last time she had seen this particular document had been in Andorra, where it had been taken away by Dr Deborah Black for tests.

"She has, and, while at first I was prepared to dismiss it as a fake, I'd like your opinion on it." He opened a report and flicked through to a series of images. "When we examined it at home, you spotted a Roman numeral and suggested it was a regnal number."

"It was a 'IV'," replied Perdita, "but it didn't fit with the dates of any British monarchs who had that regnal number. Does it refer to a foreign monarch?"

"Possibly, although doubtful because the rest of the document has clearly been issued in Britain," he said. "England to be precise. After X-raying it, Deborah managed to make out the name next to the regnal number."

"What was it?"

"Richard," said Kit. "The document was issued under the seal of a Richard IV."

"But there was no Richard IV. It must be a fake."

"Or a clue?"

Perdita considered this for a moment before returning to her own desk and opening her notebook, scanning her notes. "What were the dates again?"

"February 1659."

Flicking backwards and forwards, she carried the notebook back to Kit and sat beside him, before raising her eyes and searching the timeline on the wall.

"In February 1659, the Protectorate was beginning to crumble and there were noises for the Restoration of the Monarchy," she began. "From 1648 until 1662, there was a great deal of unrest. It was the time after what is known as the Second Civil War, which led to the execution of King Charles I on 30 January 1649 and eleven years of Oliver Cromwell and the Protectorate."

"Do you think it could be significant?"

Perdita shrugged. "We shouldn't rule it out, but I can't see how it would be connected," she said, after examining the images.

"How are you doing with finding the locket?" Kit asked.

"Not well," she admitted, "but Jenny and Izabel are coming in to talk me through the remaining letters in a bit. You never know, there might be something useful in there. Do you want to come?"

"Yes please," he replied. "I'll email Deborah's report to you, too. You might see something I've missed."

CHAPTER THREE

"Hi Izi," Perdita called, as a slim blonde woman wandered into the office. Izabel Barnes was Jenny Procter's assistant, as well as her granddaughter, and had been instrumental in helping to decode the Lady Pamela Johnson letters during their stay in Andorra.

"Nan's on her way," said Izabel, plonking herself down on one of the squashy leather sofas and putting a mug and her tablet on the long table in between them.

Perdita gathered the images she had printed, grabbed her laptop and a notebook, and sat opposite Izabel. Moments later, Jenny arrived with a stack of papers in her arms.

"Hello," said Jenny as she joined Izabel on the sofa, arranging the papers into four piles in front of her. "Transcripts and scans of the final letters, as well as translations, with a summary on the top."

Kit slid onto the sofa next to Perdita. She smiled at him and moved along to give him space.

"Shall we start?" asked Izabel, and Perdita nodded. "As you know, the Lady Pamela letters cover quite a broad time period from 1541 to 1662, which is a total of 121 years," began Izabel. "In the first five years, there were only 41 letters written. The numbers for the next few years are also quite low, but then there's an explosion of correspondence from 1586 until 1589, covering the events running up to the Armada."

Perdita said, "There was a gap again after that, wasn't there?"

"Yes, that's what our first quick summary of the letters seemed to show, but since studying them more closely, it seems things aren't quite as straightforward as we thought."

"In what way?" asked Kit.

"Many of the letters are dated incorrectly," said Jenny. "There are some with no dates at all, and many that had been dated from the later period of 1648 to 1662 had to be recategorized. When we read their content, we realised these letters had been written towards the end of the 16th century and the beginning of the 17th. New comments had been added to them and then they were re-sent between the later years."

"How peculiar," said Perdita. "Is there any indication why?"

"Not really," said Jenny. "However, they do give a very unusual view of the transition of power from Elizabeth I to James I. These letters are some of the last written in code and, although we've managed to interpret most of it using all our original ciphers, we're a bit baffled by the content. They seem to be about a disputed marriage and yet another unknown claimant to the throne."

"Catherine Howard's missing son?" asked Perdita, her voice hopeful.

"No. These refer to a married woman with a daughter," said Jenny.

"Really?" said Perdita, considering this for a moment. "There were quite a few claimants at the time, even though James I is always presented as the most logical option."

"Who else had a claim?" asked Izabel. "We might be able to work out who the letter mentions if we look at the other potential heirs."

Perdita screwed up her eyes in concentration as she thought. "Lady Arbella Stuart, first cousin of James. She and James both had claims through Margaret Tudor, Henry VIII's elder sister. Henry also had a younger sister, Mary, who had been married to Charles Brandon, the duke of Suffolk."

"Did Mary have children?" urged Izabel.

"Yes, two daughters: Frances and Eleanor. Frances married Henry Grey. Their daughters were the famous Grey sisters: Lady Jane Grey, the nine-day queen, Lady Katherine Grey and Lady Mary Grey. Mary married but had no children. Lady Katherine, however, had two sons."

"So could she be the married woman with a child?" asked Kit. "Although, you said it was a daughter?"

Izabel nodded in confirmation.

"What are the dates, Jen?" said Perdita.

"This woman is referred to as having a child around the spring of 1599," the librarian replied after checking her notes.

"It's too late to be Katherine Grey, then," said Perdita, walking over to her timeline. "She died in 1568."

"What happened to her husband and sons?" Kit joined Perdita, staring at the wallchart.

"Katherine had eloped with Edward Seymour in December 1560 and didn't tell her cousin, Queen Elizabeth. At that point, Katherine Grey was suggested as being Elizabeth's heir presumptive, so her marriage was one of great interest to everyone, particularly the monarch."

"Did her husband have a claim to the throne too?" asked Izabel.

"No, but he was the son of Edward Seymour, duke of Somerset, who had been Queen Jane Seymour's brother and Lord Protector to his nephew, King Edward VI. He might not be royal, but he was well connected and wealthy," clarified Perdita. "When Katherine was eight months pregnant, she tried to find someone to plead for her to get her back in favour with the queen. She tried Bess of Hardwick first, who refused, saying she didn't want to be implicated, so she went to Robert Dudley. Robert was furious with Katherine and told Elizabeth about the clandestine marriage. Husband and wife were both locked in the Tower of London. Katherine gave birth to Edward Seymour in 1561, then thanks to the kindness of Sir Edward Warner, Lieutenant of the Tower allowing conjugal visits to the duke, she gave birth to a second son, Thomas Seymour in 1563. However, in 1603, when it was, supposedly, suggested that one of Katherine's sons could ascend the throne, Elizabeth was said to declare that 'no rascal' would wear her crown."

"There was also the very distant claim of the Infanta of Spain, Isabella Clara Eugenia," mused Jenny, "through her descent from John of Gaunt, the third of the five sons of King Edward III."

"None of these seem to fit what we found in the letters though," said Izabel.

"Did the letters reveal anything else useful, Jenny?" asked Perdita.

"There's nothing obvious," Jenny admitted, "and no direct references to the missing heir."

Perdita considered Jenny's comments. She had not really thought they would be lucky twice with the Lady Pamela letters, but she had hoped they would have given her a few more clues. Kit threw her a look of commiseration.

"What about information on Ralph Fitzalan, or his wife, Mary Seymour?" asked Perdita.

"From the few mentions we managed to find for Ralph, it seemed he died in 1587. After this, Mary Seymour moved back to the family seat, Orleton Hall in Leominster, Herefordshire with her son, 'Prometheus' as he was codenamed in the letters. After 1587, Mary seemed to stop corresponding with the Ladies of Melusine. Strangely enough, after 1603, the codenames lessen too and real names are used, so there is less confusion over identities."

"And are there any mentions of the heirs in these later letters?"

"Not many," Jenny replied. "It's as though the urgency of the original secret seemed to lessen. I suspect that with each passing generation, the impact of the heirs' existence receded. However, there is a story about a woman escaping from some soldiers by running across a field while her housekeeper pretended to be her. The woman and her maid managed to escape to the Netherlands. The letter mentions a locket the woman says was given to her by her nephew for safekeeping."

"Do you think it could be our locket?" asked Perdita.

"I'm not sure," Izabel replied, "but I thought I'd flag it up because it was one of the few mentions of a locket. The letter was addressed to someone called Eaffrey, and signed, *Your Dear Friend*, which is most unhelpful."

"Are there any suggestions about the real name of 'Prometheus'?" Perdita asked.

"Sorry, love, none," responded Jenny.

"How frustrating."

"Don't lose hope yet," smiled Izabel, "we have made some discoveries."

"About whom?"

"Penelope Fitzalan."

Perdita's eyes widened in surprise. She pulled out one of her printouts and placed it on top of the paper-strewn tabletop. "Me too," she exclaimed and as the others examined the image, she felt a thrill of anticipation.

Jenny picked up the image. "Where did you get this?" she asked.

"It's one of the ceiling bosses in the chapel," replied Perdita. "There are only four different female faces repeated throughout. I took these the night Kit and I had to escape to Andorra. Each woman had her initials carved beside her: AB — Anne Boleyn; CH — Catherine Howard; AS — which I think is Arbella Stuart, particularly as the sunken ship in the bay has the same name — and PF. I'm guessing PF is Penelope Fitzalan."

"This is extraordinary," murmured Jenny.

"What did you discover about Penelope Fitzalan in the letters, Izi?" asked Kit, while Jenny rose and walked over to examine the other printouts Perdita had pinned to the wall.

"I think you were correct when you suggested the letters your great-great-great grandmother, Lettice, discovered were actually part of this collection. They fill the gap perfectly. Penelope was writing to Dorothy Spencer, Countess of Sunderland to tell her that she intended to stay here at Marquess House despite all that was happening in London. She mentions a secret and how she must be on hand to guard the truth, that it was necessary for her brother to know he had a safe haven should it be required."

"Her brother?"

"Yes, but she doesn't name him, which is irritating…"

"What year was this?"

"1649 was the first mention of the secret and her brother," replied Izabel. "The need to keep this secret becomes more frantic as the next few years pass."

"Are there any responses from Lady Dorothy Spencer?"

"A few, but there isn't anything significant in them."

"And this is the Lady Dorothy Spencer who was the great-granddaughter of Lettice Knollys?" said Perdita.

"Was she?" asked Kit in surprise.

"Perds, I didn't know that," said Izabel.

"Yes," replied Perdita, joining Jenny by the wallchart, "look, this is Lettice's family tree. Her younger daughter, Dorothy, first married Sir Thomas Perrot of Carew Castle and after he died, she married Henry Percy, 9th Earl of Northumberland. It was an unhappy union made mostly for political reasons, but they had four children. The eldest was a daughter, also named Dorothy. She married Robert Sidney, 2nd Earl of Leicester and their daughter, another Dorothy, married Henry Spencer, 1st Earl of Sunderland."

Perdita pointed to a printout and Izabel ran her finger down it, comparing the dates and names.

"Oh my goodness, you're right!"

"It seems the connection between the families continued down through the generations," said Jenny.

"But it still doesn't explain who Penelope was and where she fits in? Unless there's anything else?" finished Perdita, but the hopeful lift in her voice was snuffed out by Izabel's shake of her head.

"There are no clues that link Penelope with anyone other than the fact she seems to be at the heart of the letter writing. We wondered if she could be related to Katherine Newton, who was a Paston by birth, as it was Katherine who collated the original Melusine letters. Penelope seemed to be the one gathering and compiling this cache."

"Katherine Newton had four daughters," said Perdita, walking along to another family tree. "Anne, Margaret, Elizabeth and Frances, but there are very few records beyond their names, and I've searched extensively. One of Katherine's sons, Theodore, married a Penelope Rodney and they had a daughter also called Penelope, but the dates don't tally."

"There is another odd thing," added Izabel. "After one of the references to her brother, there was a scribbled postscript about the secret being hidden in a chest passed down to them from their mother."

"A chest? Were there any more clues about it?"

"Not unless we've missed something," said Izabel. "You have a far greater working knowledge of this period of history, so you may spot something we didn't notice when you read the transcripts."

Jenny was still studying the printouts on the wall. "When did you discover this, Perdita?" she asked, pointing at the image of Penelope Fitzalan. "There's no denying the connection."

Izabel peered at it again, realisation dawning. "Oh my God!" she gasped.

"Kit?" questioned Perdita. "What do you think?"

Kit, too, considered the image then gazed at Perdita. "We need to go up to your room, Perds," he said. "This is remarkable. Why did none of us ever notice it before?"

Perdita led the way, letting them into her apartment. A portrait of a woman in a gold dress dominated one wall. When she had first moved in, Perdita had found the image daunting, but she had since come to view the woman as an integral part of her space. The most startling thing about the image was the likeness to Perdita herself.

Now, as they stood staring, Perdita took the printed image of the ceiling boss from Jenny and pinned it beside the portrait.

"Penelope Fitzalan," she said, staring at the woman's unusual grey-green eyes, so similar to her own. "She was hiding in plain sight all this time. We should have guessed — after all, she chose to attach letters to her own portrait."

"*If* she was the one who put them there," said Kit. "There's no denying it's her, but what's the significance?"

"What do you mean, Kit?" asked Jenny.

"We're looking for the locket. Not Penelope Fitzalan," he stated. "I know she mentions a brother, but if we believe that the missing heir was Ralph Fitzalan, there's no way he could be Penelope's brother because she wasn't around for at least another 50 years after his birth."

"You're right, Kit," said Perdita, and for the first time she felt a shadow of doubt at her discovery. "Do you think she was referring to a different secret then? Her letters are mostly from 1649 — that's nearly a hundred years after Catherine Howard was buried in the chapel."

"But her letters did lead Mary to discover the hidden box, which she left for you to find," said Jenny.

"The hidden box that was designed to hold all three pieces of jewellery," reminded Kit.

Perdita considered Kit's words before she spoke. "For some reason then," she said, her mind making connections as she considered all this new information, "Penelope must have owned all three pieces of jewellery at some point. She knew the secret of the heirs and was custodian of the rings and the locket. Maybe she knew what connected the three pieces to reveal this secret."

"It's possible," said Kit. "And her connection to Ralph Fitzalan? They do share a surname."

"I'm not convinced there's a blood-link between them despite the shared surname, but look at the painting more closely," said Perdita, taking his hand and leading him forward.

"Perds, this is unbelievable, do you think Dad realises? The house in the background must be an earlier incarnation of Marquess House," said Kit, "and on her fingers are two rings."

"Ruby rings," added Izabel.

43

"And dangling from her other hand is a locket," finished Perdita. "I've looked at this painting so many times but never really registered what I was seeing. It was only when I noticed the likeness from the ceiling boss, I came up here and studied it properly."

"But what does it mean?" asked Kit.

"I'm not sure yet," admitted Perdita, "but it has to mean something. I've asked Piper if she can take it out of its frame and examine it properly. Perhaps this portrait has more secrets to reveal than we realised."

CHAPTER FOUR

Perdita hurried into the library, striding through the endless rows of books, heading for one she felt might now help her unravel her thoughts. The portrait of Penelope Fitzalan had been removed from her wall and Piper was examining it in more detail. This would include the removal of its frame to see if there was anything hidden within the casing.

Piper was not only a talented artist, a skill she had inherited from their late father, James Rivers, she also had a master's degree in Art History and had spent many years working at galleries and museums. Perdita realised Piper's expertise in deciphering the many clues in the painting was more vital than ever as she continued her quest for the silver locket.

As she considered the task ahead, Perdita felt her spirits rise. Her instinct had always told her the clues to solving this mystery were in Marquess House, and now she felt the ancient manor was giving up its secrets at last. *Perhaps I had to earn its trust*, she mused, as her feet led her to the far end of the vast Tudor library. Above her were five stained glass windows, each depicting a different Greek goddess, which Perdita had admired on many occasions. At sunset, the rays of the dying day streamed through the coloured glass, throwing rainbows of light into the library.

Despite her eagerness to reach The Dairy and begin delving into the newly discovered trunks from the old grotto, Perdita paused to drink in the beauty of the images. The windows had been created at different points in history and the styles of the art varied accordingly, but they were all original and none were later than the seventeenth century. Perdita stared at the images of the five women. The first was a depiction of a dark-haired woman as Iris, the Greek goddess of the rainbow. From the image, Perdita had deduced this was supposed to represent Anne Boleyn.

The woman in the next window was much younger than the raven-haired, dark-eyed Anne. She was smaller in stature with flowing auburn hair, startling blue eyes, and an obvious pregnancy. Above her head was the name Demeter, the Greek goddess of the harvest and fertility, who was traditionally presented as being pregnant. Perdita was confident this was supposed to be Catherine Howard, particularly as around the woman were a number of other symbols. Bordering the top of the window was a delicate tableau of angels and mermaids, while to one side was a crown with a rose with no thorns woven around it — this hinted at the phrase Henry VIII had famously used to describe his fifth bride: his rose without a thorn. On the other side of the image were two rings, their stones a deep red, and hanging between them a silver oval with a brilliant white diamond shape in the centre. The three pieces of jewellery connected to Catherine and her children.

Elizabeth I as the Greek goddess Atalanta, the virgin huntress, was in the third window. Her red hair was a wild tangle of curls, a bow to one side and behind her a silver full moon. The next window showed a woman wearing a crown and with a phoenix rising behind her, depicted as Persephone, the daughter of Demeter. Again, there was the border of angels and mermaids and the image representing the two ruby rings and the silver locket. There was also a hare in one corner. Perdita was confident this image represented Mary, Queen of Scots.

For Perdita, the most curious image was the fifth window. It contained a romanticised version of Arbella Stuart as Pandora, who in Greek mythology was the first human woman. Arbella was kneeling before a carved wooden casket, and the furies were streaming past her into the sky. Hope, in the form of a guardian angel with what appeared to be a mermaid's tail, hovered above her right shoulder, while behind her on a distant hill stood a house with two figures, a boy and a girl, in the doorway. It was a strange image, but there was no doubting who the woman was supposed to be as her name was written in the elaborate scroll work at the bottom of the window.

Wondering again about the significance of the windows and whether she was trying to find connections that were not really there, Perdita hurried to retrieve the book she needed, *The Llyn Cel Mermaid and Other Local Legends*. Her previous encounter with the book had been short, having glanced through it after her grandmother had listed it as a primary source for her unpublished manuscript, *The Catherine Howard Anomaly*. Although Perdita had looked through the ancient book, her interest then had been in the ancient codex comprised of letters and diary pages written by Catherine and her inner court, so she had returned the book of legends to the storage stacks. Now, though, she felt this ancient tome might hold information she had not understood the first time it had presented itself to her.

"Hi everyone," she called as she arrived in The Dairy, watching with eager eyes as Jenny and Mark supervised the delivery of the trunks from the grotto. The three paintings were being delivered to Piper in her studio, complete with their wax wrappings, where she would examine them.

A huge plastic sheet had been rolled out across the floor of the boardroom and on top of this was a lint-free cotton covering. The long boardroom table had been moved against the wall and was also covered in a protective sheet, so it could be used as a finds table. This left the centre of the room clear for the three trunks, which were being lined up side-by-side.

"This looks incredible," called Perdita over the babble of noise. "Are the trunks heavy? Is there anything in them?"

"They weigh a ton," responded Mark, joining her by the door. "There's definitely stuff inside, so I'd advise wearing a mask. Two of them have locks, and the other is held together with leather straps. If the locks have seized, we might need some expert help getting into them. Geraint said he can pop by in about half an hour to open them if necessary."

"Thanks, Mark," grinned Perdita, already itching to begin delving into the trunks. Mark had been instrumental in helping her and Kit escape from MI1 the previous year, and she was fond of the quiet restorer.

Jenny joined Perdita and Mark.

"The original of *The Llyn Cel Mermaid and other Local Legends* is in your office — would you like me to put that copy with it?" she asked, nodding to the book in Perdita's arms.

Dragging her eyes away, Perdita followed Jenny, dumping her handbag onto her office chair, and struggling into the white protective suit, laid out, waiting for her, on the desk. Rummaging in her bag, she found a hair band and swept her hair into a long plait, fastening the end and tucking it down the back of her suit.

Her only pang of disappointment was Kit's absence. She had thought he would be here. *Perhaps he has stuff to do for Jerusalem*, she thought, but it did not entirely placate her.

"I thought Kit would have been here by now," said Mark, as though he had read her mind.

"Where is he?" asked Perdita, trying to keep her voice casual.

"He took Izi out for lunch," said Mark with an edge of irritation.

"What?"

Perdita was stunned. Why had Kit taken Izi out for lunch? Despite the many moments when they had veered towards each other, Perdita was yet to resolve her feelings for Kit. Even after their kiss a few months ago, he had never pushed, understanding she needed more time. Had he decided enough was enough and begun looking elsewhere? *No*, she scolded herself, *Kit and Izi are old friends, there's nothing in this*, and relief flooded through her as sense reasserted itself. Mark and Izi had been going out with each other for years.

"He's not moving in on your girlfriend, is he?" asked Perdita, attempting to keep her voice light-hearted.

Mark shot her a strangled look. "Izi and I have split up."

"Oh, Mark, no, I'm so sorry."

"Izi decided she needed some space," he muttered, then turned towards the trunks and said, with the deliberate air of someone changing the subject, "Shall we start on the trunk with the straps? It's the heaviest so is probably full of all sorts of junk. It'll keep us occupied until Geraint has a chance to look at the locks —"

"Great, you haven't started yet," interrupted a cheerful voice. Kit was behind Perdita, already dressed in a white protective suit. "Good look, Perds," he laughed.

She knew her usual reaction would be to laugh and offer a retort, but she was still reeling from the news that Izi was single now, as well as being beautiful, accomplished, and funny. She and Kit had worked together for years. Was Kit interested in her? Unable to process this, Perdita shot Kit a blank look, marching towards Mark without a backward glance, while she tried to control her unexpectedly teeming emotions.

"Hey, what's up?" Kit asked, hurrying after her and taking her arm, turning her around to look at him.

49

"Nothing," she snapped, shaking off his grip.

Kit stepped back, holding up his hands as though in surrender, and Perdita moved around Mark, so he stood between her and Kit.

"Would you like to do the honours, Perds?" asked Mark.

Looking down at the battered container, Perdita hauled her mind back to the moment, pushing all other emotions aside, allowing the thrill of anticipation at what they might be about to discover to take precedence over her other thoughts. It reminded her of an old-fashioned school trunk. As Perdita stared down at the cracked red leather, she was reminded of all the things she had once stored in her own: her diaries, her stories, treasured mementos, and things she wanted to keep secret. Would the previous owner of this box have used it for storing similar important items?

Mark handed her a pair of gloves, then Perdita knelt down in front of the ancient box and, picking up a soft cloth, gently wiped away the dust. Hoping for a monogram, she was disappointed when nothing revealed itself. Knowing that Mark would examine the outer casing with his team of restorers in more detail, she reached over to release the leather straps. The first came apart in her hand and she turned to Mark, who smiled and took it from her, placing it carefully on the nearby boardroom table and labelling it. The other strap was held in place by a rusted buckle, which she struggled to remove.

Kit leaned over and examined it. "Would you like me to try?" he asked, his voice wary.

Perdita felt a pang of guilt about her snappiness and nodded, moving aside, so Kit could take a better grip.

After a few moments of fiddling, the strap moved and Perdita held her breath as, with great care, Kit inched the leather through. When it was free, he turned to her and grinned. Her heart was beating in excitement. It reminded her of being on a dig when every trowel full of earth might offer up a secret. Kneeling in front of the trunk, as though she were praying at an altar, Perdita pulled a mask across her face, the others mirrored her, then she gripped the edges of the lid and eased it open.

A huge cloud of dust enveloped them and all three spluttered, but as it cleared, Perdita gasped in delight. Inside the box was a tapestry, folded in on itself so the pattern was hidden but the reassuring smell of camphor suggested it might have survived the ravages of hungry moths.

"When were mothballs invented?" asked Mark.

"About 1819," replied Perdita.

Kit laughed. "How can you possibly know that?" he asked.

"I remember all sorts of nonsense," she replied but despite her best efforts, she still could not get her voice back to normal.

Kit gave her a perplexed look, then turned away.

"Let's get it out," said Perdita.

For the next half an hour, working with painstaking care, the three of them lifted the folded tapestry and with two more of Mark's team, they unrolled it, placing it on the boardroom table.

"It's a family tree," exclaimed Perdita. "Look, Lettice and William are at the bottom and there's a dedication: 'From your loving younger sister, Seraphina, on the occasion of your marriage'. Lettice had a sister, yes, there she is… Oh," Perdita traced the line across, then she was silent.

"What is it?" asked Kit.

"They were twins, they have the same birthdates."

"It obviously runs in the family," he said, his smile gentle.

"Yes," she said, but with Mark standing beside her, poring over the tapestry, she did not feel she could explain the up-rush of feelings this discovery had created.

"This goes back to the eighteenth century," Mark said. "Look, Arabella Talbot, she married Sir Philip Courtenay in 1736 and they had a daughter, Penelope…"

"Arabella Talbot? Are you sure?"

"Yes, she was born in 1716, although we don't have her parents listed," said Mark.

"But Arabella Talbot wrote a book that's in the Marquess House library," explained Perdita. "I used it when I was first searching for information about Catherine Howard. I knew she'd lived here, but I didn't know she was an ancestor."

Kit was also examining the delicately wrought names.

"Penelope Courtenay is here, too, Perds," he said. "Wasn't she the woman who had the stained-glass windows repaired? You mentioned her as being in the bundle of eighteenth-century paperwork you were studying."

Perdita leaned towards Kit, her arm brushing his. "Penelope Courtenay is Arabella Talbot's daughter. Oh my goodness, this is incredible, do you realise what this family tree shows?"

"Your ancestors in the female line," said Mark.

"It shows the list of succession of the women who inherited Marquess House," Perdita corrected him. "Kit, you remember what your dad told us — the house could only be passed down to the next female relative."

"But didn't Penelope Courtenay sell it?" said Kit.

"Yes, but from what I've read, it was to a female cousin," replied Perdita. "She was an artist, the family fortune was at a low ebb by then and Penelope couldn't afford to keep the house, so she sold it and the house nearly crumbled away, but then Lettice bought it and restored it."

"Why would the covenants still hold then?" asked Kit.

"Perhaps they were reinstated with The Milford Haven Treaty?" suggested Perdita.

Mark had returned to the trunk, but Perdita remained by the tapestry, reading the list of distant ancestors from the top to the bottom where Lettice and William's names were festooned in gardenia and white roses. Arabella Talbot; Penelope Courtenay; Dorothy Callington; Honor Fitzpatrick and, finally, Lettice and her sister, Seraphina. Nearly 150 years of family history laid before her, women she had never heard of before, women whose blood ran in her veins, women who had paved the way for her and Piper. It was a touching moment. Even more surprising was her connection to Arabella Talbot, the woman who had written a history of Marquess House.

Reaching over to one of the phones, Perdita called Jenny, requesting the Arabella Talbot book.

"Izi's in the library at the moment," Jenny said. "I'll ask her to bring it across."

Perdita was about to say she would fetch it herself, but Jenny hung up. Still unable to shake her irritation with both Kit and Izabel, and aware that Mark might not be comfortable if Izi appeared, she was annoyed the afternoon she had been looking forward to with such excitement was unravelling into something unexpected and awkward.

Staring down at the tapestry again, she took a deep breath. *Pull yourself together*, she scolded herself. *Smile at Kit and apologise for being so childish, he hasn't done anything wrong and you're the only person ruining this for yourself.* But, as she turned back to the trunk, she realised Mark and Kit were making the most of her temporary absence to have a whispered and, from their expressions, serious discussion.

"Sorry, mate," she heard Kit murmur, "I did my best to persuade her to stay, but she's determined."

"Has she met someone else?"

"She wouldn't say. I'm so sorry."

"And when does she plan to leave?"

"In a few months. She handed her notice in this morning, but I wouldn't accept it until we'd had time to talk it through properly. I've persuaded her to stay until the end of the summer when the dig finishes."

Mark was silent for a moment, then he shrugged and stood up. "Thanks for trying, Kit. You're a real mate." He turned to Perdita. "Back in a bit."

Kit watched him go with concerned eyes.

"What was that about?" whispered Perdita, joining Kit on the floor by the trunk. He shot a wary glance.

"Izi handed her notice in this morning — it's caused a bit of a stir."

"What do you mean?"

Kit narrowed his eyes at her. "So now you're speaking to me," he said, folding his arms and glaring.

Perdita fought back an unexpected giggle. "Yes, I'm sorry, I behaved like a brat. Mark had told me you'd taken Izi out to lunch…"

"Were you jealous?"

"No!" she exclaimed. Kit was silent, one eyebrow raised. "Maybe, a bit," she admitted. There was still no response. "All right, yes, I was bloody annoyed."

Kit grinned and Perdita rolled her eyes.

"All right, you can have your Smug-Mackensie-Kid moment," she sighed, "then tell me what's going on."

Kit's amused expression faltered, and he screwed up his face as he spoke, his voice quiet and serious. "You don't have to be jealous of Izi," he reassured Perdita, "she's like my little sister. I agreed to talk to her because her sudden announcement that she intends to take a year off is completely out of character, and everyone is worried."

"Where will she go?"

"Her plan, if I was in agreement, was to take a year's sabbatical, to travel and decide what she wants to do next. She completed her master's degree a few months ago, but she'd like to do a PhD and is considering going abroad to study. I agreed to keep her job open as it is for a year, but if she does increase her qualifications, then I've promised to help her either find work elsewhere or create a position within Jerusalem or Marquess House. She's Meg's best friend, after all."

Perdita felt a pang of loss. Izabel was such a key member of their team that it stung to realise she only saw it as a job. However, she knew it was important for Izabel to follow her dreams and she pushed her own sense of disappointment aside.

"Did you agree a leaving date?"

"Yes, three months from today, this is why everyone is so upset. Although Izi's been thinking about this for a while, she hasn't discussed it with anyone, so it's been a bombshell. Mark is devastated. She ended their relationship at the weekend. They've been going out with each other since they were 14."

Perdita stared at Kit in amazement. "14?"

"Yes, they were real childhood sweethearts. It's part of the reason why everyone is so bemused by Izi's behaviour."

"Do you think she's met someone else?"

"Sadly, I do," admitted Kit. "I tried to keep things work-related because her private life is nothing to do with her position here, but a few of the things she said made me wonder if there was another man in the background. The main

55

one is this sudden desire to travel — Izi has always claimed she would never want to leave Pembrokeshire."

Perdita turned back to the trunk, unsure what to say. If she was honest, then she understood Izabel's need to fly free for a while, to have an adventure with a handsome stranger and live her dreams.

"On a professional level, what do you think about it all, Perds? If we hadn't discussed this today, I was going to arrange a meeting with you and Piper to talk things through; after all, ultimately Izabel works for Marquess House, so you're her employer and you'll have to sign off on the paperwork."

"Izabel is a talented young woman," said Perdita. "We must do all we can to help her."

"Even though you were jealous?"

Perdita scowled at Kit. "I've said sorry for my momentary lapse, but, yes, even though, for a few moments, I was jealous."

Kit grinned and turned back to the trunk, examining the few remaining items that had been under the tapestry.

"What?" said Perdita, nudging him. "What does that grin mean?"

Kit picked up an old hat pin and turned it over, examining it carefully.

"It means I have hope," he replied, and the look he shot Perdita made her blush.

CHAPTER FIVE

For the next few days, Perdita and Kit sorted through the trunks. After the excitement of discovering the tapestry, the first trunk offered up nothing more than junk: several hat pins, a broken music box and two battered umbrellas. The locks were recalcitrant, and it took a locksmith, as well as Geraint, to penetrate the rusted mechanisms. Both trunks were stuffed full of books, documents, and sketches. Jenny had gone into rhapsodies over the discovery.

"We'll need to catalogue these," she said. "Who knows what we might discover in here?"

Perdita stared down at the two overflowing trunks.

"I wonder who put all this in the basement and walled it up?" she mused, returning to the tapestry that was still resplendent on the boardroom table. "We know that Granny Lettice built the grotto because we have the letters and bills from its construction, so I doubt she would have boarded it back up. It wasn't Gran, so that means it must have been either her mother, Eleanor Fitzroy, or Eleanor's mother…"

"Margaret Cecil," supplied Kit, reading from a piece of paper.

"Pardon?"

"Dad drew me a rough family tree to bring this one up to date," he said, handing Perdita the A4 sheet. "He checked the old records left by his father."

"Lettice had one daughter, Margaret, who married Peter Cecil in 1905. They had two children, Cedric Henry, and Eleanor Laetitia, who was Mary's mother. Cedric died in 1934 from diphtheria. Eleanor married David Fitzroy and they had

Mary and Cecily," read Perdita. "This is fascinating. It must have been either Margaret or Eleanor who blocked up the grotto. Would your dad know?"

"He isn't certain, but he said when his great-grandfather, Robert Mackensie, worked here, Margaret Cecil undertook a number of modernisations, mostly bathrooms and heating, but he wondered if she may have blocked off the grotto. It would have been quite old by then and might have needed repairs, so blocking it off might have been easier."

"It would make sense," she agreed. "Thanks Kit."

Perdita returned to the trunks. Izabel was kneeling beside her grandmother, sorting through the papers.

"This trunk is all loose documents," she said, as Perdita and Kit approached. Moving to the other trunk, Perdita crouched down, her gloved hands moving through the top layers of old envelopes and piles of paper, but as she shifted the surface documents into a pile, ready to hand over to Jenny, her eyes widened in excitement.

"Books," she said.

"What kind?" asked Kit. "Are they published books or ledgers?"

"Ledgers, notebooks and sketchbooks," replied Perdita, handing Kit the loose leaves of paper, so her hands were free to peruse the new treasure.

"Any account books?" asked Izabel.

"A few, I think," replied Perdita.

With Kit, Jenny and Izabel's help, Perdita unpacked the trunk, laying each book on the boardroom table. When they had finished, Perdita was not the only one buzzing with anticipation. The books ranged in size from a number of large leather-bound accounts ledgers, to smaller sketchpads, a family Bible, and numerous notebooks. For Perdita, though, the most intriguing was a series of small, matching, green leather-bound notebooks. With great care, she had opened the cover of one and gasped: on the frontispiece was the familiar mermaid from the walls of Marquess House. The next page was handwritten and was clearly a diary, even though there were no prominent dates that she could discern.

"Jenny, I'd like these taken into my office," she said, stripping off her gloves.

"We usually take everything straight to our department and check them before anyone reads them…" began Izabel, then halted. "It was how we did things for Mary," she finished with an edge of defiance.

"Which was my grandmother's choice," said Perdita. "However, I would like to be the first to examine them, so will you please arrange for them to be sent to my office."

"Of course," said Jenny, with a smile, shooting Izabel a curious glance. "All the books, or just this series of notebooks?"

"The notebooks for now, and if you would catalogue all the other finds, then I'll let you know in which order I'd like them dealt with," replied Perdita.

Jenny gathered the notebooks together and left, with Izabel walking behind her.

"Do you think there might be something useful in them?" asked Kit.

"Maybe," replied Perdita. "After all, the image of the mermaid from the walls is drawn on the first page. When I read them, it might transpire they're from the wrong era or nothing to do with our mystery, which will probably be the case. Whatever they reveal, it'll be interesting."

Kit nodded. After a pause, he added, "Why did you snap at Izi?"

"I shouldn't have done," she admitted, "but she seemed so proprietorial of the books, as though she should read them first. Even if Izabel hadn't handed in her notice, it isn't her place to try and stop me reading the notebooks."

"True," said Kit. "I suppose she was following the rules as they were laid down by Mary."

"She was," agreed Perdita, "but Mary isn't here anymore."

Perdita saw Kit's eyes cloud with uncertainty, then he turned back to the books on the table and reached for the family Bible. She watched for a moment, then strode into her own office. Jenny had laid the books on cotton covered foam wedges. Perdita picked up the one closest to her and began to read.

PART TWO: ENGLAND, 1603

CHAPTER ONE

The words would not come; inspiration had fled. With a sigh of frustration, Lady Arbella Stuart replaced her quill in the inkwell and rubbed her eyes before reading the few lines she had managed. Wrinkling her nose at her efforts, she pushed the parchment aside. A soft murmur from the chair beside the roaring fire caught her attention, and she hurried over to the little girl who was stretched out, asleep. The concern in Arbella's eyes faded to relief as she gazed down at the slumbering form. This morning, her daughter had been complaining of head pains and, with her own ill health a constant shadow on her life, Arbella had been concerned Ennie might be showing similar symptoms. It seemed her worries had been misplaced — Ennie slept peacefully, and her cheeks were their usual healthy pink.

Settling into the chair opposite her daughter, Arbella took simple pleasure in watching her sleep. Ennie would be eight years old in the summer. It was time to consider a marriage settlement, as well as a household of her own where her status would be fully recognised. There was a person she was considering as a suitable match, but she suspected those around her would see it as a subversive union.

Before this though, Ennie would need to be established in her own house. It saddened Arbella that they were not living there now. A bitter smile played across her face as she surveyed the room around her. It was sumptuously furnished with the embellishments of luxury that befitted her status as a member of the royal family, but it was not her house. The property where she and Ennie currently resided belonged to her grandmother, and Arbella was not at liberty to leave. *House-arrest*, she thought, *a prison of great of luxury, yet it remains a prison, owned by the person I love and hate equally.*

The fire crackled and Arbella closed her eyes as she returned to considering Ennie's future. Marriages between members of the royal family were matters of state, yet she feared Ennie might suffer the same fate as she had: years of disappointment as foreign prince after foreign prince was dangled to solve whatever trade deal or political upheaval was vexing the Privy Council, only to be snatched away when the issue was otherwise resolved. It was only when Arbella had taken matters into her own hands and eloped that she had achieved a man who had reached her requirements for a husband. Narrowing her eyes, she vowed to herself that Ennie would never be used in such a callous manner by the Privy Council. Her daughter would marry an English noble and remain here.

The creak of the door interrupted Arbella's musings and Bridget Sherland, her chief lady-in-waiting, entered the room.

"My lady, your grandmother has sent word she will be here shortly," she whispered, then glancing over at Ennie, said, "How is she?"

"Much recovered," replied Arbella in a soft voice.

"The Dowager Countess will be relieved."

A flurry at the door announced the entrance of Arbella's grandmother, Elizabeth Talbot, the dowager countess of Shrewsbury, better known as Bess of Hardwick. Bess was, as usual, dressed in splendid style, as though she were at court. It was often commented that she presided over her vast mansion of Hardwick Hall like a queen. 'More glass than wall' were the words to the snide poem sniggered by those who viewed Bess as a social climber, thanks to the huge and ostentatious windows of her magnificent manor. There was no other property to rival its grandeur, and the sheer spectacle of the house had turned Bess into a living legend.

Arbella's elopement with William in 1594 had horrified Bess, but she had helped Arbella to conceal her marriage. Bess had experience in such matters, as the marriage between Arbella's parents had caused a scandal and the dowager countess had narrowly avoided a stint in the Tower herself. Arbella and William's nuptials had coincided with continuing rebellion in Ireland and an unfolding economic crisis after a series of wet summers and poor crops. Queen Elizabeth, who had been distracted by these greater matters of state, had not been told of the marriage of one of her potential heirs.

When Arbella had begun to show signs of pregnancy, Bess had ordered her back to Hardwick Hall, where she remained, keeping in touch with her friends through her prolific letter writing. Much as she would have liked to show off her beautiful daughter, Arbella was a pragmatist and had agreed to keep the knowledge of her child a secret from all but a chosen few. When a few years later she had delivered a healthy son and heir, even the unflappable Bess had been concerned about the potential effect this child's birth could have on the succession.

Despite breaking Arbella's heart, the boy had been removed to a safe house. He had been handed to a distant Stuart cousin, who agreed to change their names to Steward to further disguise their connections to Arbella. The small boy had not been told of his true parentage, even though Arbella wrote to him regularly and Bess provided for him financially.

William's explosive and violent temper had driven him in directions Arbella would never have believed possible. Even now, several years later, she felt the swooping sickness of shame and guilt when she remembered William's actions and his violent end.

Arbella rose from her chair and curtseyed, as etiquette required. Bess smiled, indicating she should stand. The firelight caught her face and Arbella was struck by how old her grandmother appeared this evening. Bess was nearing her seventy-sixth birthday, and today she looked her age. *Although*, thought Arbella, *her mind is still as sharp as ever.*

"How is our precious girl?" asked Bess.

"Recovered," Arbella replied.

As Bess bent over the child, a smile broke across her lined face. "What a relief," she sighed, settling herself in the chair Arbella had vacated. "I was concerned. Children are so delicate."

"Bridget, perhaps you could take Ennie through to her bedchamber," said Arbella as the child stirred.

"Yes, my lady."

When Ennie was safely away, Arbella turned to Bess.

"I have had word from Sir Robert Cecil," said Bess without preamble.

"How is he?" asked Arbella.

Robert Cecil, the earl of Salisbury had taken over from his father, William Cecil, Lord Burghley as Lord Privy Seal to Queen Elizabeth. Arbella swallowed a secret smile. She did not fear Robert or his power, as the majority of the court did; she knew he held her in high regard and had even spoken to her of marriage. He was a widower and he was aware that a marriage to Arbella would raise his status at court. *And who knows where else*, thought Arbella, *if I am able to follow the path destiny has dangled in my lap.*

"Does Robert have news of the succession?" Arbella asked.

"Yes," replied Bess, her voice carrying a cautious edge. "At present, Robert's preferred candidate to inherit Elizabeth's crown is your cousin James VI of Scotland."

Arbella considered this information before speaking. "Does Robert think the succession will happen without a challenge?"

"It is how he hopes to arrange it," replied Bess.

Arbella felt a rush of anger. Robert might be her friend, but his arrogance on occasions was more than she could bear. "How *he* hopes to arrange it?" Her tone was derisive. "When was he appointed kingmaker?"

"It is how he has always viewed himself," said Bess.

"But my cousin James was not born in the realm —" Arbella began.

Bess held up her hand to silence her. "My sweet Arbella," she said, "we have discussed this at length over the years. The law to which you cling with such devotion is outdated and obsolete."

"Under the terms of the will of Henry VIII, only those born in England have a right to claim the throne. If this is the case, then I am the —"

"The what?" interrupted Bess, her voice ringing with warning. "Even saying those words is treason, and you are already viewed with suspicion by many men of power. The legislation to which you refer is long since out of date — you know this, Arbella. It was overturned by King Edward, Queen Mary, and Queen Elizabeth. You of all people understand the reasons why James has a superior claim to yours — you have been at the heart of this subterfuge since it began. The chances of you being named queen are slim. We only ever had hope; we never had the law on our side."

Arbella narrowed her blue eyes, her face taking on a calculated and malevolent expression. "Yes, I have been at the heart of this secret," she agreed. "Perhaps it is time to reveal it to the world. It would be manna from heaven for those who wish to stop James, a foreigner, from claiming the English throne."

Bess allowed the silence to grow between them before she responded. "But you are a woman, and the Privy Council wishes to be out from under the petticoats of queens."

"It is not their choice. It is the law."

"Which they write to suit themselves," retorted Bess. "King Henry's laws for succession are over 50 years old; they no longer bear any relevance."

Arbella glared at her grandmother. "What about my son? He is of the blood royal."

"But nobody, except a select few, are aware of his existence," sighed Bess, "and even if you were to present him at court, he is only four years old. Do you think the country would risk a child of uncertain parentage over the king of Scotland? A grown man with a wife and a dynasty that will secure the monarchy and the country for generations to come?"

Arbella leapt to her feet in fury. "My claim is stronger," she exclaimed.

"You are a woman and you are the widow of a traitor," Bess snapped. "Your husband was executed. Do you really think the country would accept you or your son as the monarch?" Bess's brown eyes looked worried for the first time. "The Tudor era is drawing to a close," she continued. "There is unease everywhere. The queen has left no will and no direct heir. The question of who will claim the crown could be the trigger for another bloody battle, one that has not been seen since the battle at Bosworth. The darkest of moods is creeping through the great houses of state, as men arm themselves and align with their preferred choice of candidate. We must protect ourselves against those who resent your claim to the throne and, for now, concealing both your children will be the wisest course of action."

"Oh Grandmamma, you ask too much." Arbella's blue eyes flashed with fury.

"We are a family; bickering is part of how we communicate, but our aim is the same and I do love you so very much, my sweet child. Keeping you here, under my supervision, was the only way we could ensure you were not attainted with treason like your husband."

It was some moments before Arbella was able to speak and, when she did, her response was guided by etiquette rather than her true feelings. "My apologies, Grandmamma," she managed in a calm tone, although her breathing was ragged and she would not meet Bess's eyes. "It's been a difficult day and I am tired. You are quite correct; we must proceed with caution."

Bess smiled at Arbella. "I have been thinking of your cousin, Lady Jane Grey," she said, her voice low and calm.

Arbella was not fooled and felt her stomach lurch. "The nine-day queen." She shuddered. "The Protestant martyr."

"She has been on my mind all day," admitted Bess. "I believe my feelings are a warning, Arbel."

"Grandmamma, you are tired — these are the notions of a worried mind, nothing more," Arbella responded, but Bess would not be deflected.

"Remember what happened when your cousin Jane was placed on the throne," Bess said. "Mary Tudor fled to her East Anglian heartland where she declared herself queen and gathered support. Nobles flocked to her, raising armies and support, clearing the way for her to claim her throne as they escorted her to London. By the time she arrived, it was clear

Jane's tenure as monarch was over. The rightful heir had arrived with men of rank at her side."

"What has this to do with me?" sighed Arbella.

Bess turned her shrewd eyes to meet her own. "Robert Cecil has summoned you to London."

"What?"

"Perhaps by placing you in London, he hopes to avoid a similar procession across the country with you at its head, accompanied by men of power who are resistant to a foreign prince wearing the English crown."

"You said the Privy Council was ill-disposed to be once again under the petticoats of a queen," Arbella protested.

"And so I believe it to be true, but there are always some who would prefer a controllable female to the unknown perils of a foreign male. By having you only a few miles from the court in London, Robert Cecil has neutralised your ability to process through the north, raising an army to challenge the succession."

Arbella gazed at her grandmother in horrified awe. "Do you think he suspects this of me? Of us?" she stammered.

"Robert is a wise young man. He will leave nothing to chance, and perhaps he has heard the rumours."

"What rumours?"

"Lord Beauchamp is gathering an army."

"The nephew of Lady Jane Grey? If he is, then it will be because *he* desires the throne, not because he's planning to fight for me," said Arbella.

"There are also rumours that your friend, George Chaworth is your secret lover and plans to rally troops to support your claim."

"Grandmamma, we have also heard whispers that Cousin James is my secret lover," Arbella countered, "and we both know this is nonsense."

"Treasonous charges have been brought against princesses of the crown with less evidence than the rumours which swirl around you now, Arbel," Bess warned. "You tread on many men's dreams and ambitions simply by being alive. You are a potential queen and, despite our belief that you will be passed by, there are always men who will use your name to further their own ambitions. You must proceed with caution in the next few weeks, my dear. The Ladies of Melusine and I will do all we can to protect you, but as the sands of time shift, we must flow with them until we see what power remains to us."

"Very well," sighed Arbella. "I will do as you advise. When am I to leave for London?"

"Cecil is sending his man Sir Henry Brounker to accompany you. It is planned that you will stay at Osterley House, a few miles from Richmond Palace where the court resides. You will be the guest of Sir William and Lady Gertrude Reade."

"The cousin of your friend, Lady Katherine Newton," interrupted Arbella. "I like Katherine. She is a clever woman and has remarkable penmanship."

"It's not surprising. She and Frances are both Pastons by birth — now there is a family who reveres the written word. We are entering strange times. The queen will no longer be on the throne by the spring. We will discuss your requirements for your journey to London while we eat. It is best you are prepared."

"Prepared for what?" Arbella asked.

"All eventualities," was Bess's enigmatic response.

CHAPTER TWO

"My lady, a package has arrived." Bridget Sherland hurried into the warm, brightly lit greeting chamber. "It's from your friend, Viscount Chaworth."

"At last," Arbella said, discarding her quill and rising from her writing desk as she took the package. "George promised he would send word as soon as he had a reply."

Pulling off the heavy hessian wrapper with eager fingers, Arbella's eyes widened as she removed the three slim leather-bound books. "What a treat!" she exclaimed as she examined each title. An old copy of *The French Historie* by Anne Dowriche, which George knew she wanted to read again; a new copy of The Book of Common Prayer that she had requested and a third book, bound in dark green leather and embossed with gold. A length of green ribbon was tied around it.

"This must the one, *Ane Godlie Dreame* by Elizabeth Melville, Lady Culross."

Bridget glanced around, her eyes darting towards the door. "How do you know, my lady?" she whispered.

"This is fresh from the printer, Robert Charteris in Edinburgh, and it is wrapped in green ribbon. Is there a note? It may contain the cipher."

Bridget searched the hessian wrappings and pulled out a folded piece of parchment, which she passed to Arbella:

"'To my dearest Arbel'," Arbella read aloud, "'to help you through the dark days of winter. Your friend, George Chaworth'."

"Maybe they are only books," said Bridget, her voice full of disappointment.

"You've always been too quick to admit defeat, my dear," said Arbella. She pulled a candlestick towards her and held the short note from the viscount in front of it. As if by magic more words appeared, this time written between the lines. "Invisible ink," said Arbella. "My cousin, Bessie Pierrepont, taught me this method of passing messages. She was situated with my Aunt Mary, the Queen of Scots, and they often used it to pass information. It was one of the many subterfuges perfected by the Ladies of Melusine. Write this down. 'Between the fourth, eighth, twelfth and sixteenth leaf,'" she read.

"But how do you know which book?"

"It is always the volume tied with the green ribbon," laughed Arbella. "It was the secret symbol that there were messages hidden within."

Discarding the silken cords, Arbella flipped through the pages, scouring each one for information, but on first sight there was nothing. Holding up a single leaf to the candle, a message emerged. Taking the quill from Bridget, she scribbled down the random selection of letters that had been secreted between the lines of poetry. Returning to her writing desk, she felt underneath, releasing the catch on the secret drawer, and removed a leather roll from which she took a series of ciphers, each written on a thin strip of paper. Checking the information she had gathered from Elizabeth Melville's poetry book, she began translating the message. Moments later, a look of fury flooded her beautiful face.

"The old fool Hertford has betrayed us," she spat.

"Sir Edward Seymour?" gasped Bridget, horrified, and Arbella gave a terse nod.

"The message that my man John Dodderidge took to him before Christmas, suggesting a marriage between my daughter and his grandson, William, has sent him into a panic. He says that if a union between two children with such strong claims to the throne is discussed without involving the queen, it will be viewed as treason. He has sent my letter to Robert Cecil, who has shown it to the queen. It seems Sir Henry Brounker and his unsavoury lackeys will not only be escorting me to London; they will be questioning me first. Oh, this is intolerable."

"Do you think the queen will send you to the Tower of London?"

"We shan't be sent to the Tower, Bridget," said Arbella. "The earl is being overcautious. He was incarcerated there after he secretly wed Lady Katherine Grey. I should have written to Edward Seymour's daughter-in-law, Honora, instead of the old man; she's the most sensible person in that family."

Running her slim white fingers through her abundant auburn curls, Arbella paced the room as she considered the best way to deal with this irritating situation.

"George says that from what he has heard, our friend Sir Henry Brounker is sure I was acting alone," she said. "He has reported to the queen that I am hysterical and therefore shouldn't be taken seriously."

"Seymour's behaviour is a betrayal of trust," muttered Bridget.

"Perhaps," agreed Arbella, "but the other letters we sent concerning this suggested marriage have reached their marks and have not been revealed to Robert Cecil. Even this letter from George has made it through. If Robert were seriously concerned about us committing treason and subterfuge, we would never have received this package from George. He would have diverted it and sent us a feint instead."

73

"Are you sure the letters were not intercepted?"

"George is but a lawyer from Nottinghamshire who shows too much interest in the stage and the playhouses," Arbella replied. "His notes are far too low on the scale of importance to be on Robert Cecil's list of potential deviants, especially at present while Robert is placing all his energies into securing the throne for my cousin, James Stuart."

The final scraps of the letter succumbed to the flames, shuddering into white ghosts, and floating with elegant grace up the chimney, their secrets lost forever.

"We must prepare, Bridget," said Arbella, her voice brisk and business-like. "My grandmother will no doubt hear of this, and I shall have to ensure she is satisfied with my responses."

"What will you say?"

"My grandmother and I have decided that for now it is prudent to keep the knowledge of my children limited to those we can trust. Therefore, if I am questioned about this, I shall suggest I was enquiring after a betrothal between myself and the earl's son."

"What about the Ladies of Melusine? Shall I inform them of our predicament?" asked Bridget.

"Yes, that would be most helpful. Use the usual codes in case the letters are intercepted."

"Do you think that's possible?"

"Oh yes," said Arbella, "although at present, with Robert Cecil so preoccupied, I think our letters will be passed over. Robert Cecil knows there are potential heirs other than his chosen candidate, the Scottish king, which is why he is trying to draw anyone with a claim to London, where they are under his power. My position in the order of succession is well-known and Robert was always suspicious of my husband, which leads him to doubt my loyalty to the crown. This is why

Ennie is being sent away. She will travel with her own court to the house bestowed upon me by Queen Elizabeth. It is far from London, so Ennie will be safe."

Bridget gathered the wrappings from the parcel and hurried from the room, intent on her purpose to write to her fellow secret keepers.

Arbella stretched her arms above her head, feeling the muscles in her back release. Her hunched position over her writing desk often led to tensions and pain, a problem that was exacerbated by the ill-health she had battled since she was a child. For months at a time she would be well, then an episode would engulf her and she would be bedridden for weeks. It was a frustrating way to live, always wondering when the next bout would bring her low.

Shaking her head to rid it of such dispiriting thoughts, she resumed her pacing, reviewing her plans and evaluating their continuing viability. She had grown up surrounded by strong women and had learned from the nursery that in order to protect oneself in the uncertain world of the court and the aristocracy, it was essential to remain forever alert and to build around oneself a trusted network of friends, influencers, spies and informers. This was even more important when royal blood flowed through your veins, as it did through hers, making her a potential heir to the throne of England.

Arbella came to a halt in front of one the bay windows and stared out over the winter grounds of Hardwick Hall as she considered all the possible outcomes of Edward Seymour's betrayal. With luck, if Cecil and Brounker believed she was mad, she would receive nothing more than a patronising reprimand, which, while insulting, would be preferable to the potential humiliation of being locked in the Tower of London.

Despite what she had said to reassure Bridget, this was a real possibility.

Sighing deeply, she sank into a cushioned chair, wondering if she would ever be allowed control over her own life again or whether she would be tethered to this tedious incarceration forever.

CHAPTER THREE

"Arbella, my dear, you look well rested after your long sleep," exclaimed Lady Gertrude Reade as Arbella entered the Withdrawing Room at Osterley House.

Gertrude was in her early 50s but looked far younger and exuded energy. Her light brown hair was drawn back from her face in a soft cap and her hazel eyes sparkled. Formerly Gertrude Paston, she was a cousin of Lady Katherine Newton and another member of the Ladies of Melusine.

Osterley was ideally placed between the royal palaces of Richmond and Hampton Court, and the Syon estates of the Earl and Countess of Northumberland, to allow Gertrude to act as both a link for correspondence between the Ladies of Melusine and a safe place of refuge. It was for these reasons that Bess had chosen the house as Arbella's base, despite the invitation offered by Robert Cecil for her to join him at Cecil House on The Strand in London.

"Thank you, Gertrude," replied Arbella with a warm smile, relaxing as she gazed around the elegant room with its roaring fire. It had been an arduous journey south. The day before she had left Hardwick Hall, a coded letter had arrived from Lady Frances Brooke, telling her there was a rumour that Arbella planned to travel south at the head of an army of three hundred horses. *If only*, Arbella had thought. "I had hoped Anne would be home," Arbella said, glancing around at the gathered guests.

"My daughter is with her husband, Michael Stanhope, in Sudbourne, Suffolk," replied Gertrude. "She is incredibly sad to have missed your visit, but with the court in such disarray due to the queen's illness, they felt it would be prudent to absent themselves for the present. However, you shall not be bored, my dear."

Although it was never spoken of, everyone was aware that Michael Stanhope's father had been executed in 1552, when he had been convicted of conspiring to murder John Dudley, 1st duke of Northumberland. Many considered Stanhope to be a hero, as he was trying to stop what he saw as a coup against the crown and the legitimate heir, Mary Tudor. As there was once again a feeling of unease about the succession, Arbella agreed with the wisdom of their decision to remove themselves from any potential danger.

Gertrude led Arbella and her two most senior ladies-in-waiting, Bridget Sherland and Anne Bradshaw, to the women in the corner. They had abandoned their card game to greet the newcomers with deep curtseys. Arbella indicated for them to rise.

"Arbella, ladies, it's good to have you here, at last," exclaimed Lady Elizabeth Brooke. "How was your journey, Arbel?"

"It was as pleasant as can be expected when you are accompanied by Robert Cecil's lackey, Sir Henry Brounker. Especially when he thinks you are insane because you dare to question his judgement."

The women exchanged knowing glances. Brounker was ill-liked and they had all encountered him at some point in their lives.

"Frances, how is your mother?" asked Arbella, turning to Lady Frances Brooke.

Lizzie and Frances were sisters-in-law, married respectively to the Reverend Sir George Brooke and his elder brother, Henry Brooke, 11th baron Cobham. However, Frances was also the daughter of Lady Kate Carey, who, with Lettice Knollys, Lady Katherine Newton, and Bess, had been the core of Queen Elizabeth's trusted Ladies of Melusine.

"Like the queen, she knows her time is near," said Frances, her grey eyes filling with tears. "My brothers and sisters and I have said our goodbyes; she wants only my father with her."

"My dear, I am so sorry," murmured Arbella, squeezing Frances's hand.

"Gertrude said I could remain here in case Mother changes her mind and sends for me."

Turning away from Arbella, Frances walked to the window, her face hidden from the sympathy of the women as she strove to compose herself. The door opened and a petite, dark-haired woman with deep brown eyes entered, her air of confidence marking her out as aristocracy.

"And here is our final guest — Lady Raleigh," exclaimed Gertrude, although her eyes were full of concern for Frances.

Arbella's eyes widened in surprise. Lady Raleigh, the wife of Sir Walter, the explorer and pirate, as well as the Captain of the Guard, was a curious addition to the group. Despite her marriage, Arbella always thought of Lady Raleigh by her maiden name, Bess Throckmorton, who had a blood connection to the majority of noble families.

"My lady," said Bess, sweeping a curtsey to Arbella, who smiled and gestured for her to rise.

"My dear, Bess," she said, taking her arm and leading her to the card table.

As though this was the signal they had been waiting for, the other women moved to their activities. Noticing the serious expression on her mistress's face, Anne Bradshaw, an heiress in her own right, swept to the harpsichord and prepared to play. Bridget Sherland followed, renowned for her beautiful singing voice.

Shooting them a complicit glance, Arbella took her position at the card table and, gathering the deck together, began to shuffle. Anne and Bridget would use the music to make it difficult for her and Bess to be overheard. Moments later, Lizzie and Frances joined them. Gertrude returned to her writing desk.

Glancing around the room, Arbella felt a small glow of satisfaction. Men might think they were the only ones who understood the subtle art of spy-craft, but each of these women were part of her especially selected network of writers, what she and her grandmother referred to as the cadet branch of the Ladies of Melusine. These were the key figures who had helped Arbella to develop her own codes and create new methods of passing on vital information.

"How were things when you were last at court?" murmured Arbella to Bess.

"The mood is dark," Bess replied in kind. "There are those who believe the country needs a king and, in James, they have not only a king but a dynasty as he has children and a wife. They believe this will ensure the safety of the country for many decades to come."

"You said, 'there are those'," replied Arbella, laying cards as she spoke. "Is the feeling at court that James has the only real claim and should ascend to be king without considering other potential heirs?"

"Some men favour Beauchamp's claim," said Lizzie, "but many find his arrogance and mercurial temper a worrying combination. His claim is also thought by many of the Privy Council to be very weak."

"Do any mention my name?" asked Arbella, the tremor of her fingers giving away her nervousness.

"There are many who think you are the rightful heir," whispered Lizzie. "My husband, George, is fervent in this belief."

"As is mine," confirmed Frances.

"They have other men willing to place you on the throne if you will promise to favour them once you are queen and allow them to worship as they wish. They prefer the Catholic mass to the Protestant," added Lizzie.

Arbella's heart pounded and she could feel her palms perspiring. "Who else?" she whispered.

"Thomas Grey; my brothers, Arthur and Nicholas Throckmorton," said Bess. "There is also Sir Griffin Markham and his brother, William, who I believe are friends of your grandmother. Our other allies are Dorothy Percy and her sister, Penelope Rich, but they have yet to persuade their husbands to our cause. Robert Catesby, his cousin Francis Tresham and his wife, Anne; Thomas Winter and his wife, Gertrude; John Grant and his brothers-in-law, John and Christopher Wright."

Arbella closed her eyes as she absorbed this information. These were people she had known for many years. They were willing to risk their lives and their liberty to put her on the throne. A rush of adrenalin coursed through her and she could not suppress a smile.

The four women continued to play cards, re-shuffling the deck and dealing a new hand.

"What do they intend?" murmured Arbella as they once again began laying cards.

"To capture James on his progress to London and place you on the throne in his stead," whispered Lizzie.

"Do they intend his murder?"

"If it is necessary, I believe they will," said Lizzie. "George claims he would prefer it if the matter were settled peacefully and James returned to his own realm to rule. However, should James resist this offer, then they are gathering men and gunpowder to ensure a quick and efficient victory."

"There are also those who suggest the kidnapping of his heirs, Prince Henry and Princess Elizabeth, but this is considered to be unnecessary by others and is causing some divisions," added Frances.

They continued to play for a few moments, then Bess spoke. "Frances knows more. Her husband, Henry, has been making plans with Walter and Thomas."

Frances, already pale, seemed to lose even more colour. "Indeed. Henry is to receive help from the Archduke Albert and his envoy Charles de Ligne, the comte d'Aremberg. Henry is to travel to Brussels, then on to Valladolid and Madrid to raise funds before returning to Jersey, where Raleigh is governor and will give him safe haven. They will use this money to raise an army to place you on the throne in James's place."

"Surely this will take time and, by then, James may already be king."

"Do not forget the nine-day queen," murmured Lizzie.

Arbella felt a cold shiver run down her spine. These were the words her grandmother had used. Was this their plan? To allow a smooth succession, then a coup shortly afterwards? This way, they would pacify Robert Cecil and those members of the Privy Council who wanted a king, but it would also allow the new monarch long enough to disgrace himself, perhaps through another plan. "Is Robert Cecil the puppet master?" whispered Arbella, her voice betraying panic for the first time.

The women exchanged a concerned look.

"No, I don't think so," said Lizzie, but she sounded uncertain. "I believe it was Henry and Walter who created the plan, perhaps with some help from Bess's cousin, Robert Catesby."

Arbella shivered — she knew Catesby; he had been a loyal friend to her husband. "Very well," she whispered.

"And, if this was suggested to you, my lady, would you approve the plan?" Lizzie asked.

The faces of her aunt and her husband flashed before Arbella. Heirs who would never inherit. Did she desire the power enough to risk her life? Yes, she did. After a lifetime with little or no control over her own affairs, the aphrodisiacal thought of complete power over all who had spurned, ridiculed, or humiliated her was a treasure to behold. Yet even with this rush of excitement, caution from years of watching her grandmother navigate the power games at court made her consider: what would she do in this situation? The answer flowed into her mind as though Bess was standing beside her: Bess would agree but would refuse to implicate herself.

"I believe it to be a good plan," whispered Arbella, aware her words would trigger a sequence of events over which she would have no control, "but I will commit nothing to paper and I claim the right to refuse all knowledge if my life is in danger."

"Very well, Arbella," said Lizzie, looking at Frances, who nodded. "We will tell our husbands you approve of their jape and we will await their next suggestion."

Frances gathered the deck of cards together with an air of finality. "I shall write to Henry," she said and bobbed a curtsey to Arbella.

"When I see Walter this evening, I shall pass on your interest," said Bess Throckmorton. "He is never happier than when he is planning a new jest."

Curtseying, Bess, too, swept from the room. As the door closed behind her, the music came to a natural end, casting the room into an unexpected silence. Standing, Arbella nudged the table with her wide skirts and a playing card, the Queen of Hearts, fluttered from the pack and landed in the fire. Arbella reached forward to try and rescue the card but she was too late; the eager flames had grabbed its edge and were consuming it with gleeful jaws.

Arbella felt a jolt of fear as the card was consumed, crumbling to ash before her eyes, wondering if this was an omen of ill-luck.

CHAPTER FOUR

The sting of the air on her face made Arbella feel alive. It had been a morning of riding, hunting and mischief with a group of friends she knew were loyal to her and her cause. Osterley House was surrounded by ornamental gardens and vast parkland and as the weeks of winter frost had given way to softer, warmer air, the hint of spring was like a long-forgotten promise suddenly recalled. Daffodils undulated in the breeze, while the brave snowdrops withered and died.

After two weeks cooped up in her bedroom at Osterley House due to a bout of her illness, Arbella was relieved to be well again and outside enjoying the first of this spring sunshine. Laughter and shouts surrounded her as she pushed her horse to catch up with Anne Bradshaw, who galloped at the front of the hunting party.

"I can see Syon House," called Anne from her vantage point at the head of the crowd of riders. "Dorothy said they would meet us in the water-meadow, and we can ride through their estate along the river towards Kew. There is the usual crowd of Henry's staying."

Arbella, who was now level with Anne, shouted, "She'll meet me first!" and urged her horse forward until it was a nose ahead of her friend, who laughed and pushed her horse to catch Arbella's. They raced good-naturedly for the last few hundred yards, jumping the fence into the vast water-meadow where they could see Dorothy waiting in the distance. Beside her was her groom, Parker, but apart from him, she was alone.

Anne and Arbella exchanged a concerned look.

"Do you think something has happened?" asked Anne, slowing her horse.

"It's possible," replied Arbella. "You wait here for the others; I'll speak to Dorothy."

Anthony Byron, Arbella's head groom, rode to join her. "My lady, it's unsafe for you to continue alone, allow me to accompany you."

"Very well," she called, ever conscious of her status as a member of the royal family and the precarious position this left her in. Since childhood, she had been schooled to understand she must always entertain caution as she was a target for kidnappers, thieves and blaggards of the worst sort. This constant vigilance had left her a nervous adult, a situation she knew was exacerbated by her illness. The pains in her side, the paralysis it brought, and the bouts of extreme fear and unease felt like a shadow-self lurking in the corner of her eye, waiting to consume her.

Walking her horse towards Dorothy Percy, Arbella wondered what news she was about to receive. Dorothy shook her reins and walked her gentle mare forwards, her face pale. The strained look on Dorothy's face was one Arbella recognised well. There was death in the air and no matter how they tried to disguise it, the women close to the queen wore its pall on their faces.

"Your mother?" were Arbella's first words to Dorothy as their horses drew level, but Dorothy shook her head.

"Aunt Kate," she replied. "She's asked to see Frances. Is she with you?"

"Yes, she's riding at the back with Henry. Anthony, will you ride back and fetch Lord and Lady Cobham? I shall be safe here with the countess."

Bowing his head, Anthony turned his horse and trotted to the group that was now gathering around Anne at the edge of the field.

"The queen asks for you too, Arbella," said Dorothy. "Robert Cecil has organised a barge from the Isleworth Stairs. It is barely a mile from here."

"Robert has organised this?"

Dorothy gave a curt nod. "Our Lord Privy Seal is ensuring all runs to his plan," spat Dorothy, her eyes narrowed in anger. "He sends Mountjoy, my sister's lover, into danger, he rallies against his old enemies, he behaves, in short, as though he were king."

"He believes he is a kingmaker."

"When really there should be no Scottish king at all. We both know there is another —"

"Enough Dorothy," hissed Arbella. "This is treason. We must always proceed with caution."

"But, Arbel, how do you stand it?" Dorothy's brown eyes were wide with despair.

"Because I have seen too many women crushed by the men in power, and I do not intend to become the next. My son is safe where he is, and he is but a boy. It is not yet his time, but if it is mine, then I can ensure he will follow in my footsteps."

"Arbel, do you know nothing of Cecil's intentions?" asked Dorothy, her fear making her impatient.

"Of course, my grandmother is one of the best-informed people in the country. Her spy network rivals even that of Cecil. We are aware that George Nicholson, Cecil's chief intelligencer has been carrying correspondence informing him of the queen's health for the past few weeks. He has also called together all the noblemen within a fifty-mile radius to make a pact to uphold the Privy Council until the new king arrives."

"What do you mean?"

"The moment the queen dies," explained Arbella, "the Privy Council should be disbanded and only resumed when there is a new monarch to approve the offices of power. It will take a few days to alert James to his new position and even longer for him to traverse the long road to London to claim his realm. In the days with no visible head of state, disaster could strike. Cecil has tried to destroy the evidence that was written by Queen Elizabeth discounting James from the succession because of his tendency to sympathise with the Spanish Catholics…"

"Tried?" asked Dorothy.

"It is safe at Hardwick Hall with my grandmother," whispered Arbella. "My grandmother is an old lady and is nervous of the power this letter would wield. She is uncertain whether even owning it could be an accusation of treason."

"Did Aunt Elizabeth name her heir?"

Arbella shook her head. "Alas, no, if she had, then we wouldn't have this treacherous atmosphere."

"She must have thought there would be time," said Dorothy.

"We all thought there would be years for her to resolve the issue," murmured Arbella. "I was only a child, but even I understood the gravity of the situation." Her voice petered out as the remainder of the group from Osterley House rode towards them, Lady Frances, and Lord Henry Brooke at the head.

"My mother…?" Frances began.

"All is arranged. We must ride to the Isleworth Stairs, where a barge for Richmond awaits," called Dorothy, then with a complicit nod to Arbella, turned her horse and headed towards the river.

Arbella, followed by Frances and Dorothy, hurried along the winding corridors of Richmond Palace. It was some years since she had visited, but the old building remained the same. The detailed scroll work on the panelled walls, the beautiful tapestries, the gentle light of the candle sconces and the floor coverings of sumptuous Turkey carpets.

This was the home Queen Elizabeth had always referred to as her "warm box", a place where she spent as much time as possible. It had always been Kate Carey's favourite royal residence, too, and that was why they were here. She had chosen the house where she felt most comfortable as she submitted to this final task for her beloved cousin and queen. Even though Queen Elizabeth was unaware, the Ladies of Melusine knew she would approve of their plan to bring her reign to an end.

The door opened the moment Arbella tapped, admitting the three women into the darkened chamber. Frances let out a sob as she hurried to the bed where her mother's near-lifeless form lay on the enormous canopied bed. The women at the bedside included Frances's sisters: Margaret and Elizabeth, who gathered her into their arms, drawing her forward, while Philadelphia Scrope and Eleanor Carey moved on silent feet, attending to their elder sister's final needs.

Arbella and Dorothy moved away, wishing to give privacy to the grieving women; both also trying to refrain from gagging at the stench of death permeating the overheated, stuffy room. Figures moved like ghosts in the gloom, all with the same objective, the desire to ease the last hours of Kate Howard, countess of Nottingham.

"Dorothy? Arbella? My dears, it is so good to see you both."

A stooped figure shuffled towards them, leaning heavily on a bejewelled walking stick.

"Mother," said Dorothy, relief in her voice as she sank into a curtsey and waited for her mother's gnarled, arthritic hand to bless her. Arbella, too, sank to the floor.

"Rise, my dears," said Lettice, her voice still melodic and warm. "My days as queen are over, I may return once more to my title of dowager countess of Leicester. I feel I would like to be remembered with more style than simply Lady Lettice."

"How fares Aunt Kate?" asked Dorothy, seemingly unable to cope with her mother's attempted levity.

"It will be soon," said Lettice, reaching for Dorothy's hand. "She has suffered for a long time, and the end will be a blessed release."

"And then, Aunt Lettice? What will happen?" asked Arbella.

Lettice shuffled to a nearby chair and sank into it. "I shall return to my home in Drayton Bassett in Staffordshire. Kate will be buried in Elizabeth's tomb as queen, and our subterfuge will be at an end. Finally, I shall have the time I need to mourn my beautiful cousins: Elizabeth Tudor, Mary Stuart and Ralph Fitzalan."

Arbella wiped away the unexpected tear brought on by Lettice's words. "And the succession?"

"Robert Cecil has doubled the guard around the palace. This is why you cannot stay, Arbel," she said. "However, there is one last task I must complete before my queenly duties are over."

Lettice signalled to another woman who had been hovering in the shadows throughout this exchange. Lady Katherine Newton, formerly Paston, and chief scribe for the Ladies of Melusine hurried forward. In her arms she carried a wooden chest.

"My lady," she said, curtseying to Arbella, who indicated she should rise.

"What is this?" asked Arbella, her voice harsh with nerves.

"When your Aunt Mary, the queen of Scots, died she bequeathed you her Book of Hours and her ruby ring, the one given to her when she was a baby."

Arbella nodded. "They are my most precious possessions," she confirmed.

"There was also a silver locket, set with a single diamond."

Lettice smiled when she saw Arbella's expression of surprised understanding. "You know about the locket?"

"My mother-in-law, Mary, gave it to me upon William's death. She told me it was of the utmost importance, but she would not explain further."

"She was correct, it is of the utmost importance. Poor Mary, she was never strong," sighed Lettice. "The locket was a present to Queen Catherine from Lady Isabel Baynton upon Catherine's arrival at court." Lettice paused, her face suddenly livid with pain. After a few moments, the attack passed and she continued. "When the Lady Cleves was dying, she summoned the Princess Elizabeth to her bedside and bequeathed her this casket. It holds the proof of our secrets. The signed confession of the Duke of Norfolk. Lady Margaret Douglas also explains the part she played in the hiding of Catherine's children, the true heirs. There are letters from Elizabeth and Mary, the ciphers to all our codes and, more recently, Katherine has written the truth about what happened to Queen Elizabeth. Kate Carey has added her confession, as have I. This casket is yours, Arbella. You may do with it as you wish. If you believe it will endanger your life, then you must destroy it. If, however, you think it might keep you and your children safe, then you must devise a place to hide it."

"There are three keys," said Katherine Newton, stepping forward and placing the casket on the table beside Lettice's chair. From a hidden pocket within her sleeve, Katherine produced the three small golden keys and placed them in Arbella's hand. "You must turn the centre key first, then the remaining two will turn together and the lock will release. This is a new addition. We felt it would protect the contents."

Arbella stared at Lettice. "The confessions," she asked, "are they signed?"

"Yes, and witnessed. They also bear the seals of all those who have written their stories for the casket."

"But if this were found…" began Arbella, her mind frantic. "It is treason."

"Unless you believe this proves the pathway of the rightful heir, then it is deliverance," whispered Lettice. "However, as we do not have windows into other men's souls and have no control over their pitiful brains, you are quite correct to react with fear. This is why you must leave before Robert Cecil's guard arrives and the palace is sealed off. But there is one last bequest." Lettice reached into the leather pouch hanging from her waist on a long golden chain. "My fingers are too swollen to wear this anymore," she said, "but it will sit well on your beautiful hands."

Arbella looked down as Lettice slid the heavy ruby ring onto her finger, the twin of the one she already owned.

"Now, my dear, if you are willing, we must disguise you as Katherine's maid. She is the only one who has permission to leave before Robert's men take over, and you must be away with the casket."

"Of course, Aunt Lettice," murmured Arbella, still unsure as to the meaning of all that had passed between them.

"You will remain with Katherine at her house this evening. We shall send word to Gertrude, so she doesn't fret."

"But the succession?" asked Arbella again.

"You must prepare for James to succeed, my dear. It is safer to let the men play their games of power. For now, at least." Breaking all etiquette, Lettice pulled Arbella into a maternal hug. "God speed, sweet Arbel," she whispered. "Until we meet again." Then she dropped into a curtsey as low as she could manage before returning to Kate's bedside.

"Come, my lady," whispered Katherine. "It is important we take you to safety."

Arbella allowed Katherine to throw a cloak around her shoulders, then fell into step behind her, relieved to be leaving behind the gloom of the death chamber as they hurried away into the gathering night.

CHAPTER FIVE

"But I can't," Arbella gasped as the letter from the College of Arms fell from her hand onto the table.

"You're the old queen's most senior female relative," said Lady Gertrude Reade, picking up the heavy vellum scroll and casting her eyes across it. "You must be chief mourner."

Arbella had returned to the safety of Osterley House in the days after the death of the old queen and the declaration of James as king.

Anne Bradshaw peered over Arbella's shoulder to examine the demand. "It says here that as chief mourner you are required to hold the banquet after the funeral, which must be paid for in full by you, and you must also provide black cloth for all members of the funeral procession," she read. "My dear, this would cost many thousands of pounds — how would you pay for it all?"

The assembled women all knew that despite the great wealth of Bess of Hardwick, Arbella herself was penniless. When she had married, her allowances and the manors bestowed upon her by Bess had become William's. His death and attainder had meant the majority of the lands had been claimed by the crown. Only a few minor manors remained in Arbella's hands, and these brought in a very small income.

"The money could be found," sighed Arbella. "Grandmamma would pay, but with everything that has happened — particularly William's betrayal — it would be hypocritical to agree to follow the coffin." She turned to face her companions. "I must refuse," she said. "I shall say that as the queen did not wish to have me in her company in life, then I will not force my presence on her in death."

"Oh Arbel…"

"There is nothing to be done," she snapped, fearing the welling sympathy in the room would undo her firm resolve not to cry. "Bring me some paper and a quill. I shall write to the College of Arms to refuse this invitation." Even as she spoke, a wave of anger rolled over her. If the succession had fallen in her favour, she would have been financially equipped to preside over a lavish funeral for the final Tudor queen. All the scandal created by William would have been swept away and she would have been able to honour her predecessor in the correct manner.

Closing her eyes, she imagined the scene. She would be walking at the head of the funeral procession, behind the purple draped coffin bearing the life-size effigy of the queen: a sceptre in her hands and a crown on her head. The coffin would be drawn on a chariot by four grey horses with flowing black caparisons draped from their saddles. Next to her would be Charles Howard, earl of Nottingham and only her trusted Ladies of Melusine would know the real reason why Charles would weep; that it was his beloved wife, Kate, who lay in the coffin, not Elizabeth Tudor.

"But who will take your place?" asked Bridget.

Arbella shrugged. "Someone will step in; I have no doubt."

"It will probably be Helena," said Lizzie Brooke. "As dowager Marchioness of Northampton, she is the highest-ranking woman in the land after the new royal family and yourself, Arbel."

"But the expense?" queried Anne.

Lizzie shrugged. "Her husband, Thomas, will pay. He will see it as his duty. He is connected by blood to the old queen.

Remember, he was second cousin to Anne Boleyn, who was Queen Elizabeth's mother."

Arbella stared bleakly at her half-written letter; to refuse this honour was heart-breaking, yet she knew there was no alternative. Swallowing her tears and taking deep breaths to calm the inner trembling she could feel beginning, she wrote a short terse note which she passed to Anne.

Turning to the other letter she had received that morning, Arbella slit open the seal and unfurled it. Her eyes narrowed as she read the official summons from the new queen consort, Anne of Denmark.

"Have you been invited to court, Arbel?" asked Lizzie.

"Yes," replied Arbella. "The queen has written, personally inviting me."

Sickened though she was at this thought, she knew the invitation represented safety, for now at least. To be at the heart of the royal household would provide her with a home, an income, and the ability to assess the situation from within. The idea of meeting her cousin James and his children was bittersweet. In her heart, she would prefer to be inviting them to her own royal court rather than being offered the crumbs from James's table.

"You must inform your grandmother," said Gertrude. "I have been told that Dorothy Percy and Penelope Rich will be accompanying you."

"What about the Raleighs?" asked Arbella.

"They are at court, but the rumours are that once Cecil is given his head, he will strip Sir Walter of his position as Captain of the Guard. It is likely he will lose many of his lucrative import licences too. Cecil and Walter have clashed for years; this will be Cecil's moment of revenge."

Arbella felt her anger at Robert Cecil surge again.

"No doubt there will be women from the Scottish court in Queen Anne's train," said Lizzie, "as well as the wives of those men who the new king will appoint to his privy chamber."

"Scottish lords, I should think," added Anne. "Do you think they're as wild and savage as the rumours suggest?"

Arbella laughed, the first genuine sound of mirth she had made for some time. "Oh Anne, you are funny. They are only men, not wild creatures."

"How disappointing," sighed Anne. "It might have been fun to paint ourselves blue with woad and pretend to be savages."

Arbella and Lizzie laughed, but Gertrude shot them a scandalised scowl. "It's no laughing matter," she snapped. "The new regime won't want to be reminded of the past. The Tudors are dead, the Stuarts reign supreme. What was it that the old queen once said: 'Men always turn towards the rising sun'? There is a new family in the palace; those who wish to advance are best reminded that the Stuarts rule now. Their word is law; all that went before is brushed aside as they invent us anew."

A silence settled over the women, each contemplating Gertrude's words and the changes that would soon engulf them. Arbella wondered where she would sit in this strange new world: on the side of the devil or the angels? If Henry and George Brooke were to push on with their plan, would the country accept her as a Tudor or reject her as a usurping Stuart? For the first time in his life, she felt relieved her son carried neither name even though the blood of both ran in his veins.

Once again, she wondered about the wisdom of the plot the Brooke brothers were spinning around her. Few people outside the immediate royal court understood Arbella's lineage and, therefore, her claim to the throne, and the number who knew of her marriage and her two children was considerably smaller. If she were to rise to such a position, the casket of confessions given to her by Lady Katherine Newton could be her way to hold the crown and present her children as the rightful heirs. Equally, a box full of such dangerous, treasonous documents could be the signature on her death warrant.

"Will you leave Henry in his current lodgings?" asked Lizzie, her voice breaking through Arbella's teeming thoughts.

"Yes, and Ennie will remain at Marquess House in Pembrokeshire," said Arbella. "She is safe there."

Arbella rose, unable to remain still. It was a relief to know her children were safe, but the mere fact they had to be hidden infuriated her. While she was trapped in the Withdrawing Room at Osterley House, the games of politics were being played by men with lesser educations than her own, men whose own agendas ruled their decisions and their judgement. Each one hoping that they would be able to get close to the king, to elevate their position through the court, in a way that had not been possible for men under the reigns of Jane, Mary and Elizabeth. Women had held the balance of power for so long, the greedy men of the Privy Council wanted to wrest it back into male hands. No matter the cost to the country.

"Damn you, William!" Arbella exploded, startling the women around her.

"Arbel?" asked Bridget. "Are you feeling quite well?"

"Don't worry about my sanity, Bridget," she replied. "I was thinking about this tangled web of lies, the succession, the hidden heirs and I damn my fool of a husband. If he were here, then we would have the opportunity to argue for our rights but with him dead, attainted for treason, my position is worsened. Not only am I a woman with what is considered a weak claim to the throne, I am the widow of a traitor and, as such, not to be trusted."

The door to the Withdrawing Room opened and they turned to see Lady Gertrude's steward.

"My lady," he said with a deferential bow, "there are visitors for the Lady Arbella. Viscount Chaworth, Mr Edmund Shakespeare and Mrs Emilia Lanier…"

Gertrude indicated for them to be shown in with all haste.

"What news from London?" said Arbella, hurrying towards the trio.

The two men both dropped into deep bows, while Emilia curtseyed.

"Stand up," Arbella snapped, then regretted her sharpness, and softening her tone, she ushered the visitors to a settle near the fire. "Tell me, what has happened?"

"As you know, my lady, a week ago, Robert Cecil and his men declared King James's authority on the tilt yard green opposite Whitehall," began Edmund Shakespeare, the younger of the two men. "Then, the grandees of the Privy Council and the Guilds formed a procession to Ludgate in the City of London, where they read the proclamation twice more before claiming the possession of the Tower in the name of the king."

Arbella could not disguise her shudder as an icy hand seemed to trace itself down her spine. Everywhere she turned, the past was reaching out to wrap its tendrils around her, drawing her ever closer to the heart of the secret. The route Cecil had taken had been the same as that of her husband when he had attempted his own misguided and thwarted raid to claim the throne. His, however, had ended in capture, followed by the humiliation of being attainted as a traitor. He was executed a few days later. Robert Cecil seemed to mock her with his every move.

"I know this," she said, her voice hard with anger and disappointment. "My cousin James is king of both England and Scotland."

"This might be so, my lady, but things are not as they seem…" began Emilia Lanier.

"You must not lose heart."

"What do you mean, Edmund?" Arbella asked, as he interrupted Emilia, his green eyes twinkling with excitement; coupled with his blond curls and freckles, he appeared far younger than his 23 years. It was why, she thought, he was such a successful actor; he had the youthful looks that made him the perfect Juliet, the ideal Rosalind, the feisty Beatrice, or a cheeky Viola.

"My brother, Will, has heard rumours from his noble sponsors."

"What rumours?" prompted Arbella.

"He claims that Lord Beauchamp is in the west gathering forces. He intends to challenge the king…"

"There is another rumour too, my dear Arbel," interrupted George Chaworth. "There is word that in Brussels, the Archduke Albert and the Infanta Isabella have been declared king and queen of England and will soon set out to take their thrones by force. This is the real reason why Cecil and the Privy Council have retreated to the Tower; they are preparing for battle."

"My lady, this is shocking," gasped Anne, her face growing ever paler.

"The plague is another factor," added Edmund. "It is virulent. Thousands of Londoners are dying, and there are rumours it is a curse brought about by the foreign king. William thinks its outbreak may delay James's arrival. He offers his support to your cause, as he believes this period with no monarch is the ideal time for other claimants to take advantage of the situation."

"Thank you, Edmund," said Arbella. "You may tell your brother, Master Shakespeare, that I am grateful for his support. However, he would do well to distance himself for the present. It is safest for us both and will allow him the freedom to move among his sponsors. His information is always reliable. If we are in need of his connections, I shall send one of my women. However, warn him to commit nothing traitorous to paper."

"Yes, my lady," said Edmund, and with a nod of farewell to each of the women, he bowed himself from the room.

"Go with him, George," Arbella said. "You know how easily he is distracted — one glimpse of a pretty face on the way back to Southwark and he won't deliver the message to Will for several days."

George bowed his compliance and hurried from the room.

"Emilia, do you believe these rumours?" Arbella asked.

Her friend gave a small, tight smile. "Yes, Arbel, I do," she replied.

Arbella allowed the words to sink in. James might have been declared king, but it seemed all was not lost. Henry Cobham had said as much. Allow James to take the throne, then when he had proven a disappointment, it would be easier to clear the way for the rightful heirs. *If Lord Beauchamp and the Infanta do not get there first*, she thought.

PART THREE: MARQUESS HOUSE, 2019

CHAPTER ONE

"What I don't understand," said Perdita, once she had found Piper in her artist's studio, "is how these diaries ended up in that trunk. They're hundreds of years old. The story being told in them happened in 1603."

"And you think the diaries could have belonged to Arbella Stuart?" asked Piper.

"It's possible, or, if not her, then someone very close to her," replied Perdita. "You know I've been convinced for ages that Arbella Stuart was linked to this somehow, but I couldn't work out how?"

"Yes, you might have mentioned it a few hundred times…"

"The historical record says that Arbella Stuart didn't marry until she was in her mid-thirties. She apparently eloped with William Seymour, 2nd duke of Somerset, on 22 June 1610. William Seymour was the grandson of Lady Katherine Grey. With both Arbella and William having a blood claim to the throne, they should have asked permission from the king to be able to marry, and not to do so was tantamount to a declaration of treason."

"The king being King James I?"

"Yes, Arbella's cousin. James was annoyed about the marriage and both Arbella and William ended up in the Tower. They tried to escape, and William was successful, but Arbella was caught after a dramatic sea chase. She was nearly in France when the ship was ordered to stop and reveal its passengers. Arbella was captured and returned to incarceration. Meanwhile, William Seymour made it to Ostend. There are no remaining records telling us about Arbella's stay in the Tower of London.

The acts of the privy council would be the usual place to find this information, but the acts from 1605 until the end of 1612 are missing. Destroyed in a fire at Whitehall."

"Convenient," said Piper.

"Isn't it? Arbella was held in the Tower for the rest of her life, dying on 25 September 1615, although no reports say what killed her. Some historians have suggested starvation, others poison, but there are no official records. Arbella and William Seymour were said to have had no children. After Arbella's death, William married Lady Frances Devereux, the granddaughter of Lettice Knollys. They apparently had eight children.

"But the diaries I read last night suggest something entirely different. These books do claim that Arbella married someone called William, although, frustratingly, there is no reference to a surname or title; well, not yet anyway, but I don't think they refer to William Seymour."

"Why not?"

"The dates don't tally and the William in the diaries was executed for treason sometime before 1603, which was when Queen Elizabeth I died. The letters also suggest Arbella had two children: a son, Henry, and a daughter, Ennie. The son was hidden with relatives in the east of the country, while Ennie was sent to Arbella's home in the west."

Perdita watched Piper's eyes widen.

"Not here?" Piper said.

"Yes. Marquess House is named as a property left to Arbella by the queen at an unspecified date. From what I can deduce, it was where she sent Ennie to establish her in a home of her own."

"Perds, that's insane. Are there are any other records from that period in the archive?"

"There are no account books — I checked with Jenny this morning — and even the new ones we found in the trunks don't cover this period, but she said she would see if there was anything else. It's later than the information Granny would have used for her books, so there might be something lurking which hasn't been researched before that would help. I've emailed Deborah at Jerusalem to ask her if they have anything relevant."

"Was there anything else?" asked Piper.

"Quite a lot. There are a number of new names and people I need to check, but there was one thing I looked at this morning that is quite strange."

"Go on, explain your anomaly."

"Remember the woman named Lady Katherine Newton?"

"Wasn't she connected to Catherine Howard somehow?"

"She was her great-niece. She was born a Paston before she married Henry Newton. It transpires that Henry had a sister, Frances, who married William Brooke, 10th Baron Cobham. It was their son, Henry Brooke, who was responsible for a plot that is being discussed in these diaries, named as 'Main Plot'. The basis of the plot was to kidnap James I and replace him on the throne with Arbella."

"Really?"

"It gets stranger. Henry Brooke was married to Lady Frances Howard, who was the daughter of Kate Carey."

"And Kate Carey, who became Kate Howard in marriage, was a key member of the Ladies of Melusine, right?" confirmed Piper.

"Yes. Ready for another crazy twist? Henry Brooke had a sister, Elizabeth, who married Robert Cecil, son of William Cecil, who had been the queen's chief adviser. When William died, his son Robert took over his position. By the time the

'Main Plot' took place, Elizabeth Cecil was dead but her brothers, Henry and George, were the instigators of the Main Plot. George was executed for his part in it and Henry was imprisoned in the Tower of London."

After a few moments' consideration, Piper spoke. "You're saying Robert Cecil was responsible for the execution of his brother-in-law?"

"Not directly, but he was involved in the interrogations and the trial. He doesn't seem to have done anything to try and save George."

Piper looked horrified. "There was no such thing as family loyalty back then, was there?"

"Not always," agreed Perdita. "What I find so strange is that these people have been virtually forgotten, yet at the time, they were at the heart of the battle of the succession."

"History is written by the victors," said Piper, quoting Winston Churchill.

"You're right," said Perdita. "The other weird thing is that all these people are connected to each other and somehow they are all linked to Marquess House, even though it was hundreds of miles away from their family homes in west London."

There was silence for a moment as the twins considered the new discoveries, then Piper spoke: "In this diary, you said Arbella mentioned a casket with three golden keys?"

"Yes, why?"

Piper hurried across the room to a vast walk-in cupboard, returning a moment later with a detailed maquette of the golden cup that had been discovered on the shipwreck named *The Arbella Stuart* the previous year.

"Pipes, it's beautiful," gasped Perdita as she cleared a space on the table before circling the model, examining it more closely.

"As we're casting the cup, we'll need moulds, but I thought building it in clay first would give me a chance to get to know all the quirks of the design. The clockwork interior is another matter entirely."

"What do you mean?"

"It's a unique and intricate design. I also think it was a later addition."

"Why?"

"The bowl and stem of the cup are two separate pieces and I think the stem, with the mermaids and the clockwork mechanism, was added a number of years after the cup was first created. The gold is different, and the style of the craftsmanship is finer than the original carving on the cup."

"How odd," said Perdita, but Piper shook her head.

"Not when I show you what I've discovered in the gold outer-casing."

Sorting through the large pile of intricate plans and designs that were strewn across the table, Piper selected a stack of X-rays, which she slotted into lightboxes attached to the walls, similar to those found in hospitals. Flicking on the lights, scans of the ancient mermaid cup were revealed.

Perdita let out a small exclamation of impressed surprise as she hurried to her sister's side in order to examine the extraordinary images. "Where did these come from?" she asked, gazing at the transparencies in awe.

"Olaf and the lab," replied Piper. "The cup is too delicate for me to have here to examine, so they booked time in any scanner or X-ray suite they could persuade to help and shot images of the cup from every conceivable angle in order to help me recreate it. It's how I was able to build the maquette. It was while I was working out the dimensions, I noticed the anomaly in the cup." Piper turned back to the lightboxes and pointed at the central image. "Do you see the gaps in the stem?"

Perdita nodded. "Wear and tear?" she suggested. "This cup is incredibly old. Perhaps they once held gems? There were garnets all over it."

"I thought the same thing until I examined the image more carefully," Piper said and shone the red beam of a laser pen onto the shadowy spaces. "They're very thin and flat."

"Agreed," said Perdita. "So, not gems?"

"I don't think so," replied Piper.

"What then?"

"There were three keys in the box with the cup. I always thought they were there by chance, you know, valuable things stored together, but I have a different hypothesis now." Piper turned to her laptop and flipped it open, selecting the digitised version of the image on the lightbox and zooming in on one of the three unexplained spaces. "When you see a close-up, it becomes more obvious," she said, stepping back so Perdita could examine the picture.

"No," breathed Perdita in wonder. "These are slots and they're shaped —"

"Like keys," finished Piper. "Whereas we always thought the mermaid cup was simply a pretty and high-status bauble for Penelope to demonstrate her wealth, it was, in fact, a secret hiding place for three golden keys. I won't know for sure until I've finished the model, but from what the images show and from my sketches, it seems that each key slotted into the stem of the cup then clicked into place so they were hidden within the mermaid design. My artistic interpretation suggests that when the keys were in place, they would have been almost invisible, blending in with the rest of the patterns on the stem."

"And you think these were added at a later date?" clarified Perdita.

Piper nodded. "It's a perfect hiding place," said Piper. "The cup is light and portable, and the keys are disguised."

"Incredible," enthused Perdita, "but I wonder why they were loose in the wooden box, rather than slotted into place?"

"Perhaps Penelope had been using them and didn't have time to put them back in place when the ship ran aground?" suggested Piper.

Perdita stared at the images, considering this new discovery. "Do you think these could be the three golden keys which Arbella was given? The ones that supposedly opened a casket containing all manner of confessions that prove this secret irrefutably?"

Piper pulled a sceptical face. "It's quite a leap," she said. "We still don't know if Penelope and Arbella were connected."

"They were both linked to our house," mused Perdita. "Although, Penelope may have rented it from Arbella, or whoever claimed the property after Arbella's death in 1615 — the tapestry family tree doesn't go back that far. Anyway, according to MI1, it's the three pieces of jewellery that are supposed to prove the secret, not three golden keys."

"Do you think the casket still exists?" asked Piper.

"Much as I want to say yes, I think it's unlikely."

"Really?"

"Can you imagine how dangerous owning such contentious information would have been? It's more probable that these documents have either been lost or separated. I wondered if that was how this whole thing began — the documents were redistributed and a few of them were discovered, prompting the beginning of MI1 and its destruction of historical discoveries that don't fit their official version of events."

"You could be right," agreed Piper. "Although, if such a thing did exist, let's hope it wasn't on board the ship."

"Definitely," said Perdita.

"Morning," called Kit as he and his father entered the studio. His eyes were drawn to the maquette. "What have we missed?"

As Piper explained her finds, Perdita allowed her mind to wander, not ready to discuss the diaries yet, and also not wanting to distract Kit and Alistair from Piper's discoveries. She tried to fit this new information into her research. At present, she could not see the link, but this felt as though there had been a small step forward, which after months of dead ends, was a relief.

"The paintings," said Piper, bringing Perdita from her reverie. "I'll begin with the de Critz of Penelope Fitzalan, followed by the three we found in the grotto."

"You think it's a John de Critz then?" asked Alistair.

"It would have to be authenticated by specialists, but yes," Piper said, with a smile. Alistair looked impressed. "Now I've had to chance to examine it properly, the quality is extraordinary. It's oil on panel, similar to the famous image de Critz painted of James I, which also puts it into the correct time scale for this picture, too."

"Was there anything unexpected in the frame?" asked Kit, hope in his voice.

"No, sorry," Piper replied. "The portrait has been scanned and X-rayed though, and there does seem to be something under the painting. It's quite faint, but it's circular and has a series of patterns around the edge — it looks like ivy — and in the centre is a female figure."

"Is this common?" asked Alistair.

"It isn't uncommon," replied Piper. "Artists often reworked paintings or reused materials."

"Do you think the circular image is connected to the portrait?" asked Kit.

Perdita was gazing up at the X-ray image. The circle seemed deliberate to her. The edges were clean, and it fitted within the painting. Backing away to get a deeper perspective, she said, "The circle surrounds Penelope."

"I noticed that, too," said Piper. "I wondered if there had been a thought to use a circular frame. Unfortunately, though, there were no other secrets or surprises within the painting. I think it is nothing more than a portrait and the letters were the one remarkable thing about it."

Perdita stared at it, disappointed, but before she could comment, Piper ploughed on.

"The three paintings from the grotto are an odd mix," she said, flicking up more images. "They're going to need proper restoration because they're filthy, but from what I have been able to ascertain, there are two portraits of men and one of a woman. The larger of the three features a young man with a shock of red hair; it isn't dated, so I've used the clothes of the subjects as a guide to their provenance and his attire places him in the mid-Renaissance: the late 1590s or early 1600s. The other male portrait is more curious because it's painted in the style of a coronation portrait."

Piper flashed the image onto the large screen so Perdita, Kit and Alistair could study it in more detail.

"Do you recognise the man?" Piper asked them.

"No," replied Perdita. "Do you recognise the artist, Pipes?"

"It's no one obvious," she replied, "which makes me wonder if it's a Victorian fake."

"Why do you say that?" asked Alistair, walking closer to the image in order to examine the facial features in more detail.

"It's not a very good portrait and the man is unrecognisable; I wonder if it's an amateur painter who was trying to copy a different portrait and put someone else's face in it instead of the real monarch."

"Would an artist do something so strange?" asked Perdita.

"Artists do many strange things," replied Piper, then grinned. "The final one, I think you'll like — it's of a very beautiful young red-haired woman wearing a sumptuous velvet dress and distinctive jewellery."

Perdita stared at Piper.

"In the background," continued Piper, "is Marquess House with its wild lake, Llyn Cel, and a shadowy mermaid figure. There were no names and the portrait, a remarkably good one, was unsigned. The only clue to her identity is the word 'catulus' scratched onto the reverse of the canvas."

"Which means kitten," murmured Alistair.

Piper clicked her remote control and Perdita gasped as the woman smiled at her across the centuries, her blue eyes clear and focussed.

"Catherine," she gasped. Alistair and Kit looked at Perdita in surprise. "It's Catherine Howard."

"Are you sure?"

"Reasonably," replied Perdita. She pulled her phone from her pocket and sent the image of the ceiling boss to Piper, who flashed it up next to the portrait. "They're too similar to dismiss the possibility that this is finally an image of Henry VIII's fifth wife."

"My goodness, if we are able to have this authenticated…" began Alistair, then stopped. "MI1 would no doubt seize and destroy it," he finished, regret in his tone. "It's a remarkable find, though, and a wonderful addition to your art collection."

"However, what's even more remarkable is the fact that if

this is Catherine Howard, it isn't the only image of her in Marquess House," said Piper. Perdita stared at her in amazement.

"What?"

Piper flashed up two more images. One of a young red-haired woman in Tudor dress, the other a young man with the flowing locks favoured by the Cavaliers during the Civil War.

"These are in my living room," she said. "I've been looking at them for a while and last night, I compared the image of this woman with the one we found in the grotto. It isn't identical, but there are enough markers — the shape of her eyes and her hairstyle — to link it in with this one and the ceiling boss. What do you think, Perds?"

Perdita stared at the familiar image.

"Why didn't we notice?" she said, with wonder in her voice.

"Ridiculous though it sounds, Perds, it's because we weren't looking. We'd both accepted the image as being of an unknown but possibly minor noblewoman. There is no provenance in the catalogue other than 'Marquess House, 1870', which could mean that was when it was found somewhere here, or Lettice bought it or it was acquired for the collection. We've had so much else going on, we weren't going to spot everything immediately. The other thing that intrigued me, and which I think might give a symbolic clue to her identity, is the flower painted around the border."

"What is it?" asked Kit. "It's similar to the one of the Jerusalem logo that's wrapped around our central image of the portcullis."

"It's a flower called angrec," said Piper, "and symbolically, it referred to royalty."

"It would make sense," mused Perdita. "Especially as we know Catherine did live here…"

"And the cavalier?" prompted Alistair, before the sisters could go too far off the point.

"I'm not sure," admitted Piper, "and until the other pictures have been cleaned it's hard to see if they're connected but, from a cursory examination, I wondered if it might be the person in the strange coronation portrait. The jawline is similar. Although, they may be completely unconnected and I'm seeing things because I'm trying too."

There was silence as they contemplated the images.

"What about the other two?" asked Kit. "Do you think they're worth investigating further?"

Perdita wandered back to the stool and perched on it. "Would they take much restoration?" she asked her sister.

"There's no physical damage," Piper said, "and they were well wrapped. It was dry down in the grotto, so the main problem is dirt. It wouldn't take long to clean them so we can examine them properly."

"Let's do that, then," said Perdita, standing up and gathering her things as she prepared to leave. "As you said, Alistair, they're part of the Marquess House collection and should be treated in the same way as all our other artwork, even if they aren't relevant to the search for the silver locket. As for the image of Catherine, I'd like her to be hung in my room, along with Penelope."

With a smile, she left, excitement bubbling inside her, feeling at last she was on the right path.

CHAPTER TWO

"Ah, there you are, my dear," said Alistair, tapping on Perdita's office door and peering inside. It was a week since Piper's revelations, and Perdita had been buried in new lines of research ever since; now she looked up from behind her pile of folders, books, and printouts. "I tried calling you, but you're obviously very busy."

"Sorry, Alistair," said Perdita, "I put my phone on silent. Why didn't you use the internal phone?"

"I did, but it was engaged."

Perdita glanced over and noticed a biography of Bess Throckmorton, the wife of Sir Walter Raleigh, had knocked the handset off the base. Reaching over, she replaced it.

"Oops," she said and looked up, finally focussing on Alistair and, for the first time, noticed his grave face. "What's happened?"

The door opened again, and Kit entered with Piper. Kit looked as pale as his father.

"What's going on?" demanded Piper.

"Please sit down, my dear," said Alistair.

Perdita and Piper exchanged a worried glance.

"Over here, Pipes," said Perdita, springing up from her desk and guiding her sister towards the sofas. "Alistair?"

Kit and his father sat opposite the twins.

"Perdita, Piper, I have some distressing news," Alistair began. "I have received a call from the British High Commission in New Delhi, who have had word from their Consular Office in Kolkata. You put my number as the one to be contacted should there be any news of Jeremy."

Perdita glanced at Kit, who gave a small shake of his head, and she braced herself for bad news.

"They've found the body of man answering Jeremy's description…" Alistair continued.

"No!"

The noise that came from Piper was more of a wail than a word. Perdita pulled her shaking twin into a hug. She nodded for Alistair to continue, knowing it would be better to hear everything at once, then they could break each piece of the devastating news down into something more manageable as they made a plan.

"The body was discovered in a hotel room yesterday morning. The man had checked in under the name of Jem Copper. The hotel maid found the body this morning. Jeremy's passport was in the room, along with a large sum of money, which correlates with the most recent amount of money withdrawn by him from your joint account."

"What money?" snapped Perdita. "Do you mean your savings?"

"No," sighed Piper. "Perds, I'm so sorry, there are some things I haven't told you. Alistair and I have been working with new divorce lawyers because Jeremy's demands were becoming preposterous, and neither of us believed he was the one behind some of the stranger demands…"

"Such as?" asked Perdita, pushing aside the momentary pang of hurt that her sister had not confided in her.

"Access to Marquess House."

"Why would he want access to this house?" Perdita asked, amazed.

"A question we both asked too," said Alistair. "At Piper's behest, I employed a private detective. I'm afraid, Perdita, I broke my word to you. I know you requested I put a tail on

Jeremy without telling Piper, to protect her, but when Piper issued the same request, I felt it was prudent to show her all the information we had gathered on Jeremy. We knew he was travelling in India, although we were startled when a new report was filed a few weeks ago."

"Where was he?"

"He and Kirstin Chaplin were photographed staying at a bungalow in the grounds of the home of Randolph Connors in Darjeeling."

"No," Perdita gasped, a cold chill running down her spine.

"This is why Piper was reluctant to tell you," Alistair said. "She didn't want to worry you if it was merely a coincidence."

"He was staying with Randolph Connors, Mum's cousin and possible murderer of Granny Mary," snapped Perdita. "How can it be a coincidence?"

"There is no way it can be," Alistair agreed, "but since then, things have taken another peculiar twist."

"Which is?"

"Ten days ago, Jeremy removed a large amount of money from our joint bank account," said Piper. "I've kept a sizeable sum in it, mostly so if Jeremy needed it to get home from India, he had access to funds."

"How much is large?" asked Perdita.

"£50,000," replied Alistair, and Perdita gasped. "He hasn't been seen or heard from since. His bank card hasn't been used and his mobile phone hasn't been switched on."

"I thought he'd taken himself off somewhere to get his head together," said Piper, her voice breaking as she contained a sob. "I was convinced he'd bought a new phone and was living in luxury while he decided what to do next. I half-expected him to arrive here at any moment."

"But Pipes, you're practically divorced — did you change your mind?"

Piper shook her head. "No, my relationship with Jeremy was over. I never would have been able to trust him again, but I didn't hate him. If he were in danger because of his association with Connors and Chaplin, I thought it would be preferable for him to come here and be protected by The Milford Haven Treaty. I emailed him suggesting it a few weeks ago, and he said he would think about it. It was the last message he sent me."

"Even though he wanted access to Marquess House?" queried Kit, unable to stop himself.

"Piper and I felt Jeremy would be safer here and we would be able to contain events if he realised he was protected by The Marquess House Treaty," Alistair replied. "Piper and Jeremy are still married, so under the terms of the Treaty, he would have the same level of protection as you two. Jeremy was behaving erratically, and we both suspected it was out of fear. He may have realised the danger he was in, thanks to the trap he had been lured into by Mrs Chaplin."

"There's more," said Kit. "Kirstin Chaplin is still at Connor's plantation, but rather more concerning, so is Inigo Westbury. We do have three people within the house working for us, and two of them have managed to plant electronic bugging devices. We don't have any intel from them yet, but it might help us to discover what is happening."

Perdita sank back into the chair, shock coursing through her. When they had been willed Marquess House, neither her nor Piper had realised another, far more dangerous legacy was attached to the property. Was it possible Jeremy was dead because of their inheritance? Another life lost because of this poisonous secret?

"Have you alerted Stephen Haberfield?" she asked.

"No," Alistair replied, "but I will if you'd like me too."

"Maybe not," she said. Perdita swallowed the lump in her throat, then, her voice constricted, she whispered, "I thought this was all behind us; the fear, the danger."

"MI1 Elite has stepped back," said Alistair. "Haberfield and I have agreed on a truce, but Randolph Connors is another matter entirely. He doesn't have to honour The Milford Haven Treaty — it only binds the hands of the Secret Services, protecting you from arrest. In extreme circumstances, it states that, should it be necessary, their protection can be called upon. This was why I turned to Haberfield earlier in the year."

"But why would the treaty include protection from the Secret Services?" asked Piper.

"It was one of the odd clauses included when Lettice Lakeby signed it in 1886," Alistair explained. "I noticed it when I took over the running of the estate from my father. After your mother died, I was so angry that I photocopied the clause onto a sheet of A3 paper and sent it to the head of MI1 Elite, showing him he had broken the terms of the Treaty and therefore should step down from his position."

"Did he?"

"Yes, he was replaced by Inigo Westbury's uncle, Jonty."

"What?" said Kit.

"Jonty Westbury was a good man. It was how Inigo managed to rise through the ranks so swiftly, the consensus being that he might be like his uncle. Sadly, this was not the case."

"Alistair, how do you stand this?" Perdita exclaimed. "How do you know who to trust?"

"You learn to follow your instincts," he replied.

Perdita shook her head in disbelief. His answer seemed too simplistic. "And your instincts tell you the body found in Darjeeling is Jeremy?"

Alistair did not reply.

"How did he die?" asked Perdita.

"Until the body has been identified, they won't give me any details," said Alistair in a strained voice.

"But you know something," said Perdita. "You always know something, Alistair — one of your sources always has information."

"It has been suggested it might have been foul play," he admitted.

"Murder?" whispered Piper.

"Yes."

"When and how will we know if it's Jeremy?" asked Perdita.

"The Kolkata police have requested that someone go to identify the body," replied Alistair. "Until there is a formal identification, they will not confirm anything else to me."

"It might not be him," whispered Piper. "Someone might have stolen his passport and money. It might not be Jeremy."

Perdita did not reply — she did not want to give her sister false hope. The name under which Jeremy had signed was one too familiar for her to ignore. When they were children and they had played at being spies, Jem Copper had been Jeremy's preferred secret agent name.

"Do Jeremy's parents know?" asked Perdita.

"Not yet," said Kit. "Piper is still legally Jeremy's wife, so she's his next of kin and would be the person informed by the authorities."

"I have to call them," said Piper, wiping her streaming eyes with her sleeve. "Then I have to go. I need to know if it's really him."

Within a few hours, Piper and Alistair were ready to leave. They were being flown to Heathrow Airport by Elliot, where they would meet Celeste and Dominic Davidson before travelling first class to New Delhi. Here, they would change for an internal flight to Bagdogra, the closest airport to Darjeeling, where they would be met by a representative from the Kolkata Consulate. He would then accompany them on the three-hour drive to the city and remain with them while they helped the police to establish whether the dead man was Jeremy Davidson or another unfortunate soul.

Perdita had wanted to travel too, but Piper had insisted she remain at Marquess House.

"I'll be with Alistair, Celeste and Dominic. I'll have all the support I need," Piper had said, dry-eyed and shocked as they had moved around her bedroom, packing her suitcase. "If there's a murderer on the loose, I want you safely here under the protection of The Marquess House Treaty."

"But Pipes…" Perdita had protested.

"No, Perds, for once, please do as I ask," Piper had interrupted. "We're in enough danger as it is. Let's not risk both our lives."

"I can't lose you, too, Piper," Perdita had exclaimed.

"You won't. I'll be with Alistair. He and I have discussed it — he can easily protect me, but both of us going would involve serious security, especially you, as the eldest. I'm the spare, remember? I'm not as important."

"What are you saying?" Perdita had been aghast. "We inherited equally…"

"But you're still the eldest, and if Jeremy has been murdered, it's probably on Randolph Connor's orders. He's insane, and it'll be you he'll target. I don't want to lose you either, so please Perds, I'm begging you — stay here safe with Kit."

They had stared at each other, both overwrought, scared, and full of irrational guilt that this might somehow be their fault. Perdita had gazed at Piper's pinched, tear-streaked face and nodded. "I'll stay here, but you must keep in constant touch."

"Thank you, Perds," Piper had said, enveloping her in a rib-cracking hug. "You can do something for me while I'm away, though."

"Of course."

"Sort things out with Kit."

"What do you mean?" Perdita's eyebrows shot up in surprise.

"You need to stop messing him around. It isn't fair. Life is short and brutal, Perds — if you feel anything for Kit, do something about it before it's too late and you spend the rest of your life regretting it."

Perdita had stared at Piper in alarm. "I'm not messing Kit around!"

"You're not being straight with him either," her sister retorted. "Kit has made it very clear how he feels about you, but, apart from a bit of flirting and a few kisses, you're still holding him at arm's length." Perdita nodded but did not speak. After a pause, Piper continued. "It's been seven months since you split up with Warren. Yes, he treated you like crap, so I understand why you're hesitant to start a new relationship, but you know the feelings you have for Kit are more than just friendship."

Part of Perdita wanted to shout at her sister and have a massive row in the way that only siblings who love each other can, but she stayed silent.

"Kit is in love with you, but he'll never pressure you into reciprocating his feelings or even discussing them." Piper's nervous but determined voice cut through the storm of Perdita's emotions. "He won't make any more moves on you, but if you do have feelings for him and you want more than friendship, then the next move is yours to make. You have to stop being selfish and realise Kit has feelings and needs too. It isn't all about you. Otherwise, you might lose him. Cal told me Kit is considering moving to Andorra for a while because he's convinced you've decided not to take your relationship any further, and he's having trouble dealing with it."

Perdita stared at her sister. Kit was planning to move to Andorra? How was that possible? Kit was always here, at her side, supporting her, challenging her, pushing her and, she realised, loving her. The thought of losing him shot through her like a physical pain. Was she being selfish, hiding behind her broken relationship with Warren, using it as an excuse? Her reasoning had always been that if things went wrong with her and Kit, it would be difficult to spend the rest of their lives working together. Perhaps she was being childish. They were adults. If they tried and it did not work out, well, they would be able to deal with it.

Having thought she was being careful and protecting herself from more heartache, she now understood she had been cutting herself off from living and in doing so, she had caused great damage to someone she cared for deeply, even loved. Her cheeks flamed with emotion and, at last, she looked at her sister. Expecting to see admonishment, Piper's clear face with its small, sad smile was an unexpected lifebelt in their sea of woes.

CHAPTER THREE

With Piper and Alistair in India, Perdita had decided the best way to stay sane was to keep herself busy. Contemplating the row of her grandmother's works in the centre of the bookcase in her office, Perdita wondered if there were any comments in them that she had missed on her first exploration. This complete set of Mary Fitzroy's books were her grandmother's own copies, and she had left instructions in her will that should either of the twins request to see her collection, these were the versions they were to be shown.

Perdita had discovered why the moment she had opened the first volume, *The History and Symbolism of Names*, a year earlier. It transpired that Mary had used them as private diaries and had written marginalia concerning her everyday life throughout the many volumes. The only book in the series that remained empty, except for one devastating comment, was the seventh: *The Missing Heirs of Henry VIII*, which had been published shortly before the death of Louisa Woodville, Mary's only daughter and the twins' mother. Perdita wondered if the two covering the Stuart era would offer any clues.

"*The Scottish Link: A Study of the Trade and Personal Links Between the Tudor and Stuart Courts* and *The Winter Queen: Elizabeth of Bohemia — The Forgotten Stuart Princess*," read Perdita aloud as she removed them from the shelf. "Never one for a snappy title, were you, Granny?" She picked up *The Scottish Link* and took it to her desk.

An hour later, fascinating though she had found the book and her grandmother's notes, Perdita had found nothing new to add to their research. She braced herself for more disappointment as she reached for *The Winter Queen*. Searching the notes before scanning the text, Perdita kept thinking, *Next page, it'll be on the next page*, but the further she worked her way through the volume, the more her hopes began to fade. Finally, as she turned the last leaf and stared at the end papers on the inside of the back cover, she noticed there was a short note, dated two weeks before her grandmother's death: "Check letters found by Lettice on the reverse of the portrait. Letter five. Penelope Fitzalan. Check *The Llyn Cel Mermaid* original. Ennie?"

Perdita's blood ran cold. Ennie? Why would her grandmother have written Ennie? It was not a name she had come across before she had read about Arbella's daughter in the mysterious diary. Reaching for her laptop, Perdita opened the scans she had of the letters found by Lettice Lakeby that had once been attached to the reverse of the portrait in Perdita's bedroom.

She read:

My dearest cousin, your kind words have kept me company as I make my decision. Be not angry, sweet lady, I cannot take refuge by your side. As we have seen with his recent actions, my brother will stop at nothing to fulfil what he sees as his destiny. He knows the truth of our history and determines to restore his rightful power. He is beyond reason. You, too, know the secret history of our family, you are one of the trusted Ladies of Melusine who has done all that is possible to protect the truth; perhaps together we can persuade him away from his desperate path. To restore our country to peace must be our aim. If only the Blessed Child had lived to tell the tale, then we may have been spared the fear of this terrible war. However, her secret will only be told when the mermaids meet in the Tudor Hall and the lock opens. Tonight, I will leave in the way we used as children and wait on the island for the help which has been promised. I shall travel to London to speak with my brother and encourage a change of heart. If my plan fails, I shall return to the west. If I fail in stopping him, perhaps then, I shall travel to your side. Until we meet dearest cousin, I am in God's hands. Your faithful kin, Ennie. Penelope Fitzalan, March 1649.

Each word now rang with new meaning. When Perdita had skimmed these letters months ago, she had not really noticed the signature; now it made her wonder what else she had missed. She retrieved the high-quality printout of the original letters, picked up her eyeglass from her desk and began to examine them in minute detail. By the signature and the magical name, Ennie, she stopped.

In pale ink, faded over the years, was a symbol. Not a mermaid, as Perdita would have thought, but something entirely unexpected, yet an image which was drenched in familiarity: the three-ringed symbol representing the two rings joined with the locket in between.

Staring down at this new discovery, Perdita ran her fingers through her hair, thinking fast, then reaching for her phone, she dialled a number.

"Hey Perds, you OK?" Kit answered on the second ring.

"Have you got a minute? I think I've found something."

Perdita was pacing around her office in nervous anticipation when Kit crashed through the door.

"Have you found the locket?" he asked.

"What?"

"You sounded so excited that I thought you might have found a clue in Mary's books."

"No, not the locket, but something nearly as important: Ennie's real identity."

126

Kit's eyes were as wide her own. "And…?" he prompted.

Perdita took a deep breath. "Ennie is Penelope Fitzalan."

She watched Kit as he processed this enormous piece of information. He walked to her vast wallchart and followed the lines from Arbella.

"How?" he said, turning back to her. "Explain."

Perdita beckoned him over to the desk to show him the letter. "It was Granny who spotted it, although I don't know if she realised the significance."

Kit was quiet as he read Ennie's words, absorbing this new strand of information. "So, Penelope's brother was the unknown son of Arbella Stuart, and he was trying to whip up a rebellion. Penelope's cousin had offered her a safe refuge, but Penelope refused it, preferring to try and persuade her brother to see sense. Could the cousin have been Dorothy Spencer, countess of Sunderland? The content is remarkably similar."

"No, I don't think so," replied Perdita. "My first thought was Dorothy Spencer, too, and a possible connection between this and the letter Izi told us about. They were certainly written within a few months of each other, but in this one Ennie is planning to travel to London; in the letter to Dorothy, she hadn't yet reached the stage where she felt the need to confront her brother. Her 'cousin' has offered her refuge and while Ennie has refused it, there's something about the tone of this letter that hints at the fact she may have realised her plan to stay at Marquess House and keep it as a potential refuge for her brother might not be viable."

"It's a shame she didn't give us a bit of a clue as to which cousin she was writing to, though," said Kit.

"True," said Perdita. "Arbella Stuart, and therefore by default Ennie, had hundreds of cousins, any one of whom could be this person. Dorothy Spencer wasn't related to Arbella or

Ennie." Perdita glanced down at her grandmother's book. "Do you think Elizabeth Stuart is involved somewhere and this is why Granny put the note in this book? They were royal cousins."

"Remind me again, where does Elizabeth Stuart fit in?"

"She was the daughter of James I."

"Which makes her the sister of the second Stuart monarch, Charles I," confirmed Kit.

"Yes, is that relevant?"

"Maybe," said Kit. "The date on the letter is 1649. Charles I was beheaded on 30 January 1649, so the country was in a state of unrest. The letter was written in March of the same year, so the shockwaves of the monarch's death were continuing to reverberate through the land. Did you notice, Perds, she mentions the 'Blessed Child', which we know was the codename used for Catherine Howard?"

"Yes, which adds weight to our theory that Penelope had spent time preserving the story of the heirs and that Catherine had been the secret she was prepared to die to keep."

Perdita swung backwards and forwards on her office chair, considering this new information while Kit continued to study the letter.

"What does it mean about the mermaids meeting in the Great Hall, though?" he mused.

"It's strange, isn't it? The syntax is odd again. Do you think it's more code? The Ladies of Melusine used plenty of unexpected words to disguise their real meanings in their other letters. This might be more of the same."

"I think you're right."

"This means we now have considerable evidence suggesting Penelope Fitzalan was Arbella Stuart's daughter. Yet, historically, Arbella was said to be childless. The diaries suggest she had two children — a son and a daughter — something else which is confirmed by this letter because Penelope refers to a brother. I don't have any clues to the identity of Arbella's son at present, but I do know that Penelope Fitzalan has been obliterated from official historical records and, if she has, then her brother has probably suffered the same fate."

"What do you mean?"

"When we began this search, the very first things I requested were the two primary sources Granny had listed in her notes for her unpublished manuscript, *The Catherine Howard Anomaly*. These two items were *The Catherine Howard Codex* and *The Llyn Cel Mermaid and Other Local Legends* by Penelope Fitzalan. I also did a comprehensive search on Penelope Fitzalan and she has vanished. There are no references to her anywhere on the internet; no one of that name seems to have ever existed and I searched extensively. My instinct was always that Penelope Fitzalan was key to this entire mystery, and now we can place her at the heart of it and begin to discover her exact connection. By being Arbella's daughter, she is also the great-granddaughter of Margaret Douglas and Bess of Hardwick — two formidable women. But what happened to her, Kit? We can place her here until 1662, which is the last date on her letters in the *Lady Pamela Collection*. It's possible she died but I'm not sure. Then she seems to have been systematically removed from history."

"Do you think The Scribe is responsible?"

"Probably, but under orders from whom?"

Kit considered this for a few moments, then asked, "Have you checked the burial records for the chapel?"

"Not yet. Although it had crossed my mind."

"Shall we take a look?" he suggested, turning to smile at her and, for a moment, Perdita was transported back to the first time she had suggested checking the burial records. It was while she had been collating the pieces of the puzzle about Catherine Howard. Despite being dubious of her suggestion that Henry VIII's fifth wife might be buried in the chapel, Kit had nevertheless agreed to help her.

Their race to the chapel through the pouring rain unfurled itself in Perdita's mind as though she were watching a film. He had hurried to find the records, while she had climbed one of the scaffolding towers in the chapel to look at the ceiling bosses, then they had discovered Catherine's grave. It had been an emotional moment for them both, followed by their exploration of the tunnel and the discovery of the ruby ring.

Before we had to run for our lives, she remembered. Yet Kit had never faltered. No matter where she had insisted on going in this quest, he had been beside her.

How could I have been so stupid, she thought, *wasting all this time?* If she was honest, her feelings for Kit had been there almost from their first meeting, when he had scowled at her and Warren upon their arrival at Marquess House. Since then, there had been so many opportunities for the two of them, yet she had turned away from them all. Piper's words that he was considering returning to Andorra reverberated around her head, and she felt her heart clench with dread at the thought of Marquess House without Kit.

I should have had more courage, she thought. *I should have trusted him, trusted myself.*

"Perds?" Kit asked.

Piper's voice seemed to echo around her head again: *The next move is yours to make. You have to stop being selfish and realise Kit has feelings and needs too.* Perdita took a deep breath. "Wait a moment."

"Is everything OK?" Kit asked, concern on his face.

Perdita lifted her head, summoning all her courage. "Kit, I need to apologise."

"Whatever for?" he asked.

This close to him, able to breath in the lemony tang of his aftershave and to feel the overwhelming presence of him, her voice faltered. His blue eyes looked tired and sad; there was even the faint hint of laughter lines around them, which made him look older, more troubled. When she did not continue, his voice was gentle, encouraging. "Perds, please, you can tell me anything."

"Oh Kit," she said. "I'm sorry, I've been so selfish." To her horror, tears welled in her eyes. *Now*, she scolded herself, *is not the time to cry*.

"You couldn't be selfish if you tried," he said, using his thumb to wipe away the tear that had fallen.

"Yes, I can, and I have been," she said. "You've been so patient and…" Her voice tailed off. Words were her tool, her means to her career, to the world; but now they had abandoned her. She gave Kit a beseeching look. "Kit, I have to tell you about Rory," she managed at last.

"Your other ex-fiancé?" he said, but his tone was gentle.

"Yes." She hung her head. "I'm not proud to have two broken engagements behind me."

"Is he the reason you won't…" Kit broke off without finishing the sentence. "Have you heard from him? Are you planning on going back to him?"

"What? No! My engagement to Rory was always a massive mistake. I told Rory I wanted to end our relationship, but he asked for one last chance, so I agreed to go with him to his parents' wedding anniversary party. I didn't want to upset them because they had always been good to me, but when he was making a speech about his parents' happy marriage, he called me on stage and proposed in front of the crowd of 150 members of his family and his parents' closest friends. To make matters worse, his mother, Doreen, slid her own engagement ring from her finger for Rory to give to me. What could I do, Kit? I was cornered. I felt I had no option but to accept. Rory thought it would solve all our relationship problems."

"What a horrible trick," said Kit.

"I know. He spent the entire journey back home telling me I had issues and it was because of my strange childhood and my mother dying that I couldn't let anyone love me," she whispered, trying to keep her voice steady, having only ever spoken about it to Piper. "By the time he'd finished, I felt as though I should be grateful he had taken me on. It's easy now to see he was manipulating me, but when you're in the middle of it, you doubt yourself."

She explained how, against her better judgement, she had stayed with Rory, even agreeing to put money into the flat he was in the process of buying.

"We'd barely completed on the flat when Rory went away for three weeks to Peru on a conference and I met Warren. I'm not proud of my subsequent behaviour and the fact I was unfaithful to Rory. By then, I'd realised Rory didn't love me, he just wanted to control me. Warren made me feel strong again and with him by my side, I was able to make the decision to leave Rory. I haven't spoken to him since I moved out of the flat. The sale of the property was handled by my father's solicitor. And then everything that happened with Warren… I'm sorry, Kit. I should have explained why I've been acting the way I have, but I felt foolish because I've allowed myself to be tricked so stupidly in past relationships."

"You have nothing to feel foolish about," Kit said, wrapping his arms around her. "Both Rory and Warren were thoroughly unpleasant."

"And us?" Perdita said in a small voice.

Kit rested his chin on the top of her head. "Is there an us, Perds?" he asked. "You know I'd like there to be, but I do understand you've had a rough time. The decision is yours now."

Perdita knew that if she did not take the chance, there would never be another and, as Piper had said, she would regret it forever. Taking a deep breath, she reached up and kissed him. Not the chaste suggestions she had for so long bestowed upon him, but a deep, lingering expression of all she knew she felt for him but had spent so long denying.

At first, Kit did not respond, pulling away and looking deep into her unusual storm-coloured eyes. "Are you sure?" he murmured, and she saw the hope flaring in his face.

"Yes," she replied.

The grin that unfurled across his face was like the sun coming out after a storm. "Thank goodness for that," he murmured.

CHAPTER FOUR

When they finally managed to tear themselves away from one another, Perdita and Kit made their way out of the research centre and across the lawn towards the chapel.

"It's a year today since I moved into Marquess House," said Perdita as they strolled towards the formal gardens.

"I know," Kit said. "Dad has it marked on the calendar on his computer. A lot has changed in a year. Think of all we've discovered: the two rings, the secret about Catherine Howard, the true story of what happened to Mary, Queen of Scots and her real identity."

They let themselves into the ancient chapel. Perdita, as ever, was struck by its beauty. The shimmering stained-glass windows, the blue and gold of the ceiling, the bosses with their serene faces watching the years pass and the mermaids swimming through the shadows.

Since her return to Marquess House, she had regularly laid flowers on Catherine's grave and now she walked on silent feet to the front of the chapel, folding back the altar cloth and sitting on the cool tiles, contemplating the ancient stone covering the youngest of Henry VIII's brides. She saw again the Latin motto *spe et nereidum* — hope and mermaids, which she had encountered throughout her quest.

"Seen anything new?" asked Kit, sitting cross-legged beside her, holding the large leather-bound burial book.

"No, not this time."

He opened it with great care and together they searched, but half an hour later, having gone through the entire volume, they discovered no trace of Penelope Fitzalan.

"What a shame," said Perdita. "It would have been far too simple though."

"I'll put this back; then shall we go down to the maze?" suggested Kit.

Perdita smiled at Kit. "Yes," she replied, standing in one elegant move, "let's enjoy the sunshine."

They set off towards the Elizabethan knot garden and the rolling lawns beyond that led to the maze.

The grounds of Marquess House were enormous, with several acres around the house set out as cultivated gardens and parkland. This gave way to farmland, much of which was rented out. It had been months before Perdita and Piper had seen everything their inheritance included. The maze was a place Perdita enjoyed wandering, especially as at its heart was another sculpture of a mermaid. There were five in total scattered throughout the grounds, but the one at the centre of the maze was her favourite. There was a delicate beauty to it, and the verdigris over the tail gave it a magical sense of movement when the water flowed across it.

As they made their way towards the scented paths of the knot garden, Perdita continued to ponder the absence of Penelope Fitzalan from the chapel. It struck her as odd, particularly as they had proof that she had once lived at Marquess House and her imprint seemed to be part of the fabric of its ancient walls. If she had loved the house and lived here for most of her adult life, why was she not in the chapel? Where had she been buried?

Then Perdita remembered something, another letter, one she had dismissed as being unconnected, but now she saw it could be a key part of the story. So great was her sudden realisation, she came to an abrupt halt.

"In the Lady Pamela collection, there was a letter to Lady Katherine Philips of Tenby stating that Lady Somerset and her companion, Anna, were due to leave by 'a vessel owned by her ladyship and she will meet Anastasia Howard, the daughter of her cousin Lady Alethea Howard, in the Netherlands'. Lady Alethea Howard was a cousin of Arbella Stuart. A cousin?"

"What about it?" asked Kit.

"Tenby isn't far from here — what if Katherine Philips was another Lady of Melusine? A ship, Kit, a woman escaping on a ship. Do you think this could be connected to the letter Izi mentioned?"

"Which letter? There are so many."

"The woman escaping across the muddy field," Perdita said. "Do you think she's somehow connected with Penelope, too?" Kit gave her a blank look. "Izi flagged it up during our meeting because it mentioned a locket." Perdita pulled her phone from her back pocket, entered a few passwords, and pulled up a transcript of the letter. "This is it," she said, passing it to Kit.

Kit looked dubious but he took her phone and began to read aloud: "'My Dear Eaffrey, the passage was tolerable but then I have always been a good sailor. However, our escape was something which may one day sit well in a play. We were making our way to the harbour and my beloved ship, when the warning came from my loyal retainer that soldiers were on the road. It was a bitter blow because my belongings were already aboard, and we had no chance to rescue any of my beloved items. My housekeeper, a brave woman, insisted she set off towards the harbour pretending to be me while I escaped. I was unhappy about her taking such a risk, but she was insistent.

"'In due course, Anna and I set off across the fields to St Brides where Mr ap Morgan, Mr Poell and Mr Laugharne harboured The George. It was bound for France and from there, we could make our passage to Holland. The going was very wet and heavy through the clay soil. After much stumbling, I suggested to Anna that we divest ourselves of the bulkier items we carried. She agreed and we packed what we thought we would need: money, small victuals, a silver dagger for protection and valuable items, in case we needed to sell them. Our remaining plate and books, I wrapped in a shawl and placed in a stout leather bag.

"'An oak had blown over in the autumn storms and I knew it had been cleared but that the hole from the roots had yet to be ploughed back into the field. It is here I deposited our goods. Freed of our burdens, we made good time over the field and made our escape aboard The George. I heard later that my beloved ship was sunk on the king's orders. Although, it was with great relief I was told the crew had escaped unharmed and are now safely back at my family home until my staff can secrete them aboard other vessels. Perhaps they will find passage to Ireland with you, my dear, on one of your missions.

"'My only heartbreak is the loss of my brother's locket; it was passed to me by my nephew for safekeeping but in my haste to get away, I forgot it was hidden with the plate. It was the foolish mistake of a flustered old woman. Maybe one day, I shall be able to return to claim it. Write soon my dear, we are safe here, perhaps you would be able to join us'."

"It's signed the Marchioness of Hertford," said Perdita, "but I haven't been able to trace who she was yet, especially as there is no date. This was one of the 'Miscellaneous' letters in the collection."

Kit stared at her. "Do you think this could be connected to the shipwreck?"

"I did wonder but with no dates, it's hard to be certain. It's as though whoever was writing it was being deliberately vague."

"The Ladies of Melusine were experts in deception and distraction," said Kit. "This woman, whoever she was, clearly had it down to a fine art."

"Do you remember the Ladies of Melusine letters also mentioned a casket of letters containing confessions that allegedly back up everything we've discovered so far?" asked Perdita.

"Yes," replied Kit, handing her back her phone. "Does Arbella mention a casket of letters?"

"Yes, she inherited it, apparently, but before you get too excited, apply some logic. I'm pretty certain a cache of such incriminating evidence would have been destroyed or, at the very least, divided up in order to spread the blame should it ever be discovered. History might have painted Arbella Stuart as a madwoman but from reading these diaries, if they are hers, she was far more astute than we've been led to believe."

"Why do you say that?"

They were entering the intricate Elizabethan knot garden with its avenues and hedgerows, accented with colourful beds of aromatic herbs, which Perdita stroked as she passed, adding their perfume to the soft summer air. "From reading Arbella's biographies and checking with The National Archives, there are no remaining letters from Arbella Stuart from before 1603, which was the year James I ascended the throne of England," said Perdita. "She was also supposed to have been a talented poet but again, none of her poetry has survived. Throughout her later letters there are also references to a secret lover, yet no one has ever been named or identified in this role. The only letters from her that remain, and there are quite a lot, are those that enforce the idea of her being hysterical and unreliable."

"We're back to the Catherine Howard syndrome," said Kit. "The only surviving evidence is incriminating letters and confessions that support the story told about her affairs and lewd living."

"Exactly," said Perdita. "I've been wondering if the disappearance of all Arbella's letters and poems was deliberate."

"Destroyed by The Scribe?"

"Maybe, or even Arbella herself," said Perdita. "Remember, she was brought up by Bess of Hardwick, who was a consummate survivor. She probably taught Arbella from a young age not to incriminate herself on paper. If her early letters revealed too much and implicated her and a possible lover, perhaps Arbella decided it was safest to have the powers that be, aka, the Privy Council, believe she was a hysteric and could not be held responsible for her actions. She may have decided to destroy any evidence herself that would prove otherwise, so she burned her letters and poems."

"Would she have wanted to be remembered in that way though?"

They had arrived at the maze where two ancient lilac trees guarded the entrance. The branches had grown together, forming a green archway; the heady flowers were dying back, but the leaves cast dark shadows through the first section of the yew maze. Perdita always felt as though this was the entrance to a magical, otherworldly place. It was the reason she liked spending time there.

"Arbella, then," prompted Kit as they entered the shadows, "do you think her intention was to be viewed with pity and derision?"

Perdita wrinkled her nose as she spoke. "No, I don't expect so, but if she was responsible for the destruction of her personal correspondence, I'm not sure she was looking at the long-term. Remember, we're viewing her actions with hindsight, we know how things ended for them all, they didn't: they were living through events. They had no way of knowing what would happen next, and I doubt very much if anyone was thinking about posterity. Their main objective was survival."

"You're right, Perds," he replied. "When we discuss history, it's easy to forget the people whose lives we're studying and dissecting had no idea what effect their actions would have."

"It's why we have to be careful when we hypothesise or make judgements on events. We need to see it from the point of view of the people while they were in that terrifying or wonderful moment. It's another reason why I'm wary of the 'madness' label attributed to Arbella. Arbella wouldn't be the first woman to be inaccurately labelled as a hysteric or mad because she refused to conform and stood up for herself. Arbella wasn't a conventional Tudor or Stuart woman. Her upbringing had trained her to be a monarch, yet she was pipped at the post by her cousin, James, leaving her with this incredible education and nothing to do with it. Not only that, despite her intelligence, she was controlled by others: first her grandmother, then her cousin, James.

"Throughout her life she was dangled in front of foreign rulers as a potential bride, but no official betrothal was ever agreed upon. Frustrated and in need of the status being married brought, she took matters into her own hands and eloped; whether this was with William Seymour, as the history books tell us, or someone else, I'm still unravelling, but we know she was headstrong and willing to take risks.

"If you search, there are many comments about her loyal friends and servants, people with whom she plans plot after plot and who accompany her on most of her travels. If you read between the lines of her official biographies and the copies of her letters that remain, it's apparent she had a loyal entourage encompassing people from the higher echelons of society to her servants to playwrights, actors and poets, including Edmund Shakespeare, the lesser known brother of the more famous, William."

Kit raised his eyebrows in surprise. "Do you have any thoughts on who The Scribe might be?" he asked.

"A few," said Perdita. "It occurred to me that whoever undertook such a vast revision of events was someone who was used to writing."

"A playwright?"

"I think so," said Perdita. "In the 1660s, when Charles II was invited to become king again, the theatres, that had been closed under Cromwell and the Puritans, reopened and the court became known as a place of pleasure. Plays were one of the most popular forms of entertainment, and it has always been suggested by historians that the theatre became a reflection of the court and politics of the day. One of the criticisms of Charles was that the court lived as though it were performing on stage and the theatre companies echoed this with plays reflecting this artifice. The king also had several mistresses who were actresses: Nell Gwyn is the most famous."

"And you think it was around then that The Scribe was forced to rewrite events?"

"We know Charles insisted on the wholesale changing of statutes when he was restored to the throne, so in official documents at least, his reign would follow on from the execution of his father Charles I without the eleven-year break.

I think he was probably the person who employed The Scribe, and there was a proliferation of writers who could have been pressed into service."

"You must have an idea then — a suspicion about the identity of The Scribe?"

"There are a number of options," said Perdita. "There were the four playwriting Howard brothers: Edward, Sir Robert, Colonel Henry and James Howard. They were all Royalist sympathisers throughout the Civil War, and any of them would have been happy to help their new monarch. But we know The Scribe was writing under duress, which means we have to discount them. Also writing at this time there was John Lacy, John Wilson, Samuel Pepys, Sir George Etherege, William Wycherley, Sir William Davenant, and Thomas Killigrew, but these men remain well known, so I don't think it can be any of them. It has to be someone more obscure."

"Were there any female playwrights?"

Perdita's eyes twinkled at Kit's words. "You're learning," she grinned. "There were a few — the most famous is Aphra Behn, and I do think she might have been involved, perhaps as one of the Ladies of the Melusine but I think we have to discount her as being The Scribe."

"Why?"

"For the very fact she is famous and we know about her," replied Perdita. "If it was Aphra, then she would have been scrubbed from the pages of history."

"She was for a long time though," interjected Kit.

"True, but I still think she's too high profile," repeated Perdita. "However, I wonder if the Eaffrey in the letter about the escape across the field might have been Aphra Behn. Aphra's name at birth was Eaffrey Johnson. And the Marchioness of Hertford makes comments about plays. Aphra was most famous for being the first woman who earned her living by writing. Her early life is shrouded in mystery, but there were many rumours after the Restoration that she was both Charles II's lover and a spy. There are no surviving records of her husband, Mr Behn, and her biographies suggest she had strong connections to the Netherlands. All of that fits in with the letter I showed you."

"So, any other thoughts on who The Scribe could be?"

"There was a woman called Anna Trapnell who is a potential candidate. She was a self-proclaimed prophetess during the Protectorate, and she published a number of accounts of her visions proclaiming the death of Oliver Cromwell."

"I bet she was popular."

Perdita grinned. "She's another one who was considered 'mad'. There are a few other potential female playwrights: Jane Cavendish and her sisters Margaret Cavendish and Elizabeth Egerton, who have distant links to Bess of Hardwick. My main hunch, though, is Katherine Philips. She was a poet and author from Tenby, which we know was once a place of importance for the Tudors, and we have the fragment of the letter addressed to her concerning Lady Somerset, so she was connected to the secret somehow. At the moment, however, it really is a theory based on circumstantial information: age, location, occupation."

"You're bound to find a clue somewhere. Perhaps the rest of Arbella's diaries will give you some suggestions."

"Arbella died in 1615, so she would have far predeceased The Scribe."

"But maybe Arbella's is another death that was not as it seemed."

Perdita paused at a fork in the maze and followed the left path, arriving in a small clearing dappled with sunshine before turning left again and heading to the centre of the maze where they could hear the fountain playing.

The clearing at the heart of the maze opened before them, a dell of golden sunshine with benches and tables positioned around the beautiful mermaid fountain. Perdita sank onto the seats closest to the water. Kit settled beside her and after a moment gazing at the arcing rainbows formed by the fountain, Perdita continued, "What I don't understand though is why the Lady Pamela letters end when they do."

"1662, if I remember correctly."

"Gold star to you, Dr Mackensie," said Perdita. "I've read the transcripts from the final letters and it's clear that as time passes, the link to the secret of the missing heirs becomes less vital. By the time this cache of correspondence ends, we've moved on over 120 years, we've had several generations of women writing to each other and the tale of the heirs has been lost somewhere in the mix. Especially as during the period from 1642 until 1649 there were the Civil Wars and then, after the execution of Charles I, there was the Protectorate. This lasted until 1660, when Charles II was invited back to be king. There is very little about the missing heirs, but the letters do show how female espionage became a recognised field during the wars."

"Really?"

"Women, particularly aristocratic and upper-class women, were able to travel more freely than men and many of them took huge risks to pass on information. Others held castles and fought invading forces on both sides: Parliamentarian and Royalist. It was a fascinating period in women's history. The Lady Pamela archive is a huge source of new information about female intelligence gathering, but I don't see where the heirs fit in or why the letters stop in 1662. My theory is that any further letters have probably been lost over time."

"Perhaps the thought of two missing Tudor heirs seemed unimportant when the Civil War was raging?" suggested Kit.

"It's possible," agreed Perdita. "If only Lady Pamela was still alive, then I could ask her more about the context of the letters. There might have been something else with them that she missed but would give us the information we need to make sense of all this."

Kit looked at her in surprise. "What do you mean, Perds?"

"I wish I could discuss the archive with Lady Pamela but she's dead, isn't she?"

"No, Perds, I thought you knew — Lady Pamela is alive," Kit said. "She lives in Patshull in Norfolk. Dad speaks to her at least once a week."

PART FOUR: ENGLAND, 1603

CHAPTER ONE

"This feels wrong," muttered Arbella as she seated her maid, Margaret Byron, on a chair and began to paint golden stars in an arc around the child's hazel eyes.

"Insulting," agreed Bridget Sherland, who was decorating Anne Bradshaw's face in a similar manner.

"We must be seen to be obeying the new regime," responded Emilia Lanier as she laced Elizabeth Talbot into a gauzy costume.

"And you are quite sure this is what the king demanded, Emilia?" confirmed Arbella, smiling at the little girl as she finished her make-up.

Margaret was bursting with excitement at being included and Arbella was delighted the child was having fun, even if to her, the performance was a monstrous insult to Queen Elizabeth. Not able to remain still any longer, Margaret scooted through the gathered women, hurrying to find her costume. Arbella sank onto the stool and watched as her friend, Emilia Lanier, shook her thick dark hair from her face and began applying her own stage make-up and nodded.

"Your cousin, King James, has left Edinburgh and is making his way south to claim his throne," Emilia confirmed. "Yet, beyond appointing Helena Von Snakenborg as the chief mourner in your place, he still won't give permission to organise the funeral for Queen Elizabeth. Despite his claim to 'do all honour' to her, he refuses to wear mourning and will not admit anyone into his presence if they are wearing black anywhere in their attire."

Around her Arbella heard mutters of discontent from her female companions.

"Instead, he is encouraging entertainments such as our masque, the suggestion being that he is providing entertainment for his subjects, especially women, who, according to the king, adore dancing in masques," continued Emilia contemptuously. "He travels with a troupe of players, and he behaves as though he has been king for years and is enjoying a merry progress through his land. He hunts, he gambles and he spends time with his favourites enjoying the hospitality of the great houses of the land."

Bridget shook her head in disgust while Anne tutted as she pulled her rainbow costume over her head. She was to play Iris, the messenger of the gods.

Arbella was unsurprised by this comment. "James has never understood dignity or respect," she said. "He believes he is playing complicated games of control over men and they will find this impressive. He doesn't realise it belittles him in their eyes to behave with such childishness towards the woman who has made him a powerful, wealthy and respectable monarch." The fury in her voice was evident. "The man has no heart," she continued. "He flounces like a petulant child while there are better candidates to wear his crown."

"Careful, Arbel," warned Elizabeth. "This is treason."

Arbella shrugged. "Who will hear us? Anyway, I'm supposed to be mad, so my words can always be denied."

Five days earlier, she and her entourage had arrived at the magnificent Wrest Park, home of her cousin, Elizabeth Talbot, who was married to Sir Henry Grey. The two women had grown up together, along with Elizabeth's two sisters: Alethea and Mary. They were the daughters of Gilbert Talbot and Mary Cavendish, Arbella's maternal aunt. The little girls had always included their royal cousin in their games and often referred to her as their fourth sister.

When she had refused to take up the position of chief mourner at the queen's funeral, following advice from both her grandmother and Helena, dowager marchioness of Northampton, who would be her replacement, Arbella had decided it would be prudent to quit the capital until the funeral was over. Wrest Park was 50 miles from the capital, giving her a great enough distance to be viewed without threat while also being near enough to return at speed should it be necessary.

The women were gathered in Arbella's rooms preparing for an elaborate masque on the command of the king. A letter had arrived the day after Arbella, suggesting members of the king's entourage might be arriving and would need entertaining. Elizabeth and her husband, Henry Grey, had immediately called together their musicians and staff in order to prepare for a feast and masque involving the women. Using costumes from a previous performance, the women had devised a spectacle suitable for a royal visitor or his representative.

The man sent by the king had arrived that afternoon, bringing with him an uneasy tension. James Hudson was a Scottish agent of the new monarch; he had recently been ennobled at the first meeting of the Privy Council. Despite protestations that he was merely looking for a bed on his journey to London, no one was fooled. He was there to see whether James's instructions for a potential royal visit had been taken seriously. As such, they had no option but to continue with the entertainment even though all those involved felt the insult and humiliation of the king's orders.

"To issue instructions to put on a masque while the queen remains unburied is barbaric," snapped Bridget, whose furious expression was at odds with her glittering face as her maid dressed her as the goddess of the harvest, Demeter.

"All he will see is his dutiful cousin following his whims, even while they sicken my heart," said Arbella, then turning to Emilia asked, "Does Kate's — I mean, the queen's body — remain at Whitehall Palace?"

"The instructions left by the queen have been followed," Emilia replied. "There was a written document stating she did not wish to be embalmed. The reason given is that she did not want her virgin body to fall into the hands of strange men after her death. Instead, Kate has been wrapped in cerecloth, which will protect her body."

Arbella felt tears welling in her eyes as she thought of the cloudless night at the beginning of April when the body had been moved. A black-draped barge lit by torches had carried the coffin along the Thames from Richmond Palace to Whitehall as Kate Carey completed her last task for her beloved cousin and queen. Until the new king gave his assent there could be no funeral, and with James wending his way south, enjoying the attention and acclaim of his new courtiers as they galloped the length of the country, the final rest of Queen Elizabeth seemed far from his mind.

"Your information has been vital to our cause," said Arbella to Emilia. "Is your son safe?"

"He is in the north with some friends of his father," Emilia replied. "Far from London and danger."

Emilia had once been the lover of Henry Carey, son of Mary Boleyn and the Lord Chamberlain of England. When their passionate affair had led to her pregnancy, Henry had arranged for her to marry her cousin Alfonso Lanier, devastated that he was unable to marry her himself. However, the marriage had been a cover for the continuing relationship between Emilia and Henry and she had given birth to a son, named Henry, after his father.

Their shared love of the theatre had always been at the heart of their relationship and with Henry Carey the sponsor of the leading company of players, the Lord Chamberlain's Men, who held the rights to the plays of William Shakespeare, Emilia was part of this contrastingly glamorous but seedy world. As a poet, Emilia was respected in her own right and she remained a central figure in the burgeoning artistic scene. Her aristocratic connections to the Clifford family gave her the ideal background to flit between the two worlds of high society and the theatre, enabling her to feed Arbella with information from both.

"It is believed James will next head for Berwick-upon-Tweed," said Emilia, turning around so Elizabeth could lace her into the flowing silver and grey gown she was wearing for her depiction of Persephone, goddess of the Underworld. "Those riding to join him hope for high positions and increased power in the new court. It has also been said that many wish to impart to him a warning to avoid London."

"Why?" asked Arbella, alert to the implications of this comment.

"Plague, my lady. It grows ever more calamitous. The Lord Mayor has told the Privy Council that ships coming from the east which are infected with the plague should remain unladen below Woolwich for 40 days."

"What good with this do? The goods will be damaged if they are held in dock for so long," exclaimed Arbella.

"The Lord Mayor claims these measures will ensure the goods are safe," said Emilia. "He believes they must be aired in open fields to avoid contagion. However, there are great problems. The goods are heavy, and there are no cranes to unload them so far from the warehouses. The cargos include soap, ashes, pitch, tar, copper, and barrelled fish. None of which are likely to take an infection."

"My husband says many merchants have agreed to these terms but there are far more who are sceptical," said Elizabeth. "They claim their goods would be held far away from people in warehouses, where they can be safely stored and there is no risk of theft or destruction. There is much unrest — the sailors and captains are concerned they will be made scapegoats for the current virulent plague. It adds to the growing unease within the city."

"Many believe the plague is a curse because the new king will not allow his subjects to bury the old queen," said Bridget in a low voice.

"And what do the fellow candidates for the throne make of this situation?" asked Arbella, seating herself while Emilia fitted her with a long blonde wig.

"The Privy Council has ordered local magistrates to arrest all letter carriers, suspicious persons and 'dubious looking foreigners' in order to try and stem any violence."

"Is it working?"

"There have been a few scuffles, according to the Ladies of Melusine," said Anne. "I have received word from Lady Gertrude Reade at Osterley that our writers report a general feeling of unease. At present there is no open rebellion, but the towns are tense, as though everyone is anticipating trouble."

"And George Chaworth? Is there word from him?"

"He is with Lord Beauchamp and they have returned to Bryanston in Dorset, where his father-in-law, Sir Richard Rogers, lives," said Elizabeth.

"Is Honora with Edward Seymour?" asked Arbella.

"We believe so," said Bridget. "She wrote to us in code the day before they left, suggesting Lord Beauchamp has retreated in order to allow the intrigues to develop. However, he is gathering men and support. The possibility of an uprising continues."

"But until we have had a funeral, we are held in a state of uncertainty," mused Arbella. "Do you think James does this on purpose?"

"Yes," replied Elizabeth. "James is testing us all — can't you see it, Arbella?"

"What do you mean?" Arbella twisted to look at her cousin who was dressed as the Greek goddess Atalanta, the swift-footed virgin huntress.

"While he wends his way through the country, handing out largesse, forgiving past misdemeanours and creating an impression of the bountiful monarch, he believes he is winning the favour of his people. Meanwhile, those who also have a claim are becoming frustrated and it is possible they will act with rashness, sealing their own fates. James is pushing his rivals to see who will show their hand first, then he will retaliate. However, we have had word from Lady Frances Brooke."

"Is she not at court, in mourning? I had been told no letters are being allowed to leave unless they have been passed by the Privy Council."

"You're correct, but she was able to write before the more rigorous searches of the post began," said Bridget. "Although Robert Cecil has heard rumours concerning the Ladies of Melusine from his late father, he like so many men doesn't believe we mere women can be writing about anything of importance, so when Frances cried and begged him to send the letter, he did so without a fuss."

"Clever girl," smiled Arbella. "The guile of women is never to be underestimated. What did she say?"

"Beauchamp may have retreated for the present, but he is not to be regarded as a spent force and must not be dismissed as such," Bridget replied. "Her other news was regarding her husband; he has asked for permission to travel abroad but it has not yet been granted."

"Why not?"

"The Privy Council is suspicious of his motives and, while the rumours of the crowning of the Infanta and the Archduke have been reported to be false, there is still concern that the Spanish may offer help to other candidates."

"In what way?"

"There are rumours of financial aid in order to raise an army to overthrow the new king, but the price would also involve the promise of a return to Catholicism."

"This would never happen," dismissed Arbella, as she stepped into an embroidered golden tunic to play the part of Pandora. Turning away, she gazed out at the lashing rain, missing the terrified exchange of looks between the women at her words. "Was my name mentioned?"

"No, your name is never mentioned in the letters, not even in code, but from the information Frances has gathered, it seems there are many who believe you are the rightful queen and they will support you in your quest, should you choose to pursue it."

"Are these supporters women or men?"

"Both," finished Elizabeth.

Arbella resumed her contemplation of the silver raindrops sliding like tears down the diamond-paned windows. Her life seemed to have been a series of movements from grand house to grand house followed by an interminable wait for action. In the brief years she had been married to William, the homes had at least been hers to command. Now, she was once again at the mercy of her relatives and their generosity, and it left her feeling infuriated and humiliated.

It should not be this way, she thought. *Once again, my life has been stolen, snatched from under my nose. If it were not for the Ladies of Melusine I would be powerless, yet their letters and their words give me an insight into events that could still turn to my advantage.*

"Where is Bess Raleigh?" she asked, turning back to watch the activity of the women as they put the finishing touches to their costumes.

"She is with Sir Walter in London, I believe," replied Anne.

"Then we must write to her," said Arbella. "She holds great influence over her husband and brothers. Perhaps they will be able to advise us of the true feeling in the capital."

"And Viscount Chaworth?" asked Bridget.

"When this ridiculous masque is over, would you write to him on my behalf please, Bridget?" asked Arbella. "Tell him the excitement of the entertainment, which was at the request of the king, has left my nerves is tatters. There is no choice but for me to retreat to a darkened bedroom where I rage with fever."

Her words were delivered with much theatrical swooning which made Emilia laugh.

"But why?" asked Anne.

"He will be able to show the letter to Lord Beauchamp, who will assume I am no longer a potential contender for the throne," explained Arbella. "This might encourage him to tell George more than he would be inclined at present. When it is written, we shall draw the symbol of the three rings in the corner and we will write in alum between the lines, explaining to George that we need more information on Beauchamp's plans."

"Is this wise, Arbella?" asked Elizabeth.

"We must know the truth, and George hopes that if he gives me enough information, I will look kindlier upon him when he proposes."

"He wouldn't dare," gasped Bridget.

Arbella raised her eyebrows in amusement. "George is my friend but he, like so many men, finds the potential of a crown alluring. My heart has never been George's and it never will. It doesn't stop him trying though."

A tap on the door and a call from Lady Frances Kirton, another of Arbella's loyal entourage, interrupted the conversation. She summoned them to the gathering point for the masque which would take place in the great hall. Elizabeth, as lady of the house, left first. Bridget was a few paces behind, accompanied by Margaret Byron, their gauzy dresses causing a shimmer of light against the sullen greyness of the April day.

"There is also a rumour that James may lodge with your aunt and uncle at Worksop," said Emilia, as she and Arbella gathered the elaborate props their characters needed for the performance before following the others towards the great hall.

"That isn't a surprise," Arbella replied, tucking the ornately decorated box she would carry as Pandora under her arm. "Gilbert and Mary are the earl and countess of Shrewsbury. They are important and well-connected, not to mention extremely wealthy, and from all I've heard, James admires abundant finances in his courtiers."

Emilia gave a derisive laugh before adding, "Doesn't it irritate you?"

"Of course, but it's no surprise that he plans to question those related to me," said Arbella. "I would do the same —

test the ground, see who was loyal. If only I had been born a man, then there would have been no question. I would have been king."

They had arrived in the antechamber where the performers would wait until it was time to take their turn on the newly built stage. The women were performing an elaborate dance of goddesses worshipping Zeus, who was being played by Elizabeth's husband, Sir Henry Grey, as a tribute to the new king. The usual excited atmosphere Arbella remembered from waiting in the wings of other masques was absent; instead, the performers gathered in sullen groups, muttering at the inappropriateness of the event.

Emilia glanced around to check there was no one in earshot. "All may not yet be lost, Arbel," she whispered. "The other rebellions are fading, but this doesn't mean the transition of monarchy will continue in this peaceful manner. Remember Jane Grey? Her father believed he had succeeded, but the loyal people of the realm would not allow a courtier to determine the succession."

It was a moment before the implication of Emilia's comment made its impact. An alertness flooded Arbella and she, too, looked around the room, ensuring they would not be overheard.

"What do you know?" she asked.

"I've had a note from Dorothy Devereux concerning the first Privy Council meeting," Emilia said, her voice low. "I didn't want to mention it in front of anyone else because she sent it with a mermaid symbol."

Arbella felt a flush of excitement creeping up her neck. The mermaid symbol was one the Ladies of Melusine rarely employed; it signified content that could be treasonous and which must be discussed by only the most senior members: the inner core of women who were descended from the original creators of the group. "Tell me." Her voice was harsh, urgent, eager to discover the news before she was summoned on stage.

"The meeting took place on Easter Monday, and Charles Blount was sworn into the Privy Council. The king created him Earl of Devon," Emilia began, moving aside as Margaret Byron rushed past, eager to make her debut. "He has given him and Lady Penelope permission to marry once she has been divorced from her first husband, Baron Rich. The king will also legitimise Charles and Penelope's children so they can inherit his title."

Arbella's raised her eyebrows in wonder. Lady Penelope, daughter of Lettice Knollys and elder sister of Dorothy Devereux, had created a scandal by leaving her husband, Lord Rich and living openly with her lover, Mountjoy, bearing him four children out of wedlock. It seemed James was going out of his way to make friends with those he saw as the future of the court. Penelope was well-connected, with blood links to the majority of ancient noble families.

"Were any other new members sworn into the Privy Council?" she asked.

"John Erskine and Lord Kinross, one of the king's many favourites. He also admitted Esme Stuart, James Elphinstone, Lord Balmerino and Sir George Home."

"A preponderance of Scottish lords," said Arbella in wonder. "Was Robert aware of this plan? It would not have been in his interest to have this sudden influx of unknown foreigners sworn into the Privy Council. They will tip the balance of power in favour of our new sovereign."

"He appeared to be as stunned as everyone else," confirmed Emilia. "Many of the old lords are furious too. Robert was apoplectic when James started dropping huge hints about Theobalds."

"The Cecil family home?"

"Yes, the king has taken a liking to it and is hoping Robert might let him have it."

Arbella could not suppress a vengeful smirk. "Robert's father built Theobalds — it was his life's work. Robert loves the house. It appears things are not going as he planned."

"We all knew Robert had overstretched himself, and now he's discovering he doesn't wield as much power as he believed," said Emilia. "However, the most insulting appointment was the Mastership of the Hospital of St Cross and Almshouse of Noble Poverty in Winchester."

"What happened?"

"Queen Elizabeth had promised it to Lizzie's husband, Reverend Sir George Brooke, but instead it was given to James Hudson." She nodded towards the great hall, where Hudson was being feted as the king's representative. A furious expression crossed Arbella's face. "There are suggestions that rather than gaining friends, as he believes, the king is storing up enemies for the future," finished Emilia.

Bridget hurried over. "We're on in a moment, do you have your props?" she asked. Arbella and Emilia lifted them and Bridget nodded, chivvying them into the line with the other women.

"George Brooke has a terrible and unforgiving temper when crossed," whispered Arbella to Emilia, considering the new appointments. "Lizzie, too. They won't take this well."

A moment later the signal was given, and the women twirled onto the stage. Arbella skipped to the centre of the brightly lit arena, holding Pandora's box aloft while the other women began to weave and sway around her. She might be smiling at

James Hudson with all innocence, but her mind was whirring. She knew Lizzie and George would be furious; she had not seen them since leaving Osterley several weeks earlier, but she was confident Lizzie would encourage George to act, to refuse to accept this insult. Running through the noble families in her mind, assessing potential allies, locating new enemies, Arbella began to form what she thought of as her war council in her mind.

Moving into the line of women, Emilia appeared beside her and whispered, "George's rage has not yet abated," as though their conversation had not been interrupted by the masque. "He is one of many who are finding the new incumbent on the throne rather troublesome. But if all Dorothy has heard is correct, you may not have to wait much longer for your proper position to be recognised."

"Emilia, take care," whispered Arbella as two of Hudson's men who had been enlisted to take the parts of Apollo and Ares, the god of war, danced past. "There are only so many treasonous words we can pass off as playacting within the masque. Your words are laced with danger. Remember what my grandmother has always taught us: to watch and wait as the demure women we are — to make no comments and commit nothing to paper."

"Arbel, you have a son — he should have been the heir after you, not James," hissed Emilia as they linked arms and crossed the stage with the others in a stately pavane.

"A son who is hidden."

"But why? With the combined blood running in his veins from both you and William, he is a Tudor prince. He could continue the Tudor line; would you not prefer this to the usurping Stuarts?"

"Of course I would," retorted Arbella, "but he is four years old. Do you think the country will go to war for a child?"

Once again, she skittered towards the centre of the stage, placing the box on the floor while looking around, her face a picture of delicate confusion. The players on one side of the stage begged her to stop, while the other encouraged her to give in to temptation and open the box. As the music built to a crescendo, she flipped open the lid, pulling out a darkened cloth to represent the furies. The dancers wailed in sorrow, before the cloth was pulled aside to reveal Margaret Byron dressed as Hope, who had been trapped with the furies in Pandora's Box.

As the assembled guests clapped, Emilia was once more at Arbella's side, taking advantage of the chatter and applause.

"Your son is a true prince," she murmured, her dark eyes wide. "There are many men who would follow his banner and guide you as Regent until the day your son was able to take his majority."

"And if he didn't?"

"Then you also have a very quick-witted and able daughter."

Arbella shook her head, curtseying as was required before hurrying off the stage with the others. The conversation was dangerous, and she refused to risk her children's safety. With an air of finality, she said, "Ennie would never consent to being used as a political pawn. My daughter has few ambitions beyond marriage, family and a happy home."

"You sound disappointed."

"Not in the least. Ennie is happy with her world."

Emilia and Arbella traversed the corridor back to her rooms, where they would change before joining the rest of the guests for dancing; *another insult to Queen Elizabeth*, thought Arbella. As Emilia began to unlace her from her costume, she said, "Ennie has suggested that now she is settled in her new home, the manor of Marquess House, she could take charge of the storage of the letters Lady Katherine Newton has chosen to keep."

"This is a wise thought," agreed Emilia. "When we return to London, I will advise Lady Katherine of the situation. Perhaps we could visit Ennie. It would be pleasant to breathe in the fresh Pembrokeshire air."

"And lead the king and his spies straight to my daughter? I think not," retorted Arbella. "I will write to Dorothy and inform her that she must continue to make plans. James may yet make things easy for us by upsetting too many people, and if he does, we must be ready to move with calm deliberation."

Emilia gave a wide, wicked smile. "Of course, Your Majesty," she murmured and dropped a low, deferential curtsey.

CHAPTER TWO

"My sweet cousin, Arbella. We two meet at last."

From her position in a deep curtsey, Arbella did not respond but she was gratified to hear the tone of surprise in James's Scottish vowels. She had been supplied with an impressive entourage of beautifully attired ladies and gentlemen, displaying blood-links to every noble family in the land, and she herself was dressed in the most extravagant manner the sumptuary laws allowed for her rank. Her rustling purple silk gown was embroidered with the three cinquefoils found on her grandmother's coat of arms; two tiny stags representing the house of Cavendish, her mother's maiden name, pranced on the edge of each white-lined satin sleeve, while the golden kirtle sweeping down the front of her skirts was dotted with a three-ringed pattern.

Although no one could see it, there also a small embroidered mermaid, the symbol of the Ladies of Melusine, hidden in the lining of her bodice. It was an affectation begun by Lettice Knollys, but one which the new generation of Ladies had adopted with enthusiasm. All their items of clothing bore an embroidered mermaid somewhere, often worked into the delicate patterns or hidden in a sleeve lining or an inner panel.

To complete her regal attire, Arbella wore her magnificent pearls. Her abundant red hair was coiled at the nape of her neck and covered with a shimmering golden net studded with amethysts and pearls. *James would have to be an imbecile to miss my message*, she thought as she waited for him to raise her from her supplication.

"Dear Arbella," he exclaimed, "this most beautiful palace of mine here in Greenwich is the ideal backdrop for so momentous a meeting of royal blood."

Insincerity dripped from his every word and Arbella, now standing, was surprised to find herself as tall as James. "Greenwich is, as you say, a magnificent palace; however, the wonders of Richmond and Hampton Court are not to be dismissed. Have you seen them yet? Oatlands, too, is a wonder."

Smiling with all the sweetness she could muster, despite her shaking hands, Arbella saw James flinch as though she had hit him.

"These are places we are yet to discover," replied James, his smile wide but his eyes cold. "Perhaps one day you will have the honour of showing me the remainder of my realm. At present, I have been enjoying the sport at Theobalds. I was also most impressed with Sir Robert Chester's hunting grounds in Royston. It seems both these homes in my county of Hertfordshire will soon become new royal favourites."

Behind the king, Arbella noted Robert Cecil shifting uncomfortably from foot to foot. His face was impassive, but his hands were gripped into tight fists. Was it Robert who had begun the rumour that had so recently reached her ears? Edmund Shakespeare had written saying it had been reported in the Southwark alehouses that Arbella was imprisoned in the Tower of London, awaiting execution for treason.

"Is there anything from Emilia?" she had asked after reading Edmund's short note.

"She confirms the rumour reported by Edmund," Anne Bradshaw had told her.

The information had unsettled Arbella — had the rumour been a hint of what was to come out of this meeting with James?

Taking the seat he indicated, she gave him her most unthreatening and demure smile. Lounging near her cousin were two young men.

"Arbella, have you met my friends?" asked James. He pointed to the younger. "This is Philip Herbert, earl of Montgomery, a favourite hunting companion."

Philip swept his hair to one side, a habit which appeared to delight the king, who shot him a sly smile. The young earl glared at Arbella from under his eyelashes, his expression haughty.

"And this is John Ramsey, earl of Holderness," continued James, pointing to the other young man. "He used to be a page at my court, but he's become such a close friend I've promoted him through the ranks of my household, and he is my boon companion."

Fury emanated from John Ramsey, who Arbella estimated was a few years older than Philip.

"What a happy group we are," enthused James, who appeared amused by the rivalry between the two young men.

Arbella remained silent, observing her cousin as he paced the room before seating himself beside her. Many horror stories had reached her ears warning of James's fearsome appearance. One claimed he was unable to speak properly because of an overlarge tongue; another that he did not walk but lurched on crippled legs, while his eyes protruded monstrously from his head. The man sitting beside her was middle-aged, of medium height with short dark hair streaked with silver. His beard was sparse and cut square, but what interested her most were his mismatched eyes; one was a dark green, the other an unusual grey, which reminded her of storm clouds.

If either eye matched the other, they would be his most interesting feature, she thought, watching as James settled himself. As it was he was unremarkable, neither handsome nor a hideous ghoul. It was, however, the pomposity and arrogance he radiated that shrouded him in the unpleasant air of which she had been warned.

"How is your health?" he said, his voice the one he might use when addressing a fractious child.

"Very well, thank you, Your Majesty," replied Arbella. "And yourself — were you tired by the journey?"

"No, we hunted and raced our way across my new land, making friends and meeting fellow travellers as we traversed."

Ramsey laughed and James winked at him, enjoying a private joke. Ignoring the schoolboy-esque giggles, Arbella continued, "It was a great shame your arrival in the City of London was affected by the plague."

"A mere trifle. We travelled to Whitehall by closed coach, then by river to the Tower of London. I was able to inspect the treasure house and it is most impressive. My admittance into Middlesex was gratifying. There were 60 or more men in their livery cloaks, and the Lord Mayor and the aldermen were accompanied by 500 prominent citizens, all on horseback, wearing cloaks of velvet and chains of gold. The crowds of common people were so dense it was impossible to count how many had amassed. It is clear my people are relieved I have arrived to take the crown and bring great glory and honour to this realm once more."

"How pleasant for you, cousin," Arbella said, her voice demure.

"Most delightful," said James, looking her in the eye, "as was our trip to Hinchingbrooke House near Huntingdon in Cambridgeshire."

Arbella felt herself go rigid with shock but forced a smile to her frozen lips. This was information that had not reached her.

"Cambridge is not a city I know," she replied, dropping her gaze.

"It is a wonderful county and I met with the masters of Cambridge University," continued James. "They were most gratified by my interest."

"An honour for them, Your Majesty."

"Yes, they seemed relieved to have a man once more guiding their charters and overseeing their curriculum. Hinchingbrooke House was one of my favourites. It belongs to an interesting man. Do you know of it?"

Arbella raised her goblet to her lips with trembling hands. "As I said, Cousin, Cambridge is not a city I know, and I have never visited this house."

She met James's curious stare with an insouciant expression.

"You should; I believe you would find it most rewarding," said James "The man who owns it is Welsh by descent and related through marriage to the former Privy Seal, Thomas Cromwell. This man's name is also Cromwell. Oliver — a good strong name. He runs a household of great men. It pleased me to see the youngsters from noble families who have found their way to his halls. The man is a strong Protestant, a soldier by bearing, and will train those boys to be loyal subjects."

"It is something for which we should all praise God," replied Arbella, her breathing becoming ragged as panic threatened to overwhelm her.

"Perhaps one day, my sweet Arbel, if we are able to arrange it, you too will enjoy the delights of raising sons."

Arbella looked up. Anne Bradshaw was directly opposite her and their eyes locked in shock. James, meanwhile, had summoned Cecil and was whispering in his ear. A moment later, Cecil had given instructions for the crowds of people surrounding the two cousins to be ushered away. Arbella took this interruption in the conversation to recover and soon only Arbella, James, Robert Cecil, Anne Bradshaw, Bridget Sherland, Philip Herbert, and John Ramsey remained. As the door closed on the extended entourages, James slumped in his chair, taking a deep drink of wine.

"How do you bear all this pomp?" he asked, his Scottish accent more pronounced, his face opening into the first real smile he had yet presented to her.

"You learn to accept it," Arbella replied, finding herself as wrong-footed by this sudden change of tone as James had been by her dramatic entrance.

"Aye," he sighed. "It must be even more difficult for you. At least we men don't have to wear such armour as you women trot about in all day. Fetch more wine, Philip," he called, "and you, John," he said, pointing at Ramsey, "stop sulking and join us."

Cecil was also welcomed into the group, as were Bridget and Anne.

"Your grandmother did well by you today, Arbel," said James, taking the goblet of red wine passed to him by Philip and running his finger along the back of the man's hand in a suggestive manner. "I wasn't expecting to find myself facing an alternate court."

Arbella blushed, but laughter bubbled up in her throat. "Well, Cousin, I wouldn't want you thinking there was no one snapping at your heels."

James appraised her as he swallowed a huge mouthful of wine. "You are not as I expected from the reports sent to me over the years," he admitted. "I thought you would be fainting and flailing…"

"Or speaking in tongues, perhaps?"

"Perhaps."

Arbella waited. She had no desire to lead the conversation — it was the king's duty to set the agenda, her role was to listen and respond. Despite the convivial atmosphere James was creating, she did not trust him. The threat of the Tower loomed again in her mind.

"The reason I cleared the room was so we could discuss your marriage," he said.

Arbella braced herself. "My last marriage or a new one?"

"Your first marriage," James said. His tone was light, but his eyes were serious.

"From what I have read in the reports my Lord Privy Seal has been keeping," began the king, and Arbella shot Cecil a look of white-hot contempt. Robert smiled back, unmoved by her anger. "You and William Fitzalan eloped in February 1594, marrying in secret in his chapel at the Hereford family seat of Orleton Hall."

"We did," said Arbella. "We were in love and we were bored with the caution preached to us from all sides, so we took matters into our own hands."

"How did the queen react?"

"Anger, at first, then she forgave us."

"Elizabeth was a curious and contrary creature," muttered James. "It is no doubt because, like you, she was a woman."

Arbella remained silent.

"And you were happy?" continued James when it was clear she would not react to his taunt, returning to the subject of her marriage.

"Yes."

"It was a full marriage?"

Arbella blushed but she raised her chin in defiance. "Yes."

A look of great cunning stole over James's face. "And you bore William Fitzalan two children."

Arbella's breath caught in her throat.

"Don't deny it, Arbel," said James, his voice cold. "You have a daughter, Penelope, and a son, Henry."

"I do," she managed to gasp, her heart thundering.

"Where are they?"

Arbella did not reply. After a strained silence, James gave her a spiteful smile.

"It doesn't matter. They are irrelevant, as are you," he said. "Another marriage will be arranged for you, and soon. You are both an asset and a threat to my throne. Not only do I wish to rid myself of troublesome heirs around whom a rebellion could be built, I also wish to give you a better life. You have existed in limbo for years and this is unfair. You are still a young woman, Arbel, you deserve happiness."

His torrent of contradictory words unnerved her further. How could he describe her as a threat, then wish for her happiness? *The madness runs in his blood*, she thought, *not mine*.

"Very well," she said.

"My wife, Anna, will leave Edinburgh in a few weeks. When she arrives in London, you and your chosen ladies shall be placed in her court, until such time as I have arranged a suitable union for you. Be prepared, you will be travelling abroad. Unlike our dear Uncle Henry, I shan't make a habit of executing my possible rivals. There is no need when I have two sons and a daughter to make the thrones of England and Scotland secure for generations to come.

"However, other men are fools and might view you as a rallying point, therefore it is safer for all pretenders to be away from my eye. It occurred to me to annul your marriage and make your children illegitimate. There seems to be no point though, and I am not petty. Your son can bear your late husband's title, but should he ever try to lead a rebellion against me, then your family will be destroyed."

A ringing silence followed James's speech. Arbella stared at him in horror. Did he think she would faint? Throw herself on her knees in either supplication or gratitude? Dissolve into heart-wrenching sobs? Meeting his lopsided gaze, she did the only thing she could under the circumstances — she smiled.

"This is most generous, Your Majesty," she replied. "Where shall I stay until the queen arrives? It would be inconsiderate to continue to impose upon my cousins. My properties were all absorbed by the crown after William was attainted for treason. I have received no money since the queen died, as my pension ceased while we awaited your arrival. My welfare is now your responsibility."

James rose from his chair and poured himself another goblet of wine. "You could return to your grandmother at Hardwick Hall," he suggested, but Arbella shook her head. "Where would you like to stay, Arbel?" Once again, he employed the patronising tone of pomposity he had used at the start of their encounter.

Arbella's mind was whirring as she considered the most suitable home at which to lodge. It must be near London but far enough away to keep her safe from the dangers of the plague. There must also be people she could trust, courtiers who were on her side and hers alone.

"Richmond Palace," she said, her blue eyes meeting the king's mismatched gaze. "It is now the home of Helena van Snakenborg and her husband, Sir Thomas Gorges."

James glanced to Robert Cecil for confirmation and the Lord Privy Seal nodded his agreement. "Very well, sweet Arbel," James said. "You shall be a guest of the Dowager Marchioness of Northampton until such time as my wife arrives. Now, I would like you all to leave. My friends and I have a game to continue."

He leered at the two young men, who pouted and giggled in response. Arbella exchanged a bemused look with Bridget and Anne. Gathering her dignity, she stood. Bridget and Anne fell in behind her and Robert Cecil took the arm she proffered.

"Good day, cousin," she said to James, curtseying deeply, "until we meet again."

"Yes, my dear, until then," he said, but he had eyes only for Philip, who was once again playing with his hair.

The footmen threw wide the doors and with a final curious glance at James, Arbella left the room.

CHAPTER THREE

"How did he know about Henry and Ennie?" snapped Arbella a week later as she nocked an arrow in place and turned towards the archery target. Arbella focussed on the bullseye, frowning in concentration, imagining she was aiming at the king's face before letting the arrow fly. There was a thud as she hit the target, but it was wide of the centre. Arbella scowled, then moved aside to allow Lizzie Brooke to take her turn.

They were at Richmond Palace. It had been a favourite with all the Tudors, particularly Elizabeth, who had enjoyed hunting in the deer park. Its close proximity to the river made it well connected, only nine miles from the Palace of Westminster to the north-east and fewer in the other direction to Hampton Court Palace.

"Could he have intercepted one of our letters?" asked Helena Von Snakenborg.

"It's possible, but I would suspect not. The worries of women are below James — he is interested only in blood sports and his mewling favourites," said Arbella, her voice laced with contempt.

"What of my dear brother-in-law, Robert Cecil?" asked Lizzie. "Would this be his work?"

"It's possible," said Arbella, "but despite all he has done, I'm unsure whether Robert would risk the revelation of another potential male heir. He was eager for James to succeed, and his plans have come to fruition, so pointing his protégé in the direction of a rival would be foolish."

"Unless he hoped the king would assert his authority and have Henry declared illegitimate, therefore removing him as a threat."

"It's possible," agreed Arbella.

"What I don't understand," said Lizzie, returning from the targets, where she had shot two bullseyes in succession, "is why the king didn't take this opportunity. He could have removed Henry and Ennie from the royal succession with the stroke of a quill."

"To remove them or deny them, he would first have to admit they exist," explained Arbella. "Even the king has to consult parliament in order to pass legislation, and many members of the Privy Council are unaware I have children. James prefers it this way. It is far better that they should fade into obscurity than to have their names interred forever on a legal document disclaiming their legitimacy. Documents can be altered, as James is aware. It's a pity though, because there are a number of council members who may have supported Henry's claim."

"What were his views on your late husband, William Fitzalan?" asked Lizzie, shading her eyes as she watched Helena fire straight and true at the target.

"It was most peculiar," replied Arbella. "I was expecting a far more serious discussion, but it was as though he didn't know who William was — he even agreed to allow his title to pass to Henry. My son is now the third duke of Hereford and will be proclaimed so in the College of Arms, despite being a huge threat to James's throne."

Helena returned and Arbella walked forward for another turn. Once more faced with the targets, she nocked an arrow and this time hit the bullseye, her other two arrows following in a neat row. The other women cheered, and they retired to the chairs situated under the shady enclave of the trees.

"Considering the fact they're related, how could James not know of William's bloodline?" asked Lizzie, surprised.

"Remember, there are few outside the Ladies of Melusine who know William's true heritage," said Helena. "Many believe his father, Ralph Fitzalan, was an illegitimate son of Thomas Howard. Even fewer people know that through his mother, Mary Seymour, he was also connected to the Seymour and Parr families."

"Only a select few know that William was actually descended from the marriage of Catherine Howard and Henry VIII," stated Arbella. "Unfortunately, after our marriage, when William's mother told him the truth about his royal lineage, the knowledge of his true Tudor blood drove him insane. My mother-in-law died a few months later, and I found myself with child, which was when William became obsessed with becoming king.

"As you all know, on 25 February 1601, he instigated his coup and tried to the claim the throne. If Sir Robert Devereux and Sir Christopher Blount had not been killed trying to protect the queen, I believe William might have escaped with his life, but once he was caught, the queen had no choice but to attaint him for treason, and the punishment was execution."

A cool breeze rippled the leaves around them, causing Arbella to shiver and reach for the woollen shawl draped over the back of her chair. For a moment, she was lost in memories of her husband, a man with a quicksilver temper. When his temperament had been sunny, he had made her feel as though the world was a glorious place and theirs for the taking, but when his mood had soured, she shuddered in remembrance of his ugly and violent temper.

"Would you feel strong enough for an entertainment this evening?" asked Lizzie, drawing Arbella back to the present. Pushing away her memories, Arbella threw her friend a quizzical look, surprised to catch the timbre of excitement in her voice.

"What form will it take?" she asked.

"It's to be a surprise — something my husband and his brother have arranged."

"Who else will be attending?"

"Their friend Thomas Grey, Sir William Markham, whom I believe is an old friend of yours, and Lady Bess Raleigh. Of course, the Gorges family will be in attendance too — those who are currently at home, anyway. It will be an eventful evening," said Lizzie. "When my husband and his brother are in the same room, things are rarely quiet for long."

Arbella and Lizzie exchanged a knowing glance. The Brookes brothers were legendary in their ability to disagree and argue; whether the topic was serious or whimsical, they seemed to delight in taking opposing views and sniping at each other until one stormed away.

"Yes, my dear, that would be delightful," said Arbella, "especially now my health is fully restored."

"Alas, my husband and I will be unavailable for these games," said Helena. "We must attend a dinner with Henry and Dorothy Percy at Syon Abbey. I believe the Reades from Osterley House will also be attending. The topic of discussion will no doubt be the pomp and circumstance finally afforded to the queen and her funeral a week ago."

Arbella nodded her understanding. Helena and Thomas were wise to absent themselves — there must be some members of her entourage with whom she could claim to have been should this evening of subterfuge become too dangerous.

CHAPTER FOUR

"My lady, it has been far too long," exclaimed Sir William Markham, kissing Arbella's hand. "You look well, Arbel. The country air suits you."

Arbella smiled in delight at seeing her old friend. They had been at either end of table for the delicious meal served for the assembled Gorges family and their guests — too far from each other to catch up on local news and mutual friends. William Markham's family lived near Hardwick Hall and they were part of the same social set.

"What news from home?" she asked, as the burly nobleman smiled down at her.

"All is well. Queen Anna has left Edinburgh and will be in England within the month," he replied.

"Now Queen Elizabeth has been laid to rest, has a date been set for the coronation?" asked Arbella.

"It will be in July, but it has been suggested it will be a small affair. The plague in London is still rife. There are reports that the death toll is now in the tens of thousands."

"This will infuriate the king," murmured Arbella. "From reports I've heard, he was hoping for a lavish celebration of his good fortune."

Markham chuckled. "I'm sure it will be an impressive sight, but maybe not quite so sumptuous as he had imagined. If he doesn't have the coronation soon, there will be none but ghosts left in London to line the streets and cheer his carriage."

Arbella shuddered at the bleakness of this image. "Emilia wrote this week telling me the theatres and taverns are closing," she continued. "Partly through fear of contagion, but

177

also because there are so few people left in London. The players are performing to near empty houses and the beer is going rancid in the barrels with no one to drink it."

"Is Emilia planning to remain in London?" asked Markham in surprise.

"No, she has removed herself to Londesborough Hall in Yorkshire. It is one of the many homes owned by the Clifford family, and Emilia has been friends with young Lady Anne Clifford for many years. They will be safe away from the horrors of London and the plague."

"This is wise, indeed."

"What do the people make of this terrible plight?" asked Arbella.

"There is increasing anger at the death toll," replied Markham. "Every day, they are beginning to question the validity of James's position as monarch. There are many who are convinced this plague is a punishment from God for allowing a foreign prince to sit on the throne of England."

Arbella was unable to stop a smile from erupting on her face. "Then let us hope the anger continues to grow," she murmured.

They were in one of the smaller retiring rooms off the great hall of the palace. A fire blazed in the grate, taking the chill off the cool spring evening. The moon glimmered her silver magic through the windows and stars were appearing in the deepening sky. Within the room, convivial conversation and the playing of the virginals by Elizabeth Gorges while her betrothed, Sir Hugh Smyth of Ashton Court, turned the pages of the music, created a bright atmosphere. It reminded Arbella of the occasions when her grandmother had entertained. When she had been a small child, evenings such as these had been a regular occurrence, but as Bess had aged, the music had dimmed and the house had become quiet.

A burst of laughter caught her attention and Arbella glanced over to the group playing cards. Bridget was seated beside Thomas Grey, who was leaning towards her, teasing her about the card she had chosen to play.

"Thomas seems taken with Lady Bridget," said Markham, following Arbella's gaze.

"He has been attentive to her all evening," she agreed. "It would be wonderful for Bridget to make a good match. She is a sweet and loyal soul who deserves happiness and security."

"You care very much for your ladies, don't you?"

"We are together all day, every day — they are more like sisters than ladies-in-waiting," she agreed. "My aunt, Mary, Queen of Scots, once told me that to treat those around you with kindness, love, respect and friendship is to shower yourself with the same sentiments in return. Her court was loyal to her throughout her troubled life. They loved her. Watching her taught me a great deal about human nature and, in return, I choose to treat those around me with care, whether they reciprocate or not."

They had traversed a circuit of the room and arrived at a gaming table set for backgammon.

"Shall we?" asked Markham, and Arbella smiled her agreement.

Within moments of settling themselves, Henry Brooke arrived carrying goblets of wine. "Would you mind if my brother George and I joined you?" he asked, his handsome face open and friendly.

Markham glanced at Arbella, who as the cousin of the king was the highest-ranking person in the room. She nodded her consent.

"Please, Henry, make yourself comfortable," said Markham.

A moment later, George slid into the seat opposite his brother, delivering more goblets and a jug of wine. The men were of a similar medium height and light build, but while Henry's hair was dark brown and matched his neatly trimmed beard, George's was a startling blond, almost white. Over Markham's shoulder, Arbella watched Lizzie send the page for chairs, indicating he should place them at their backgammon table. Bess Raleigh detached herself from the group around the virginals and, linking arms with Lizzie, strolled across the room to join the group with Arbella. The two women settled themselves beside her. Lady Frances Brooke was noticeable by her absence.

"Have you had word from Frances?" asked Arbella.

"I had a letter today this morning," said Henry. "She has reached Berwick, where she will take charge of the king's daughter, the Princess Elizabeth. We felt we should be seen to be showing our loyalty."

Arbella raised her eyebrows, anger registering on her face. "Your loyalty?"

"My lady, it is a feint, but we must play this game wisely."

Arbella held his gaze, then dropped her eyes. "William, why don't you and Henry amuse us by playing backgammon?" she said. "We ladies shall listen idly while you men make important conversation."

"Although I doubt we will understand anything we hear," chimed Lizzie.

"Being mere women, our minds are far too busy concerning themselves with trivial affairs," finished Bess.

The men around the table exchanged an amused look, then Markham threw the dice. "What news?" he asked, glancing at George.

Arbella's eyes swept around the group. As she looked from face to face, she felt a new tension fill the air at William Markham's words.

"We have two riddles," said George. "One is mine and one is my brother's. Mine concerns my faith and a suggestion to the king to aid his Catholic subjects. Our intention is to make an overture of friendship, to persuade him to tolerance."

"And if my cousin refuses your offer made in friendship?" asked Arbella.

"Then we may have to consider other alternatives," said Henry, throwing the dice and taking his turn.

Arbella met his gaze, understanding flowing through her as he leaned forward and drew the outline of a crown on the table with his finger. Balling her shaking hands into fists so no one would notice, she tried to control the tumult of emotion these words had triggered. For once her fingers trembled from excitement rather than weakness, and she did not wish anyone to misinterpret her response.

"Yes, Your Majesty," murmured Henry, "in our eyes, you are our rightful monarch."

Looking at the gathered faces, Arbella realised they were all in support of Henry's comment. Each wore a similar expression of determination and respect.

"My wife informed you that I had requested permission to travel?"

"She mentioned it," demurred Arbella.

"Yesterday, I was granted leave to go abroad," added Henry. Beside her Markham was taking his turn, while George topped up the drinks.

"Where will you visit?" asked Bess, as though they were discussing a pleasure trip.

"Brussels," replied Henry, "then, my plan is to travel to Spain, to stay with a friend."

"Do we know your friend?" asked Lizzie.

"It is the Count of Aremberg. He has many acquaintances within the Spanish court, people who offer help to our cause…"

"Is it wise to trust the Spanish?" asked Arbella, unable to stop herself from interrupting as Henry's words cut through her teeming mind.

"We believe so," continued Henry. "Once on the Iberian coast, I shall make contact with our Spanish go-between who will provide the finance. When the money is in place, I'll return to England via Jersey, where Sir Walter Raleigh is governor. He will hide the funds until such time as we have been able to enlist our loyal supporters — those who wish to see their rightful queen crowned."

"And Sir Walter has agreed to this plan?" Arbella asked. "It was mooted before, but he had not given his consent."

"He is in agreement, my dear," said Bess. "Walter is unimpressed with the new regime. As a token of his loyalty, he wished me to present you with this Spanish doubloon. It is the twin of one he gave you when you were a child on your first visit to Queen Elizabeth's court."

Allowing Bess to slide the golden coin into her palm, Arbella considered the gesture and gave a gracious nod. She had encountered Sir Walter Raleigh on many occasions, usually finding him brash, arrogant, and self-serving. However, Queen Elizabeth had always forgiven him his many faux pas, something which had added to his arrogant swagger. Unfortunately, the queen's favour had warped Raleigh's true perspective of his popularity and ability. Now, with his royal protection gone, he was suffering the wrath of Robert Cecil and was finding the reign of King James extremely uncomfortable.

The only time Arbella remembered Walter acting in a selfless manner was when as a child she had been scared by the roar of one of the lions in the menagerie at the Tower of London. Sobbing in fear and unable to find her grandmother, Sir Walter had come to her rescue, scooping her into his arms and placating her with the golden coin. It now resided with Ennie, who had always found it fascinating.

"What has happened to your husband?" asked Arbella.

"He's been stripped of his position of Captain of the Guard," replied Bess.

"This is insulting indeed," Arbella said. "Who has replaced him?"

"The title has been given to Thomas Erskine, the earl of Mar's cousin, another of Cecil's confidants," replied Bess. "He has also lost the monopoly for the sale of wine, which was our main source of income. Without this contract his credit has collapsed, and we are facing bankruptcy."

"*You* will not lose out though, brother," mused George, his eyes narrowing as he looked over at Henry, a hint of spite in his tone. "I believe the monopoly has been passed to Charles Howard, earl of Nottingham — your father-in-law."

"What my father-in-law chooses to do with his money is no concern of ours," dismissed Henry, his temper flaring. "Frances and I do not rely on his charity; I have wealth enough to support my family."

"It is true you and Walter have been ordered to quit Durham Court, Bess?" asked Lizzie, laying a placating hand on her husband's arm and shaking her head, calming his fiery temper.

"It's a monstrous insult," said Henry. "You have resided there for 20 years, Bess. Part of me wants to blame Robert

Cecil, but this seems too petty for him. He and Walter may have sparred, but this demand is not of his making. He might have denied Walter of the wine monopoly because we all know he was abusing his position, but Cecil would never have made Walter's family homeless."

"We have Sherborne Castle in Dorset," said Bess.

"But no London residence," interjected Markham.

"Walter has re-evaluated his loyalties and he realises these lie with the person he views as the true monarch," finished Bess.

"And what then, Henry?" Markham asked. Arbella watched as he threw the die and moved his counters across the board. "With the Spanish money in Jersey with Walter?"

"We raise an army, ride on Westminster, and make it plain to James Stuart that he is not welcome here. It was not Cecil's job to cast himself as kingmaker when there were other, worthier candidates."

Closing her eyes while she assimilated the information laid before her, Arbella felt both wonder and terror course through her. To wear the crown was her wish — it had been her dream since she was able to understand her place in the succession. It was this that had led her to memorise the family trees of all the noble lines, searching endlessly for others who might have a preferential claim to her own. Her cousin, James, had always been the one who blocked her path. Henry Brooke was convinced she should be queen, and the idea was heady indeed.

"What would my role be in this?" she asked.

"None, at present, my lady," said Henry. "You must be kept away from the plot, then, should we be betrayed, as is always possible, you are in a safe position to deny all knowledge of our endeavour. Whatever happens to us, our priority is always your safety and the continuation of the Tudor line through your heirs. You are the last of the Tudors and it is your blood that should be on the throne. After you, your son will be the next King Henry."

"Very well, Baron Cobham," she said after a pause, using his formal title to show her seriousness and belief in his plan. "You may continue with this scheme; however, I will put nothing incriminating on paper and should the plot be discovered, will deny all complicity."

"Of course, Your Majesty," he replied. "Our intention is to keep you safe, no matter what might happen to us."

Overwhelmed by the weight of the conversation, Arbella rose, beckoning to Bridget and Anne. She left the room, but as she traversed the corridor to her chambers, her cheeks burned with excitement and her heart beat with joy.

James might have the throne for now, she thought, as she entered her rooms, *but it may yet still be mine.*

PART FIVE: MARQUESS HOUSE, 2019

CHAPTER ONE

The weather is no respecter of grief, thought Perdita as she zipped up her black dress. When she felt the sky should be grey, rain teeming to match their tears, it was a day of perfect summer sunshine without a cloud to mar the endless blue. Sliding her feet into black sandals, Perdita swallowed her sadness, determined to be strong for Piper and for Jeremy's parents. With one final glance in the mirror to check her sombre appearance, she picked up her sleek black handbag and let herself into her grandmother's old suite. Piper was already waiting, her face white, her hair a cloud of red curls cascading down her shoulders. Jeremy had always been fascinated by Piper's vivid hair and she had left it loose in his honour.

"Ready?" asked Perdita.

"No, but when will I ever be?"

Perdita slipped her arm through her sister's and led her down the stairs to the Tudor Hall where Jeremy waited in the shining wooden coffin. It would follow the same path taken by their grandmother's a year earlier. This funeral felt sadder, more visceral, because Jeremy had been taken from them in violence and, despite the endless reassurances from Alistair and Susan, neither twin could quite shake off the feeling that he was dead because of the tainted secret that was part of their legacy.

This feeling had been exacerbated when Alistair had updated them on the report from his own team of investigators who had been working with the Indian police.

"A woman matching the description of Kirstin Chaplin was picked up on CCTV at the end of the street on the night of Jeremy's murder," he had said. "However, the official line of enquiry is that Jeremy was killed by a drug dealer to whom he owed money. This person has disappeared and the case has been left open, pending further enquiries."

"What?" Piper had exclaimed. "Jeremy had many faults, but he abhorred drug use…"

"And if he supposedly owed someone money, why was there nearly £50,000 cash in the room, along with his credit cards and his passport?" Perdita had finished, her voice shaking in anger. Alistair had held up his hands to calm their furious tirade.

"I agree," he had said. "The police don't believe this either but, can't you see, they are being leant on and forced to cover up the truth."

"By whom?" Piper had snapped.

"Randolph Connors," Alistair had replied. "Jeremy had served his purpose; Connors was concerned he might come back here and tell whatever secrets he had discovered, and he could not allow that to happen. Connors is a wealthy and powerful man; Jeremy's death will never be traced back to him or Chaplin."

Tears had streamed down Piper's face.

"Then it was our fault…" she had whispered.

"No, Piper, this is Randolph Connors's fault, not yours," Alistair had implored, but it did not sit comfortably with either twin.

Piper took her place between Celeste and Dominic, while Perdita walked behind them with Kit beside her. Only a few of Piper and Jeremy's friends had journeyed to Marquess House and they were joined by Alistair, Susan, Sarah and Alan Eve, Jenny and Izabel, and Callum.

As they walked behind Jeremy's coffin into the bright sunshine, Perdita's mind returned to Mary's funeral, then to her father's, only six months before her grandmother's. *We've seen too much death*, she thought as they filed into the chapel, the air heavy with the scent of flowers. *How much more will we have to endure?*

The words of the service washed over her, but it could not capture the boy who had been their constant companion when they had been growing up. The man who had married her sister and was the closest thing she would ever have to a brother. *This could easily have been my funeral*, she thought, *or Piper's or Kit's or Callum's, after the brushes with danger we've had, first with MI1, then with Randolph Connors earlier this year.* It was a chilling thought, but Perdita knew it was true and as she realised how close they had all come to sharing Jeremy's fate, a renewed determination flowed through her.

She was the only one who could end this terror. She was the one who had to unravel the secrets through her research and finally fit them into place. Until she did that, they would never be safe. The discovery of the locket was essential and must be her sole focus from now on. There could be no more days of mourning.

But where is it? she thought. If it was the locket referred to in the strange letter about the escape across a field, then it was buried somewhere. She had scoured the remaining Lady Pamela letters for more clues but, to her frustration, had found none. Her mind shifted to Lady Pamela and the confusion she had felt at Kit's revelation that she was still alive.

Perdita had cast her mind back over all the conversations they had shared about this old friend of her grandmother's. Perdita had realised she had never asked about Lady Pamela, assuming as a friend of her grandmother's she was probably dead.

"How old is she?" Perdita had asked Kit.

"She'll be 80 this year," Kit had replied, "although you wouldn't know it to look at her — she looks 20 years younger. She attended Mary's memorial service with her stepdaughter, Kathryn…"

"What? Why didn't you introduce us?"

"She didn't stay for the reception. They left after the service, or one of us would have done. She'd probably be delighted to hear from you. Dad has often told me that Lady Pamela has always taken an interest in you and Piper."

"Why did no one tell us then?"

"Perds, I'm sorry, no one was deliberately keeping this information from you — it was an oversight, honestly." He had pulled his phone from his pocket and pinged her a message. "Here's her email address and telephone number."

Perdita had headed straight for her office and dialled the number.

"Hello?" a cheerful voice had answered.

"Hello, am I speaking to Lady Pamela? My name is Perdita Woodville-Rivers…"

"Oh, my dear," Pamela had interrupted, her voice ringing with joy, "is it really you? How wonderful to speak to you at last."

Since then, they had spoken at least once a week. While Pamela was not a historian, she was a woman who had lived a wide and varied existence and Perdita enjoyed their conversations. She was also impressed by Pamela's insight into their research and her ability to analyse details with pinpoint accuracy.

Kit touched Perdita's hand, bringing her back to the present. Everyone was standing. Piper was white-faced but dry-eyed as she walked past, still between Celeste and Dominic. Perdita took Kit's hand, and he squeezed it as they stepped out of their pew to follow Jeremy on his final journey. There would be a reception in the Lady Isabel room.

"Perds, I can't face speaking to anyone," Piper whispered as they made their way back to the house after the interment.

"I've got this," Perdita said, hugging her sister. "You go and do what you need to do."

Piper had nodded and disappeared down the path towards her studio. Perdita moved towards Celeste and Dominic and the three of them led the group back to Marquess House for a painful hour of polite conversation before everyone left and they could begin to deal with their grief.

"Perdita, my dear," said Alistair as the room emptied, "I thought we could go for a walk. There is something I'd like to discuss."

This was the closest Perdita had been to Alistair all day, and she was hard pushed not to recoil at his appearance. He looked exhausted — his skin had a greyish tinge, there were dark circles under his blue eyes and, for once, he looked his age. Ever since his return from India, Alistair had been in a strange mood. Perdita hoped she was about to discover why.

"Perhaps it would be better if you left your bag here," he said. "You will understand in a moment."

Bemused, Perdita placed her handbag on the chair beside Susan and followed him on to the terrace, and then down one of the three flights of steps that led into the formal gardens. From there, they walked towards a secluded walled garden. It was a beautiful spot with a long canal filled with koi carp. Two ornate bridges were situated at either end of the glittering water. The walled garden faced south and was a suntrap — semi-tropical plants grew against the mellow walls and the beds housed a collection of specimens that were listed in their own right as a separate collection from the Grade One listing of the building. They strolled to the far end of the garden where a bench was positioned, giving a view of the canal.

"What's the matter, Alistair?" asked Perdita when they were finally seated on the bench. "Why didn't you want me to bring my handbag? Has something else happened?"

"I'm afraid so," he said, "and, with the exception of Susan, you and Piper are the only people with whom I feel able to discuss this development. I wanted to ensure we were alone with no electronic devices. A precaution."

A coldness gripped Perdita's stomach as she steeled herself for more terrible news. "Tell me everything, please," she said.

"This is difficult for me, Perdita," he said, "so please excuse me if I stumble over my words."

Perdita squeezed his hand, trying to keep her face impassive, while imparting some of her strength to him. "Alistair, you're scaring me, what's happened?"

"While I was in India, I discovered through one of my spies within Randolph Connors's household that we have a mole within Marquess House. Someone who has access to our most sensitive information and who has been feeding this to Connors for at least a year."

"A year," echoed Perdita. "You mean since I arrived."

"Yes."

"Do you think I'm the spy?" Her tone was light, but she was horrified.

"Perdita, it pains me very much to say this, but for a while, I did think you might have undisclosed links to Connors and that you were working with him. My dear, I must apologise — this is the reason why I didn't disclose everything Mary had discovered immediately."

Perdita was silent as she absorbed this revelation. "There were times," she said, "when I knew you were lying to me, but I couldn't work out why. Neither could Piper — in fact, she was convinced you were the untrustworthy one and that we should cut you loose: banish the Mackensies from Marquess House and go it alone."

Alistair raised his eyebrows, his surprise as evident as Perdita's. "When did she suggest this?"

"After Callum arrived at Castle Jerusalem. She suggested we leave immediately because she didn't trust any of you and was convinced you were about to sell us out to either MI1 or Randolph."

Despite his seriousness, Alistair was able to raise a wry smile. "Your sister is quite a force to be reckoned with," he said. "What dissuaded her?"

"Me. I told her I would trust you with our lives. I explained that if Mary had trusted you so implicitly, then I did too. Once she was over the shock of seeing Callum, she agreed to stay but I'm not sure her mistrust has totally been put aside."

Alistair fell silent. After a few minutes, he turned to her and spoke. "I would like to ask your forgiveness, Perdita, for ever doubting you."

"Of course," she said. "You had your reasons."

His blue eyes searched hers for a moment, then he continued, "While we were in India, one of my spies contacted me and said it was too dangerous for her to continue within Randolph's household. Her name is Asha and she has worked as Connors's personal assistant for two years. It was she who discovered the leak within our walls, but she hasn't been able to locate the source. Whoever this person is, they have access to the highest level of security…"

"And you thought it might be me or Piper?"

"As I said, at first it crossed my mind, but something Asha told me a few days ago made it impossible for it to have been either of you," he said.

"What did she tell you?"

"The first indication of the leak was actually a few weeks before Mary died, before you or Piper even knew we existed. I suspect this person was the one who gave the details to Connors that the dig personnel were no longer staying here."

Perdita felt sick; she knew what was coming next. "This person left the window open…?" she asked.

"Either the window or a door, and the broken window was staged afterwards to make it look as though there had been a break in," concurred Alistair.

"This person let in Granny's murderer and they're still here?" She was trying to control her anger, but it was taking every ounce of her self-restraint.

"I'm as horrified as you, Perdita," said Alistair, "that someone who calls Marquess House home was instrumental in Mary's death."

"You must have your suspicions," she said.

Alistair looked pained. "This is the hardest part, Perdita. There are only a few people who could have access to the information that has been passed to Connors."

"Who are they?"

"Susan, you, Piper, me, Jenny, Sarah, Alan, Kit, Meg and Stu."

Perdita groaned. She could not believe anyone who Alistair had named could betray them, would have aided a killer.

"You've already discounted Susan, me and Piper," said Perdita. "I also know it isn't you, because if it was, we wouldn't be sitting here now."

"Which leaves Jenny, Sarah, Alan or my children," said Alistair, looking desperate.

"Could it be Jenny?"

"It's possible, but my instinct tells me no," he said. "Whoever has been feeding this information has also leaked financial details relating to the estate, and Jenny has no access. Neither does Alan."

"So we can discount them?"

"Yes, I suppose we must."

"Does Sarah have access?"

Alistair nodded. "For the housekeeping, but I find it hard to believe she would be involved. She's worked here since she left school — your mother was her best friend; she is godmother to both you and Piper. Why would she sell you out — what would she gain from such behaviour?"

"Alistair, we have to put sentiment aside; this a question of proof," said Perdita, surprised at the calmness of her voice. "Is there anything that we can use to discount her? What else did Asha say had been passed to Connors?"

"Financial details, information about our research centres…"

"Sarah doesn't have clearance for information on anything to do with research. It can't be her," interrupted Perdita, relief in her voice, but it was short-lived when she realised the implications of discounting her godmother from the list of names. "What else has Connors been told?" she persisted, trying to push the gathering panic from her mind.

"This is the most distressing part: he has been told some, but not all, of the details from your research into the rings and the locket." Perdita felt bile rise in her throat but did not interrupt. "Also, peculiarly, information about the cleaning of the chapel."

Perdita's and Alistair's eyes locked as understanding washed through her.

"No," she said, the force of the word bringing her to her feet. "No," she repeated. "Not Kit. You can't suspect your own son."

The horror in her voice resonated around the walled garden and the world seemed to grow dark. Her mind refused to contemplate such betrayal. Was it Warren all over again? Had Kit deliberately targeted her? Had the man she had fallen in love with sold her out to the enemy?

"Every single piece of information given to Connors covers the work Kit does," he said, misery dripping from every word.

"No! No. It can't be," she gasped. "Not Kit."

They stared at each other, both horrified, but as Alistair seemed to crumble under the vastness of this discovery, Perdita found her mind was clear. In all her years of following clues and tracking down research, she had learned to listen to her instincts and to follow the facts. Her heart was telling her she could trust Kit, despite what seemed to be evidence to the contrary. She must push emotion aside and be strong for both herself and Alistair as they examined the evidence. There had to be an explanation.

Pushing her hands through her hair, she walked towards the closest bridge, pausing to look down at the lazily swimming koi as she tried to draw sense from this terrible situation. Would Kit betray her? His family? Every instinct within her told her he would never behave in such a manner. Yet the information being passed to Connors was all connected to Kit.

A chill ran through her when she recalled something Kit had said recently concerning families and how not all relationships were built from love and support but could be built from resentment and rage. Had he been referring to his own situation?

The thought was shocking, and Perdita understood why Alistair had looked so dreadful since his return from India. Would Kit betray them? As she considered all Alistair had told her, Kit's face burst into her mind: smiling, serious, gentle, teasing, cheeky but always honest. A new thought occurred to her: if it were Kit, he would cover his tracks — he was too smart to leave a paper trail straight to his own door. As this thought reached her like a lifebelt in a stormy sea, Perdita felt herself breathe properly for the first time since Alistair had made his revelation.

"Someone is framing Kit," she said, her voice low.

"Who and why?" asked Alistair.

"What would tear apart the fabric of Marquess House and Jerusalem more than discovering the heir to your job is a traitor?" she said, hurrying back to join Alistair on the bench and taking his hands. "Alistair, I'm going to ask you some questions. Let's try and resolve this between us before we discuss it with Kit, because when we tell him, and we will have to so he can protect himself, he's going to need our support to get through it."

"Very well," said Alistair. "What would you like to ask?"

"Does Meg, as the eldest, have any reason to resent Kit's position here?"

From the expression of surprise on his face, Perdita realised this was not what Alistair had expected.

"No, none at all," he said. "When the children were growing up, I always made it clear that while I would love them all to join me in Jerusalem, I didn't expect it and would support them in whichever field they chose. Meg considered becoming a doctor, but this changed during her teens when she discovered business studies and an aptitude for investigation. When she approached me about working with me after her degree, I asked her where she would prefer to be based and she chose Andorra. Meg is loyal to Jerusalem but has no interest in running the legal side of Marquess House, which is a huge part of my job."

"So there is no reason to think that Meg would want to disgrace Kit in your eyes?"

"None whatsoever."

"What about Stuart?"

"Like Meg, he approached me about working in Jerusalem, and the original plan had been for Stuart to be trained to take over from me. Kit was always the one who I presumed would want to be out in the field, searching for relics and paperwork, but it became apparent as the boys grew older that Stuart was the one who relished being out in the wide world while Kit had a decisive legal brain and a desire to remain in Pembrokeshire, so they swapped jobs and there has never been an ounce of bitterness."

Perdita stared at the canal, considering Alistair's words. "So we can discount a family rift," she said. Alistair's face seemed to gain some colour as Perdita said these words, and she saw the relief in his eyes. "Does anyone else have access to Kit's computer?" she asked.

"Me, Susan and… No, it couldn't be."

"Who?"

"Izabel."

Perdita's eyes were wide with horror. "No," she gasped.

"Izabel and Kit work together on the research grants, she has access to all his files…"

"And all mine too," gasped Perdita. "She's been acting as my assistant for the past three months."

"But why?" whispered Alistair. "Why would Izabel betray us?"

"I have no idea but, without us realising, she has been given the same level of clearance as me, Piper, you and Kit. Even Susan isn't able to view all the files Izabel has had access to for the past year."

"Izabel has grown up here — she's Meg's best friend and she's family."

"Is she?"

"Jenny and I are second cousins. Izabel is related to the Mackensies, albeit distantly. Why would she betray us? Betray you? Jenny's her grandmother, I can't believe she would deliberately endanger her. They've always been so close."

"Izabel is the only other person with the level of clearance needed to pass on the leaked information."

"But Kit…"

"If it were Kit, would he really leave a trail that leads directly to him? He's far too intelligent to do anything so stupid," snapped Perdita, angry with Alistair for continuing to doubt his youngest son.

The harshness of her tone seemed to bring Alistair back from the depths of his despair, and for the first time since their conversation had begun, Perdita saw his brain kick into action.

"Perdita, I do believe you're correct," he said, hope burgeoning in his voice. "If it was Kit, he would have covered his tracks far more thoroughly." Relief washed over Perdita. "We need to set a trap," he said, his tone once again its usual decisive self. "It's the only way we'll be able to prove whether it's Izabel or someone else who's been framing Kit."

"You say Asha has left Connors's employ?" said Perdita.

"Yes, she's terrified he might find her, so we've set her up in a safehouse in Denmark. There is no way to trace her."

"In that case, we need to lay a false trail that appears to lead to Asha and ensure Izabel is the only person with access to these details. Although she won't know that — she'll think Kit is the only other person we've told, and if Connors sends someone to this address to discover Asha, then we'll know for sure it's Izabel."

"Simple but effective," he said, smiling. "Leave this with me. Perdita, perhaps we should keep it between us for now."

But she shook her head. "No, for his own safety, we have to tell Kit. If it is Izabel, then she might be setting him up for other things too. He needs extra security until we've resolved this matter."

Alistair stared at her for a moment, then he took her hand, his eyes brimming with tears. "Thank you, Perdita," he said.

"What for?"

"For believing in my son."

"I love him, Alistair. I knew it couldn't be him."

CHAPTER TWO

The conversation with Kit and his father was one of the most difficult Perdita had ever endured.

"For your own safety, we had to tell you," she told Kit, holding his hand as his face blanched of colour. He wore an expression of such bleakness that for a moment Perdita shivered as he became almost unrecognisable.

"You thought I would betray you?" he hissed at Alistair, who hung his head in shame.

"No, but I couldn't see a way around it. Kit, will you ever be able to forgive me? It was Perdita who realised you were being framed."

They spoke at length, deciding on a plan of action and, when the two men were calmer, Perdita left them to resolve the unspoken anger resonating between them.

Two hours later, Kit knocked at her door, exhausted but looking more his usual self.

"Thank you," he said. "You saved more than my reputation; you stopped a huge rift developing in our family."

Perdita looked up into his dark blue eyes. "I love you, Kit. I knew you would never betray anyone. It isn't in your nature."

Taken aback, he stared at her and Perdita wondered whether she had revealed her true feelings too soon.

"I love you too," he replied at last, and a grin played around his lips. "You have no idea how long I've waited to say that and how often I've planned this scene, but I was always the one who said it first."

She laughed, but for the next few days Kit seemed fragile and she knew it would take time for the breach between him and Alistair to heal. In the meantime, they all had to behave as though nothing had changed so as not to arouse anyone's suspicions.

Perdita insisted Piper be told and took her sister for a walk along the cliff path to ensure they could speak with no fear of being overheard.

"I'll do my best to remain calm around Izabel, but I can promise nothing," Piper said. "She has Jeremy's blood on her hands as much as if she pulled the trigger herself. She is also responsible for Granny's death. We need to deal with this situation with speed. Should we pass this information on to Stephen Haberfield?"

"It occurred to me that we should," Perdita agreed.

"I'll do it," Piper said. "You have enough going on. Then I'm going to clean those paintings to see if there are any clues on them. I've contacted Vivienne Dorothy, who I used to work with at the Tate Modern; she's a spectral imaging expert."

"A what?"

"It's a particular form of photography using special cameras that utilise 16 different wavelengths of light in order to capture images that are often invisible to the human eye. I thought I'd ask her to check the images we found in the grotto and the portrait of Penelope."

"Whatever you think is best — you're the expert."

"When I have the results, we need to consolidate all our sources of information and solve this, Perds — no one else must die because of us."

That night, unable to sleep, Perdita read further into the diaries. As she immersed herself in the new story, a hypothesis had begun to form, driving her early from her bed in the morning, leaving Kit asleep as she slid outside in the watery light of dawn.

The shadowy early morning silence of the research centre was like a balm. Working, she had discovered, was the best way for her to deal with the endless maelstrom of emotions engulfing Marquess House. For the first time since she had moved to the ancient manor, she craved solitude and was determined to have it in order to lose herself in her research. This need was exacerbated by the fact that there were only a few days left before Olaf and Maggie arrived to begin the dig. Perdita had agreed to spend a couple of days on the land-based site and a day with Olaf on the wreck. Although she was excited to be with her old friends again, she felt her real research was slipping away, and each day without answers was another day when those she loved were in danger.

Within moments of arriving, Perdita sent an email issuing instruction that she was not to be disturbed by anyone other than Piper or Kit, and shut herself in her office, pulling down the blinds over the enormous windows that faced the corridors. The previous day, Jenny had delivered the two copies of *The Llyn Cel Mermaid and Other Local Legends* to Perdita's office, which she now removed from the safe and positioned on foam wedges on her desk, her cotton-gloved hands treating the books with gentle reverence.

Positioning the foam wedge in front of her, she opened the cover of the book. During her previous encounter with this document, she had focussed on the legend of the mermaid, scanning the other stories but not reading them properly, but now she wanted to check one of the titles to see if it fitted with a new hypothesis she was forming. If she was correct, it was possible there were other clues within the text, references which had made no sense a year ago, but might now point her towards a connection.

Making notes as she went, Perdita began to write an assessment of the book. It was printed, rather than handwritten, but there was marginalia and hand-inked illustrations that had been added afterwards.

Her next task was to list the contents. As she wrote, she cross-referenced them with her father's copy of the book and realised he had not only altered the order of the tales, but he had updated the titles as well. In the original volume, the mermaid was the first tale, followed by 'Lady Skribenten, The Curse Changer', then 'A Faithful Fellow', 'Passage to Monacha' — the Latin word for nun — 'The Women of Glass', 'The Lost Prince', 'The Mermaid Ship' and the final story, 'The Clockwork Window'. In her father's edition, 'A Faithful Fellow' was now 'The Enchanted Garden', and 'Passage to Monacha' was 'The Secret Tunnel'. Why had her father changed them?

Returning to the title pages of each one, she noticed a line of text was written under each inscription: "Carved from wood, it reflects the glass," she read aloud.

Was that an old proverb or motto? She put the thought aside for the moment and spent the next hour reading each story, making notes, and comparing them with the versions in her father's updated edition.

Rising periodically to check facts and try to resolve questions, she made copious notes. Her theory was growing and by the time she had finished the final tale, she could feel the rush of excitement building within her as she wove together the information she had discovered. A knock on the door brought her back to the present.

"Hey, Perds, are you OK?" Kit called from the corridor.

Hurrying across the room, she unlocked the door.

"What's going on?" he asked, indicating the key.

"Nothing. I wanted to be able to vet people before they wandered in," she replied, locking the door behind him.

"I woke up and you were gone. I was worried," he said, slipping his arms around her. "Would you like me to leave you alone?"

For a moment, she accepted the solace of his arms, then she disentangled herself with as much gentleness as possible. "No," she said. Now he had offered the possibility of solitude again, she found she did not want it.

"What are you doing?"

"Reading the book of legends. The original is quite different from my dad's version. Do you know who rewrote the stories?"

"When you first got this out, I mentioned it to Dad and he said it was my mum who worked on it with James. It's why he did the portrait of us to go on the page opposite the one he did of your family."

Perdita reached for her father's book, opening it to the painting of the Mackensies.

He wandered over to study the ancient document. "Have you found anything interesting?"

"Possibly," she replied. "It really is a curious collection."

"In what way?"

Perdita paused. "It feels like a treasure map," she said, after considering her words with care.

Kit laughed. "How did you draw that conclusion?"

"Every tale seems to be leading somewhere." Glancing at Kit, she gathered her thoughts, then pointed to the list of codenames. "Prometheus," she began.

"Bringer of fire to the human race, according to mythology," said Kit.

"Exactly. Prometheus was also the codename we were never sure about in the Ladies of Melusine letters. All we had managed to ascertain was that he was the son of Ralph Fitzalan, the missing Tudor prince. If what the diary says is correct, then Prometheus was named William and after his father's death, he inherited his title to become 2nd duke of Hereford…"

"And he was the rightful heir to the throne," interrupted Kit.

"Yes, and he married Arbella Stuart. They had two children, and one of them was a son."

"So, even after Ralph Fitzalan died, he had a son, William, who had a son of his own — two more legitimate Tudor princes," said Kit. "But what happened? Didn't the letters from the Ladies of Melusine say Lettice should step aside for the son after pretending to reign as Elizabeth for six months?"

"They did…"

"Why didn't Lettice step aside then?"

"I haven't worked out all the details yet," admitted Perdita. "Maybe the Ladies of Melusine were concerned that William's temperament was too similar to his grandfather's and decided to proceed with caution until he proved himself worthy."

"That never happened, though. James I became king. The line of the female twin took precedence over the male Tudor line."

"Because I think William was already dead by then, executed for treason."

"What?"

Perdita pulled Kit over to her wallchart and pointed to the timeline spreading across the wall.

"It was your dad who made me realise it," she explained. "Last year, when we discovered both Elizabeth and her half-brother, Ralph Fitzalan, had been killed at the siege of Fotheringhay Castle and Lettice had masqueraded as queen, your dad asked if I minded if he played devil's advocate. He reminded me that Lettice's son, Robert Devereux, was beheaded on 25 February 1601 at the Tower of London, along with his stepfather, Christopher Blount. Would Lettice really execute her own son and her third husband? In 1601, Robert Devereux was said to have ridden through the streets of London, trying to gather support to overthrow the queen. What if the rebellion was never led by Robert Devereux? What if it had been a coup by William Fitzalan, trying to take the throne?"

"It would make sense…" began Kit with his usual caution.

"And what if Robert Devereux and Christopher Blount were killed in the skirmish? What if they were defending Lettice when they died, and this was why she had no choice but to execute William?"

"And Arbella?"

"It would explain why she is always being described as being a virtual prisoner at Hardwick Hall. Maybe Lettice put her under house arrest, as Mary Tudor once did to Elizabeth. Whether she had condoned the coup or not, Arbella had to be removed from London."

Kit considered this for a moment, his eyes moving across the pages of the books Perdita had spread across the table. "Don't shout," he said, and Perdita rolled her eyes, "but even if that's the case, why would they bother to imprison Arbella? As one of the Ladies of Melusine, she wouldn't have colluded with her husband — she was invested in keeping the heirs safe."

"But Kit — Arbella and William had a son!" Perdita exclaimed. "He was the rightful king of England, not through Arbella's weaker claim, but through his father, who was the grandson of Henry VIII and Catherine Howard. Arbella's son was the king of England, but he was a child. The country would have been ripped apart by war again if his true identity had been revealed. The wars of the roses had decimated the country; who would knowingly want to plunge the land into civil war again for an unknown child? Perhaps Arbella was removed to Hardwick Hall for her own safety."

Kit did not reply but continued to study the wallchart.

"From the letter Granny pointed us to, we know that Penelope Fitzalan is Arbella's daughter, therefore making her sister to the rightful king of England. She should have been Princess Penelope. Arbella's son must be the king who was written out of history. I think he followed in his father's footsteps and seized the crown, and I think he was successful, then when Charles II won his throne back for the Stuarts, he had the usurper written out of history by The Scribe. In her book of legends, one of Penelope's stories is called 'The Lost Prince'. Penelope was leaving clues. The stories are not based on local legends. I've been checking. They are something entirely different, and I am certain they're important to this secret."

Kit listened. She could see him processing the information, but his face remained closed, unreadable.

"What's the matter?" Perdita snapped.

"This is all very well, Perds, and now you've expanded your theory, I concur with your analysis, but who was Arbella's son?"

Perdita ran her hand through her hair and a frown creased her forehead. "I don't know," she admitted. "Arbella refers to him as Henry, but beyond that, I have little else to go on."

"There were hundreds of Henrys," said Kit in despair.

They stared at the piles of books, the notes, the wallchart, as though waiting for the answer to appear magically in front of them.

"We need the locket," Perdita said into the growing silence. "It must be the clue that brings it all together."

CHAPTER THREE

"Olaf! Maggie! How wonderful to see you both!"

Perdita hugged Dr Olaf Dade before turning to Maggie and grinning. Professor Maggie Cartwright had once been Perdita's boss and, even though they no longer worked together, Perdita did not feel so comfortable throwing her arms around her. Moments later though, Susan Mackensie, Sarah Eve, her sons, Billy and Larry, and Kit joined them on the driveway and there was a chorus of effusive greetings.

"We're back and this year, it's going to be even bigger and more exciting," Olaf exclaimed, opening the back doors of the van to enable Billy and Larry to unload the dig equipment. "And, for you —" he pointed at Perdita — "we have a surprise."

"Really?" she asked, a certain amount of unease in her voice. Surprises unnerved her, especially these days.

"Don't worry," enthused Olaf. "It's a good surprise. Maggie has it stowed in the boot of her car. We thought it would be safer than flinging it in here with all the hardware."

Maggie had been appraising the exterior of Marquess House. Now she turned to Perdita and grinned. "Nice place you've got here," she laughed, raising her eyebrows.

"Piper and I have learned to cope!"

"Is it Tudor?" asked Olaf, standing back to take in the beauty of the old manor.

"At its heart, yes. There were a lot of Jacobean alterations though, and there's a Victorian wing which was added by our great-great-great grandmother," said Perdita. "The dig and all the personnel will be housed there."

"Perds, it's incredible," said Maggie as Susan led them inside. "Why did you never tell us you were related to Mary Fitzroy?"

It was the question Perdita, Alistair and Piper had spent some time preparing to answer.

"My father and grandmother were estranged after our mother was killed in a car accident," said Perdita, keeping her voice steady and not rushing through the explanation; she did not want it to sound as though she had learned it by rote. "Although we knew Mary was related to us, we believed Dad when he said she found it too difficult to be around us because it reminded her of the loss of her daughter, our mum, Louisa. We were only seven when we left Pembrokeshire, and we had no reason to doubt Dad. However, after Mary died last year, it became apparent she had wanted a reunion, but she had been worried we might reject her. Leaving us all this was, so Alistair told us, Mary's way of apologising."

There were elements of truth within Perdita's story and as both Maggie and Olaf accepted it without question, she breathed out in relief.

Olaf trailed behind them into the magnificent Tudor Hall, where they paused for Maggie to admire the exquisite tiled floor and the carpet woven to both replicate and protect it, as Perdita had done on her first visit.

Kit hung back to help Billy and Larry organise the equipment, while Sarah disappeared back to the kitchen.

"Do you actually live in the house?" asked Maggie. "Marquess House is legendary as a research centre and funding body, but where do you actually live?"

"Upstairs. I have an apartment; so does Piper."

"It's incredible, Perds," said Maggie. "I understand why you resigned when you were given all this. I'd have done the same."

They walked across the Tudor Hall, wending their way down the tiled corridor which would once have been hidden behind a green baize door but had now been opened up so it could be used as a shortcut through the house to the vast Victorian wing where the archaeologists and volunteers would be staying throughout the dig.

Perdita had expressed surprise about this, as the previous summer they had all been housed in The Orwell Hotel. Susan had explained, with as much gentleness as possible, that the reason was because of Perdita herself.

During the initial planning stages, Mary had recklessly invited them to stay in the Victorian wing. However, as the dig had drawn closer, scared for Perdita's safety, Mary's nerve had failed and a few weeks before the team arrived, Susan had sent an apologetic email to Maggie saying there was a problem with the roof and as a precaution Mary had booked accommodation for them at The Orwell Hotel, all expenses covered by Marquess House.

"If we'd been here, she might not have died," Perdita had said to Piper upon discovering this. "She was murdered while the dig was taking place. Perhaps if everyone had been staying here, the killer might not have risked it…"

"Or you might have been killed alongside Gran," Piper had interrupted.

She had stared at Piper; the thought had not occurred to her, but now it sent chills down her spine.

"It must have been a bit of a surprise when you discovered the dig was actually on your land, Perds," said Maggie.

"Yes," Perdita admitted. "When I joined you last year, it never occurred to me to ask about the land and whose property we were excavating. You must have known it belong to Granny — Mary Fitzroy."

"We did, but we had no contact with her. The dig was organised first through Stuart, who had worked with Olaf on other projects, then through Kit and Alistair. Kit's assistant helped too — Izabel. Is she still here?"

"She is but she's handed in her notice. She wants to go travelling for a while," said Perdita, proud of herself for keeping her voice even. "She isn't Kit's assistant though, she works in The Dairy most of the time as assistant to her grandmother, Jenny Procter, our chief librarian and archivist."

"Quite the family business," said Maggie, and Perdita nodded, not trusting herself to speak.

Kit and Alistair had laid the trail for Izabel a few days earlier, but they were still waiting to see if she had taken the bait. Izabel, meanwhile, continued to work in her usual way: bright, smiling, and helpful, so much so that Perdita was beginning to wonder if they were incorrect in their suspicions. In a way, she hoped they were, but she was also nervous about who else could be involved if it were not Izabel. The next few days would prove things irrefutably.

"It makes life easier for us that you own the land," said Olaf, bringing Perdita back to the present.

"Why?" she asked.

"I'm hoping you'll give us access without the usual six-month delay due to paperwork that we always seem to encounter."

Perdita laughed. "Of course," she replied, her eyes twinkling with mischief. "I'll ensure there's never more than a three-month delay."

"I'm very excited to see the plans for the museum," said Olaf, his enthusiasm engulfing the room.

"They're all laid out, waiting for you to inspect," said Perdita, leading them through to a sitting room off the large dining area. "It's a large space, and one gallery is being purpose built for *The Arbella Stuart* when we're finally able to raise her. At least this year we can take another step closer to securing her."

"I wonder if we'll discover any more doubloons," Olaf said. "The one you unearthed last year was the only coin of its kind to be discovered. I'm still hoping for a treasure chest full of them somewhere in the hold."

"Wouldn't that be amazing?" sighed Perdita. "It would give you plenty of dating evidence."

"Well, we have the mermaid cup with its inscription 'PF, June 1642', so we know it must be later than 1642, which negates my theory of an Armada vessel blown off course. Incidentally, the images of Piper's early work on the replica look stunning. I can't wait to see it. How is she? You know, after Jeremy?"

"She's doing OK," said Perdita, then in order to distract Olaf, continued, "I've checked the local nautical records from that period to gather the names of the most influential ship-owners in the area. Sailing out of Dale there were three main dealers: Thomas Poell, sometimes written Powell, who was master and owner of the *Sondaie*, an eight-tonne ship crewed by four men that was licensed to trade in Ireland, North Wales and the upper Severn valley."

"Was *The Arbella Stuart* listed anywhere?" asked Olaf.

"The other two specifically situated in Dale, who were both owner and master, were Peter Holland and Thomas Steven. They had licences to trade in the same area as the *Sondaie*. Thomas Steven had a boat named *Mary Motton* but, curiously, the name for Peter Holland's craft has been redacted."

"Do you think he could have owned *The Arbella*?"

"It's possible, but I haven't been able to find any more details."

"Would you email me the information and your notes on your primary sources…?" Olaf paused. "Sorry, I'd forgotten you don't work for me anymore."

"I typed it all out," she laughed. "If you check your inbox, you'll find it's attached to the note I sent you earlier with the directions."

Olaf beamed. "Always efficient, that's my Perds!" His eyes strayed back to the plans. "These are incredible. I can never thank you enough for helping me fulfil my dream of raising this shipwreck."

"It's wonderful that we're able to help," replied Perdita.

Olaf squeezed her arm in a gesture of thanks. "I'll be back in a bit; I need to fetch your surprise from the car." He hurried away, calling over his shoulder, "If I'm not back in an hour, you'll know I've got lost in your massive house…"

Perdita laughed.

A moment later, one of Sarah's catering team arrived with a trolley of refreshments.

"What are you hoping for on the land-based site?" asked Susan as they settled into the squashy chairs, once they were furnished with tea and cakes.

"We found some interesting pieces last year," said Maggie. "There was a cache of Tudor pieces, which makes me wonder if Henry VII had a camp here when he first landed at Mill Bay in August 1485. The perceived knowledge is that he and his army marched straight on from the coast, but a few may have deserted and stayed here. Whatever we find will be interesting."

"What was in the cache?" asked Perdita. "Any jewellery?"

"They were an eclectic mix," said Maggie. "The items were in what appeared to have been a simple leather bag with no embellishments. We considered that is might have been buried by someone of low status — and we haven't dismissed this hypothesis yet — but the contents are very ornate. One theory was that it could have been a cache of stolen items that the thief never returned to collect. Our new Perdita…"

"Sorry, your new what?" asked Susan.

"Her name's Dr Rachel Stanmore, but she's taken over Perdita's old job and we refer to her as our new Perdita sometimes. We shouldn't do it, but she doesn't mind. Anyway, her theory was that it wasn't swag but had perhaps been buried by a more high-status person, perhaps a woman, who was escaping during the Civil War."

"There was a lot of unrest around here in that period," said Susan, earning her a surprised glance from Perdita. "Oliver Cromwell seemed to have a particular fascination with Milford Haven and Pembroke Castle. Kit explained it all to me once. I wondered if it was because Cromwell had Welsh ancestry."

"It's possible," agreed Perdita, making a mental note to ask Kit about these connections.

"Anyway," continued Maggie, "the individual items from the leather bag are Tudor but the anomaly that stops us from assuming too much is the purse of coins. The dates are much too late to be Tudor. They range from 1659 to 1661, which is at the end of the Protectorate and into the Restoration. Rachel wondered if the pieces of jewellery were family heirlooms that someone was trying to save. Whoever it was must have buried the bag with the intention of returning, but never did, whether because they were caught or another reason. The items were a mixed collection: silver plate in the form of several platters and two pewter tankards, a silver comb and…"

"Here we are!" exclaimed Olaf, erupting through the doors with a large box in his arms, followed by a grinning Kit. "I got lost, but your lovely son rescued me, Sue. Now, I need a table and somewhere away from Perdita so I can lay out her surprise. Come on, Kit, you can help."

Kit rolled his eyes good naturedly, but Perdita could not focus — she was stunned by Maggie's revelation.

"This way, Olaf," she heard Kit say as he led him into the ballroom. "We've already laid out a finds area in the Victorian conservatory, you can put the surprise there."

Turning back to Maggie, hoping to question her some more, Perdita was frustrated that the conversation had moved on and the two women were discussing details about the volunteers. Perdita did not feel she could interrupt, but she was burning with curiosity to know what else had been discovered the previous year. She was already on her feet and heading towards the conservatory to ask Olaf, when Kit called to her, his voice harsh and urgent.

"What's the matter?" she asked, rushing into the glasshouse. "What's happened?"

Olaf was staring at Kit in bemusement. Perdita took in Kit's ashen face and followed his gaze.

"No," she gasped, knowing she too had paled.

"What's going on?" asked Maggie, her voice sharp, following them.

Perdita did not hear her; she was staring at the items Olaf had laid out with such care. "Are these the finds from last year?" asked Perdita.

"Yes, we finished working on them a few weeks ago but we decided to bring them with us as a surprise for you," said Maggie. "Is something wrong?"

"No," said Perdita, "nothing is wrong. Olaf, I need your gloves," she said, and he hurriedly handed them to her.

"What's the matter, Perds?" he whispered, but she did not reply. Her focus was on the item in the centre of the finds table.

Kit was beside her, and she could feel him trembling as they stared in disbelief at the cache of artefacts found a year ago in her grandmother's field. In the centre of the table, gleaming in the summer sunshine, was a silver locket.

"Oh my God, Perds, is that it?" said Kit, his voice low and tense.

"It might be," she replied.

Barely aware there was anyone but her and Kit in the room, she reached forward and picked up the silver locket. Her heart pounded and her hand trembled as she smoothed her fingers over a small dent in the top, a scar from its burial for hundreds of years. At the centre was an indentation where a stone had once decorated it, but what made her gasp was the engraving. Etched around the edges were tiny mermaids, identical to those on the walls of Marquess House, and when she turned it over, three Latin mottos wound themselves around each other like vines: *Spe et Nereidum*, *Semper Sorores* and *Iuncta Sanguine*. Her hands shaking with emotion, Perdita opened the locket and her face blanched.

"What is it?" asked Kit, leaning forward. "What does it say?"

"'To my son, King Richard IV'," she gasped.

"Do you think we've found our missing Tudor king?" Kit asked.

Perdita looked back at the locket and nodded her head. The locket glinted in the afternoon light, fat and substantial on her gloved palm. "Catherine's locket," she said at last. "The third jewel. Now we have to work out how these three pieces of jewellery fit together to reveal the truth behind the biggest secret in history. Thank you, Olaf. Thank you, Maggie. This is a wonderful surprise."

Without another word of explanation to her former colleagues, she turned on her heel and left, the locket grasped in her palm.

PART SIX: ENGLAND, 1603

CHAPTER ONE

"Her Majesty, Queen Anna." The heralds raised their trumpets and the fanfare rang out. The doors to the receiving chamber were flung open, and Arbella sank into a curtsey. Behind her, Bridget Sherland and Anne Bradshaw followed suit.

"Dearest cousin Arbella," came a melodious voice, "at last we meet, but I feel we have been as close as sisters for years."

More theatrics, thought Arbella, waiting for the customary royal blessing before she was allowed to stand up. After writing a long letter to her grandmother, it had been decided it was unnecessary for Arbella to stage a grand entrance when meeting the queen. Instead of the extravagant purple gown she had worn to meet the king, Arbella had chosen a modest outfit in a light green fabric, known as Tudor green, which she felt echoed her roots without issuing a challenge. Silver embroidery glimmered in the summer light, highlighting the borders of flowers and mythical creatures that frolicked around the hem and down the seams of the bodice, while tiny mermaids swam around the trim on her sleeves. There were no heraldic symbols, nothing that could be interpreted as confrontational. It was a gown suitable for the warmer weather and for meeting her new royal mistress.

"Arbella, rise, rise — we are all friends here. You know many of my ladies," said Anna with a casual flick of her hand towards the women who had followed her into the chamber.

"Yes, Your Majesty," replied Arbella, nodding to Penelope and Dorothy, the daughters of Lettice Knollys, as they glided into the room. Behind them were Robert Cecil's nieces, Elizabeth, and Susan de Vere.

"These ladies have travelled with me from my Scottish court," said Anna, leading Arbella towards two women who were organising the others. "This is Margaret Stewart, the daughter of James Stewart, 2nd Earl of Moray." The smaller of the two women gave an elegant curtsey. "And this is Jean Drummond, the daughter of Lord Patrick Drummond."

Jean smiled and Arbella gave a small bob to each woman in turn.

"We shall all soon be such friends," trilled Anna, taking Arbella's hand and leading her to two chairs positioned by an open window which overlooked the magnificent, sun-drenched parkland. Arbella waited for the queen to give her permission to sit, aware Anna was known to take sudden dislikes to those who she saw as trying to slight her. With a gracious incline of her head, Anna smiled, and Arbella slid into the seat beside her. They were off on good terms, and Arbella breathed a sigh of relief — a rivalry with the queen would have been tiresome.

"What a journey we have had," sighed Anna. "It is a relief to be able to stay somewhere for more than a few days. Though we did enjoy Sir Thomas Griffin's house very much, and at Althorp we were met by Queen Mab and her fairies as we entered through the magical woods. I must speak to my husband about promoting dear Sir Robert Spencer in gratitude for giving us such a delightful welcome."

"It must have been informative to see so much of your new kingdom and to meet so many people," said Arbella.

"Yes, it was interesting, though I believe the version of the country I have been shown is not completely accurate. There were some groups of people who appeared to show anger at our presence. My husband's choice as monarch is not to the satisfaction of everyone."

"The sweeping changes of a new monarch will always bring suspicion," replied Arbella.

"You are quite correct, my dear," replied Anna. "These are strange times."

Arbella gave the smallest of smiles in response, and a shrewd expression flickered across the queen's face.

"Arbel, I believe you are a poet and have many friends who are creatives: Emilia Lanier and Elizabeth Melville, in particular," continued Anna, changing the subject.

"Emilia and I are friends, but I have only had the pleasure of reading *Ane Godlie Dreame* by Elizabeth Melville. Are you familiar with the work? I know it was printed in Edinburgh," replied Arbella, wondering if, once again, her loyalties were being tested.

Elizabeth Melville was a Presbyterian and much opposed to James's ecclesiastical policies; Arbella was surprised the queen was interested in her. From the rumours she had heard, Anna professed to being a Protestant in public in support of her husband, but she was a Catholic behind closed doors.

"I have a copy but have not yet read it," admitted Anna. "When I have, it would be my pleasure to discuss it with you and share opinions."

"It would be a delight," said Arbella, her voice full of genuine enthusiasm.

"This makes me happy. Now, Arbel, we are a court of women and there is something I would like to ask you. Do you like performing in masques?"

"Why, yes," replied Arbella, surprised at the direction the conversation was taking. "In recent years there has not been much cause for masquing at Hardwick Hall, but when I was a young girl and at the court of Queen Elizabeth, I was once crowned Queen of the May and danced in a number of entertainments."

She did not include the recent debacle at Wrest Hall, still feeling the keen sting of the insult to Queen Elizabeth in its performance.

"Good. You see, while my husband has taken it upon himself to licence a troupe of players, The King's Men, it infuriates me that women are not allowed to join them on stage."

"The King's Men?" asked Arbella in confusion. "Who are these players?"

"They were formerly The Lord Chamberlain's Men," replied Anna. "The men who hold the licence to Mr Shakespeare's works."

"When did the king become their patron?"

"Very recently. The patent was put in place on 19 May, and since then my husband has requested double the previous number of performances."

"James is making the most of his new-found fortune," murmured Arbella.

Anna chuckled. "Women may not be able to tread the boards at The Globe or Rose Theatres, but it is deemed allowable for women to present masques; therefore, I have a proposition — I would like my court to produce such spectacular events that we are remembered for centuries to come as the women who rivalled the men on stage. It is time the men understood they are not the only creatures on this planet who have the ability to express themselves creatively."

A laugh rose in Arbella's throat. "Your Majesty…" she began, but the queen raised her hand.

"Anna, please. We are cousins."

"Anna, you are not what I expected," said Arbella.

"Nor you, Arbel."

The two women exchanged a look of understanding.

"You heard I was a scatter-brained fool, no doubt," said Anna, smoothing out the skirts of her dress as she spoke. Arbella noticed the tell-tale sign of fury in her busy fingers.

"Those were some of the stories spread by the Privy Council," Arbella admitted. "While I suppose you were expecting a gibbering idiot, foaming at the mouth?"

"Such gossip had reached my ears."

"It seems to me that many men fear women who have their own opinions," sighed Arbella. "Therefore, in order to discredit us, we must be ridiculed. It is a stigma I have suffered all my life."

"And my suggestion of creating the greatest masques ever to rival our male player?"

"I would be honoured to help," replied Arbella.

"Do you think your friend Emilia would lend her brilliance?"

"At present she's in Yorkshire, where she's hoping to the avoid the plague, but when she returns you might be interested to read some of her sonnets. And perhaps, with time, it might be possible for me to write some verses too."

Anna smiled, a genuine expression that lifted her face to one of shimmering beauty. "Oh Arbel, it is good that you have come to join me. We women must support one another." A look of loneliness flashed across Anna's eyes, and Arbella felt a pang of empathy. "However, until we are settled somewhere and my children are with me, we will not be a complete household, so it will be difficult to perform as I intend. There is also the planning for the coronation, after which we shall be going on progress. The plague continues to make London uninhabitable, and my husband wishes to see more of his new kingdom. You will accompany us and, perhaps, within our own court, we can while away the days deciding on our first entertainment."

Anna stood and swept away with a suddenness that startled Arbella. A moment later, Dorothy Percy was at her shoulder.

"Well done, Arbel," she said. "The queen likes you. She told Penny that she makes up her mind about people instantly and never alters her position."

There was a fanfare, then the queen and her inner circle left the room. Arbella joined the other women in a deep curtsey.

"Come, my dear," said Dorothy, "it's a beautiful afternoon, let us stroll in the gardens."

Dorothy took Arbella by the arm and led her through the maze of corridors of the ancient stronghold to the ornate pleasure gardens surrounding the living quarters. They were followed by Bridget Sherland and Anne Bradshaw, who walked behind at a discreet distance. As they made their way through the milling waves of courtiers, Arbella considered Anna's words.

The demand for more play performances was not a surprise. News had filtered through from the Ladies of Melusine that James was taking full advantage of the royal coffers and was extravagant with those whose loyalty he wished to secure. Snippets of the letters she had received ran through Arbella's active mind:

…his journey from Scotland has, according to my husband, cost the nation over £10,000…

…gifts totalling £14,000 have been handed out to nobles…

…my son has suggested that The Master has spent over £17,000 on the funeral of our dearly departed queen. This is more than was necessary and much of it went in bribes…

The Master was the codename for James; it was one of the few the Ladies of Melusine still employed when communicating news.

Her cousin's unnecessary extravagance continued to rankle; however, before her resentment could ruin her mood, Dorothy whispered, "There is a letter from Frances."

Before replying, Arbella glanced around to ensure they would not be overheard. "What news?"

"Her husband has been granted permission to travel."

"This is wonderful," replied Arbella. "It means the plot hasn't been discovered, or Cecil would have kept Henry at court."

"Unless Cecil is setting a trap for Henry to ensnare himself," Dorothy suggested.

Arbella shuddered. "What do Lizzie and Gertrude say?" she asked.

Dorothy turned around and beckoned for Bridget and Anne to join them.

"We haven't heard from Lizzie for some weeks," said Anne. "There is concern that George may have been arrested."

"Gertrude has written to her again to try and discover what is happening," added Bridget.

"But why would George have been arrested?" asked Arbella.

"He and his friends were more interested in asking the king for tolerance for Catholics than in joining Henry and his men. George continued to raise men and money to kidnap the king," said Anne.

"They believed if they held him somewhere comfortable and appealed to his better nature, he would be lenient on Catholics," finished Dorothy.

"George hinted as much when we were at Richmond Palace," said Arbella. "He is a fool to have gone ahead with such a hare-brained scheme."

"Sir Thomas Grey believed the men to be disorganised, and he distanced himself from their scheme," whispered Bridget. "He has thrown in his lot with Henry and Sir Walter Raleigh."

"While Bess Throckmorton wrote to say her cousins Robert Catesby and Francis Tresham have been formulating a plan to kidnap Prince Henry and Princess Elizabeth to hold as hostages while the king is persuaded to the way of thinking of George and his men," added Anne.

The women had reached the centre of the walkway where a fountain played and stone seats created a circle in the bright sunshine. Arbella sank onto the bench, staring at the sparkling water as it cascaded into the pool.

"Has Robert Catesby not learned his lesson?" muttered Dorothy, sitting beside Arbella and fanning herself.

Arbella winced. The name of Robert Catesby still felt like a curse. He had been a friend of her husband's and had supported him when William had tried to seize the throne. Catesby had escaped punishment, but from the many letters he had sent her in the aftermath of William's execution, she knew he burned with the desire to avenge his friend. His ferocity unnerved her, and she had been careful to distance herself from him in the past few years. It seemed his need for retribution continued to burn brightly.

"Catesby and his men are radicals," she said, "despite their blood connections to the Throckmorton family; not to mention links to the Hungerfords, the Ardens, the Treshams and the Breretons. They run wild."

"I thought Catesby was one of the recusants Robert Cecil and his men had locked up?" said Dorothy. "My husband mentioned it. He had been working with Catesby on another project when he was arrested."

"Cecil and his lackeys were eager to keep the more vocal elements under control while the king was travelling, but now James is in London, it's probable Catesby has been released as long as he remains in Warwickshire," Arbella replied. "Robert Cecil wouldn't dare upset so many noble families at present, and by keeping Catesby imprisoned he might lose the goodwill and patronage of his kin."

"Would Robert Cecil care?" asked Anne.

"The surge of Scottish lords to whom James has given positions of rank and honour has changed the balance of power in the Privy Council," replied Arbella. "Cecil needs the support of the old guard and, while Catesby might be a Catholic, he has influence. I suspect Cecil has released him with the instructions he must stay out of sight. It's what I would do if Catesby and I were still on speaking terms."

"Your words are wise, Arbel," said Bridget, squeezing her hand in a gesture of sorority.

"Who else has George involved in this ridiculous plan?" asked Arbella.

"Two priests, William Watson and William Clarke, who are opposed to the Archpriest, George Blackwell," supplied Bridget. "They are the instigators of the belief that if they speak to the king with gentleness and sense, he will understand the Catholics mean him no harm, particularly as there are rumours his wife is a supporter of the Catholic faith."

Arbella absorbed this information but chose not to reply. The accusation of being a fervent Catholic had been thrown at her in the past, and she would do nothing to further these rumours. Her grandmother had always advised that the topic of religion was one on which it was best to be practical.

"Griffin Markham also believes these matters can be settled without bloodshed," added Anne.

"This is such nonsense," snapped Arbella. "These men have lost all reason. Have they forgotten this is not a battle of religion? This a fight for the throne. My cousin, James, behaves in a manner that is not befitting for the king of such a dignified realm. However, when the rightful heir is in power, then all matters of religious intolerance will be solved."

"Better that he behaves badly now," replied Dorothy, a shrewd expression on her face. "It will allow other potential heirs to take advantage of his misjudgements."

Arbella frowned. "In all the discussions about potential heirs, we forget that James has two sons and a daughter," she said. "Prince Henry is nine years old and from the reports we have heard, he is an intelligent, athletic and personable young man, the stuff of true kings and princes. Elizabeth will be seven in a few months and will no doubt be used for a political marriage, and even if Henry does not reach his majority, there is the baby, Charles. I believe he will be three at the end of the year."

"What are you suggesting, Arbel?" asked Bridget, a note of fear in her voice.

"Nothing," replied Arbella. "I am merely stating that the removal of James may not leave the way as clear as these men believe."

She gazed out over the beautiful gardens, wondering if she should use her illness as a reason to leave court and return to the peace and safety of Hardwick Hall. The task of removing James and his family from the royal line was overwhelming.

"Do not fear, Arbel," Dorothy said. "If you remove the head of a family, unless the heir is of age, there is a period of loss and disarray. You forget, Henry is a foreign princeling. His father is Scottish and his mother is Danish. He was born in a foreign land. Your son has English parents, he was born in England and he is descended through the male line of the Tudors. Should there ever be a question over which Henry has the right to succeed, I think your son will have the blood advantage."

A silence grew between the women, full of respect, understanding and hope. However, after a while, the heat began to overwhelm Arbella and she stood. "I shall retire," she said. "The sun has given me a headache."

"Of course, my lady."

Arbella swept back down the shaded walkway, craving solitude after a trying day of tension and intrigue. As she emerged from the shadow of the walkway, the relentless sun flashed across her eyes and for a moment, she was blinded by its white glare. Around her the world seemed to shift as the colours blurred and the ground undulated. A familiar fizzing sound began in her ears, and the pounding of her head overwhelmed her.

Gasping, trying to bring breath into her lungs, Arbella felt fury and frustration suffuse her. This was a battle she had fought and lost all her life, and the moment for a bout of her crippling illness could not have been more inopportune.

"Oh no," she moaned, "not now…"

The edges of her sight blurred, and her legs buckled beneath her as she threw out her hands, groping for something to catch hold of to break her fall. Behind her, she heard running footsteps and the shouts of concern from Dorothy, Bridget, and Anne, then all went black.

Arbella's bout of illness left her bedridden for over a week, her body wracked with pain, her mind a frenzy of fear and paranoia as demons crawled up her bed to whisper terror in her ears. Knife-sharp pains had sliced through her abdomen, and her eyes had slid from sight to blindness while her temperature raged.

On the ninth day, she was woken abruptly by Bridget shaking her. "George Brooke has been arrested. Robert Cecil's men took him to the Tower at dawn."

"Is he the only one, or has the whole plot been exposed?" Arbella gasped, once the meaning of the words had seeped into her sleep-soaked brain. Fear coursed through her. Would there be soldiers arriving at her door any moment to take her to the Tower?

"At present, he is the only one. They were betrayed by the Jesuit priest, John Gerard — the man whom Griffin Markham insisted would be loyal to the plot."

"What about the Markham brothers? William and Griffin — have they been caught?"

"Not yet. We only know about George because a letter has arrived from Lady Gertrude Reade. Lizzie Brooke is staying there with her twin daughters; she is distraught about her husband."

Arbella accepted the small ale handed to her by Anne Bradshaw. She noticed Margaret Byron was not in the room and was relieved — if events were about to take a dangerous turn, she would concoct a reason for the girl to be sent home; she did not want to risk the child's life along with their own.

"Was there any mention of Baron Cobham and his alternate plot?"

"No," replied Anne. "All those apprehended are concerned with George's plan to try and coerce the king into treating Catholics with tolerance. It is believed that a number of Catholic informers discovered the plot and wrote to Robert

Cecil. He is in a difficult position; George Brooke is his brother-in-law."

"Robert and George have always squabbled…" Arbella began.

"But this is treason," said Bridget, her voice rising in panic. "Do you think Cecil will help him?"

"I doubt it," said Arbella, her voice matter of fact. "They have never been friends, despite their relationship through marriage, and Cecil is a shrewd man. He will see this as a way to prove his loyalty to the new regime. My biggest concern is George's temper. Cecil will know how to provoke him, and he will use this to try and draw information from him. Our greatest danger is whether or not George has details of his brother's plot."

"Why?" asked Anne, white with fear.

"If George tries to save himself by selling out his brother and revealing Henry's far more dangerous plan of removing James from the throne, bypassing the prince and crowning me instead, then we may all find ourselves on a barge to the Tower."

"Would he be so disloyal?" asked Bridget, shocked.

"Not intentionally," replied Arbella, "but we all know how George is when roused — he doesn't know what he's saying. He shouts and screams, blaming all around him for being fools and blaggards, before the recrimination of regret once he has resumed serenity. He may let slip information that cannot be withdrawn, no matter how much he apologises when calmness has returned."

Although her voice was restrained, Arbella was fighting to control her fear. When she had been inveigled into approving the plot, she had thought it was exciting, but now George was being questioned, the full weight of the scheme hit her. Jane

Grey had been executed for less; would she, too, end her days on the block? The room swayed and Anne caught her elbow, easing Arbella back onto her mound of pillows.

"Did Lady Gertrude have any more information?" Arbella asked when she had recovered from the dizziness.

"She has warned us to deny all knowledge of the plot and not to write about it, even among ourselves," Anne replied. "Robert Cecil is a wise man, and she is concerned he may finally have realised the Ladies of Melusine have been discussing court business for years under his nose. Until the danger has passed, Lady Gertrude suggests everything is to be written in code."

There was silence as the enormity of the situation unfolded around them. Arbella looked from one familiar face to another.

"Ladies," she said, doing her best to keep her tone calm and reassuring, "we have committed no crimes, we have worked hard to protect ourselves, both through our codes and the strength of the bonds of the Ladies of Melusine. We must keep our heads and continue as usual…" She stopped when the two women exchanged a nervous glance. "What else has happened?" she asked, the serenity draining from her voice.

"My lady, a letter arrived for you a few days ago purporting to be from Henry Brooke, but his writing is wild…"

"Why did no one show me?"

"You were suffering from your illness, madam, and we were more concerned for your recovery than bothering you with a letter we believe may be a feint."

"Show me," Arbella demanded, holding out a slim white hand. She was relieved to see that for once it did not tremble.

Hurrying to one of Arbella's wardrobe chests, Bridget knelt before it and released the secret compartment hidden in the side wall, removing the letter. Arbella closed her fingers around the roll of parchment, smoothed it open and began to read, her eyes narrowing with fury.

"Henry claimed he would write nothing incriminating," she scowled, looking up from the scrawled and blotched parchment. "Yet this is full of intolerable and treasonous demands. He has informed me that I should write to Philip III, king of Spain, promising that when I am queen I will offer tolerance to Catholics, that there will be a cessation of help to the Protestants in Holland, and I will agree never to marry without his consent. He has also suggested I write in a similar manner to the archdukes of Austria, the governors of the Netherlands, and the duke of Savoy in order to gain their support, too. What is wrong with the man? These instructions are in complete contradiction to our previous conversation."

Furious, Arbella considered burning the letter, not because it incriminated her but because she was astounded at Cobham's arrogance and his belief that should he become the vessel for placing her on the throne, he would have any command over her. All her life, she had been surrounded by people who believed they knew her mind better than she knew it herself, who thought they were wiser, cleverer, more attuned to the subtleties of politics, but Arbella had been educated to be queen. Her understanding of the nuances of court life had been learned at the knee of the most formidable woman of her generation, Bess of Hardwick.

Throwing back the covers, she swung her legs from the bed and stood. There was strength in them again, and she sent up a small grateful prayer of thanks. *Illness*, she thought, *is my greatest debilitater. It is a ruthless enemy and I am powerless against it.*

Aware she could easily slide back into the nightmare of her condition, Arbella knew she must not overexert herself for a few more days, but Bridget's shocking news seemed to have energised rather than debilitated her recovery.

"Prepare the copper bath for me, Bridget; I wish to wash away the lingering odour and clamminess of this repulsive condition. My hair is stiff with sweat from the fever. Once I am dressed, we must summon our war council. If Cobham did write this letter, then we must cut him loose, for he is a liability. However, I suspect Robert Cecil's hand in this scheme, and we must consider the implications before we act."

CHAPTER TWO

"My lady, once you are rested, the queen desires your presence."

"Thank you, Bridget. If you and Anne will help me prepare, we will join her shortly."

Arbella had been gazing out of the window of her carriage at the procession of horses, carts, and people as they plodded into Base Court within the confines of the magical palace of Hampton Court. With the queen now reunited with the king, the Privy Council had urged the royal couple to remain in the leafy countryside, away from the plague-filled streets of London until the coronation. As a member of the royal family, Arbella had been compelled to follow suit.

She led Bridget and Anne into her bedchamber and allowed her mind to wander as they tidied her hair and straightened her attire. Despite their sojourn in the great houses of Berkshire, Middlesex and Surrey, letters from the Ladies of Melusine had continued to find her, keeping her abreast of the situation throughout the country. The most disturbing news had been the unexpected change of regime in the household of the young Princess Elizabeth. Lady Frances Cobham had been the head of the princess's household, but she had recently been removed and replaced by Lady Anne Harington.

"I fear Henry's true intentions have been discovered," Frances had written. "He remains abroad but must return soon."

That comment made Arbella feel the letter she had received, purporting to be from Henry, was even more suspicious. Word had also come from Honora Rogers. In a coded note, she had informed Arbella that her husband had, for now, decided to accept James as king, conceding his own claim was not as strong as that of the Scottish monarch. However, her postscript had stated that Beauchamp would offer his army should another claimant come forward.

Arbella had shredded and burned this information. Her confidant, Sir George Chaworth, continued in Beauchamp's service, also providing her with regular updates, and he had confirmed the number of horses and arms available should it be required.

The Reverend Sir George Brooke remained in the Tower of London and with each passing day, Arbella waited for the knock on the door. In her dreams she saw Robert Cecil's sorrowful face as he arrested her and led her to the barge, ready to take her to the Tower. Every letter delivered to her rooms seemed to echo with screams of fear, and yet still George Brooke was bearing the responsibility for the plot to kidnap the king. Bridget's voice pulled Arbella away from her dark thoughts.

"You are ready, my dear," she said, passing Arbella the silver-backed looking-glass for her to inspect their ministrations.

"Thank you, ladies," she said, "once again you have tamed my wildness and made me respectable. Without you, my hair would be a monster I could not control."

As she walked through her receiving rooms, Arbella paused, taking in the activity of the loyal members of her entourage as they made her living quarters comfortable: Lady Frances Kirton, Anne Newdigate and Anne Somerset whisked from room to room, their voices soft but industrious as they called to one another, determined to make the chambers as elegant and comfortable as possible. Arbella's status as a member of the royal family was one her loyal retainers intended to make clear by creating an entertaining space that reflected her regal blood.

"Ladies, forgive me," said Arbella. "I have been inconsiderate. You've worked so hard to make my rooms comfortable, thank you." As she spoke, the women paused in their work, waiting for her words. "As you know, we shall remain here until the coronation, on 25 July. After this, I am sad to say many of you may have to return to your own homes and families. Under the king's command, the court will be on progress and there will be no room for you all to accompany me. Perhaps, when things are more settled, we shall be reunited, but until then you will be in my thoughts and prayers."

"Whenever you need us, my lady, we will always be ready to hurry to your side," said Lady Kirton, curtseying, while the other women nodded and murmured their agreement.

"Come, Arbel," said Bridget, "we should join the queen."

With a final nod to the gathered women, Arbella swept from the room. Moments later, she was being announced to the gathered crowds of the queen's new rooms. Lady Penelope Rich beckoned Arbella forward, and she was welcomed into the queen's private drawing room. Many of the women who were of a lower rank to Arbella curtseyed as she passed, so she seemed to cause a rippling wave through the brilliantly coloured dresses of the women.

The queen, who was having an animated conversation with Jean Drummond and Lucy, Countess Bedford, reached out a hand in greeting, pulling Arbella into the heart of the conversation. Penelope joined the group on Arbella's other side.

"We have been appraising the work of Master Shakespeare with that of Mr Benjamin Jonson," said Anna. "However, I suggested that Emilia Lanier and her sonnets are as worthy as any poetry by either man. Do you agree, Arbel?"

"I believe Mr Shakespeare has a far broader range when he writes," Arbella said with a considered smile, "while Mr Jonson has a tendency to fall back on caricature, but I find Emilia's words exquisite…"

"My views exactly," interrupted Anna in delight. "I wrote to her, and she replied saying she is working on a poem entitled 'Salve Deus Rex Judæorum' or 'Hail, God, King of the Jews', and in one poem within the piece she argues that Eve is wrongly blamed for the Original Sin, and some blame should be put on Adam."

There were scandalised gasps from a few of the assembled women, but Arbella nodded at the queen's words.

"She has also sent me a copy of this poem in its draft form," said Arbella, "and I believe her argument is that Adam must share the guilt because he is depicted as being stronger than Eve; therefore, he should have been able to resist temptation and help Eve to overcome her confusion."

"A valid defence," said Anna.

"Have you read her dedication to the brave women who followed Christ to the cross?" asked Arbella.

"Not yet. She has only recently sent it to me, but I am most eager to study her argument. Perhaps we will soon be able to persuade her to return to London."

The doors opened and Margaret Stewart was announced.

"Excuse me, my dear," said Anna, smiling an apology, "I have business to discuss with Margaret."

Arbella curtseyed as the queen glided away, followed by her loyal ladies, while she remained with her own inner circle:

Dorothy, Penelope, Bridget, and Anne. Penelope stepped forward.

"Arbel," she whispered. "Take this, read it and destroy it." Pushing a small square of parchment into Arbella's palm, Penelope then moved closer, allowing Arbella a moment to slide the message into her sleeve.

"Please tell the queen I am tired after my current illness and shall retire to my rooms," she said to Penelope, who dropped a curtsey.

"Yes, my lady, I hope your health improves soon."

Arbella walked from the room, her movements measured so as not to draw attention, but the moment Bridget had closed the door to her bedchamber, she pulled the note from her sleeve.

"It's from Emilia," she gasped, gazing down at words that seemed to scorch the page with their message. "It says, 'Cecil knows about the letter sent to you by Henry Cobham. The words are not from the Baron. It is a trap set to ensnare you. The Baron has returned to London. All is well. Emilia'."

Arbella considered the last comment. Henry Brooke was back in England and all was well. The money must be safely with Sir Walter Raleigh in Jersey. A thrill of fear ran through her. The plot was advancing, but it seemed Robert Cecil was aware of some form of subterfuge even if, at present, he did not have all the information he required for an arrest. Despite the potential danger, Arbella could not ignore the excitement coursing through her at the thought that they were still eluding Cecil.

"Burn the note," instructed Arbella, moving to the large canopied bed and perching on the edge while she thought. "Do we still have the letter that was supposed to have been sent by Cobham?" she asked Bridget.

"Yes, my lady."

"This evening, when we attend the revels, it must be secreted about my person."

"Arbel, this is most dangerous," said Anne from where she was shredding the note into the fireplace.

"Robert Cecil will be in attendance, and I trust Emilia's words," Arbella replied. "I shall surrender this letter to him with a few tears, saying I am frightened for my life. This feels like a test of my loyalty."

"But what if it isn't?" asked Bridget. "You would be betraying Lord Cobham. He has returned. The feint letter might be all Cecil needs to arrest him."

"It is my fear that George has broken and revealed his brother's plot. This is Robert's way of testing to see whether there is any truth in George's words."

"Would George betray his brother?" gasped Anne.

"Under torture, we would probably all say whatever was needed to save ourselves any more pain."

"Do you think Robert Cecil would try to trap you in such a way?" asked Bridget. "You and he have been friends for so many years."

Arbella gave a harsh laugh. "It wouldn't be the first time Cecil has intercepted mail and rewritten it to suit his own ends. But it is our supposed long friendship that I will play upon this evening, and trust that he will not sell me to the king."

CHAPTER THREE

Above Arbella's head, the night sky exploded in a shower of brilliant green stars. A fire-breathing dragon flew towards her from its perch atop a wooden tower with a terrifying scream, rockets shot towards the twinkling stars before plummeting back to earth with crashes and shrieks, while two vast girandola — horizontal spinning wheels of fire — lit up the twilight of the summer sky. Screams of fear and excitement echoed around the gardens as the storm of the fireworks broke overhead, adding to the mystery of the revels. Arbella, seated with her most senior ladies and friends, applauded in delight as the extravagant entertainments unfolded around them.

To her relief, Arbella's health was improving each day, a situation which was being helped by the queen. Anna had taken it upon herself to send fresh figs and spiced wine each morning, hoping these would aid her "sweet Arbel" to gather her strength for the coronation.

The passing days of summer carried an endless stream of dignitaries to Hampton Court Palace in preparation for the double coronation of James and Anna. There were hunts, jousts, river parties and dances. Every evening, the players swirled around, providing entertainment, their words filling the golden air with amusement and intrigue. This evening, a rumour had reached Arbella that the newly named King's Men would be performing a play.

Taking the shawl handed to her by a concerned Bridget, Arbella selected a spiced cake to nibble while she listened idly to her friends guessing at the possible play to be presented.

"Charles suggested *A Midsummer Night's Dream*, but we are well past the summer solstice," said Penelope, accepting a drink from a page.

"Perhaps *Twelfth Night*?" suggested Dorothy, arching her eyebrows in amusement.

Arbella laughed. "A play about deception, most appropriate."

"As we are about to attend a coronation, do you think it might be one of the histories?" suggested Bridget.

Arbella grinned. "It depends on Will's mood," she said. "Things are never as they seem in Mr Shakespeare's plays, as is so often replicated in the life of the court. When he invited my late husband to a showing of *Richard II* — the story of a feeble and indecisive king who allows the country to fall into ruin — it inspired poor William to go ahead with his siege. Whichever of his repertoire we are treated to there will be a hidden message, whether it will be Will's choice or the king's. We shall soon see."

Dorothy wandered from her seat to the fire pit beside Arbella and, while warming her hands, said in a soft voice, "The king rode to meet my husband at Syon House this morning. He wished to partake of our deer parks. While they were riding, he spoke with Henry at length about his alchemy and other experiments."

"Really?" said Arbella, surprised.

Dorothy's husband was known as the Wizard Earl, but Arbella had never really thought Henry had managed to make more than foul smells and the occasional explosion.

"James claims to have an interest in witchcraft. He felt Henry's experiments would help him to understand sorcery."

"Does the king plan to arrest your husband for heresy?" asked Arbella.

Through the Ladies of Melusine, they were aware of James's fear of and fascination with the occult. In 1597, he had published a dissertation on contemporary necromancy entitled *Daemonologie*. It had followed a famous case in Scotland known as the Berwick Witch Trials.

"The king's true interest is gunpowder," replied Dorothy. "He believes it is a form of magic. Henry has been working on a new way of producing it, a method which he believes makes the process less volatile."

Arbella noted the edge of irritation in Dorothy's comment and gave her arm a reassuring squeeze. "Are things well between you and Henry?" she asked.

"Henry is as prickly as before we had our reunion; I would hate for him to lose his temper and be rude to the king. James takes offence easily, and my husband is quick to remonstrate with anyone who disagrees with his pronouncements."

"Would you like me to ask Charles to intercede?" said Penelope, referring to her lover Charles Mountjoy, the newly created earl of Devonshire. "The king has become so attached to him he can barely allow him out of his sight. Charles has the skills of a diplomat and can soothe most troubles."

Before Dorothy could respond to her sister's offer, Anne Bradshaw emerged from the shadows, her face glowing with excitement. "My lady, your graces, I've been sent to fetch you," she announced. "There is to be an entertainment and we have been requested to move to the entrance of the fountain park where we should await our surprise."

"Surprise?" asked Bridget, and Anne nodded.

"How very intriguing," replied Arbella, smoothing down her skirts as she stood.

"Come, Arbel," said Penelope, offering her arm. "Let us see what mischief is in the king's heart this evening."

Arbella allowed the conversation to ebb and flow around her as they traversed the gardens. Flaming torches positioned along the pathway beckoned them forward, drawing them towards the eerie lilt of piped music as it floated over the song of the cascading water. Despite her fears and the constant rustle of the letter hidden in the lining of her sleeve, Arbella could not help but smile with delight at the magical world that had been created in the gardens of Hampton Court. A shadow fell in front of them, causing Dorothy and Bridget to gasp in surprise.

"I am Cobweb," said the fairy, who had flowing white gossamer wings and was clad in shimmering, clinging fabric. "Follow me."

The sprite danced in front of the women, guiding them to an enchanted clearing. Silken awnings were draped above seats piled with cushions. Torches flamed, throwing wild shadows into the sky, and coloured lanterns swung in the trees.

"Welcome to Fairyland," trilled the sprite. "I must away to join my friends."

"Ladies, you are well met by twilight," called a voice, and the slim form of Edmund Shakespeare emerged from the shadows. He turned a perfect cartwheel, landing in front of Dorothy. "Countess," he exclaimed, "let me lead you to your lord."

In turn, he took each of the women and delivered them to the seat beside their husband or lover, until only Arbella remained.

"My lady," said Edmund, returning to collect her, "you will be most pleased with your choice of companion." He flipped a somersault, landing with practised ease in a bow, before taking her hand and leading her in the first steps of the pavane. As Edmund capered around her, he whispered, "Laugh at what I am about to say, then our kingmaker will not be suspicious.

George Brooke has given up his brother; you must distance yourself from Henry Cobham's plot."

Doing as he had commanded and laughing, Arbella looked at him with terrified eyes. He continued the charade, but for a moment his face set in an expression of the utmost seriousness. Then he led her forward. "My lady, may I present you to Sir Robert Cecil, the Lord of Misrule," exclaimed Edmund, his face once again a mask of mischief.

"Arbella, how wonderful," said Cecil, as she took the chair beside him.

As her eyes adjusted to the gloom of the tent, she saw she was seated to the right of Queen Anna, with Cecil on her other side. The queen's face was glassy and expressionless. It surprised Arbella when she felt Anna's cool fingers slip into her hand and squeeze, as though seeking reassurance. A moment later, Arbella understood why. On Anna's other side was her husband, but James seemed oblivious to the presence of anyone other than Philip Herbert.

James was lounging on the silken cushions, a goblet of wine held loosely in his fingers, his cheeks flushed while Philip Herbert leaned close to him, their shoulders touching. As they whispered and giggled together, Philip would occasionally feed James a slice of peach, using his fingers to wipe any juice that ran down James's chin. Queen Anna stared ahead in fury.

A discreet cough drew Arbella's attention to Robert Cecil. Arbella was unsure how to respond to him. She had seen him so rarely since the succession, but she still considered his behaviour to have been duplicitous. However, her grandmother's caution was deeply bred into her bones and, despite her own personal annoyance with the man, offending him would be foolish: he was the Lord Privy Seal, one of the most powerful men in the land, and could make her life difficult.

"You are angry with me, Arbel," he said, his voice as soft as the silken throw he passed her to drape across her legs in the cool night air.

"Do you blame me?"

"Not in the least, but you understand why I had no choice."

"Don't justify your subterfuge to me, Robert," she hissed. "You had a choice. Are you pleased with your decision?" Shooting him a contemptuous look, she was gratified to observe the despair on his pale face as the new king fed his young friend sips of wine from his goblet, his hand resting high on Philip Herbert's thigh.

"Things are somewhat different than I had imagined," Cecil managed. "The reports from my spies were, I thought, an exaggeration by the enemies who wished to keep the Scottish monarch from the English throne."

"And now?"

"He is as the rumours suggested." Cecil paused, taking his own deep gulp of wine as the king belched then laughed uproariously. "And far less refined than I had been led to believe."

Arbella narrowed her eyes and shot him a scornful look. "And all because you and your friends on the Privy Council were desperate for a king," she sneered.

Another high-pitched trill pierced the air and Arbella looked over at Philip, who was holding James's hand. Despite her own terror that the plot revolving around her had been discovered, she wondered how Anna bore the embarrassment of James behaving so lewdly in public. *But he is a king,* she thought, *and in this world men are able to behave as they choose, especially those who are powerful.*

"My lady," continued Robert Cecil, drawing Arbella's attention away from the spectacle of the king. "Let us speak of other things. It is a relief to see you returned to health."

"Thank you, Lord Cecil," she demurred. Despite his sweet words and silky tone, she viewed him as a serpent, ready to strike at any moment. Before they could continue the conversation, shadowy figures emerged onto the low stage. Torches threw a stylised garden into sharp relief and two gentlemen appeared, ready to set the scene for the coming drama. Seeing their clothes, a cold fear grasped Arbella's heart.

"Who chose the play we are to view this evening?" she whispered to Robert Cecil.

"I believe it was the king."

He knows, she thought. *This is the strangest play to choose at such a time, and it is the only one he could use to torment me.*

"What play is this, Arbel?" murmured Anna. "I am not familiar with this opening scene."

"It is *Cymbeline*, Your Majesty," replied Arbella. "It is a tragic tale of two lovers torn apart after they have exchanged tokens of jewellery: a ring and a bracelet. There are missing princes who were stolen at birth and misunderstandings between the lovers. I believe some of the action takes place in Wales —"

"Milford Haven, to be precise," interrupted James's cold voice. "The far-flung port that serves the houses in the Tudor heartland of Pembrokeshire."

Arbella stared at her cousin. His mismatched eyes glittered with malice.

"What an unusual choice," said Anna, her voice cold. "You are a constant surprise, James."

They returned their attention to the story unfolding on the stage and Arbella stared at her hands in horror, not hearing a word of the drama. The message was clear: James had discovered Ennie's hiding place. This was not simply an evening of entertainment; this was a warning. Milford Haven was only six miles from the village of St Ishmaels, where Ennie now resided in Marquess House. Arbella swallowed her panic. If the king knew of her daughter's whereabouts, had he also discovered her son's location?

Trying to calm her rising fear, Arbella began to plan which of the Ladies of Melusine would be able to provide her with the information she required. Those nearest to her son's hiding place would be the most useful, but she would avoid direct contact in case Cecil was intercepting her letters. If Henry were indeed in danger, she would move him somewhere more discreet. The letter in her sleeve rustled, and as the players stopped halfway through the play, giving the audience a break for refreshments, Arbella knew the time had come to act.

"Bravo!" called Robert Cecil, clapping along with the others as the actors melted away into the shadows. Arbella smiled widely and clapped with equal enthusiasm.

Bridget leaned forward and said, "I shall fetch you some wine, my lady; you stay in the warmth of the tent." She left on the arm of a tall, good-looking man.

"I believe Bridget is being wooed by Thomas Grey," said Robert Cecil, watching the laughing couple walk away.

"He has long admired her," agreed Arbella, "and this would be a wonderful match."

"Wouldn't you miss her if she wed? She would have to leave your service."

"I would never stand in the way of her happiness," said Arbella. "We have been friends for many years, and it would delight me to see her married, especially to someone as intelligent and attentive as Thomas."

"And what of Anne Bradshaw? Is she betrothed? She is an heiress in her own right."

"Her father is in negotiation with a suitable husband. If they can agree terms, it's possible Anne will be leaving my service next year."

"Your women are loyal, Arbel."

His words held a strange timbre and to her overwrought and nervous ear, they sounded like a threat. Concentrating on keeping her voice light, she replied, "They are my friends first, and friends are loyal."

"You would stand by them, no matter what?"

Unsure where Cecil was leading her, Arbella took refuge in feigned ignorance. "Robert, my ladies and I have been together for many years; we will always support one another."

Another long pause grew between them, broken by a servant sweeping upon them with offers of small cakes and spiced wine, which they both accepted.

"What of Lady Frances Brooke?" Cecil asked when they were alone again. His words were like deep dark pools of despair in the bright lights of the stage.

"We have been friends since her first marriage to Henry FitzGerald."

"And her second husband, Baron Cobham. Are you his friend?"

"No," snapped Arbella, fear making her respond with a speed she knew had betrayed her.

"Sir George and Lady Brooke? Do you count them as friends?"

Arbella turned to look at Cecil. His face was in shadow. "Robert, why do you ask these questions?" she said, attempting a tone of light-hearted dismissiveness but, even to her own ears, sounding terrified.

"George Brooke has been arraigned for treason," he said, his voice like velvet in the raucous atmosphere. "He has admitted to trying to apprehend the king, and he told me there was another plot led by his brother, Baron Cobham. He claims his brother wishes to question my decision to place James Stuart on the throne. George suggests there is another Stuart whom his brother would prefer to see wearing the crown of England."

Arbella did not reply — she was frozen to her chair, her mind blank with fear.

"My men are arresting Baron Cobham as we speak. His wife, Lady Frances, has had the care of the Princess Elizabeth removed and the young royal is now with Lord and Lady Harington. Lady Raleigh has taken refuge with her brother, Arthur, because we have arrested Sir Walter, who is a conspirator of Baron Cobham. Neither will be leaving the Tower tonight, or perhaps ever again." Cecil placed his hand on her wrist, and Arbella flinched. "We have been friends for many years, Arbel," he said, and now his voice was urgent. "This plot has been suspected by the Privy Council for many weeks. My dear, do you know anything about it which could be of use to me?"

Arbella could hear the blood thundering in her ears. Despite Cecil's soft words, she knew the wrong word could cause this conversation to end in disaster. She might still be leaving the party with a royal guard of her own. Thinking of all she had been taught by her grandmother and all she had witnessed at the skirts of those two formidable queens, Elizabeth Tudor and Mary, Queen of Scots, she composed herself. The silence lengthened, then with a tentative touch to his hand, Arbella whispered, "Robert, are we friends?"

"Why, yes, Arbel, of course," he reassured her.

Taking a deep breath, she pitched her voice to imitate a level of terror that would have impressed the actors had they heard her. "I am in fear for my life," she gulped.

"What has happened?"

"A letter arrived while I was ill, purporting to be from Baron Cobham, but I know his hand and it is not a good likeness."

"And the contents?"

"Telling me to write to Spain for help, to offer terms to the Catholics as though I were Queen. To make promises about the Protestant Netherlands…" She allowed her voice to ebb away, as though she could not bear to speak the words aloud for fear of incriminating herself. With trembling fingers, she slid the letter from the lining of her sleeve and passed it to Robert Cecil.

"And you do not recognise the handwriting?" he asked, unfolding the tattered piece of parchment.

"No, my lord."

"You did the right thing, telling me of this," said Cecil, patting her hand in a patronising manner.

She nodded, biting her lip in anxiety. "What do you mean?" she whispered.

"It was to ensure you were not involved in the planning of the plot," he replied. "If you had not passed the letter on to me, I would have been arresting you this evening, but your wonderful innocence has protected you once again. Don't fret, Arbel, I will protect you."

Arbella gazed at Robert Cecil. "You sent the letter?" she asked.

He shrugged. "The next few days will reveal the truth," he said, sliding the crumpled piece of parchment into the lining of his sleeve. "If you have any other correspondence that might incriminate you or those you care about, destroy it when you return to your rooms this evening. Leave nothing out. I am not the only person investigating this plot, and there are many who continue to view you as a threat to the throne and would have you removed permanently. If there is even the smallest trace of evidence against you, even I may not be able to save you from befalling the same fate as your cousin, Jane Grey."

There was a brief pressure on her arm, then Robert Cecil turned his attention back to the play, leaving Arbella alone with her fear.

CHAPTER FOUR

"Baron Grey of Wilton has fled to the Netherlands," said Bridget three days later, as she and Arbella settled themselves on a barge. "His man sent word to me this morning."

"Why has he done this?" asked Arbella in surprise.

"Since the arrest of Henry Brooke, he fears he will be next," Bridget said. "We spoke of this at the palace while we watched *Cymbeline*. He departed for his London house that evening and from there by boat under cover of darkness."

Arbella twirled a stray curl around her finger as she considered Bridget's words. Was Thomas Grey another who had been sent a message by Edmund Shakespeare to distance himself from the plot? "But surely there is no evidence against Baron Grey," said Arbella.

"Lady Kirton told me Robert Cecil has also had the poet Anthony Copley arrested," added Anne Bradshaw in a low voice. "It seems he has produced a list of all the people involved in George's plot, including William Watson, William Clarke, Sir Griffin Markham and Baron Grey."

"We must proceed with great caution," Arbella murmured. "These are dark and dangerous days."

The previous evening, she had followed Robert Cecil's advice and burned all her correspondence, even her letters from the Ladies of Melusine. Unbeknown to her ladies-in-waiting, Arbella was keeping a record of events in a collection of small notebooks that she secreted at the bottom of her jewel chest. No one knew of her journals and this was the way things would stay, unless they were required to save her life. In them she had detailed everything concerning the plot. If ever she felt these annuls were dangerous, she would dispose of them in a heartbeat.

"Do you think the men will remain loyal to each other?" asked Anne from beside Bridget.

"We can only hope there will be honour among them," said Arbella, "but Walter Raleigh, like George Brooke, has a fiery temper. Henry Brooke has a stout sense of justice and will be happy to bear the responsibility for his own planning but will not allow others to use him as a scapegoat."

"You have an idea someone will lower themselves to this device," said Bridget, a shrewd expression on her face as she watched Arbella.

"Walter Raleigh will pass the blame to anyone if it paints him in a better light," replied Arbella. "He has behaved in such a manner throughout his days at court, and I see no reason why he will change now. His wife, Bess, is using her family connections to try and win Raleigh a pardon but, at present, she is unsuccessful. It has reached my attention that there are members of the Privy Council who are trying to suggest she, Lizzie and Frances are the true instigators of this scheme, so I have warned them to take care."

Bridget looked horrified. "Why would the Privy Council think that?" she asked.

"I suspect Robert Cecil's hand in it. He wants to try and minimise the impact of this plot."

"Why?"

"His choice of monarch is not proving popular — James is upsetting so many of the senior nobles of this country, and Cecil fears his machinations could still backfire on him. The last thing he wants is for the disaffected members of the aristocracy to realise that there is an alternative to the new monarch. If he suggests the plot he has uncovered is a scheme created by shrewish wives, it will be taken less seriously than if it had been proposed by senior members of the old Elizabethan court. Cecil will paint the wives as unnatural harpies, hellbent on the destruction of each other and full of devious intent in destroying the friendships their husbands have forged for many years."

Arbella stopped as with an unexpected lurch and much shouting, the lavish barge was pushed away from the pier at Hampton Court Palace, floating out into the centre of the mighty River Thames as they headed to the Palace of Whitehall and the preparations for the coronation of King James and Queen Anna.

"Isn't it all too late now?" asked Anne. "In a week's time, James will have been crowned. There is nothing anyone can do to halt it."

Arbella shrugged and leaned back against her cushions, closing her eyes to enjoy the sunshine and the lulling plash of the oars in the water. Anne was correct — the coronation marked the end of the period of unease. James would be the anointed king, the representation of God on Earth and, once again, her status would be in a state of flux. A member of the household, a woman of royal blood, but with no power. It was infuriating.

"Have you heard the other news?" asked Bridget.

"What news?" asked Arbella.

"The queen has insisted Sir Robert Spencer be raised to the peerage; he will be Baron Spencer of Wormleighton."

Arbella smiled. "Anna is not the passive wife I was expecting," she said. "In her, James really does have an equal. When will the promotion take place?"

"This evening," replied Bridget.

"Then on 23 July we have the debacle of the honours being presented — those that can be bought," snorted Anne.

"Don't fret, ladies," Arbella said. "The more James irritates his contemporaries, the more power our cause gains. James is losing his popularity and he hasn't even been crowned yet."

"There will also be the ceremony to create new Knights of the Bath," said Anne.

"A ceremony that can only take place on the night preceding a coronation," sighed Arbella. "It makes me wonder what James is up to with his choice of dignitaries to be honoured."

"What do you mean?"

"One of those selected for this rarefied position is Oliver Cromwell of Hinchingbrooke House. As soon as we arrive at the palace, I must write to his wife and warn her that my son is no longer safe in their household. Annie will understand; she is a shrewd woman and her Dutch blood makes her the most practical woman I have ever met. She is loyal to our cause and will help us secure a safer home for Henry. James is making it clear he knows where my children are hiding and that he can gain access to them any time he chooses. I would hate to leave the king with the idea he is one step ahead of me."

A week later, Arbella walked two paces behind Queen Anna in Westminster Abbey, their heads covered by the golden canopy of state. Her royal blood decreed she should accompany the queen at the head of the procession of the countesses, but each step they took increased the fury rising in Arbella.

All around, the dignitaries who were brave enough to risk the plague-ridden streets of London watched the spectacle. To one side, Arbella saw Charles de Ligne, Count of Aremberg, the Catholic ambassador from Spain, the man to whom Henry Brooke had travelled in order to raise funds for the Main Plot.

If the rumours she had heard were true, Aremberg was at the coronation to boost his denial of any involvement. His role, according to her Ladies of Melusine, was to be that of diplomat as he tried to broker a deal to halt the endless Anglo-Spanish wars.

Yet, thought Arbella, as the count caught her eye, *a mere month ago he had been discussing providing an Armada in order to help place me on the throne. These men are despicable in their cowardice and their lack of loyalty. My women would have worked together to protect each other, rather than selling their friends and relatives out to Robert Cecil and his bullies.*

Taking her seat, Arbella watched the proceedings. As James was anointed with the sacred oil, she tore her gaze away. "It should have been William," she hissed to Dorothy Percy, who was seated beside her.

"Or you," her friend responded. "But we have no choice, Arbel, we must see it through."

Arbella felt her fingernails biting into her palms as she clenched her fists, but she nodded. Earlier that day, as they had processed through the streets of London, Penelope Rich had informed Arbella that the hoped for Coronation Day pardons had not been forthcoming to any of the men involved in what were becoming known as the Bye and Main Plots.

"We are concerned that James means to make an example of the plotters in order to show he will not forgive threats to his throne," she had whispered.

Half an hour later, this seemed to be confirmed by a new addition to the ceremony.

"I present the king to his people," announced the Archbishop, "calling on any who denied James the Sixth of Scotland and First of England to be legitimate King of England to say so now, otherwise he would be held a traitor!"

Silence followed this announcement, although Arbella felt the delicate touch of Dorothy's hand on her arm, as though holding her in position. No one spoke into the hallowed silence of the Abbey, but Arbella understood the significance of this addition even if others were less well informed. Word had come to her that during the questioning of the two priests who had been George Brooke's accomplices, they had claimed their plot could not be viewed as treason because James was not yet an anointed monarch. Robert Cecil had included this charade to refute their argument and enable himself to lay a guilty charge upon them.

Five hours later, Arbella finally left the Abbey for a reception at Whitehall Palace. As she was ushered into her awaiting barge, she felt a hand on her elbow.

"My lady, may I travel with you to the palace?" came the soft tones of Charles, Count of Aremberg.

Although the count had helped to raise the money for the plots spun around Arbella by Cobham and Raleigh, his collusion had not been detected and he was one of the few Catholic envoys who had accepted an invitation to the coronation. Looking into his handsome face, Arbella's instinct was to refuse; then she saw the fierce expression in his eyes and, wondering what news he wished to impart, she gave a gracious nod of compliance.

"The pleasure would be mine," she said, and allowed the count to hand her down into the beautifully appointed barge.

Bridget and Anne moved away to a discreet distance as Arbella and the count took their positions on the embroidered cushions in the covered area at the centre of the golden boat. The grey day had given way to teeming rain and unseasonable cold for July; the heat of the brazier was welcome.

"It must have been difficult for you to endure the coronation, my dear," said the count in his impeccable English once they were in the main flow of the river.

"More than I could explain," she replied. "However, these things happen, and I accept my cousin and his wife as my superiors."

Charles gave her a long, shrewd look. "No, you don't," he replied. "I was watching you, and you believe the crown should be on your beautiful head."

"To even think it is treason."

"As is plotting to overthrow the king," he replied. "Have you had word from Cobham or Raleigh?"

"They are in the Tower being questioned," she muttered, nervous about admitting to even knowing the men, despite the fact they were in the middle of the choppy waters of the Thames and could not be overheard. "The king has refused to grant them clemency. Their letters are being read before they are sent, so I have had no news from either man."

Her words were true, and she felt there was no need for the count to be told she had other ways of receiving information about the prisoners in the Tower of London. The Ladies of Melusine continued to operate and it was with great relief she had been told that all the men who had plotted to make her queen were being treated with consideration. There were no reports of torture. *Not yet, anyway*, she thought with a shudder.

"The rumours I have heard are that these men are to be made examples of, in order to quell any other potential challenges to the throne."

"Perhaps," said Arbella, her tone dismissive. "Robert Cecil is probably pleased to have his rivals out of the way while he tries to salvage his reputation and position at court."

Aremberg laughed. "Things are slipping from his control," he said. "Is the rumour true that the king has taken a liking to Theobalds and is trying to persuade Cecil to gift him his beloved family home?"

Arbella raised her eyebrows in amusement. "The Lord Privy Seal is learning too late that the role of the kingmaker does not necessarily lead to a long and prosperous career. The promises he made to the English nobles have not come to fruition. Titles, lands, and prestigious positions at court have gone to the Scottish lords and there is much unrest. Many of the old guard blame Cecil for this disaster."

Aremberg pulled his pipe from the leather pouch on his belt and spent a few moments filling it with tobacco, before lighting it from a taper thrust into the brazier. Arbella watched but said nothing. The rumour that had reached her household had suggested that Aremberg had attended the coronation in order to try and smooth over the troubles caused by arrests connected to the Bye Plot and the Main Plot and to distance himself from the plotters. It seemed that while this was the impression he was busy establishing with the king, he had another agenda.

"Have you heard word from Robert Catesby?"

The swift turn of Arbella's head was, she realised, an indication of her shock at hearing this name. "No," she said in surprise. "Is there any reason why you ask such a question?"

"What are your views on the man?" he asked, ignoring Arbella's response.

"He brings trouble in his wake, and since William's death we have distanced ourselves."

Again, there was a prolonged silence as Aremberg sucked on his pipe, filling the air with the acrid smell of tobacco. "Catesby continues to burn for revenge for his friend," he whispered, leaning closer to Arbella. "He hopes the fact that James has a Catholic wife will persuade the king to our Church. Catesby aims to finish the work your husband began, to restore the Catholic faith in England —"

"Enough," snarled Arbella. "The words you speak are treason, sir, and I will have no part of this pernicious plot." Her eyes flashed with anger, and the fury on her face caused him to recoil.

"But, my lady, the rumour in the Spanish court is that this, too, is your belief."

"Your rumours are wrong. I am a Protestant."

"And your son?" he asked, his face sly.

"He follows my faith."

"How would his father feel about this? William was a devout Catholic; he would be shocked to hear you have raised his heir to be a Protestant."

"William's faith cost him the crown and his life," said Arbella, her voice cold. "His temper would have been forgiven in time, but his religious beliefs were intolerable. His arrogance and stubbornness were his undoing. You will not drag me or my children down with the same vicious rumours."

Aremberg considered her for a moment, then gave a boyish grin that made him appear years younger. "You're remarkable," he said.

Arbella stared at him in confusion at this unexpected change in his demeanour. "What's going on?" she demanded.

"Arbel, you are an intelligent woman, yet even you have missed the subterfuge being wrapped around you by Robert Cecil."

"Explain, Aremberg, I am in no mood for games." Even to her own ears, her voice carried the imperious tone of Queen

Elizabeth and she noticed Aremberg sat up straighter, the levity leaving his eyes.

"You claim Robert Catesby is a troublemaker, and yes, this cannot be denied, but he is true to his cause —"

"To return Catholicism to this realm," she interrupted.

"No, to see the true monarch on the throne."

The meaningful look in his eyes took Arbella by surprise.

"Aremberg, we are travelling to celebrate the coronation of my cousin, James, and his wife, Anna," she hissed. "The men who tried to place me on the throne are incarcerated and I narrowly escaped arrest myself."

"Why do you think you escaped?" asked Aremberg, his tone urgent.

"Because I wasn't involved." Her response was haughty.

"No, it was because Robert Cecil wanted you to be free," he replied. "He knew you were involved, yet he retained the evidence and didn't use it against you."

Arbella gasped in horror.

"In Cecil's eyes, the game is still on," he continued. "At present, he is keeping all the players active. He may yet need to put you on the throne himself if James becomes even more degenerate, but he is a contrary man and he may also decide to cut his losses and dispose of all troublesome heirs. Haven't you noticed, Arbel, all the other claimants for James's throne have vanished into the mist? You are the only challenger still standing. This is because Cecil has decreed it so."

"Are you saying I'm in danger if I stay at court?" she asked.

"I'm suggesting that of the two Roberts currently circling you, only one has your best interests at heart."

"Catesby?" she whispered.

He nodded. "He is sworn to protect you, while Cecil may well yet destroy you. The trial date for Cobham, Brookes,

Raleigh, Grey and the priests has been set for 17 November in Winchester. You will attend in the gallery. Don't be shocked by anything that happens and, remember, there are many in this realm who are loyal to you and your heirs."

The Whitehall Stairs were approaching, and Arbella indicated for Bridget and Anne to prepare her to disembark. Aremberg's words had taken her by surprise. She considered him for a few moments, then said in a voice as calm as his own, "And why should I trust you?"

"I have this," he replied, and by sleight of hand he produced a gold doubloon from behind her ear. "Raleigh gave it to me and said I was to tell you the lions can't hurt you while he is around."

Arbella stared at the golden coin.

"Do not fear, my dear Arbel," said Aremberg as he stood, preparing to help her from the boat. "Keep the faith throughout the trial and once we have seen Cecil's next move, we will play ours. Catesby will be in touch. The game is not over yet."

They were on the quayside and a crowd of courtiers swirled around them. Aremberg gave a swift bow and vanished into the wall of red created by the elaborate coronation robes. All Arbella could see was more blood on her hands.

PART SEVEN: MARQUESS HOUSE, 2019

CHAPTER ONE

Perdita understood at last. "William Fitzalan was Catholic!" she exclaimed. "He was cut out of the succession by the Ladies of Melusine because of his faith."

Running a hand through her hair, she walked to her wallchart and stared at the endless notes she had added over the months of her research. Could Arbella's husband's rebellion really have been about religion? His friends, particularly Robert Catesby, were all known Catholics, many of whom were later involved in the infamous Gunpowder Plot of 1605, so it was possible.

Had William, a devout Catholic, tried to depose the Protestant monarch following the instructions of the 1570 Papal Bull? Perdita checked her printouts for clarification: the bull was issued on 25 February 1570 by Pius V, saying it was the duty of all Catholics to remove the heretic Protestant queen, Elizabeth Tudor. It had been suspended in 1580 by Gregory XIII and reinstated in 1588 by Sixtus V after the death of Mary, Queen of Scots.

Or, thought Perdita as she gazed at the image of Lettice Knollys, had William acted because he had discovered the truth about his heritage and knew he was the rightful king of England? Any hot-blooded Tudor male would have considered it his right to depose a woman who was not even the true queen.

Perdita returned to her desk where the three remarkable pieces of jewellery they had discovered on this quest sat in their new leather and velvet box. While she had been reading Arbella's diaries, she had kept the two ruby rings and the silver locket in front of her like talismans, tangible links to the unfolding story. She stared at the gems as she considered the newest twist before a knock on the door interrupted her train of thought.

"Perdita, it's Alistair. Is everything all right?"

Hurrying to let him in, she smiled as he entered her office. "I've taken to locking it so no one can stray in by mistake," she said, securing the latch before returning to her desk.

Alistair lowered himself into the chair opposite it. "Very wise, my dear, especially with the amount of information you have on display."

"I considered taking the wallchart down," she admitted, following Alistair's gaze, "but it's extremely useful and helps me to spot patterns. Drawing the blinds and locking the door seemed a small sacrifice."

"How are your investigations going?"

"Well, I think." Perdita paused, deciding how much to reveal. "Sense is slowing prevailing over chaos, but there are gaps and, until I'm more certain, I don't want to present my theories."

"Perhaps this will help," said Alistair, handing Perdita a slim metal box.

"What's this?" she asked.

"It arrived this morning from our archive in Castle Jerusalem. It's the documents my great-great grandfather, Douglas Mackensie, bought concerning The Scribe and the original force created to protect the secret, the King's Men, or the King's Guard, as he also refers to them. They were an elite squad of trained soldiers, not to be confused with the theatrical troupe who performed Shakespeare's plays at the court of King James I," he said with a smile. "I thought it would be safer to bring them to you myself."

Perdita leaned forward in excitement. "Thank you, Alistair," she said, taking the key he offered and opening the box.

Inside were two pieces of folded parchment and a more modern envelope containing several sheets of closely typed prose and handwritten notes. Reaching into her desk drawer, she pulled out a bundle of protective cotton gloves, offering a pair to Alistair. After putting on her own, she cleared a space and rolled out the lint-free suede covering she used when examining the jewellery, then with great care, placed the documents on her desk. Unfolding the first piece, she grinned in delight. It was an official warrant, dated 1665 with a royal seal attached.

"This is the document Edward, who was Douglas's son, discovered. If you remember, it was Douglas who first unearthed the confessions," explained Alistair, pointing to the other piece of parchment. "It's an execution warrant and, rather like the Bill of Attainder created for the supposed death of Catherine Howard and Jane Boleyn, it was read to Parliament and passed, giving those accused no chance of a trial. The men listed were rounded up and beheaded on 21 June 1665, but no reason for their deaths is given in any records. Edward believed these were the original King's Men, the elite guard who was created to watch over The Scribe."

"How do you know this?" she asked.

"Edward has written his theories and conclusions — they're in the envelope. The other document is the most interesting though. It's the confessions of two of the former members of the King's Guard."

"Have you read it?"

"No, only Edward's notes. The writing is atrocious, and some of it's in Latin. However, you'll probably thoroughly enjoy unravelling it," he smiled at her, then continued, "You know, Douglas, my great-great grandfather, was actually in love with your great-great-great aunt, Seraphina."

"Seraphina?"

"She was Lettice Lakeby's twin sister," Alistair explained. "They were engaged to be married but, very sadly, Seraphina died. She had never been strong, and she contracted TB, dying unexpectedly a month before the wedding."

"Oh Alistair, how sad," Perdita said.

"Devastating for all involved from what I've been told," he said. "Lettice and William remained close friends with Douglas, even when he married my great-great grandmother, Isla Stowarth, two years later."

Perdita hesitated — it seemed rude to ask if the marriage was successful.

"It was a happy union," continued Alistair. "But your family and ours remained connected. After discovering the subterfuge in the Secret Service, Douglas turned to his friends, Lettice and William, for help."

"Why?"

"Back then, Douglas was not a wealthy man, so your great-great-great grandparents gave him the money to buy Castle Jerusalem and set himself up in business. As far as Lettice and William were concerned, the money was a gift, but Douglas was determined to repay every penny. In the meantime, as a way to repay their kindness and continuing financial assistance, he insisted upon acting as their solicitor, which was his original profession, and estate manager."

"He became their Lord Chamberlain."

"Yes. I believe it was Isla who coined the phrase as a joke, but it stuck," Alistair said. "Douglas thought it was funny. It was my grandfather, Robert, who had the astonishing business acumen that created the family wealth. He insisted on repaying all the money, plus interest, to your great-grandmother, Eleanor, but the habit of Jerusalem working with Marquess

House had stuck and by then, the two companies were intertwined, like a vast family, and the roles that were established by Douglas have continued."

"The tapestry showed Lettice was a twin, but I had no idea Seraphina died young," Perdita said. "Oh Alistair, think how different things would have been. We would have been related."

Alistair raised an eyebrow and gave Perdita a knowing look before gathering himself to leave. Perdita laughed.

"Two more things before you lose yourself in the documents," he said. "There has been a slight change of plan in the trap we have set."

"Why?"

"To protect my son," he replied. "I don't want Kit knowing the details. Asha has been moved, in order to prove categorically that he has no knowledge of events, and the trail we plan to leak has been altered. The only people who know the correct information are myself, Susan and now, you and Piper." He handed her a sealed envelope. "Please don't think I doubt Kit," he continued. "I trust him implicitly. This is to protect him in case any other organisations make counter-accusations against him."

"MI1 Elite?"

"Yes, or even Randolph Connors."

Perdita felt sick at the thought but nodded her understanding, even if she did not entirely agree with Alistair's decision.

"And the final thing. Olaf emailed us both this morning with a request to try and raise the mermaid figurehead from the boat."

Perdita turned to her screen and saw it in her inbox. Opening it, she clicked on the footage attached to the message.

"Do you see the movement around the base?" Alistair asked. Perdita could see two of the diving team examining the ornate piece of sculpture. "According to Olaf, it's extremely unstable — one storm could sheer it off."

"Is it possible to salvage it?"

"He says they'd need some quite expensive equipment, but the lead diver has a contact who could supply it."

The dig was in its final stages and, although there had been interesting finds on both the land and sea sites, there was nothing that had added to Perdita's research. The mystery as to why the ship seemed to have been deliberately sunk remained unsolved, and the new finds discovered on board shed no clues. Salvaging the figurehead would at least make the dig teams feel as though the summer had given them one extraordinary find.

"I'm up for it," Perdita said, "but Jerusalem is half-funding the dig too, so it isn't only my decision. How do you and Stuart feel about it?"

"Happy to go ahead. In fact, Stuart has already checked the credentials of the specialist crew and they seem exemplary. We weren't sure if they'd be available, but apparently they recently had a lucrative contract cancelled when a company went into liquidation, so they're trying to fill the gap."

"Serendipity," said Perdita.

"Indeed. I'll pop in and see Olaf on my way back to my office and tell him the good news."

Clicking the lock behind him, Perdita returned to her desk and once more immersed herself in the past, wondering if these documents could help her prove the theory that was forming in her mind. When the phone on her desk rang, she was tempted to ignore it but saw it was Piper calling from her studio.

"Hey," Perdita said, flicking the phone on to loudspeaker.

"You busy?" came her sister's tense voice.

"Nothing that can't wait. What's up?"

"The portrait of Penelope Fitzalan. I've got the results back from Viv. You have to see this, Perds, it's extraordinary."

"On my way."

"Bring Kit," were Piper's final words before she hung up.

"What's happened?" asked Perdita as she and Kit crashed through the doors of Piper's studio ten minutes later.

Callum was already seated on one of the high stools at the vast table in the centre of the room. The portrait of Penelope Fitzalan lay in front of him, but he and Piper were poring over images on the light box. Perdita and Kit exchanged a glance.

"Cal checks my studio for bugs every morning," said Piper, her cheeks tinged with pink as she caught the look between them.

"Does he now?" murmured Kit. "Is it only the room he checks?"

"Not now, Kit," said Perdita, aware of her sister's short fuse, although there was laughter in her eyes as Kit squeezed her hand.

Piper glared at them, then turned away. Perdita ushered Kit onto another high stool and gave Piper her full attention. She could see from the strained lines around Piper's mouth that whatever had been revealed had shaken her.

"As you know," Piper began, "I contacted Vivienne Dorothy, who I used to work with at the Tate Modern. She's a spectral imaging expert and uses a form of photography that captures images invisible to the human eye. Do you remember when we first had the painting X-rayed that there was a circle around the image of Penelope?"

"Yes," said Perdita. "We wondered if it had been put there as a cutting guide for a round frame."

"It wasn't," said Piper. She flipped the images she and Cal had been studying onto the screen on the wall. "The spectral imaging revealed this inside the circle."

Perdita felt a well of excitement surge through her as the shadowy hidden image appeared on the screen. "It's the oriel window in the Great Hall," she said.

"Exactly," replied Piper.

"Which proves Penelope lived here," said Perdita. "From what I've discovered, this was her home for most of her life."

"But why was it painted over?" Kit asked.

"The more I examine this portrait, the more bizarre it becomes," explained Piper. "I think the oriel window was the original backdrop for Penelope, but some years later the background around the image was altered to the one we can see now."

"Was that usual?" asked Callum.

"It's not something I've come across before," admitted Piper. "There are endless records of canvases being reused so you have a ghost image under the painting, but to obliterate the background and leave the main central image is unusual."

"Who would do something like that though?" asked Kit.

"This is the real oddity," said Piper. "I've been examining this new background and it still bears all the signs of being completed by John de Critz, the original artist. He painted out the old backdrop and put in this one, but there is only one image of Penelope; there isn't any over-painting. Her likeness remained the same throughout."

Perdita was staring at the shimmering image on the screen. "Would it have been a fashion thing?" she asked. "The court of James I was known for its glamour. Could it be something as simple as a change of taste?"

"We can't dismiss changing fashions," agreed Piper, "but I'm not sure we'll ever know for certain."

"What about the three pieces of jewellery in the painting?" asked Perdita. "Did they look as though they had been altered?"

Piper flashed a series of images onto the screen, each one dedicated to the three pieces of jewellery. "No, Perds. Like the image of Penelope, there were no changes made to the jewels."

Perdita stared at the image, her mind working fast, presenting theory after theory as she found her way through the twisted mass of information she had compiled.

"What is it, Perds? What have you discovered?"

Perdita looked up, realising they were all staring at her in concern. "I'm not sure," she admitted, "but this, linked with the information Alistair gave me this morning — the confessions from The Scribe — I have a theory but it's…" She checked herself. "I need to confirm a few things. Thank you for this, Pipes — it might be the missing piece of the puzzle I need."

With her heart pounding, Perdita hurried from the studio, leaving the others staring after her in bemusement. Kit caught up with her when she reached her office.

"Perds, what's going on?" he asked. "You've made a connection?"

"Perhaps," she admitted.

"Come on, Perds, you can tell me anything, no matter how strange it might seem."

"It isn't the strangeness," she said. "It's the vastness. For the past few months, I've been following a trail, but with the confession about The Scribe and the hidden image on the painting, I think this is even more enormous than we first believed…"

Kit stared at her in amazement. "Have you worked it all out?"

"Maybe, but if I'm right, Catherine was only part of this secret. I think it goes back further than her — all the way back to the Princes in the Tower, Henry VII and his defeat of Richard III at the battle of Bosworth."

"Should we tell Dad?" Kit asked.

"Yes, but there's something I have to check first. Will you help me?"

"Of course. What are we looking for?"

"The birth date of Arbella's son."

"Why?"

"Because if I'm right, he's been hiding in plain sight all along."

CHAPTER TWO

Perdita stared around at the faces of the people she loved best in the world. She and Kit had heaved the long table that normally stood against the wall into the centre of the room and put chairs around it. Callum had once again swept the room for listening devices, including a thorough check of all the electrical equipment. Despite this precaution, all devices were switched off to ensure there was no way for the information to be heard beyond the walls of Perdita's office, while Alistair had reinstated his beloved overhead projector.

The trip to the Marquess House library with Kit had confirmed Perdita's theory, and having sat up late into the night discussing it with him, it seemed they were in incredible danger. Now Alistair, Susan, Piper, Kit and Callum were waiting for her to begin.

"This is becoming almost routine, isn't it?" she said. "Me explaining the 'accepted version' of history before we destroy it entirely."

"Maybe this will be last time, Perds," said Piper.

"Arbella Stuart," began Perdita, flipping up an image, trying to push aside her nerves. "The lost queen of England, the woman who should have succeeded Elizabeth. Until about 30 years ago, Arbella had been largely forgotten by historians, her claim to the throne diminished in the face of her supposed 'madness', which was viewed as a symptom of her illness, porphyria — a condition that has also been attributed to other members of her lineage: Margaret Tudor, Mary Stuart and George III. However, the diaries we found in the grotto have given a quite different perspective.

"At first, I was bemused as to why we kept discovering all these documents in the house — the diaries, the account books, the Catherine Howard codex — but the more information I've uncovered, the less strange it seems. There is no coincidence about them being here; they were deliberately grouped together because these books were compiled for a reason."

"Which is what?" said Alistair.

"To lead us to the truth."

There was silence.

"The only piece of the puzzle that doesn't fit are the letters from the Ladies of Melusine," said Perdita. "I can't explain how they were placed in the archive of Lady Pamela Johnson, along with the Book of Hours that once belonged to Lady Kathryn Knollys because, if my theory is correct, they should have been stored here. Despite the fact Lady Pamela claims to be descended from the Baynton family, suggesting this is the reason she was custodian."

Perdita's eyes locked with Alistair's, but his expression remained unreadable. After a moment, Perdita returned to her explanation.

"Just before James ascended the throne in 1603, there was a flurry of rumours about other potential claimants trying to steal the throne. These all petered out when Robert Cecil declared James as king and the new monarch rode into London to huge accolades."

"Except he didn't," said Piper. "There were two plots in the wake of his immediate succession, followed two years later by the far more famous Gunpowder Plot."

"Correct," replied Perdita. "One plot was an attempt to kidnap James in order to persuade him to be lenient with Catholics, and the other was to remove James from the throne and replace him with Arbella Stuart. They were known as the Bye Plot and the Main Plot. They've been largely glossed over in histories of the period, which makes things even more peculiar, as they had a number of far-reaching consequences.

"It was because of the Main Plot that Sir Walter Raleigh lost his liberty. He was arrested for treason along with Henry Brooke, who was the husband of Lady Frances Howard, the daughter of Kate Howard, one of our Ladies of Melusine. Due to their involvement in The Main Plot, Raleigh and Cobham would both spend the rest of their lives imprisoned. In 1617, Raleigh was briefly pardoned by the king in order to lead a trip to Venezuela in search of El Dorado, but he was eventually beheaded in Westminster on 29 October 1619."

"What happened to Cobham?" asked Alistair.

"He was released from the Tower in 1618 but died shortly afterwards," replied Perdita. "One of the families at the heart of all three plots were the Throckmortons. Bess Throckmorton was married to Sir Walter Raleigh, and her cousins, Robert Catesby and Francis Tresham, were the main protagonists in the Gunpowder Plot. Even more unexpected, the maiden name of Robert Catesby's wife was Catherine Leigh."

There was a surprised silence.

"Leigh?" questioned Piper. "Like Lady Isabel Leigh, Catherine Howard's half-sister?"

"Yes," said Perdita.

"Were they related?" asked Susan.

Perdita pulled a disgruntled face. "I'm not sure. Despite my best efforts I couldn't find a direct link, but that's not to say there isn't one, because this selection of families is particularly convoluted. These families were like a vine, criss-crossing over one another, marrying within the branches, twisting and turning their endless plots and, at their heart, was Arbella Stuart."

"Could you clarify something for me, please, Perdita?" asked Susan. "Were the Bye and Main Plot linked to the Gunpowder Plot?"

"Not directly, but the men who were later responsible for the Gunpowder Plot were involved with both of the other plots as well. We can also link a number of the Gunpowder Plotters to the coup supposedly staged by Robert Devereux in 1601, which I now believe was a plot to overthrow the throne by William Fitzalan." She turned to Alistair. "It also explains away your comment about Lettice seemingly signing the warrant to execute her own son. Arbella's diaries tell us that the real reason William was discounted from the succession was because of his faith. He was a devout Catholic."

"Of course," exclaimed Alistair. "Elizabeth left instructions for Lettice to stand aside after six months in order to give Ralph Fitzalan the crown, but if Ralph was dead, then William was the heir."

"If he was Catholic, as well as displaying the unstable temperament of his grandfather, Henry VIII, it's possible Lettice and the other Ladies of Melusine were wary of giving him ultimate power," Perdita continued. "However, William's mother, Mary Seymour, told him the truth about his lineage before her death in March 1598. When Arbella gave birth to a son in 1599, William became obsessed with claiming his birthright."

"And Arbella?" persisted Susan. "Was this the real reason she was incarcerated in the Tower?"

"I don't think so, but she was placed under house arrest with Bess of Hardwick. Arbella's biographies tell us she wasn't incarcerated in the Tower of London until 1611. She was said to have been imprisoned because of a disastrous elopement with another potential claimant to the throne — William Seymour, 2nd duke of Somerset — which King James saw as a treasonous act. Arbella staged an escape attempt, but she was recaptured and remained in the Tower until she died of ill-health on 25 September 1615, aged 40."

"But you believe this is incorrect?" asked Alistair.

"Yes," replied Perdita, her unusual storm-coloured eyes meeting Alistair's blue ones. "The fact she never stood trial for her involvement in the Bye and Main Plots presents an anomaly that can't be ignored — one that is made even more curious when you consider she was the widow of a traitor. This brings me to another discovery. Throughout the diaries there are small comments about Lady Jane Grey — people reminding Arbella of Jane's fate and making comparisons between them."

"And how does Jane fit in with Arbella not standing trial?" asked Kit.

"This is the strange bit," admitted Perdita. "In the aftermath of Jane being removed from her nine-day tenure as queen, Mary Tudor had seemed to be lenient towards her. However, a year later, after Wyatt's Rebellion once again threatened Mary's throne, she was persuaded by her Privy Council that while Jane remained alive, she would continue to be a target for unrest and Mary would be safer if Jane was executed. Can you see the link with another monarch refusing to execute a cousin?"

"Elizabeth I and Mary, Queen of Scots with the Babington Plot," said Alistair, his voice flooded with understanding. "My goodness, Perdita, you're right. Mary Tudor resisted passing sentence on Jane Grey for over a year before finally being persuaded it was in her best interests. Yet there was no real evidence against Jane, only the persistence of her Privy

Councillors playing on her fears. The parallels are there when you look."

"What does it mean though, Perds?" asked Piper.

"It means we have another echo in history," said Perdita. "Historians focus on Elizabeth I executing Mary, Queen of Scots, one queen executing another, but it wasn't the first time it had happened. Mary Tudor had signed the death warrant for her cousin, Queen Jane. She may only have been on the throne for nine days, but Jane was still a queen. It shows that cousins are not immune to bumping each other off after the first exciting flush of securing the throne has worn off."

Kit gave her a quizzical look. "This is about Arbella, isn't it?" he asked.

"Yes," said Perdita, "and it shows more clearly than ever that Arbella's treatment after the discovery of the Bye and Main Plots is an anomaly."

"You're right," said Alistair. "Neither Jane nor Elizabeth I could be proved to be implicated in the plot against Mary I, yet one was executed and one was imprisoned, whereas Arbella was invited to attend the hearings of the plotters she was apparently involved with before returning to the royal court. It is peculiar."

"Do you think the facts have been changed by The Scribe?" asked Piper.

"I would say almost definitely," replied Perdita. "Previous to this, royal women almost always bore the brunt of the punishment, even if they weren't involved in the plots around. Meanwhile, Arbella, who had already been placed under house arrest after her husband's failed coup and was mother to two more potential Tudor heirs, wasn't even arrested in 1603. Yet, if her diaries are to be believed, she was at the heart of the plot to elevate her to queen."

"Maybe the diaries are fake," suggested Callum, "and the reason she wasn't put on trial was because she really wasn't involved in the plots?"

"Actually, Cal, that was my first thought too," Perdita replied. "Then I found a document that was discovered in the 1990s and was described as being the most comprehensive account of its kind relating to The Main Plot. Arbella's name appears throughout it, and it implicates her as being at the centre of the plot. There are details of letters written to her and received in response. However, according to the few remaining records we have of the trial, and there are very few, none of this information came out in court."

"Why not?" asked Piper.

Perdita shrugged.

"Do you think Arbella did stand trial and it's been struck from the records by The Scribe?" asked Susan.

"No, I think she always watched from the balcony," Perdita replied. "Her diaries state her patronage of the plot hinged on the proviso that if it were discovered, she would distance herself entirely. Her fellow plotters agreed to her demands and it seems none of them betrayed her, hence the reason she was able to escape prosecution."

"Interesting," said Alistair, "and this 1990 document, did it give any details of the trial?"

"No, it was mostly the case against the plotters, and it suggests that subsequent government investigations have interpreted the trial as either the hasty overreaction of a nervous king, or a potential personal settling of old scores between Robert Cecil and Sir Walter Raleigh. There is even the suggestion that the entire plot was a fabrication."

"Really?"

"The official court transcripts of both trials have vanished,"

Perdita continued. "The brief knowledge we do have is from hastily made notes from a scribe at court."

Perdita paused as everyone exchanged looks varying from resignation to alarm at her words.

"What happened to Arbella?" asked Piper.

"According to her diaries, she attended the trials that took place in Winchester in November 1603, but it's one of the few areas where she is quite scant on details. Her biographies report that she was accompanied by the earl of Nottingham, the widower of Kate Howard, and his new young bride, Margaret Stewart, the daughter of Scottish noble James Stewart, 2nd earl of Moray. Another friend listed as accompanying her was Katherine Howard, countess of Suffolk, who was the eldest child of Sir Henry Knyvet. It was her uncle, Sir Thomas Knyvet who was responsible for thwarting the Gunpowder Plot."

"And these women were Arbella's friends?" questioned Piper.

"Yes, apparently so. They had other links too, which are quite bizarre when you connect them to our story. Sir Henry Knyvet's wife was Elizabeth Stumpe, who was the daughter of wealthy clothier, James Stumpe. He's not a well-remembered figure, but he links with us because he was the third husband of Lady Isabel Baynton, Queen Catherine Howard's half-sister. Not only that, Arbella was friends with the poet Emilia Lanier, who has been credited as being the mysterious 'dark lady' in Shakespeare's sonnets. Emilia had been the mistress of Henry Carey, so there's another link, and her most famous poem, 'Salve Deus Rex Judæorum' was dedicated to the countess of Suffolk."

"Perds, how did you ever unravel all these connections?" asked Callum in awe.

"Because she's brilliant," said Kit.

Piper grinned and Perdita felt a blush creeping over her cheeks. "It's all there if you look," she said, "and once you tug at the web of connections, the plots and counterplots make more sense. History books don't delve into the family trees, which is a shame because these offer so many clues to possible motivations."

"Or, perhaps if they do, they're visited by an unmarked car full of Watchers," suggested Piper in a cold voice.

An uneasy silence followed.

Perdita and Piper exchanged a glance of defiance. "The first trial," Perdita said, her tone firm, "was for the Bye Plotters and began with the two priests, William Watson and William Clark, along with Sir Gervase Markham and Reverend Sir George Brooke, brother of Henry Brooke. They were all found guilty of High Treason and sentenced to be hanged, drawn and quartered."

"What happened to the others?" asked Piper.

"The trial of Sir Walter Raleigh has been claimed to be something a spectacle. He denied ever meeting or knowing Arbella, claiming the plot was a fabrication. Walter Raleigh and Henry Brooke battled it out, accusing each other of being the leading protagonist of the Main Plot. Sir Thomas Grey, 15th Baron de Grey Wilton, who was also accused, denied all knowledge but eventually they were all found guilty of High Treason and sentenced to death. However, the king decided to show clemency. On 10 December 1603, Henry Brooke, Thomas Grey and Gervase Markham were pardoned at the block and had their sentences commuted to life imprisonment."

"Where was Arbella when this was taking place?" asked Susan.

"Records tell us that she returned to the royal court. She is listed as joining in the masques organised by Queen Anna right up until 1611, when she was imprisoned in the Tower of London for marrying William Seymour." Perdita flipped up the portrait of William Seymour. "But, I think William Seymour actually married Arbella's daughter," she continued, "and it was this act which was seen as treason by the king. Arbella's husband, William Fitzalan, was the grandson of Henry VIII and Catherine Howard, so with a joint link to the crown through both their parents, Arbella's children had a better claim to the throne than anyone else, even the king. If Arbella's daughter then married William Seymour, their children could have posed a terrifying threat to the Stuarts.

"Arbella's children have been removed from history in its entirety, and documents have been left suggesting Arbella was actually married to her son-in-law. The Scribe has been responsible for many of these changes but, according to the confessions of two of the original King's Guards, The Scribe did not work alone. There was an assistant who I believe outlived The Scribe and continued to make changes until 1689. After this, the discrepancies diminish and stop. However, for the real truth to make sense, I think we have to look back even further."

"Why?" asked Alistair. "I thought we'd discovered all there was to find in the earlier years of the Tudors."

"There's more to the secret than we thought."

"What do you mean, Perds?" asked Piper.

"If I'm right, then everything we believe we know about the Tudors is up for debate."

"But we already know that, because of all the things we've discovered," said Alistair.

"Perhaps I should phrase it in a different way," said Perdita.

"Except for a few key elements, everything else we know about the Tudors might be nothing more than a brilliant story invented by The Scribe."

"What have you discovered?" Alistair's voice was tense.

Adrenalin was pumping through Perdita's veins. "The Princes in the Tower," she said.

"What?" exclaimed Piper, and she laughed out of nervousness. "Perds, this is madness — how can they be involved? They died long before any of this began. We're following the trail of the missing heirs of Henry VIII, not trying to rewrite the entire Tudor era."

"Someone has already rewritten the Tudor story," replied Perdita, "and it was the death of the princes that was the catalyst for Henry Tudor to ascend to the throne. It begins with them, the two royal boys who remain at the centre of one of the biggest historical conspiracies in this country."

Kit shifted in his seat again and she looked over at him. He gave her his usual lopsided grin of support and encouragement.

"History tells us that after the sudden death of their father, Edward IV, the princes were taken into the Tower of London to prepare for young Edward V's coronation, but were declared illegitimate by their uncle, Richard Plantagenet. He claimed the throne in Edward's stead and was remembered forevermore as King Richard III. By late 1483, both boys had disappeared, and their murder has been the subject of years of speculation. For centuries, Richard III was reviled as a ruthless murderer of children, but in recent years, he has been rehabilitated in the public domain, his crimes glossed over, his rediscovered remains buried with pomp in Leicester Cathedral."

"Where are you going with this, Perds?" asked Piper.

"What if there was a version of events that revealed the reason why no one has even been able to identify the killer of these two princes?" said Perdita.

"Such as?" asked Callum, giving a nervous laugh.

"What if the princes were never in the Tower of London in the first place? Ever since we discovered Catherine Howard had two children who were written out of history, I've been trying to make sense of this entire story. How was it done? Why was it never discovered? Then I realised we were looking at the detail but not the bigger picture; and last night, I remembered something, a particular date, which was why I wanted to check those books from the library with Kit," she said, looking into his blue eyes.

"Did they confirm whatever it is that you think?" Susan asked, her voice tremulous.

"Yes, Susan, they did," she replied. "You see, I think The Scribe was far more prolific than we realised. I think she — because I do think it was a woman — has rewritten the entire Tudor story."

"What…?" began Alistair, but Perdita shook her head and he halted.

"I think this person was being held under guard throughout the time they were working on this massive rewrite of history," continued Perdita. "My suggestion is that The Scribe was unhappy with her task, so she wove enough clues into the tapestry of the story for anyone to find them if they were looking."

"Perdita, that's a remarkable suggestion," said Susan.

Perdita put a sheet of paper into the projector and shone it onto the screen. "This is what made me begin to view things differently," she said. "It's a page from the old website for St George's Chapel at Windsor Castle. St George's Chapel is the burial place of Henry VIII, Jane Seymour and many other monarchs, including Edward IV and his wife, Elizabeth Woodville. In 1789, workmen carrying out repairs in the chapel accidentally broke into the vault of Edward IV and Elizabeth Woodville and discovered a blocked-up wall that led to a small adjoining vault. This tomb contained the coffins of two unidentified children. At first, they were thought to be two of Edward and Elizabeth's children who had predeceased them: George, who had died at the age of two and Mary, who died age 14.

"However, in 1810, during the excavation of the royal tomb on behalf of King George III, there was another unexpected discovery. This time it was under the Wolsey tombs, and two more lead coffins were revealed. These were labelled with plaques saying 'George Plantagenet' and 'Mary Plantagenet.' Their position, when viewed alongside the contemporary tombs, showed they were situated in a vault adjoining that of their father, Edward IV."

"Who were in the first two coffins, then?" asked Piper.

"The mystery remains," Perdita said. "In order to open a royal tomb and do any DNA testing, the monarch has to give permission, and, at present, no one has taken this strange story any further. It's as though no one in authority wants to make a fuss about two unidentified children's tombs, despite the fact their remains date to the 15th century and could possibly solve one of the greatest whodunits in British history."

"You're suggesting these coffins could be the Princes in the Tower?" confirmed Alistair.

Perdita nodded.

"But weren't two bodies found in the Tower?" asked Callum.

"More than two," replied Perdita. "Small bones that could have belonged to children were discovered in an old chamber that had been walled up, then after this in 1674, workmen in the Tower discovered a wooden box containing the bones of two children. It makes you wonder what was really going on in the Tower of London or whether these macabre discoveries were deliberate red herrings."

"How very strange that the coffins in St George's chapel have not been investigated," said Alistair.

"What's even more peculiar," Perdita continued, "is that the website for St George's Chapel has been updated, and there is now no mention of this mystery anywhere on the site. Although, you can still find it online."

"But why?" asked Callum.

"MI1 Elite," said Kit, his voice low and dark.

"Exactly," said Perdita. "I came across this entry some years ago and made a note of it out of curiosity. Back then, I didn't think it would have the significance it might now carry. What if the princes predeceased their father?"

"That would be really unlucky," said Susan.

"True, but the deaths of both an heir and a spare are recorded elsewhere. James V of Scotland and Mary of Guise had two sons, James, duke of Rothsay and Robert, duke of Albany. Robert died on 4 April 1541 and James died nine days later, on 12 April 1541…"

"But, Perds, that was years later," interrupted Piper.

"I know, but it still pre-dates The Scribe. I have long suspected The Scribe used real events and moved them around, hence the strange echoes of history we keep discovering. What if The Scribe, inspired by more contemporary events, began to spin tales of missing princes in order to increase the drama in her story? Two lost boys in the Tower of London who were the catalyst for the Tudor dynasty."

"Perds, I have a question," said Kit. "If the princes predeceased their father, Edward IV, wouldn't Richard III have been king anyway?"

"Initially, yes," agreed Perdita, "Richard would have inherited the throne but, remember, there were many nobles who felt the Yorks were not the true heirs. Edward IV had won the throne from Henry VI. Edward was from the House of York; Henry was from the House of Lancaster. These two warring families had subjected England to years of warfare. What if, after a few years of this unpopular York monarch, the Privy Council decided they'd had it with York kings? What if they had offered Henry Tudor the throne and recalled him from his exile in Brittany?"

"Why do you say that?" asked Alistair.

"The first and most obvious reason is due to Henry VII's changing of history," said Perdita. "It's a well-known fact that he back-dated his reign to the day before the Battle of Bosworth, claiming he was king and not Richard III on the day of the war. What if he really had been king then, and this document was in fact one of the few events that hasn't been altered? What if the rumours about him were begun by those who had been loyal to Richard in the aftermath of the Battle of Bosworth in order to try and discredit Henry?"

There was silence, then Piper spoke. "Why though? Why begin a rumour that Henry back-dated the books in order to change events?"

"What better way to make the Tudors and their claim to the throne seem even more dubious?" replied Perdita. "By suggesting Henry Tudor, the patriarch, had won his crown by luck and with the help of his mercenary army from France, rather than through his strength of lineage, it weakened his legitimacy to be monarch. His claim came through his mother,

Margaret Beaufort, who was descended from the illegitimate line of John of Gaunt. The Beauforts were eventually legitimised, but there were older noble families who believed they were not entitled to inherit.

"What better way than to play into these prejudices and claim Henry killed the 'real' king, when in reality the situation was reversed: Richard III was the usurper and Parliament had called on Henry to restore order. If you discredit the founder of the dynasty, you cast a shadow over the entire family. What no one expected was for The Scribe to do such a good job when she recreated the history of the Tudors, they became the monarchs who have cast the most fascination among scholars while the Stuarts have faded into the background.

"Interest in The Tudors ran amok, especially in the Victorian era, as more and more documents were being discovered and studied. The only way the Secret Service could control it was to try and maintain the version The Scribe had written, while destroying anything else that suggested there were other events."

"So, are you saying the 'history-book' version is actually The Scribe's retelling of history?"

"Yes."

"Perds, I'm confused — is The Scribe a goodie or a baddie in this scenario?" asked Piper.

"The Scribe did as she was commanded and recreated the Tudor story, but she left enough clues to point academics towards a different version of events — the true version — if you knew where to look. Then she placed the keys to these codes and clues in her own family archive, perhaps hoping that one day her descendants, the true heirs to the British throne, might be able to revive their claim."

There was silence.

"Are you saying the Tudors didn't exist?" asked Piper, aghast.

"No," said Perdita, turning to her sister, "they definitely existed, and they reigned, but they weren't as they seemed. We know at least two Tudor heirs have been written out of history. We know the stories about Henry's queens aren't the way they've been portrayed. Looking at the scope of the changes, I suggest The Scribe was writing with hindsight: she knew the outcome of all the skirmishes, and she painted a vast and dizzying portrait of a family. She's done such a good job that we're all still fascinated with the soap opera that is the Tudor dynasty, and she has completely distracted us from the biggest cover-up in history."

"Which is what?"

"The fact that our executed 17th century monarch, Charles I, was actually murdered by another Tudor. A Tudor who went on to reign as king, but whose tenure and that of his offspring has been removed from history."

"There was another Tudor king?" asked Callum.

"This man had a coronation and he passed the crown to his son," Perdita replied, "but the Privy Council were so horrified by this man as incumbent monarch, they reached out to another royal family, the Stuarts, to offer their heir the throne instead. In 1660, Charles II returned from exile to be King of England. His first task was to rewrite all the official documentation, back-dating it to the date of his father's execution, indicating he had inherited the throne immediately and there had been no 11-year gap. An action which holds echoes of Henry VII and Richard III in 1485."

"But Oliver Cromwell, and then his son, Richard, ruled during those 11 years," said Alistair, as understanding flooded his face.

"It took me a while to realise," admitted Perdita, turning to look at Alistair, "then I remembered that terrible letter in the Lady Pamela collection, the one from Arbella's cousin, Mignonne, whose real name was Bessie Pierrepont, explaining how Mary, Queen of Scots had died, yet Black Fortescue and his men beheaded her corpse. I knew I'd read something similar. In January 1661, on the twelfth anniversary of his father's execution, Charles II put the exhumed bodies of Oliver Cromwell, Robert Blake, John Bradshaw and Henry Ireton on trial. The corpses were found guilty of treason and were posthumously beheaded before being hung in gibbets."

"You're saying Oliver Cromwell, the man who dissolved the monarchy, was actually the last Tudor king?" gasped Piper.

"Yes," replied Perdita. "He was her son. He was Arbella's son and the son of William Fitzalan. He was Henry VIII's great-grandson and he was the rightful King of England. I was checking his birth date and it's one of the few things The Scribe seems to have left alone, as though she were leading us to this final secret. Oliver Cromwell was in fact Henry Fitzalan, 3rd duke of Hereford, the son of Arbella and William, born on 25 April 1599."

CHAPTER THREE

"Did The Scribe change the name of Henry Fitzalan to Oliver Cromwell?" asked Callum, once they had all recovered from the shock of this new information.

"Not as such," said Perdita. "I believe The Scribe used the name and history of the real Oliver Cromwell as background to describe the last Tudor king."

"What happened to the real Cromwell?" said Susan.

"He emigrated to America."

"What?" said Piper.

"It's recorded in most of Cromwell's biographies, but it's always glossed over. In 1641, at the time of the Great Remonstrance, when John Pym was challenging the authority of Charles I, Cromwell claimed that if the king won the vote, he would leave this land behind and go where he could worship in peace and build a better life. This was at the time when there was a flood of Puritans heading to America to build a new world. I believe the real Cromwell, furious with the monarchy and unnerved by the potential return of Catholicism, decided to strike out for a new land where he could build the Puritanical world of his choice."

"Perds, that's quite a leap!" exclaimed Piper.

"It's not as bizarre as it sounds," Perdita replied. "I've been checking the lists of Puritans who were known to have emigrated around this time."

"You're not telling me there's a Cromwell on the manifest?"

"No, but there is a Williams, which was the correct surname of the real Oliver Cromwell."

"Explain," Piper demanded.

"The Oliver Cromwell who we know as the Lord Protector was descended from Katherine Cromwell. She was the sister of Sir Thomas Cromwell, the Lord Privy Seal of Henry VIII, who was beheaded on the day Henry married Catherine Howard," said Perdita. "Katherine Cromwell married a Welshman called Morgan Williams."

"In that case, the family name should have been Williams," confirmed Alistair.

"Precisely," replied Perdita. "However, Katherine Cromwell's husband began life as Morgan ap William, his surname meaning 'son of William'. The Welsh still used the custom of referring to their offspring as 'ap' for a son, followed by the father's first name. When it came to Anglicising their surnames, the Welsh families usually added an 's' to their father's names, hence Williams. However, with the Cromwells rising to power, it wasn't surprising the family of Katherine Cromwell decided to adopt her surname, rather than Morgan's anglicised name, Williams. In order to protect their Welsh roots, the Williams' arms were used, and the family continued to add 'alias Williams' for several generations on official documents, including the real Oliver Cromwell's marriage certificate. During the Protectorate, one of Oliver's Royalist kinsmen — of which there were many — wrote to him saying he had considerable trouble being accepted under the name of Cromwell and intended to change it back to Williams."

"So, you're saying the 'real' Oliver Cromwell actually gathered up his family and sailed to the New World under the family's actual surname of Williams?" asked Piper.

"Yes."

"I still don't understand though, Perds — why would The Scribe choose to denigrate Oliver Cromwell?"

"My theory is The Scribe wanted revenge. When he was a young man and had to be hidden for his own safety, Arbella hid her son, Henry, with a man called Oliver Cromwell who lived in Hinchingbrook House in Cambridgeshire. He was the uncle of this Oliver Cromwell. It occurred to me while I was reading the confessions that The Scribe may have blamed this man for radicalising her brother and decided to vilify him."

"But Perds," said Kit, "the 'Oliver Cromwell' who ruled during the interregnum was anti-monarchy."

"Was he though? The Scribe left details of the leader during this period having a coronation. Cromwell, the republican, is recorded as having a coronation in all but name and being addressed as 'Your Highness'."

"No!"

"In 1657, the official records state Cromwell was offered the crown by Parliament and he was said to have refused. However, the ceremony reinstating him as Lord Protector on 26 June 1657 took place in Westminster Hall and, St Edward's Chair, the throne used in coronations, was brought there from Westminster Abbey. Cromwell wore purple robes lined with ermine and the sword of justice and the sceptre were used, as in traditional coronations. From then on, he was addressed as a monarch and when he died, his son Richard was named as his successor. Even stranger, on the 11 July, after this ceremony, Cromwell went on what was effectively a mini progress. He went to Bristol, where a public holiday was declared, then down through Wales to Tenby, where Henry VII and Jasper Tudor escaped through the tunnels during the Wars of the Roses, and then he went to Milford Haven."

"No way…" whispered Piper.

"Despite the fact this period is viewed as having no monarch, the evidence to show there was a king who has been hiding in plain sight all along is staggering. It was never an interregnum, it was a missing monarchy, but we're so used to accepting what we've been told over the years, none of us have ever acknowledged what has been staring us in the face all along."

There was a stunned silence.

"Richard IV," said Kit, into the tension. "The engraving in the locket. It wasn't a present from Arbella to her son, it was a gift from her son, Henry, who we know as Oliver Cromwell, to her grandson."

"And it would explain the regnal number on your New Zealand document," said Perdita.

"What document?" queried Callum.

Kit pulled a long protective tube from where it was poking out of his Fred Perry sports bag and removed the ancient document within. Laying it in the centre of the table, he produced some padded weights to hold down the curling parchment. "I bought this a few days after Perdita first moved in to Marquess House," he explained. "Although, back then, we had no idea it would prove to be relevant to her quest."

"What is it?" asked Callum, peering at the old map.

"It's a document of ownership for the islands of New Zealand going back to the 1600s, and it predates Captain Cook, who didn't discover them until April 1769. I thought it was a fake, which was why I bought it for Jerusalem. Then, when it arrived, it became clear something was awry. The parchment was wrong and there were mistakes in the document itself. It claimed that Elizabeth was on the throne in January 1558…"

"Mary Tudor was on the throne then," interrupted Susan. "Elizabeth didn't become queen until 17 November 1558."

"Exactly, Mum," said Kit. "Even more dubious, however, was a randomly placed Roman numeral of IV, which as Perdita pointed out was an incorrect regnal number for any monarchs in the seventeenth century. We dismissed the regnal number until Olaf handed Perdita the silver locket, and inside was a dedication to a King Richard IV." Kit slid another transparency on the projector and shone it onto the screen. Alistair and Susan gave stifled gulps of surprise. "It's a palimpsest, and it's tricky to read," admitted Kit as he shone a laser pen, tracing it over the letters as he spoke, "but it says: 'By the order of King Richard IV, in the year of our Lord sixteen hundred and fifty eight, I declare the pardon of my grandmother, Lady Arbella Stuart, dowager duchess of Hereford and dowager countess of Lennox'. The rest has been lost."

Kit sat down again, and Perdita reached across to place another image on the projector.

"This is one of the paintings we discovered in the grotto," she explained. "I suggest it's the coronation portrait of Richard IV, the man who was briefly king after his father had died, but who was replaced by Charles II when the Privy Council invited the Stuart monarch to return as king."

"It's possible," said Piper, staring at the image. "Despite my first thought that it was an amateur artist, it could have been in the school of Robert Walker, who was the parliamentary artist for the interregnum. It would make sense because he painted Oliver Cromwell and Henry Ireton, who was supposedly Cromwell's son-in-law. There's no reason why he wouldn't have been commissioned to paint Oliver Cromwell's son as well."

"Do you think the other one, the man with the red hair, could be William Fitzalan?" asked Perdita.

Piper considered this for a moment, then said, "The clothes would suggest the late Elizabethan period and the X-rays showed the initials W.L.M. faded in the background. I suspect it's by Hieronimo Custodis, a Flemish portrait painter who was popular towards the end of Elizabeth's reign, so this image would fit into the correct time period."

"It's possible then, Pipes," confirmed Perdita.

"I'd say it's likely," her sister replied.

Around her, Perdita was aware of the growing tension in the room and knew she had to explain the most startling discovery. "The Tudors have always been studied more than the Stuarts," continued Perdita. "The story has everything: drama, love, death, divorce, a cruel charismatic villain, an ice queen. I suspect when The Scribe was asked to create these changes, the intention was to portray the Stuarts as the glorious saviours who put the country back together after the chaos of the bastard line of monarchs. Instead, her stories were so tantalising they caused the Stuarts to be side-lined."

"But, Perds, how would this have been possible?" asked Callum. "Surely someone would have remembered real events?"

"How? It was hundreds of years ago. I bet most of us can't remember in detail historical events that have taken place within our own lifetimes. I might be wrong, but I think The Scribe was someone we've been shadowing and chasing ever since we first began this quest. Someone, who from my own admission, had been systematically written out of history."

Perdita's eyes locked with Kit's, her voice trembling slightly.

"You know the identity of The Scribe?" Piper asked, her face stark as the twins locked eyes.

"Yes," said Perdita, her voice trembling, "I believe she was Oliver Cromwell's sister, Ennie. Also known as Penelope Fitzalan."

Her final image was projected onto the screen — the portrait of the woman in the golden dress that, until recently, had hung in Perdita's living room.

"She was Arbella Stuart's daughter and she lived in Marquess House. I think this was the reason Oliver Cromwell took his triumphant march across Wales — he was coming home to Marquess House, to his elder sister, Penelope. I also believe she was held here while she was being forced to rewrite events at the behest of her cousin, Charles II, after he returned from exile. She may have briefly been part of his court, but she vanishes from the records in September 1660. I suspect she was imprisoned somewhere, although not the Tower of London, before Charles made his proposition."

"How are you so sure?" asked Alistair.

"From one of the letters Granny Lettice found on the reverse of this portrait. Penelope, or Ennie, as she signs herself, is writing to an unspecified cousin refusing an offer of refuge because she wants to go to London to try and talk some sense into her brother. She doesn't name him, but it must have been Henry aka Oliver. The letter is dated March 1649, two months after the execution of Charles I. She writes that her brother is 'beyond reason' and because he knows his true identity — the fact he's the heir to the throne — she is trying to persuade him away from his 'desperate path' and the 'terrible war'. This must have been when Henry claimed the throne."

Silence once again greeted Perdita's explanation.

"But why would Penelope have been chosen to be The Scribe?" asked Susan after a few moments. "There were hundreds of writers."

"It would be the ultimate punishment, wouldn't it?" said Perdita. "From what I've gathered from reading Arbella's diaries, Penelope was happiest when left alone to write her stories. Her book in the library is an amazing selection of beautifully written tales, but they're not local legends. If Penelope was known to be a talented writer, what better way for Charles to ensure the stories had a ring of truth? Penelope was writing about her own family history.

"That's also why I think Arbella has been presented in a far more delicate light than many of the other characters in the tale, because Penelope was writing about her beloved mother. I think Arbella and her daughter are the mysterious pair discussed in the earlier letters written by the Ladies of Melusine — perhaps they didn't know about Henry at that point because he had been hidden from birth, for his own safety. It also explains why all the relevant documents that lead to the unlocking of the clues Penelope left are in Marquess House. Although, I am yet to discover why Richard was issuing a pardon for his grandmother."

"My dear, this is incredible," said Alistair, "but how do we prove any of it?"

"With Arbella's box of confessions."

"Which you've said yourself probably doesn't exist," said Piper.

"Something I believed until recently."

"What have you discovered?" Piper asked, and there was fear in her voice.

"The jewellery," Perdita said. "Two ruby rings and a silver locket. Separately, they mean nothing, but brought together, they are the key to the biggest secret in history."

"You've worked it out…" Alistair began, but before he could say any more, there was a hammering on the locked door of Perdita's office.

"Alistair, Alistair…"

Perdita flung it open to reveal Jenny Procter, her usual elegance dissolving as tears streamed down her face. "Jenny, what's happened?"

"It's Izabel," she choked. "She's gone. She's left a note, but she's taken everything, even her passport."

Perdita stepped away, leaving Susan to comfort Jenny. Kit was by her side. Callum was holding Piper's arm, whether to restrain or support her, Perdita was unsure. Alistair's face was ashen, but his eyes were alive with anger.

"The trap has been sprung," he said. "Perdita, we will continue this later; there are more urgent matters to attend to now. Kit, with me, please. Everyone else, we go to a Code Red."

"A what?" asked Perdita.

"It's a security ranking," said Callum, following Alistair and Kit. "It means we're in lockdown. No one enters, no one leaves, and we monitor all calls, even to private mobile phone numbers."

Susan turned to Perdita and Piper. "We've only ever had to do this once before," she explained, one eye still on Jenny, "when your mother died. Please, my dears, will you ensure this room is secure? Take the jewellery to the strong room and then go to Alistair's office, where he will explain our procedures. I'm taking Jenny to our rooms."

Perdita felt an icy fear shiver down her back as she groped for her sister's hand.

PART EIGHT: ENGLAND, 1604

CHAPTER ONE

My dearest Ennie,

Your last letter was one of such joy. It lightens my heart to know you are happy in your household in Pembrokeshire. Your story about the stormy lake, Llyn Cel, made me shiver. It will not be long before you are challenging Aunt Lanier with your stories and poems.

I hope your new kitten, Alys, and your puppy, Fourpaws, are settling in well and no longer keeping you awake at night. Now that Christmas is over, I plan to leave your cousin and the royal court in order to travel to Hardwick Hall to visit Grandmamma.

During this time, I have decided to move your brother from his current residence. As you know, the king has restored Henry's title and, through his gracious generosity, has also returned to us the home of your father: Orleton Hall in Herefordshire. Your brother will move there with his own household. It is time the king and your brother knew each other.

Sweet child, I hope we shall be reunited soon. Until then, you remain in my heart,

Mother

Arbella replaced her quill in the inkwell, re-reading the letter before folding it into a square and sealing it with a shining dollop of red wax. There were no hidden messages, so she felt safe pressing her signet ring into the blood-like substance, watching as the Hereford crest of the hare and the mermaid emerged to glint in the firelight. *The Hereford crest*, she mused. *I am the Dowager Duchess of Hereford, yet still I am known as the Lady Arbella Stuart rather than by my true title. This is a court of masks. A place of disguise and subterfuge, where no smiling face should be trusted.*

Placing the letter on top of her pile of other freshly written correspondence, Arbella tried to suppress the swoop of anger that swept through her at the thought of the trials of the Bye and Main Plots in Winchester. As Count Aremberg had warned, she had been denigrated throughout, while she watched with her loyal friends from the gallery. When the sentences were decreed, she had hoped the men involved would be given short terms of imprisonment, but as each death penalty was read aloud, she had been hard pushed not to shout out in horror.

After George Brooke's execution, the king and queen had decamped to Hampton Court. No one seemed to mourn the loss of the supposed traitors, but Arbella could not dismiss the fates of the men who had tried to make her queen with such equanimity. The stress of the trials had weakened her, and the month of October had been lost through her ailments: the terrible pain, the fatigue and the terrifying dreams created when the balance of her mind was in a state of flux. These symptoms had left her bedbound and weak. Even now, her eyes remained red-rimmed and sore. Her symptoms had meant no one expected her to make anything but the briefest of visits to partake of the court's riotous and lewd celebrations throughout Christmas and New Year.

When Queen Anna had visited her, explaining her plans for an extravagant masque entitled 'The Vision of the Twelve Goddesses', written by the poet Samuel Daniel, Arbella had felt nothing but relief that she would not be well enough to partake. There were also numerous plays performed, which at least gave Arbella the chance to exchange news with Edmund Shakespeare on one of her few visits to the bustling rooms of the court.

"Walter is not bearing his sentence well," Edmund had informed her, "while Henry writes endless letters to his influential friends, trying to fathom a way in which he can persuade the king to release him from the Tower. James, however, is no longer interested. He wishes only to amuse himself with frivolities, his favourites and his hunting."

The day Bridget had arrived in a state of bitter fury with more news of the queen's masque was when Arbella realised how much she was growing to dislike her Stuart cousins, who she felt were bringing the crown of England into disrepute.

"The queen is to play Pallas Athene," Bridget had said, "while Lady Bedford and Penelope are to be Vesta and Venus."

"No doubt it will be a spectacle to behold," Arbella had murmured, her voice containing a hint of sarcasm.

"You're right, my lady," Bridget had responded, her voice shrill with unshed tears of indignation, "because the queen has given a warrant to Katherine Knyvet and Audrey Howard to take Queen Elizabeth's dresses from the Tower and cut them up for costumes."

Even now, her disgust at Bridget's words rose like bile in Arbella's throat. Queen Anna was, in many respects, an enlightened and educated woman with whom Arbella enjoyed spending time, but this act of destruction of Elizabeth's wardrobe, less than a year after James's ascension to the throne, was an insult of magnificent proportion, and Arbella, like many other courtiers, was struggling to forgive the lack of respect shown to the previous monarch.

This combined with the drunken behaviour of James and his companions, the childishness of the games favoured by the court and the vulgarity of the new courtiers were ever stoking the smouldering anger within Arbella's heart. In her view there was no reverence left at court, no respect, merely a slew of debauched upstarts emptying the royal coffers in an orgy of extravagance.

Turning to the letters that had arrived with a messenger an hour earlier, she lifted the first and removed the seal. While she had been ill, Anne Bradshaw had acted as her secretary but now with her eyes able to focus again, she had requested all letters be carried to her in person. Her nerves remained unsettled, and she continued to fear that Robert Cecil might surprise her one day with a warrant.

But Henry Cobham kept his word, she thought, *as has Walter*. Her name and her involvement had been denied. Walter had even made a joke of it while he had given his defence, distancing himself from her and ridiculing the idea of her complicity. It had been unpleasant to be laughed at, but Arbella preferred that to incarceration. Both of the men who had protected her now languished in the Tower, their sentences commuted from execution to life imprisonment.

George Brooke had not fared so well. He had been beheaded, and Arbella knew Lizzie was in despair. Along with William Watson and William Clarke, he had paid the highest price for the plot. Arbella wondered if George was made an example of because he was a man of God.

"Yet James continues with his lewd lifestyle, Anna spends money with no thought for the country, and the court earns a reputation for levity and boorishness," she muttered to herself, focusing on the letter in her hand.

"Are you well, my lady?" asked Bridget, entering with a jug of spiced wine.

"Expressing my irritation with the goings-on below in the chambers of the royal court," she replied with a smile, looking over the top of the short note from Emilia. "Do not fear, my dear, my wits have not left me. I am not conversing with shadows and ghosts."

"That's good to hear," said Bridget. "There is much discussion at present concerning the king's witch-hunting zeal and the number of people he brought to justice during the Berwick Witch Trials. If you were thought to be chattering with spirits, who knows what danger you would find yourself in. James's main topic of conversation at present is that he doesn't understand why witches in England are not burned as they are in Scotland."

"Because we are not savages," snapped Arbella, disgruntled at the idea of James and his obsession with the occult. "Emilia has decided to return to court," she added, looking up from the note, "but will leave her children with Anne Clifford at Skipton Castle."

Arbella lifted the square of parchment level with the flame of the candle on her desk, but no secret words appeared. She had not expected any — there were no key words or symbols to indicate hidden correspondence, but she was thorough and liked to check.

Placing the letter to one side, she opened the next — a message from her Aunt Mary, countess of Shrewsbury, bringing her up to date on family news. The final letter was in an unfamiliar hand, but as she read it, a smile unfurled on her face. For a few moments, she sat considering the words as a plan formed in her mind. "Now we are through the festivities and my health is improved, I intend to petition the queen to leave court," Arbella said.

Bridget's eyes narrowed. "You intend to travel through the winter snows?" she asked. "My lady, you dislike the cold — would it not be wiser to wait until the spring?"

"It will probably be spring by the time I'm given permission," replied Arbella. "You know how slowly the court works. Anyway, the king and queen intend to process into London in March to make up for the lack of pomp at their coronation. Anna has already made it clear she expects me to ride beside her, which I will do. My plan is to leave after this event."

"Where will you go?"

"I shall visit my grandmother before returning to my husband's estate," Arbella announced. "My son will join me, and we will establish a household for him. I may also take a trip to Staffordshire."

Arbella saw the surprise register on Bridget's face.

"Why Staffordshire?"

"It is very pretty in the spring."

Her blue eyes caught the worried grey frown of her friend as Bridget's face creased with concern.

"Arbella, is this wise?"

"Why yes, I believe it is. There is nothing like a short progress to establish bonds between families and, at some point, I must arrange suitable matches for my children. If I don't, you can be sure my grandmother will begin interfering in her usual bossy manner."

Arbella sipped her wine, then wandered to the windows to watch the falling snow, ignoring Bridget's searching gaze.

"What did he say?" asked Bridget, after a few moments.

"Who?"

"Do you wish me to say his name aloud? Especially as you have already dropped his note into the flames in order to avoid any form of incrimination."

Arbella laughed. "You never miss a trick, do you, my dearest Bridget?"

"Not when your life might depend upon it, my lady."

Not wishing to upset her friend further, Arbella returned to the writing desk and said in a voice barely more than a whisper, "Robert Catesby wishes to ask my opinion on a scheme."

"George Brooke was executed only a month ago," hissed Bridget in terror. "Henry, Walter, Thomas and the others are in the Tower of London. They have given their freedom, while others have given their lives to protect you, yet you dabble in another dangerous scheme and with a man who you know to be reckless. A man who was at your husband's side when he fought for the throne, a man who slipped away in the dead of night and left your husband to face the axe alone."

"Times change," said Arbella. "I agree that he's a scoundrel, but the longer my cousin sits on the throne, the worse his behaviour becomes and the angrier it makes me. My late husband was not perfect, his reign would have been fraught with problems, but we are considering my throne, not his, and I would choose to display dignity, discretion and care over my subjects. This man is cunning and might be my last hope at claiming what is rightfully mine."

"Robert Catesby is not to be trusted — you know this, Arbella. I beg you, please reconsider."

Arbella stared into her friend's white face. She understood Bridget's fear but the more she saw of the new monarch, the less she believed he should be allowed to remain on the throne.

"Either I or my son should wear the crown," she replied. "Catesby has a scheme. I shall listen to his words and if I believe the idea to be good, then perhaps he and I can reach an accord. If, as I suspect is the case, the suggestion is one of madness, then I shall spend a pleasant few days in his company before returning to Orleton Hall."

"Arbella, please see sense," whispered Bridget, but Arbella had heard enough.

Throughout her life, those around her had advised and scolded her whenever she made decisions of her own, but she was a grown woman. Her house arrest with her grandmother was at an end and her children were safe. Ennie was in her own home, and soon Henry would be established in a miniature court of his own, as the heir to the throne should be while he waited for his crown. In their veins ran Tudor blood — they were the rightful royal family, not James and his extravagant wife. No matter how kind Anna had been to her personally, the sacrilegious way she had treated the wardrobe of the old queen infuriated Arbella, and, if discussing treason with Catesby was the way to secure a future for her son, she was prepared to take the risk.

"Should anyone question my motives, I shall state we are discussing a potential marriage between Ennie and Catesby's son, Robert. They are of a similar age and a marriage could be advantageous."

Arbella sipped her wine and moved towards the chair by the fire, collecting a book that had been sent by Emilia. Making herself comfortable, she began to read, her gesture dismissing Bridget, who curtseyed and left the room on silent feet. To Arbella, the gentle click of the door held a reproachfulness which added to her annoyance. *Do none of them understand?* she thought as she gazed at the snow, allowing her tired eyes to blur with the shifting light and gloom of the day.

Despite what Bridget thought, Arbella had not burned Catesby's letter but had secreted it into the lining of her sleeve. Now she was alone, she removed it, re-reading each line with care to see if there was another meaning within its words. Finally, having decided there were no hints or clues, she decided to try one last test and held the note up to the candle. A moment later, a short message flared in the fiery light.

For your own safety, you must leave court at your earliest convenience. Word has reached me that the Little Beagle plots to have your head when the snows of winter have thawed. Beware his evil intentions and avoid him at all costs. Your friend, R.C.

The Little Beagle. Catesby's nickname for Robert Cecil. With shaking fingers, Arbella dropped the note into the fire, her heart pounding with fear.

CHAPTER TWO

The house was new, two storeys high, and with vast, red-brick Dutch gables at either end. The bright stonework glimmered in the spring sunshine as Arbella and her party approached. The noise of their horses' hooves on the immaculate cobblestones caused shouts of greeting and the scurry of preparation as she led the way through the archway to the stables.

"My lady, let me help you!"

Arbella's groom, John Good, a former member of her grandmother's household who was now part of her own loyal staff, hurried towards her, reaching out to take her gloved hand.

"Thank you, John," she said with a smile as he lifted her from her saddle. "I'm a little heavier than when you used to do that at my grandmother's house."

"You're still as light as a feather, my lady," he said, blushing to the roots of his sandy hair before taking her horse and leading it away.

"My Lady Arbel," called a voice through the noise and bustle of their arrival.

"Robert," she exclaimed as Catesby walked towards her.

A shiver of sadness rippled through Arbella as she watched him approach and for a moment, she saw an echo of her husband in the handsome man striding towards her. William and Catesby had been good friends, both assured of their great good looks and their place in society, both determined their cause was Godly and would succeed. But William was dead, a traitor to the crown, and while Catesby was still viewed with suspicion, his confidence in his own beliefs clung to him and he continued to exude an air of power. Kneeling before her, he took her hand, kissing the soft red leather of her riding gloves.

"Your Majesty," he murmured.

Despite the tremor of excitement it gave Arbella to be addressed as a queen, fear was never far from her heart. "Enough, Robert," she snapped, snatching away her hand and bidding him rise. "You were always a reckless fool."

Catesby grinned, his velvet brown eyes twinkling. "You are among friends here, Arbel," he said, shaking his dark curly hair back from his face. "Why should two old friends not meet to discuss a potential union between their adored offspring? You worry too much."

He took her hand, leading her through the crowd to the house. To Arbella's relief, Bridget and Anne fell in behind them. It had been many years since she had seen Catesby, and she had forgotten the unnerving intensity of his charm.

"This way, my lady," he exclaimed, leading her to the great hall at the centre of the house where a vast fire burned brightly. A table was being laid with food, and two serving women approached with jugs of wine. "We keep a merry house here," continued Catesby, indicating the Minstrel's Gallery above the hall where musicians, on his cue, began playing a lively tune. "Other friends are also staying and your time here will, I hope, be entertaining as well as informative."

Arbella exchanged a concerned glance with Anne and Bridget. Catesby turned away, issuing instructions. Since the death of his wife, Catherine Leigh, six years earlier, he had never remarried, relying instead on his loyal staff.

"My lady, we should leave," whispered Bridget. "He remains as wild and dangerous as in the days of his lordship."

"Perhaps you're correct, Bridget," agreed Arbella, who was beginning to wonder at the wisdom of her visit.

A door at the other end of the chamber was flung open and three people entered on a wave of laughter. The two men were the brothers Thomas and Robert Wintour, cousins of Catesby, and the woman was Robert Wintour's wife, Gertrude: a Talbot before her marriage and a distant cousin of Arbella's. Upon seeing Arbella, all three ceased their boisterous conversation and dropped into deep bows.

"Rise, please," said Arbella, her eyes once again seeking those of her ladies-in-waiting. In the flurry of greetings, Arbella reached for Bridget's hand and squeezed it. "Tell John Good to remain close at hand in case we need to leave quickly," she whispered. "I'm unsure whether to trust these games."

"Very well, my lady, I shall attend to it at once." Bridget gave a bob of a curtsey and slipped from the room.

"There is no need for fear, my dear Arbel," said Catesby. "You are safe here and, as I said in the stable yard, you are among friends."

"Recusant friends," she said, her tone light, but the men all stiffened at her words.

"Friends, nevertheless," repeated Catesby, ushering her to the largest, most ornately carved chair in the hall.

"Robert, this was a mistake," said Arbella, resisting his offer. "I should have listened to my ladies. If I am discovered in your company, especially after the events of last year…"

"You will not be discovered," Catesby assured her, "and anyway, the evening will soon be closing in. Should anyone question your presence here, you came to shelter from the inclement weather while on progress to visit your grandmother in Derbyshire. There is nothing unusual in my offering hospitality to the wife of an old friend."

Arbella gazed around the room, taking deep breaths to calm her nerves. All Catesby said was true. Her visit here could be passed off as nothing more than a convenience.

"Come, my lady," said Gertrude, hurrying forward, her ash blonde hair a flurry of curls around her head, a style popularised by Queen Anna and adopted by all who wished to be viewed as a fashionable. "Sit by the fire and sample some of Robert's plentiful victuals. He keeps a good table and I find after a journey, I, too, am often out of sorts until I have eaten."

With the air of one used to being obeyed, Gertrude indicated to Catesby's serving men to bring platters of food to Arbella, helping her to arrange a selection of items on a silver plate.

"Let us leave the men to discuss important things, while we share family news," she exclaimed, sitting beside Arbella, and indicating for Anne to join them.

Arbella stared at the plate of food and shot a look at Anne, who raised her eyebrows. "Gertrude's as bossy as ever, then," murmured Arbella, and Anne turned her laugh into a cough.

But Gertrude had been correct and as she ate, Arbella felt her energy and good humour returning. The music continued to play and while she gathered herself, Catesby, Thomas and Gertrude's husband, known to his friends as Rob, played a noisy game of skittles.

"You look better, my lady," said Catesby, wandering over to join the women when they had finished. "Would you care to take a stroll around my new garden?"

"A short walk," Arbella conceded. "It is becoming cooler outside, and I would like to rest before the evening entertainments."

He offered his arm, and his chatter of inconsequential things took them through the house and out onto a vast walkway that led down to the intricate garden below. As they left the others behind, she noticed there was an urgency to Catesby now; the careless bonhomie of earlier was slipping. Arbella shuddered; she was no fool and she could sense the danger. When she had been married to William, she had become used to this sense of crackling unease pervading the air like a bad spirit. It had been a number of years since she had felt it, and it was an unwelcome presence. When they were a distance from the house and no one would overhear their conversation, Arbella was unsurprised when Robert slowed his pace, his tone serious.

"My man, Thomas Fyshe, attended the trials and witnessed your distress," Catesby said. "I believe Raleigh was free with his defamation of your name in the courtroom."

"To distance me from the plot," Arbella replied.

"Or to save himself?"

"If that was his plan, it failed. He is imprisoned in the Tower, and the king shows no signs of leniency."

Following Catesby along a winding path, Arbella considered how beautiful it would look in a few months when the roses were in bloom. For now, the new leaves shuddered in the cooling breeze, their razor-sharp edges threatening all who might attack them and ruin the growing buds containing their beauteous flowers.

"The Reverend George Brooke didn't fare so well," said Catesby. "He and the Catholic priests were executed."

"James doesn't like recusants."

"He must hate me then," said Catesby.

"You were wise to distance yourself from the Bye Plot," Arbella conceded. "I believe it was ill-conceived, and we all knew George's temper was his weakness. Robert Cecil would have known how to provoke him."

"The Little Beagle is a cunning man," commented Catesby. He turned to look at her, his brown eyes troubled. "Arbella, there are many who taint you with William's crimes," he said. "They believe that, despite your public Protestant beliefs, in private you are really a Catholic and you would plot with the Spanish to take the English throne. Many fear that if you were queen, you would return the land to the days when Catholics unleashed cruel punishments and the Spanish Inquisition lit their bonfires across the land."

"Such rumours have been started by Robert Cecil, no doubt," Arbella replied, her tone derisive.

"Among others," agreed Catesby.

"There are always rumours, Robert," she sighed.

"Whispers begun by the Little Beagle have a tendency to be believed."

"What are you saying?" she snapped. "Tell me what you have heard. I'm in no mood for guessing games."

Catesby slumped onto a stone bench and dropped his head in his hands, as though the weight of his secret pained him.

Arbella, her body taut with nerves, perched rigid beside him. "Tell me," she insisted.

"Cecil and the king know you are popular with the people — too popular as far as they are concerned. Despite the king having three children, you pose a real threat to the stability of the Stuarts as a royal family. Robert Cecil believes he can control this volatile situation by creating you as the monster. Not only does he spread rumours that you are a Catholic, he hints that you are in touch with Spain." Arbella threw him a haughty look but before she could speak, he continued. "While the money gathered by the captured plotters to fund an invasion remains hidden, the Little Beagle suggests to those with influence that you have control of these coffers and could still cause harm to the realm."

"If he believes all this, then why doesn't he have me arrested?"

"He doesn't, but he wants other men to believe it. He intends to blacken your name and, depending on how the king acts in the future, either have you cast off as mad or discovered at the heart of a scheme, as Mary, Queen of Scots was found at the centre of the Babington Plot."

"Mary was James's mother — are you suggesting he would do to me what those men did to her?"

Catesby broke a leaf off a nearby rosemary bush and sucked the silvery-grey blades. "James is not always in his right mind," he replied in a quiet voice. "As you suffer from an illness that often leaves you in a state of confusion, so does the king, and his eldest son, Henry."

"I have become aware of his symptoms," Arbella agreed.

"The unbalancing of the king's mind leaves him vulnerable to unscrupulous men such as Robert Cecil. They would use the king's fears against him in order to retain the vision of the land as they wish to see it and, at present, you and your children are an inconvenience. This is why I advised that you leave the court. Cecil could not be seen to act too quickly after the trials of the other traitors, but I believed that every day you remained under his eye, the danger to you increased."

Arbella allowed Catesby's words to sink in. Little of what he had imparted shocked her. She had known for some time that she could no longer rely on the old friendship she had once shared with Robert Cecil. It saddened her that he would betray her, but she knew Catesby was a wily courtier, a man who would always put his own survival above that of anyone else.

"You stated you had heard of a plot. Is it in my name?"

"Not in your name, but you have been linked to it by those outside the plot."

"How do you know this?"

"The plot was devised by myself and the Wintour brothers," Catesby stated, his voice calm.

"And you would betray me too?" Arbella asked.

"Never, my lady. We plan to rid this land of our turbulent king by blowing up the Houses of Parliament when he and his council take their seats there. Our intention is then to round up and destroy all the Scottish lords who currently inhabit our English seats of office. Your name was suggested by other interested individuals — people of my faith, who believe you might be the only monarch who would allow us to worship in peace."

Arbella turned to look into Catesby's wide brown eyes. "All you wish from me is reassurance that I will not persecute Catholics?"

"Yes, my lady. We will need to be certain we are both agreed on terms, but, if you will assure us that Catholics will no longer be punished and we will be allowed to return to our churches unmolested, then it is our intention to rid ourselves of these dreadful usurpers and place you, then your son, on the throne of England."

"And your plot — how far advanced is it?"

"We are a small band of like-minded brothers who are certain of our success…"

"But where do your funds come from? Are you supported by the Spanish?"

"Not directly," he said. "However, the reason the money obtained by Henry Brooke and stored by Sir Walter Raleigh in Jersey before his arrest has eluded the king and Robert Cecil is because we moved it from Raleigh's control when the danger of capture was imminent."

Arbella stared at him in incredulity. "You have the Spanish money from the Main Plot?" she whispered.

"Bess Throckmorton helped to find a way to pass the funds to me for safekeeping."

"Bess and Walter are involved?"

"And Henry Brooke. This is the second phase of the plan. It was the reason I distanced myself from them so many months ago."

Arbella could hardly believe her ears. This was a continuation of the plan to make her queen. She had not been abandoned.

"Do you agree, Your Majesty?" asked Catesby, his tone serious. "If we are to continue with this game, do you agree to allow freedom to Catholics?"

"Yes," she replied. "You know it was always my intention to allow my subjects to worship as they choose, to live peaceably together praising God in the way each of us feels is right."

Catesby was beaming, his excitement palpable. "Then we begin —"

"Do not kill unless you have no other choice," interrupted Arbella. "I will not have the blood of innocents on my hands."

"Of course, my lady."

"And, as I insisted to Raleigh and Cobham, should this plot be discovered, I have the right to distance myself and deny all knowledge."

"Yes, my lady. Our aim is to protect you and see you safely onto the throne, not to lead you to your death." Catesby stood, taking her hand and raising her to her feet. "Let us retire before banquet this evening, where we will speak no more of this. We have your word and you have ours. Tomorrow, the plan will begin."

CHAPTER THREE

"Mamma," came the shrill tones of Arbella's five-year-old son, "there are horses arriving. I think it's Uncle Markham."

Arbella, in the room off the long gallery that she had adopted for her own private use, smiled to herself. For the past few days, she had been writing her version of recent events with the intention of taking it with her on a visit to Ennie in order to stow it in the casket. Bridget and Anne sat with her, both engaged in embroidery as they made new clothes for Ennie.

The decision to leave court was a good one, Arbella decided as her eyes travelled over the homely scene. The past month had given her peace of mind, as well as the opportunity to spend time with her son. Their afternoon strolls had afforded her the perfect occasion to explain some of his true history to him. Not enough to place Henry in danger, but sufficient for him to realise his destiny.

The sound of frantic running footsteps echoed along the wooden floor of the long gallery.

"Arbella, where are you?" shouted a female voice.

"Emilia?" called Arbella, rushing into the gallery. "What are you doing here…?"

Edmund Shakespeare and Sir William Markham were racing along in her wake.

"My lady, you are safe!" exclaimed Markham in relief as they crashed to a halt.

"Uncle Markham, Uncle Shakespeare!" came the shrill voice of Henry as he appeared with his nurse, throwing himself onto the two men.

"Your Grace," said Edmund, catching the small boy and clutching him tightly. "You've grown even taller — soon you will be biggest man in Christendom."

"I shall be a giant like my great-grandpapa," Henry squealed in excitement.

"Henry, be careful," said Arbella. Turning to Henry's governess, Lady Anne Fitton, she added, "Lady Fitton, please take Henry to his rooms. I shall visit you there shortly. Lock the doors and let no one pass but me, Anne or Bridget."

"Yes, my lady," replied Anne. "Do not fear, he will be safe with me."

Arbella swallowed a lump in her throat as she watched Henry bound off with Anne. "What's happened?" she asked, as soon as her son was out of earshot.

"Robert Cecil has issued a warrant for your arrest," said Markham without preamble. "There are soldiers on the road, heading this way."

Bridget gasped and Anne Bradshaw shushed her.

Arbella felt all the energy drain from her body as fear engulfed her. "On what grounds?" she asked, her voice shrill.

"High treason," replied Edmund. "Emilia was spending the day with Anne Clifford, who can never keep gossip to herself, thank the lord, because she let slip that Cecil and the king planned to place you in the Tower to use you as bait to ensnare the organisers of this new plot."

"Do they believe I'm involved?"

"Yes, but they have no way of proving it," said Markham. "This is a ploy to scare your fellow plotters enough to break cover so that Cecil can identify them."

Arbella stared at Markham, panic overwhelming her. "What shall we do?"

"Edmund will take Henry to his parents' house in Stratford-upon-Avon. His mother is elderly, but she has her wits and will ensure he is hidden until Sir Edward Devereux, a cousin of Edmund's through marriage, can take the boy to safety."

"To safety? Where could he possibly be safe? The king knows his true lineage…"

"To the Devereux family seat of Lamphey Hall in Pembrokeshire, where he will await a ship to take him abroad."

"And my daughter?" Arbella's voice was constricted as fear coursed through her.

"Sir Edward will take your daughter, too. She is currently at Marquess House, in St Ishmaels — it will not take long to move her to Lamphey Hall. In the meantime, you will be travelling with me to my family seat of Rufford Abbey, where we will lure the guards, ensuring Henry's safety."

Arbella's heart skipped a beat. "Lure the guards?" she queried. "You intend for me to be caught?"

Emilia pushed her way past Markham. "No, Arbel," she said. "William has explained it badly. I shall disguise myself in one of your dresses, while you will accompany Edmund dressed as his page, travelling with Henry. The plan is for you and Henry to meet Ennie in Pembrokeshire, then you will sail for France where Mary Seton, once a close companion of your aunt, Mary, Queen of Scots, will protect you. She is now a nun and has offered you and the children sanctuary. You will be safe with her while Catesby and his men work to free our land from these usurpers."

Arbella stared at her assembled friends, her eyes moving from face to face. Gathering up her skirts, she returned to the papers strewn across the desk and began shuffling them together in a pile. She handed the bundle to Bridget. "Place these with the other paperwork in the strong room; keep them safe."

Bridget gave Arbella a reassuring smile and scurried from the room.

"How long do we have?" Arbella asked.

"An hour at most," said Markham, "possibly less."

Arbella took a deep, steadying breath. It was imperative she remain calm or her recalcitrant nerves and her often weak body might fail her. However, as the adrenalin surged around her, for once she found her mind was clear and strength was her companion. "Anne," she said, "go to Henry's quarters with Edmund and explain the situation to Lady Fitton. Henry will need warm riding clothes, boots and a hat. Edmund will advise her."

The two left and Arbella could hear their feet pounding down the long gallery, receding into the distance as they headed for the east wing.

"Emilia, come with me," Arbella said. "You will require my riding habit. Where am I to find male clothes to fit me?"

"Here, my lady," said Markham, passing a large leather bag to Emilia. "Edmund brought these costumes from the court players. They should fit you well enough."

Arbella could not help but marvel at the speed with which her friends had raced to her aide.

"Thank you, William," she said. "Can I leave you to organise the horses?"

"My lady," he said with a deep bow.

"Come Emilia," urged Arbella. "We must be on the road before the hour is up. I will not risk my son's safety."

As they ran, their skirts bunched in their hands, Emilia explained what had happened to cause such a furore. "Thomas Percy, you remember him?"

Arbella nodded. "He's Henry Percy's second cousin…" she gasped as she took the stairs two at a time.

"Yes, and a devoted Catholic. He was once sent to treat with James while he was still King of Scotland to ask for clemency for English Catholics — something which James promised and has since rescinded. Tom's fury is great, and when he overheard two of Cecil's men in a tavern discussing the warrant he was persuading the king to sign, his suspicions were aroused. Catesby has informers within the palace, and he contacted them immediately. When they ascertained the arrest warrant was for you, Catesby sent his most trusted man to inform us, then Anne Clifford whispered your planned incarceration to me late last night and Edmund suggested this plan."

"To dress me as a man?"

"You will look younger in men's clothes — your smooth complexion will make anyone glancing at you assume you have not yet entered manhood, and they will take no notice of you. It's a perfect disguise."

A flurry of activity greeted them as they pounded into Arbella's rooms. Arbella's other ladies-in-waiting were already prepared and as Emilia stepped through the door, she was whisked away to be transformed into a semblance of Arbella. Meanwhile, Arbella was seated in front of her looking glass while Lady Frances Kirton began coiling her hair into a tight net and Margaret Byron rummaged through the leather bag Emilia had thrown her, producing first a short brown wig, then breeches, boots, shirts and waistcoats.

Arbella watched in the mirror as her dress was stripped away and she was buckled and laced into the clothes of a page. A slight, brown-haired youth stared back at her, and even she struggled to recognise herself.

"I am a boy," she said in wonder. A woman appeared behind her and Arbella blinked. "Emilia?"

"Why no," her friend replied in a voice so like her own that Arbella spun around to face her. "I am the Lady Arbella Stuart."

"But what will happen when the soldiers catch you?"

"Nothing, because they won't catch me. When we arrive at William's house, I will return to my usual self and there will be no charges to answer. By then, we will have distracted Cecil's guards enough to give you, Henry and Ennie time to flee."

"You would place yourself in such danger for us?"

Emilia's dark eyes softened. "You are my queen; I am sworn to protect you and the real royal family."

The two women stared at one another; then as the danger of the situation overwhelmed them, they hugged.

"William has informed your man Hugh Crompton that the staff are to deny Henry was ever here," said Emilia, pulling away. "They will say that you were here last week, when you paid a short visit, but you had left with the intention of returning to London. All will mysteriously forget where it is you intended to stay, and no one will mention Henry."

"You would all risk your liberty and your lives for me…" Arbella began in awe.

"My lady, we are loyal to you," said Lady Kirton. "As you have always cared for us, our families, our children. You would risk all for any of us, and we would protect you with equal ferocity. Now, my lady, ride fast, swift and true. We will pray for you."

Arbella called her thanks once more, then led Emilia from the room and through the servants' corridors to the stable yard, where Markham, Edmund and Henry, along with outriders from Markham's men and many of her own male staff were waiting.

"Mamma, you are unrecognisable," called Henry, his voice bubbling with laughter. "This is such a fine jape of Uncle Edmund's."

Arbella was helped onto her horse by John Good, who then mounted a huge hunter and slid his flintlock pistol into the saddle bag, bringing the horse alongside her.

"Should you be intercepted," said Markham, riding to Arbella's side, "John will protect you and Henry. Ride for Edmund's mother — she will hide you. If you are caught, deny your identity. Say you are running away from a cruel master who has whipped you once too often. The lie will not last for long, but it might buy us enough time to rescue you."

"Enough, William," said Arbella, her nerves already shredded. "Let's ride. I shall protect Henry, you will all protect me, and, with God's grace, we shall outwit Cecil's men and soon be safe on a boat to France."

CHAPTER FOUR

"In there, wench," sneered the man, his rough hands flinging her into the dank, stone cell.

Arbella let out a cry of pain as she lost her footing on the slippery cobbles, slamming into the filthy floor, her shoulder taking the brunt of the impact. A rat skittered away in the darkness, and she swallowed the sob threatening to escape her parched mouth.

Staring at her bleak quarters, she shuddered. If she had been placed in this rancid hole, what had happened to the others? Images of torture and brutality swam through her mind, and she prayed her companions had escaped. Her comfort was the knowledge that Henry was safe. They had been barely a few miles into their journey when they became aware they were being trailed by soldiers. Deciding to split their party in order to try and lose these interlopers, Henry had been placed on Edmund's saddle and he had fled. Always a daring horseman and having honed his acrobatic talents on horseback for the entertainment of theatre goers and revellers throughout London, Edmund's daring equestrian skills had been required to save the small boy.

Markham had tried to send Arbella with them, but she had known her presence would have slowed their escape, and Henry's life was more important to her than her own. Instead, she had pointed to a small group of men to accompany her, telling the others to scatter and save themselves, then she had ridden for her life, knowing it was only a matter of time before the wild horses of James's guards caught up with them. The chase had lasted for many miles and the exhilaration of the ride had left her breathless. When the captain of the guards had finally caught her, threatening her with his pistol, her response had been to pull her horse into a spectacular rear, its hooves slicing through the evening air, before allowing the men to surround her. "Take me," she had commanded, "but these men are here under duress; you have no quarrel with them."

It had not worked and the last she had seen of William Markham, John Good and Markham's friend, Sir James Croft, was them being forced to kneel in the mud, their heads bowed and their hands tied behind their backs.

"One noise out of you and you'll wish you'd never been born," leered the gaoler, bringing Arbella back to the present. "Dressing up as a boy won't stop me and my men showing you…"

"Enough, Falwell," snapped a cold voice from the shadows. "Leave the prisoner and return to your other charges."

"Yes sir," Falwell muttered and melted away into the dark dripping depths of the corridor.

Arbella raised herself into a sitting position and glared at Robert Cecil through narrowed, angry blue eyes. "'Words are easy, like the wind; faithful friends are hard to find'," she said, her voice sparkling with fury.

Cecil threw back his head and laughed. "Oh Arbel, even now you choose to display your arrogance by quoting a poem by Mr Shakespeare. All that surprises me is that it isn't in Latin."

Observing Cecil, Arbella felt her confidence rise. He might be laughing but his eyes were cold, and his hands were balled into fists, a sure sign he was on the edge of his temper. Despite appearances of control and power, Arbella could sense there was something awry.

"Why did you run, Arbella?" Cecil asked.

"Wouldn't you if you were told there was an arrest warrant issued in your name?"

"Only if I were guilty."

"Guilty? Whether guilty or not, my name, my sex and my closeness to the throne suggest I would never be given a fair trial, and I didn't wish to end my days in the same manner as my cousin, Lady Jane Grey. She suffered a traitor's death because of the behaviour of those around her. If I am to die in such an ignominious manner, I would rather it was because of my own actions."

"So, you admit to being involved with these Catholic plotters?" Cecil sneered, a hint of triumph in his tone.

"Don't be foolish, Robert," Arbella replied in a voice of bored contempt. "I am neither Catholic nor involved with whatever plot you have most recently created to try and incriminate me."

"I've created?"

"Or perhaps my cousin James is your puppet master."

Cecil glared at her through the bars set high in the solid wooden door, then he vanished from view, his footsteps growing faint as he stormed away.

Arbella listened, trying to ascertain whether there was a guard hovering beyond the wooden door. When she was sure she was alone, she heaved herself from the floor and limped to the wooden chair in the corner of the miserable cell. The straw mattress was wet, and even from a distance she could see the lice and fleas scurrying within its folds. Sitting carefully on the chair, she moved her arm and was relieved that apart from a dull ache, she did not seem to have damaged it badly when she fell.

Footsteps in the corridor brought her from her reverie and she pushed the chair in front of her, waiting with her hands on its loose back. It was a weak, spindly creation, but wielded with intention it would stop the brutish gaoler in his tracks if she needed to defend herself.

The key ground in the lock and she held her breath, ready for an attack, but two women entered. It was her loyal ladies-in-waiting, Bridget Sherland and Anne Bradshaw.

"No," howled Arbella in anguish, "you were not meant to be punished alongside me! This was my choice, my foolishness."

"My lady, no," gasped Bridget, hurrying forward to grasp Arbella's hand. "You misunderstand — we are here to remove you to better quarters and dress you according to your status. The king ails and while in his state of confusion, he can't be disturbed. The queen has insisted your stay in the Tower is to be of the greatest comfort. We are to take you to the Lieutenant's Lodgings, where you will be the guest of Sir William Waad."

"William Waad," Arbella uttered with a shudder. "The pernicious creature with delusions of grandeur. I think I might prefer to remain here."

Bridget gave her a complicit look. "You will only be at his mercy for a short while. Robert Cecil plans to place you under house arrest, but until a suitable location has been decided upon, Waad is your gaoler. From the rumours we have heard, we believe you will be lodged in Lambeth with Sir Thomas Parry."

"For now, my lady," said Anne, stepping forward, "we must remove you from this rancid hole."

As Arbella was washed, fed and dressed by her ladies, Bridget passed on the news of her fellow rebels.

"Markham and John Good are being held at the Marshalsea prison in Southwark," she whispered as she poured steaming scented water over Arbella's hair, "and Sir James is in The Fleet. We believe they will all soon be released without charge because there are no charges to bring. All have denied knowledge of the warrant and say they were accompanying you on a ride. They claim you find the costume of a page a preferred outfit in which to gallop across country. There is nothing anyone can say to suggest otherwise."

"And Henry?"

"Safe with Mary Arden in Warwickshire," murmured Anne. "Edmund will remain there until it is decided where best to place your son."

"Should we send him to Pembrokeshire?" asked Bridget.

"This would lead them to Ennie. Henry is safe for the moment," replied Arbella. "What word of Catesby?"

"In hiding again."

"The man was always able to hide."

"He has written though," added Anne, "to say their plot continues and, should it be necessary, they will send men to rescue you from wherever you are placed."

Arbella considered this as she submerged herself under the scented water, the only noise the sound of her blood pounding in her ears. Catesby was reckless, but he was loyal. Rising from the water and wiping her face with the crisp linen sheet passed to her by Bridget, she replied, "Not yet. I shall remain here to discover how events proceed, then we'll consider Catesby's offer."

The days in the Tower passed with surprising speed. Each morning, Arbella expected to be interrogated by Robert Cecil but the summons never came, and she was left in peace. After a week, she was allowed to visit Bess and Walter Raleigh in their vast apartments in the Bloody Tower. Upon arrival, she was amazed at the comfort of their rooms, which were furnished with tapestries and belongings from their home. Raleigh's key members of staff were in attendance, along with their son, Wat.

"James will soon release you," Bess assured her. "The warrant was dreamt up by Cecil, but his plan has led nowhere, and the cousin of the king can only be held for so long without causing a scandal. Have you heard? The wonderful people of London are already writing ballads about you and your plight. Soon you will be a national heroine, all of which helps with our cause."

Walter coughed and said, "Remember where we are, my dear — let us be wise with our words."

Visits to Henry Brooke were also allowed, and he too seemed certain her freedom would be secured within days. "You are too valuable a member of the royal family to remain here," he said. "When you are free, the new plot will continue; there are already missions to Spain to gather assistance."

That meeting left her more nervous than reassured, and she chose not to hurry back to Cobham's apartments.

"There must be action soon," she complained to Bridget a month later. "James can't keep me here indefinitely."

"Yes, he can," Bridget replied. "He's king."

Arbella flounced across the room in irritation. "You would say that," she muttered. "You're enjoying being reunited with Tom."

Bridget blushed, and Arbella noted she did not deny her renewed closeness with Thomas Grey, another prisoner in the Tower. Noticing a pile of books placed on the table beside her favourite chair, Arbella nodded towards them. "What are these?" she asked.

"To prove you're not forgotten," replied Bridget.

Arbella shot her a curious look, then picked up the top publication: Hugh Holland's *Pancharis*. Opening the cover, she saw it had been dedicated to her. The others in the pile all contained similar dedications. "This is humbling," said Arbella, sinking into her seat.

"Arbella, you are a beacon of hope for many of the noble English families who have been usurped by James and his Scottish interlopers. There is far more unrest than we first suspected. The king, in trying to unite the uneasy factions of English and Scots, has suggested we all be known as Britons, a proposition that has caused even more of a division. There was a fight in the Presence Chamber when a Scot struck an Englishman, but what has really caused a furore is the murder of the earl of Northumberland's page by one of the new Scottish courtiers."

Arbella stared at Bridget. "And we are stuck here, unable to act."

"For now, my lady," said Bridget, pausing in her sewing, "this is the safest place for you to be — no one can accuse you of being involved in any plots."

Two days later, Dorothy Percy came to visit Arbella.

"Arbella, my dear, these rooms are sumptuous," exclaimed Dorothy as she glided into the parlour Arbella used during the day. "You're so close to Bess and Walter — it must be most pleasant to walk together in the gardens."

"There are far worse places to be incarcerated," Arbella admitted. "Or even be forced to play childish games."

Dorothy paused in removing her elegant blue leather gloves. "You are wise to be away from the turbulence of court," she sighed. "Penelope is forced to play ludicrous games all day and wait on the queen. Anna is a pleasant woman, but she is in constant competition with James, trying to prove her court is more sophisticated than his, and there is much unrest."

"I have an area outside for my own private use," said Arbella. "Would you care to take refreshments in the sunshine?"

The two women linked arms and strolled through the large doors into a long rectangle of garden where silken awnings were strung to offer shade from the late autumn sunshine.

"It reminds me of Richmond Palace," said Dorothy, settling herself on a chair piled with brightly coloured cushions, "when you were staying with Helena and Thomas."

"How are they?" asked Arbella.

"Not well. They dislike this new regime."

"And Lizzie Brooke, how does she fare?"

"She remains at Osterley House with Lady Gertrude and is becoming close to Gertrude's son, Francis. He has been most attentive since her loss of status and the death of her husband."

Arbella tried to hide her surprise. Lizzie and George had been devoted. But, she reasoned, a woman without a husband was a burden to her family, especially one who had young children to support.

"My husband and his cousin believe she is wise to make a good match," said Dorothy. "Henry has been working closely with Francis Reed, and he has a high opinion of his scientific knowledge."

Arbella leaned closer to Dorothy. "Do you have news?" she whispered.

"Yes, the most exciting imaginable."

"Tell me."

"The Yorkshire man, Fawkes, has returned from Spain. He carried a variety of letters and messages from men at court, not all of whom were Catholics, who oppose the king and have suggested that with a small amount of military help, the new court could be overthrown. The Spanish have once again agreed to back these plans with the assurance of your complicity. There is also a new scheme to remove you from the Tower and take you to a place of safety. This way, when the battle to remove James begins, you will be far from danger and, when it is over, you will be able to ride into London in triumph once you have been declared queen."

The thrill of this idea no longer appealed to Arbella in the way it had before her capture. Yet, the idea of bringing peace and stability back to the realm she loved, which was currently splintering into unhappy factions, gave her a sense of purpose far beyond what she now viewed as her vain wish to wear the crown the previous year.

"Is Catesby still leading this plot?" she asked warily.

"He is one of many."

"Who else?

"My husband; Edward Somerset, Francis Clifford, and your uncle, Gilbert Talbot. These men are prepared to name you as monarch."

"My uncle?" Arbella stared at Dorothy.

"Yes. Your cautious, God-fearing uncle. Even he has had enough of the lewdness and extravagance of James and his court of favourites."

"And my children?"

"Ennie remains safe in Pembrokeshire."

Dorothy's sudden change of tone unnerved Arbella. "Where's Henry? Did Edmund manage to smuggle him to safety?"

"No. He was discovered at the home of Mary Arden, but do not fret, they are both safe. Henry was then placed with your uncle for a few weeks, before James insisted Henry be returned to Oliver Cromwell at Hinchingbrook House. He says it is for Henry's benefit — if he is in the household of so loyal a Protestant, he won't be corrupted by any Papist influences."

Arbella shook her head in despair at the religious references. This was an excuse, but she knew it could have been far worse. Henry could have simply disappeared. Thankfully, James had shown compassion to her son. Though she did not like Cromwell, thinking him parsimonious, he had cared for Henry well in the past and she knew her son would be safe in his care.

"James is recovering his wits a little, then, if he had the sense to send Henry back to Cambridgeshire," Arbella said. "All summer I've been receiving reports that James has been ill, raving with madness and on the brink of death. Have I been wrongly informed?"

Dorothy shook her head. "The rumours are true, Arbel, but, as we the Ladies of Melusine hid much of what happened with Queen Elizabeth from the court, James's loyal men do the same. His health is rarely discussed, but when he does appear, he looks pale and he has hardly hunted at all in the past month — a sure sign he is unwell."

"You're right," Arbella sighed. "I have heard rumours he thinks he has been cursed by a powerful witch."

Dorothy looked unsettled, then she gave a nod. "His doctors claim he is in the throes of an attack similar to those which afflict you and which struck down his mother. James believes his ailments are caused by witchcraft. His son, Prince Henry, is also beginning to show similar symptoms."

A terrible realisation seeped into Arbella's consciousness. She fixed Dorothy with her steady blue gaze. "He believes me to be the witch, doesn't he?"

Dorothy's sharp intake of breath was enough. Suddenly, her incarceration made sense. Robert Cecil had not wished to question her because he had not wanted to alert her to the real fear in the king's heart. They did not suspect another plot, as had been suggested — they were too arrogant to think such a thing could happen again — instead they were holding her here, under scrutiny, to see if she behaved in a manner conducive to being accused of witchcraft.

If James thinks I am a witch, she considered, *it is only a matter of time before he creates a reason to bring me to trial.* If the plot being led by Catesby was discovered, James would certainly suggest Arbella controlled all these men by magical forces. It was another reason to put her in the Star Chamber and make her account for her behaviour.

"So witchcraft is the root of my imprisonment," Arbella said.

"Yes," Dorothy replied. "We discovered these truths only this week. My husband and Francis Clifford attended a play at court, and James was discussing his requirements for future works. He called Will Shakespeare aside, asking if he had ever written about witches and their interference in the choosing of a monarch. Shakespeare claimed he had heard an old Scottish legend and would explore the possibility."

"Did James mention me directly?"

"No, but he was overheard speaking to Philip Herbert, suggesting the dislike of his people was not due to their lewd behaviour but due to a 'powerful sorceress spreading a pallor' over his land."

An uneasy silence grew between them. Arbella began to pace the small enclosure as she processed Dorothy's words. She had always known about the king's fear of witches. He had been famous for his persecution and burning of them in Scotland, but the English laws had stayed his hand when he had become king. Her mind flew back over the past year, the many meetings with her cousin, examining them in detail, wondering if this had always been his suspicion or whether it was a new fear brought about by the illness which they shared, the strange affliction running in their joined royal blood. The denial of a plot was easy — as long as there was nothing in her own handwriting, she could parry verbal accusations — but an accusation of witchcraft was different. Simple protestation would not be enough to save her.

With growing concern, Arbella returned to her seat. "How advanced are the plans for my escape?" she asked Dorothy.

"The tide is turning as we speak; it will be high by nightfall. Walter Raleigh has a boatman who brings him beer. When the man delivers tonight, he will take away a cargo of cotton and barley. You will be hidden among the sacks."

"And where will I go?"

"To Mary Seton."

"But my children?"

"They will be safe. It's you who is in danger. Once you are established in France, we will find a way to send the children to you." Dorothy stood, preparing to leave. "Bridget and Anne will disguise you. Edmund Shakespeare will meet you at the dock. If all goes well, you will soon be free." Her brown eyes filled with tears. "Until we meet again, my sweet Arbel, know you are our true queen."

CHAPTER FIVE

The night was dark. The moon had vanished from the sky. It was known as a witch's moon, but Arbella knew even thinking of that was a bad omen. She was clad in the rough clothes of a farm maid. Her lustrous hair had been painted with a dye made up from oak galls in order to dull its auburn hue under a shadow of darkest brown. Her pale skin had been roughened with make-up, and her slim frame had been padded to make her look as though she were with child.

She waited with a rough bag full of her belongings at her feet. The chill breeze from the wharf eddied around her, lifting the edges of her mud-brown cloak, as she hovered by the back door to the Bloody Tower. Walter Raleigh's beer delivery would arrive soon and while it was being unloaded, she would slip aboard. Edmund Shakespeare, who would accompany her, was still within the chamber but Arbella had not been able bear the confines of the stuffy room or the acrid smoke from Walter's pipe. Nerves were already making her feel queasy and inhaling the strong tobacco had made her feel worse. The door clicked and she turned, her edginess making her jump at even the most innocent noise.

"My lady, the man is moments away. Are you ready?" said Edmund, his blond curls darkened by the same gall dye as had been painted on her own.

"Yes," she replied. "Thank you for risking all to see me to safety."

Edmund smiled, his green eyes twinkling. "When you are queen, I have rather taken a fancy to an earldom," he said.

"Helping to save your life would surely be worth such an ennoblement."

Despite the seriousness of the situation, Arbella could not help but smile at his cheeky grin.

"Possibly a dukedom," she replied.

"Even better."

The splash of oars brought their conversation to a halt. A bargeman came into view and hailed Edmund, who knocked three times on Walter's door: the usual signal for deliveries. Strolling into the dark night as though nothing extraordinary was taking place, Walter and his pipe created a grey cloud against the velvet sky. Checking his hoard, Walter chatted to the boatman while the beer barrels were rolled onto the quay. Crates of cotton and barley were loaded into their place and with a nod from the boatman, Arbella stepped calmly aboard, followed by Edmund.

Sitting on the cold, damp plank that served as a seat, her rough bag at her feet, Arbella felt desperate. When would she return to her home? When would she see her children again? Reaching into the darkness, she found Edmund's hand and squeezed it, needing the comfort of another human.

The boatman was onboard; there were shouts of farewell to Walter and he raised a hand, before dropping into a deep bow. Swallowing the lump in her throat, Arbella turned for a final look at the Tower of London, then the boatman and his crew steered them through the gate and out onto the choppy waters of the River Thames.

A spectral mist felt its way towards them as the boat edged through the black water. Lights from the lanterns on other rivercrafts were blurred by the obscured air, each tiny flame hovering like a spell in mid-air.

Arbella glanced along the row of glowing dots and hoped the lights were friends rather than foes. Pulling her woollen shawl around her, she shut her eyes, pushing aside the tales she had read about the river: the sacrifices made to its watery demands, the monsters said to swim in its depths and the icy cold waves that her cousin, Charles Cavendish, had once ghoulishly told her could reach into boats and pull unsuspecting river-users to their deaths. She prayed to God, to Old Father Thames and to Isis, the female deity of the dark river, begging them for mercy, for safety and to one day be reunited with her children.

"It's not far, my lady." The boatman's voice came distantly through the mist and her fearful thoughts.

"Thank you," she replied.

"You will soon be safe, then we can rid our land of this usurper and you can return home in triumph…"

"Enough, sirrah, you forget yourself," Edmund interrupted, his voice angry, and the man gave a mumble of apology. "A French boat awaits us in the estuary," Edmund whispered to Arbella when the boatman had returned to the tiller. "Once you are aboard, it will travel to Calais where you will be met by a party of novice nuns bound for the Convent of Saint-Pierre where Lady Seton is assuming the role of Abbess. You will travel disguised as a novice with them to Reims. It will take a week."

Arbella did not reply. The events of the day continued to swirl around her mind, and she suspected the full horror of this second escape attempt would not impact upon her until it was over. At least, she hoped that would be the case. The last thing she needed now was for a bout of her wretched illness to weaken her and make it impossible for her to travel across France.

"And you Edmund?" she asked. "Where will you go?"

"Don't worry about me," he smiled. "I shall join a band of jongleurs who I know to be working the coast, then when it is safe, I shall return to London."

Around them, the calls of the other river-users crept through the mist, the muffled shouts as eerie as the cries of the dead. Arbella gripped Edmund's hand, praying fervently that they would soon be safely aboard the French bark and away from the danger of her life at court.

"This way, my lady," said the French skipper, Tassin Corvé, as they boarded the ship a short while later. "Your cabin is small, but I hope comfortable enough for our trip."

"Merci, Monsieur," replied Arbella, gazing around the tiny space, taking in the bed fitted into the wall like a cupboard. "I shall be most content."

"We shall depart within the hour."

She sank into a chair, dropping her bundle at her feet, and felt tears spring into her eyes. "Does the king truly believe I'm a witch?" she asked Edmund. His face creased with unease. "You must know — he spoke to your brother about it at great length."

"My lady, the king runs mad," Edmund replied. "You know his fear of plots and of the occult. He has been given his heart's desire, the throne of England, a country with more power and wealth than his beloved homeland of Scotland. Word has come to me that he thought his new subjects would welcome him, but he has found difficulties at every turn. Many members of the Privy Council have blocked his plans. He has been told he must limit his spending, and he doesn't understand why the populace deride and belittle him in their ballads and pamphlets, while they turn to you as their saviour."

"They do?"

"Have you not heard the ballads? They speak of your wisdom, your kindness to your tenants, your consideration and the fact you should have been queen. 'Once when I thought to have been Queen, but yet that still I do deny'," he began to sing, but Arbella hushed him.

"Edmund, no, are you insane?"

"It's a ballad called 'True Lovers Knot Untied' and is about you and William."

"No wonder the king is furious — he must think I have encouraged these rebellions."

"No, my lady. He understands that you have played no part in these uprisings, that the people do this because they would rather have you on the throne. He believed all Cecil said about the country needing a man to lead. In Queen Elizabeth's court, the men felt their power was being eroded because they could not get close to the monarch, and they decided enough was enough. But now they have a king, many are still unable to take advantage of his reign because they have been replaced by foreigners from the Scottish court. The country is a tinderbox waiting to go off, and the reason James wished to keep you hidden was to avoid giving any plotters a figurehead. That is why he spreads the rumours that you are a Catholic. He thought it would turn people against you, but, instead, it seems to have placed you more firmly in the public eye, not to mention giving the Spanish a key figure around whom to rally."

"I'm not Catholic," Arbella said.

"I know, my dear, but at this stage it doesn't matter. The people want you on the throne."

Arbella sighed. Her biggest fear while she had been in the Tower was that she would be forgotten by the people, but it seemed that had not been the case. Her name and cause had continued to be championed.

There was a lurch as the anchor was raised. Arbella heard the whip and crack of the wind as the sails filled, turning the bark towards the estuary.

A smile spread across Edmund's handsome face. "We are on our way!" he exclaimed, but Arbella could feel no joy. James saw her as a threat. Despite the confidence with which her friends had organised and asserted this plan, she could not share their belief it would go smoothly. When she was safe in Reims, she would breathe easy; until then she felt the shadows of the throne reaching towards her, gripping at her skirts, refusing to free her from the blood in her veins and the destiny she had once thought would be hers.

"I would like to rest now, Edmund," she said, and he bowed, backing from the room.

Moving to the tiny porthole, Arbella stared out at the blackness. They would travel downriver to the coast, then pull over until first light, taking the tide in the early hours. Until then, she must rest.

Throwing herself onto the narrow bunk, Arbella fell into a fitful sleep, relief only coming with the dawn when she once again felt the boat sway as they headed out to sea.

CHAPTER SIX

"To France, you say?" came King James's clipped tones. "Not Spain?"

"No, Your Highness. I believe France was her intended port, although where she might have travelled afterwards, we can't be sure."

Arbella sat in the carriage, her hands bound with cords, every inch of her body aching. The door opened and James clambered in, taking the seat opposite her. A moment later, the coach began to move.

"You led us a merry dance," said James. "Thank goodness Griffen Cockett, the captain of the *Adventure*, was in the vicinity. Did you honestly think your rag-tag plotters were a match for my navy? As soon as you failed to return to your rooms, William Waad raised the alarm." His tone was light but his eyes, boring into hers, were cold with fury.

"Am I being returned to the Tower?" Arbella asked, her tone listless. Exhaustion had muted her fear and her desire to escape. It seemed that no matter where she went, James would find her and haul her home.

"Oh no, my dear, you have too many loyal friends already housed there. You will be travelling west, to Exeter, where you will be under the guard of Sir Thomas Denys, of Holcombe Burnell."

Arbella stared at James in surprise. "The West Country?" she asked. "Why on earth would you send me there?"

"It's a very long way from court and what the courtiers do not know about, they cannot stop."

A chill of fear ran down Arbella's spine. "Will I be under house arrest with Sir Thomas Denys?"

"For a little while. Until the Bill of Attainder has been passed and I have the legal capacity to finally rid myself of you, my troublesome cousin."

"On what charge?" she asked.

"Witchcraft."

"James, you know this is nonsense. I am no more a witch than you or Anna. We are cousins. Would you really be seen to execute your cousin?"

"No one will see," he said, with a smile of satisfaction. "That is the beauty of my plan. Sir Thomas Denys and his family have experience of bonfires, of burning Protestant martyrs. They were well-known for it when our Catholic cousin, Mary Tudor, was on the throne. Sir Robert Cecil was most informative, telling me about the death of the heretic Sir Thomas Benet, the father of Margaret Benet." He paused, staring at her in fury, waiting for the significance of this comment to sink into her tired mind.

"Margaret Benet," she murmured, trying to remember where she had heard the name.

"She was a friend of Joan Bulmer's," prompted James, "and disappeared when Joan and her accomplice, Katherine Tilney, were arrested."

"They were ladies-in-waiting to Queen Catherine Howard," said Arbella, understanding flooding through her. "She also vanished around then."

"And we both know what happened to her, don't we?" sneered James. "As for those other little sluts —" Arbella flinched as spittle sprayed over her, such was the force with which James spat the word — "did you honestly think Henry would allow those women to escape? Margaret Benet was tracked to her father's house, but as she died the following day from the sweating sickness, the old king insisted her father pay the price for her sorceress ways instead. He was burned at the stake. Henry always suspected Tilney had bewitched him. Thomas Benet was burned as a punishment for his daughter's involvement in witchcraft. It seems this feminine craft follows the men of the family everywhere, but to think it's running in the veins of my cousin, the woman who tried to steal my crown. Soon, my dear cousin, you will be suffering the same fate."

"No," Arbella gasped, fear coursing through her. "James, please, reconsider. You know this is madness."

James knocked on the roof of the carriage, bringing it to a halt. "This is where we say goodbye," he said, his face white with hatred. "When you are gone, my throne and the succession of my children will finally be secure. God speed, sweet cousin." Flinging open the door, he stepped into the dazzling light of the autumn day and was gone.

Arbella stared at the pile of letters she had written. This was all she able to do now — send word to her children, to her grandmother, her aunts and uncles, her cousins and friends. Since her journey to Devon, only a select few women had been allowed to stay with her. Bridget Sherland and Anne Bradshaw were by her side, but her larger entourage had been dismissed. Most had returned to Hardwick Hall and Bess, but even the great influence wielded by her grandmother had been unable to save Arbella this time.

There had been no trial. James had passed a Bill of Attainder and it had, after much protest, been passed through the court of law. James would bear no discussion of her case, and three days earlier the date of her death had been announced to her.

Since then, she had found herself in a strange trance, writing letters to ensure her affairs were in order, wondering if her beloved William would be waiting for her at the gates of heaven.

The previous night, she had chosen not to sleep. Instead, she had sat with Bridget and Anne, talking, trying to laugh, remembering as many good things from her life as possible. When the sun had peeped over the horizon, her calm had been shattered and for the first time since she had been caught at sea by the *Adventure*, she wept. The plan had been flawed from the start, but it had been her only chance. Now she had no choice but to face the brutal truth.

"The pyre is complete," she said, staring out of the window of their comfortably appointed rooms in the home of Sir William Courtenay at Powderham Castle. The Courtenays were not in residence. Instead, the castle had been given to Sir Thomas Denys while he supervised Arbella's house arrest.

Bridget let out a sob, and Anne gripped the Bible she was reading even more tightly.

"Do you think the king will give you a last-minute reprieve as he did to the other plotters?" Anne asked.

"No, Anne, I don't," replied Arbella. "James no longer shows mercy. He has not yet realised that being given the crown is not enough to be king. The manner in which you behave towards your inferiors is what sets men and women apart. If you treat them with respect, as every person deserves, no matter what their circumstances in life, then you will be respected in return. If you treat them with contempt, then this too will be returned. I hope my cousin learns this before it's too late."

"What do you mean?"

"Catesby and his men continue," Arbella said, her voice calm. "They have heard of what my fate is to be, and they will go ahead with their plan. Their intention is still to blow up the houses of Parliament, but they will use the young Princess Elizabeth as their puppet monarch. Though I suspect they will replace her with Henry, once the truth of his lineage has been accepted by the Privy Council. Word came to me yesterday claiming that the plotters intend to light bonfires throughout the streets of London and burn effigies of James when my pyre is lit. It won't do any good, but it'll be a tribute of sorts."

Arbella's voice cracked and tears filled her eyes. With an impatient hand, she flicked them away, wanting to complete her task before the arrival of the guards. She returned to her desk and reread the letter she had been working on. This would be her final one. It was to her beloved daughter. It was filled with love, so Ennie would know her mother had not abandoned her willingly. She would understand there were sometimes higher purposes that needed to be attended to, and stopping James was one of these things.

Her letter to her son, Henry, was similar but she would not send it him to directly. It would remain in Ennie's safekeeping and when her beautiful girl felt the time was right, she would show Henry the contents of the casket and, perhaps then, he would take his rightful place as king. The two ruby rings were to be bequeathed to Ennie, while the silver locket was to be Henry's link with the past. The jewellery that had identified Catherine's children when she was parted from them would continue to create the link with her heirs.

Dropping the sealing wax onto the letter, Arbella lifted her hand to push her signet ring with William's crest into the pool of hot red wax, and then she looked at the other ring. The small golden one on her little finger. The seal of the Ladies of

Melusine. Removing it from her finger, she used this instead and smiled as the mermaid appeared.

"My dearest, Ennie," she murmured, "above all else, please remember, there will always be hope and mermaids."

The pounding on the door indicated the arrival of the guards and with her head held high, Arbella Stuart, the lost queen of England, rose to greet them, her smile in place as she prepared to step into the flames.

PART NINE: MARQUESS HOUSE, 2019

CHAPTER ONE

Tears streamed down Perdita's face. *No*, she thought, *no, not that — the worst possible ending.* As she reread it, she knew there was no denying the meaning of the final pages of the diary. Unable to sit still as the adrenalin caused by the horrific details of Arbella's end surged through her, Perdita unfolded herself from her cross-legged position on the armchair and walked into her kitchen. Pushing the door closed, she flipped on the kettle. She did not want to wake Kit, who was asleep on the sofa, having worked solidly for days with barely a break.

It had been three weeks since Izabel's disappearance and once her panic had subsided, Jenny had offered to help try and trace her. However, after sending a text assuring Jenny that she was alive and well, Izabel's phone had gone dead, her email address had stopped working and her bank account had been cleared out and closed down. At this stage, Jenny had offered to resign. Perdita and Piper had refused to accept, instead suggesting Jenny take a sabbatical with full pay until Izabel was found. Dr Deborah Black had agreed to come over from Castle Jerusalem to replace her until events had played out to their conclusion.

One of the private detectives employed by Alistair had sent images of Izabel in the French Riviera with a tall man who was several years her senior. Jenny was under the impression that Izabel had eloped with this man and had no idea of what had really happened. Alistair had identified the man as Xavier Connors, only son of Randolph Connors.

"Isn't he married?" Perdita had asked.

"Yes," Alistair had replied, raising his eyebrows in distaste, "but I imagine he's deliberately targeted and groomed Izabel in order to gain her trust and encourage her to betray us. I'm sure he sees it as a job rather than a threat to his marriage."

They had waited to see if the safehouse where Asha was supposed to be hiding would be breached by Connors. It happened within a week and when the small group of black-clad, armed men had discovered the house was a ruin, they had sped off in fury. Since then, there had been no trace of Izabel.

Three days later, a new directive from the Home Office had been issued unexpectedly, insisting upon endless legal requirements for the renewing of The Milford Haven Treaty in order to ensure everything was still valid under UN legislation. None of them believed this was a coincidence, which was why Kit and Alistair had been working around the clock to ensure they were protected by every treaty and law they could employ.

Pouring boiling water into a mug, Perdita's mind returned to the horrific final pages of the diary, considering how this version of events, should it ever be made public, would change the view of James I and the Gunpowder Plotters when another thought suddenly stuck her. "Flames. Of course," she exclaimed. "The unexplained flames in the Lennox Jewel."

Excitement pulsed through as she replaced her mug on the table and raced to her bookshelves.

Her swift movement woke Kit, who stirred and stretched. "How long have I been asleep?"

"About an hour."

"Are you OK?" he asked. "Your eyes are on fire."

"I've finished reading Arbella's diary," she said, trying to control her breathing.

"What happened to her?" Kit asked, his tone wary.

Pausing in her task, the books balanced in her arms, Perdita turned to face him. "She was burned at the stake for witchcraft."

"No," Kit gasped, horrified.

"James had trumped up charges brought against her. He issued a Bill of Attainder in September 1604 and had her executed. It was the same year he passed his famous Witchcraft Act." Perdita placed the books on the coffee table, then sat on the sofa beside Kit. "According to her diaries, Arbella was involved with the early stages of the Gunpowder Plot," she explained. "Robert Catesby was an old friend of Arbella's husband, and from what she's written, the true intention of the plot was to place her on the throne."

"History doesn't mention her being involved in the Gunpowder Plot though," said Kit.

"True," admitted Perdita, "but it does claim that on the night the plot was discovered, Londoners supposedly lit bonfires and burned effigies of Guy Fawkes. It's where the tradition of burning the guy on bonfire night came from, but I've always thought it odd because the real Fawkes wasn't burned at the stake — he was hanged, drawn and quartered on 31 January 1606."

"You think the bonfires were lit to celebrate Arbella's death?" asked Kit in surprise.

"No," said Perdita, "definitely not. When Arbella was executed, James was becoming increasingly unpopular, and, if the dates in Arbella's diary are correct, these bonfires were lit a year before the Gunpowder Plot was discovered. They were organised by a disgusted populace who were actually burning effigies of King James to show their displeasure at what he'd done to Arbella."

"The New Zealand document, the palimpsest," said Kit.

"Richard IV, as he had been styled, was Arbella's grandson and he had been issuing a posthumous pardon, but we didn't know what for; do you think it was this? He was making it clear the charges against her were false."

"Probably," said Perdita, "but even better than that, there is a famous piece of evidence to help support this theory…" Perdita began to scrabble through the pages of one of the books she had selected, opening it at a spread of images of a magnificent jewel. "But that isn't everything. I've made another connection. I need to get Piper." She reached for the phone and punched in Piper's number.

Moments later, Piper walked through the door, followed by Callum.

"Have you been checking Piper for bugs — I mean, her room for bugs again?" asked Kit, throwing Callum an amused look.

"What's happened now, Perds?" asked Piper, ignoring Kit.

"Arbella," said Perdita, and updated them on her horrific discovery.

"Do you think it's true?" asked Piper.

"Yes, and it would also explain a symbolic mystery in one of the most famous Tudor jewels in existence: the Lennox Jewel," Perdita said. "It's said to have been commissioned by Arbella Stuart's paternal grandmother, Lady Margaret Douglas, sometime around 1565, probably as a present for her husband." Perdita pushed the images of the Lennox Jewel into the centre of the rectangular coffee table they were sitting around. She pointed to the image of the top section of the jewel. "In the centre is a royal woman. She's sitting on a seat, wearing a crown, which is how we know her status: the seat represents the throne…"

"So she's a queen," said Kit.

"Yes. It shows Arbella as a queen, even though she was never crowned," agreed Perdita, "but there were many people who felt she was the true queen of England, hence the symbolism. Beside her," Perdita's voice was unsteady, "is a stake surrounded by flames, and inside the flames are roses. This image was usually translated as representing the burning of Catholic martyrs, as Lady Margaret Douglas was Catholic."

"But you think it represents Arbella being burned at the stake?" clarified Kit.

"I do now I've read the diaries," agreed Perdita. "There's the royal woman, the flames and the roses within the fire, which could be said to represent her Tudor blood. Written on a scroll above the woman's head is the motto *Gar Tel My Relaes* — cause tell my release — which has always been thought to refer to Margaret Douglas and her release from the Tower, but I now think it might be a reference to Arbella's release from the pain of the flames."

"Didn't Arbella try to escape from the Tower of London?" asked Piper. "Could it refer to that?"

"It could," said Perdita. "According to her biographies, she tried to escape from the Tower disguised as a young man, but she was captured. There's a curious line in one of Arbella's biographies stating that there were plans made for a second escape attempt, but no details remain."

"Maybe they were deliberately destroyed," suggested Callum.

"I would say it's probable," agreed Perdita, before turning back to the image. "On Arbella's other side is the two-faced winged figure of Time with cloven feet. In Renaissance culture, Time was treated as a malevolent figure, associated with the god Saturn, who in turn became identified with Satan, hence the cloven hoofs. If you consider Arbella was accused of witchcraft, the presence of this figure makes more sense because witches are supposed to consort with the devil. Time is extending his right hand to a naked female figure in a pool of water…"

"Melusine," said Kit, surprise ringing through his voice.

"Exactly," agreed Perdita. "The two scrolls beside this figure read: *Tym Gares Al Leir* — time causes all to learn — which has always been thought to be an observation on what would happen to those who persisted with their heretical ways. They fall into the jaws of hell, which you can see beneath her. But I think the hell is meant for James and what would happen to him because of his actions towards his cousin. The other thing which is interesting is the Renaissance belief in 'the naked truth', something which has always been thought to have been represented by the woman in the pool of water. Strangely, there are also parallels to the story of Susannah from the *Apocrypha*…"

"The reading at Granny and Dad's funerals," said Piper. "You read the Susannah fragment then."

"It's strange, isn't it? In the tale, Susannah was spied on by the elders of the village while she was naked and bathing."

"Could they be connected?" asked Kit. "Would your Gran have known about the Lennox Jewel?"

"She'd probably have known about the jewel, but we'll never know if she made a connection to the story of Susannah," said Perdita. "The pool of water in this jewel also has another interpretation. It's often thought to be a well, and the Tudors used wells to represent the womb. Most scholars have interpreted this to be a reference to the offspring of Margaret Douglas's womb — Lord Darnley, James's father and Charles Stuart, Arbella's father are shown as the true Catholic heirs to the throne. However, if we now conclude that this symbolism is about Arbella, perhaps it's suggesting *her* offspring are the true heirs: Henry and Ennie."

"When you explain it like this, Perds, it does make sense," said Kit.

"It irons out a lot of the confusing symbolism," Perdita replied. "In this lower section, there's also an armed warrior and his fallen foe, who are both wearing classical armour. The fallen man points to a red shield by his side and a crowned warrior holds a female figure by the hair, his sword drawn as if to slay her."

"Is that meant to depict James I dragging Arbella to the stake?" asked Callum.

"I would say it's highly likely, again tying in with the images that he is bound for hell because of his treatment of the true queen."

"Perds, I don't doubt you for a moment," said Kit, "but this jewel was said to be commissioned in 1564 — how could it possibly tell the story of Arbella Stuart's death in 1604?"

"There are no records stating where this jewel was made," said Perdita. "Experts have suggested that it could have been one of three Edinburgh goldsmiths — George Heriot, Michael Gilbert II or James Gray. However, this jewel, like the Marquess House jewels, vanished from sight after 1616. Remember, in official records, Arbella was supposed to have died in 1615, even though we now know this isn't the case, but it's curious it was around then that the Lennox Jewel also disappeared from view."

"It is a bit odd," agreed Piper.

"The next time the Lennox Jewel appears in official records is when it was purchased by Queen Victoria in 1843 from the dealer Farrar of Wardour Street. He'd bought it from the sale of the house, Strawberry Hill, the home of Horace Walpole,

4th earl of Orford. The jewel was listed among the queen's private jewellery collection following her death in 1901 and, as far as I know, it remains part of the royal collection today. There was more than enough time for these images to have been added at a later, unspecified date, leaving a new secret at the heart of the jewel."

"It was a Lennox family heirloom though," said Callum, "not a Stuart jewel."

"Arbella should have inherited the Lennox title and lands from her father, but instead they were passed first to her paternal great-uncle, the childless bishop of Caithness, then a deal was struck handing the earldom to another of James's cousins, Esmé Stuart, Lord D'Aubigny."

"So, on the strength of this jewel, you believe the things written in Arbella's diaries are true and that she was burned at the stake?" asked Piper.

"I don't want to, but these images have always been difficult to interpret, yet now they make sense," replied Perdita. "I also think the horrific death of Arbella might have been what drove Henry Fitzalan, or Oliver Cromwell as we know him, to seize power from his Stuart cousins. Not only had they murdered his mother in the cruellest manner possible, they had denied him his birthright."

"It's a brilliant theory, Perds, but how would we prove it?" asked Piper.

Perdita's eyes were shining with excitement. "Two ruby rings, one silver locket set with a perfect diamond — separately they mean nothing, but together, they are the key to the biggest secret in history."

"You've worked it out, haven't you?" said Kit, his eyes never leaving her face. "You were about to tell Dad when Jenny burst into the office."

"Penelope showed me the way," Perdita said, "but before I reveal everything I need a favour, Pipes. How are you at fitting gemstones?"

"What do you need me to do?" asked Piper.

Perdita edged past her sister and headed for the ancient mermaid tapestry in the corner of the room. Swinging it forward, she keyed in the combination, then removed the leather jewellery case containing the Tudor rings and the silver locket. Holding the leather box in one hand, Perdita reached further inside and removed a square red ring box. "It's the locket," she said, returning to the others. "For the mechanism to work, I think it needs to have a diamond in the centre."

"What do you mean, 'for the mechanism to work'?" demanded Piper. "What have you done?"

Perdita went pink as all three of them stared at her. "I had a theory about the jewellery, and a few nights ago, when I couldn't sleep…"

"What did you do, Perds?" repeated Piper.

"I decided to follow the trail left by Penelope Fitzalan in *The Llyn Cel Mermaid* in order to discover the hiding place for the missing casket, the one containing all the confessions."

"You said it was unlikely to have survived," said Kit.

"My first theory was that it would have been destroyed," she agreed, "but the further down this road we've travelled, the more I've begun to think I was wrong in such an assumption and it had actually survived. If it has, then I had an idea about its hiding place, thanks to Penelope Fitzalan pointing the way. She was here throughout the Civil War, she's a cousin of the Stuarts, we can place her at court after her mother's death and we know she was bequeathed Marquess House. I'm certain she's The Scribe, and the casket, if it's where I think it might be, will prove everything we've discovered is true, beyond all reasonable doubt. One of the few things we know about MI1 Elite is the fact they believe the three missing pieces of jewellery are the key to this entire mystery. Key being the operative word."

"Explain, Perds," said Kit.

Perdita turned to look at him. "When we were discussing this with your parents, I explained that Penelope, as The Scribe, had left a series of clues across the face of history and, if you remember, she wrote a cache of letters saying there was something in Marquess House she was prepared to die to protect. It was in the correspondence sewn onto the reverse of her portrait, and we thought she meant Catherine Howard. To a certain extent she did, but I've realised this wasn't the only secret. I think she was referring to the casket, the one given to Elizabeth I by Anne of Cleves when she knew she was dying, which was then passed on to Arbella."

"Why though, Perds?" asked Piper.

"There are clues throughout the book of legends and, a few nights ago, I realised that she left proof somewhere else too. It was something else she left hidden in plain sight, like she did with her brother."

"What are you talking about?"

"It's in the windows, Piper — she left an image behind, and once you've seen it you'll be amazed that we've all missed it for so long."

"The windows? What windows?"

"In the library — the five women in the stained-glass windows. In the first alcove is Anne Boleyn, shown as the goddess of rainbows, Iris. Her image appears in Elizabeth I's ruby ring, the one originally created for Anne of Cleves and bearing the inscription *Iuncta Sanguine*. It had the emerald clip, something which is drawn into the lid of the wooden box which had housed it for centuries.

"Catherine Howard is next, depicted as Demeter, the goddess of corn and fertility. Catherine gave birth to twins and, although we are the only people who know it, she was the real mother of Mary, Queen of Scots. Mary was sent to Scotland with her mother's ruby ring. Mary is the next image, painted as Persephone, who is Demeter's daughter, and her Tudor half-sister, Elizabeth I, follows, portrayed as Atalanta, the Virgin Huntress. And finally, we have…"

"Arbella Stuart," said Piper.

"Yes. She's represented as Pandora, the first woman," continued Perdita. "Rather like Eve, Pandora was lured by temptation and opened a box full of the furies of the world, releasing hate, malice, lust and all the other evils."

"A box full of danger," said Kit, his voice low.

"But, also hope," added Perdita. "Trapped in Pandora's Box with all the terrible evils of the world was Hope, and that was released too. Hope in the fifth window is a mermaid."

"Hope and mermaids," whispered Piper. "*Spe et nereidum*. It's all over the place — on Catherine's grave, on the walls, in the letters from the Ladies of Melusine and on the locket."

"According to the diaries," Perdita continued, "Elizabeth left Arbella the casket containing all the confessions proving the truth about Catherine and her children. I was looking at the Tudor graffiti again and as the sun began to set behind the windows, they seemed to glow. It was then I realised what was behind Arbella in her image."

"What?" asked Kit.

"A small version of the stained-glass window from the Tudor Hall. Its image is painted behind Arbella. Penelope refers to it in her book of legends."

"No, she doesn't," Kit contradicted her. "I've been reading the legends again in case it would be helpful to you in your research, and she makes no mention of the stained-glass window."

Perdita stared at him in surprise. "Thank you, Kit," she said. "It is there but it's disguised, like everything else Penelope left behind."

"Where is it then?" asked Kit.

"Penelope wrote a series of clues in her book. The collection of tales leads the way to the box and gives an outline of the things Penelope, as The Scribe, changed. Some of the titles from the stories are: 'Passage to Monacha' — which is Latin for nun — I think it's about our tunnel; there's 'The Women of Glass'…"

"The stained glass windows?" asked Callum.

Perdita nodded. "Then there's 'The Lost Prince.'"

"About a forgotten Welsh prince, no doubt," said Piper.

"Yes," said Perdita, "not to mention 'The Clockwork Window'."

"More clockwork, like the mechanism in the mermaid cup that we know belonged to Penelope," said Piper.

"Exactly," said Perdita, "and underneath the title of each story Penelope wrote a line of poetry, only it isn't simply a pretty series of words; if you read the lines together, they become instructions." Perdita rummaged around in her computer bag and produced a typed sheet of paper. She began to read:

"*Carved from wood, it reflects the glass*
From the lady who was forgotten.
No rose, no thorn, the circular path
Leads back to the beginning, to the day I was born
Turn red to the left, turn red to the right

Let the silver light shine in the heart
The world will turn and the sea maids will swim
All the secrets we have kept are stored within."

"What does it mean?" asked Piper.

"It's the wooden carving that is the replica of the oriel window opposite it in the Tudor Hall," said Perdita. "And the fact this image appears behind both Penelope in the original painting and her mother, Arbella, in the stained-glass window, makes me even more certain."

"Sorry, Perds, but how did you get to that from this poem?" asked Kit, reading it again.

"'Carved from wood, it reflects the glass'," read Perdita. "The panel opposite the window is a direct carved copy of the patterns in the stained-glass window."

"Yes, I see that," Kit said.

"'From the lady who was forgotten'. Did you know that another name for an oriel window is a Catherine window?" asked Perdita. "This is reinforced by the next line, 'No rose, no thorn…'"

"She was Henry VIII's 'rose without a thorn'," said Piper.

"What's the next bit though?" asked Callum. "'The circular path / Leads back to the beginning, to the day I was born'?"

"Penelope Fitzalan was born in 1595. That date is carved at the top of the frieze — it's the only difference between the window and the frieze."

"'Turn red to the left, turn red to the right'," read Piper, then she stared at Perdita, excitement in her green eyes. "This is the lid of the box — the one the rings were in. There were arrows pointing to the left and right, and the locket was the curve at the bottom. 'Let the silver light shine in the heart'."

"And the last two lines?" asked Kit. "'The world will turn and the sea maids will swim / All the secrets we have kept are stored within'?"

"Ennie's letter to her cousin. She refers to the 'Blessed Child', which we know was a codename for Catherine Howard, and she says, 'her secret will only be told when the mermaids meet in the Tudor Hall and the lock opens'. I think the last two lines are an echo of this sentence. When the door mechanism is activated, the mermaids swim and all the documents gathered by those at the heart of the secret will be discovered in the casket."

There was a long pause, then Kit spoke. "Do you know how to unlock this frieze?" he asked.

Perdita grinned when she saw the fire in his eyes. "I have an idea," she replied, "but that's why I think we need a diamond. A few nights ago, I took the jewellery down to the frieze and there are three indentations that match perfectly to the drawings in the lid of the box, as well as replicating the three-ringed symbol used throughout the house. The rings fit in the top two and the locket in the bottom. The two rings turned as they were meant to, but the locket wouldn't fit properly, and I think it's because it's missing the diamond. The stone would have sat at the front, and I wonder if that point is needed to make a connection somewhere."

"Or it could be that the mechanism has seized up after all this time," said Callum.

"True," agreed Perdita, "but don't you think it's worth another try? I'm certain that if it still exists, the box is hidden behind the frieze."

"And, if it is there, how will we open it?" asked Callum. "Do you want me to fetch a crowbar?"

"Hopefully not," said Perdita. "Arbella's diaries give very clear instructions that there are three golden keys needed to open the locks…"

"The keys in the stem of the mermaid cup," gasped Piper. "They must have been the keys for the chest, and the jewellery opens the door to its hiding place. Let me have a look at the locket, Perds."

Perdita passed the jewellery box to her sister. Piper examined the locket before picking up the red leather ring box and removing the solitaire engagement ring Warren had given Perdita, examining the stone through Perdita's jewellery loupe.

"It's good to know Warren's ring has proved useful," muttered Kit.

"I never met the bloke," murmured Callum in reply, "but that's an impressive ring. You've got a lot to live up to, mate. Better start saving your pocket money."

Perdita chose to ignore Callum and avoided looking at Kit's unexpectedly flushed face.

It took Piper half an hour in her studio to be satisfied with the fit of the diamond in the locket. "It isn't perfect," she said, "but taking into account the small dents in the silver and without being able to trim the stone, which I have neither the tools nor the expertise to do, this is the closest we're going to get."

Perdita stared down at it and felt her chest tighten. The locket lay smooth and sleek in its case, the fiery heart of the diamond catching the light and making the silver glow. "This is how it might have looked when Lady Isabel Baynton gave it to Catherine Howard," she said. "It's remarkable."

Piper disappeared into her storeroom and reappeared with the three replica keys from the golden cup. "Come on," she said. "Let's go and test your theory."

They made their way through Marquess House, up the narrow wooden staircase leading to the Minstrel's Gallery, which ran along one wall above the Tudor Hall. Coming to a halt, Perdita stared across the void towards the oriel window.

"Look, the Latin mottos from the jewellery are all around the edge," Kit said, reading each one aloud. "*Semper Sorores, Iuncta Sanguine* and *Spe et Nereidum*. I've read the stories, Perds — which one made you certain this was the spot?"

"'The Clockwork Window'," she replied. "It's the tale of a mouse whose house is ruined when someone places a wooden chest on top of it. Then the figure of Hope appears and leads him to a new and better home. The description of the panel the mouse lives behind is carved with magical mermaids, and the mouse 'hears' keys being placed at certain points in the panel. When these are turned, they release the clockwork mechanism above his head and the lock opens."

"Perds, you're amazing," sighed Piper.

"Thanks, Pipes," replied Perdita, "but keep your praise until we've found the box."

Perdita moved closer to the carving and, after running her fingers over it for a few moments, she grinned. "Look here." She moved aside so the others could peer at the oval indentations. "And there's one opposite and down here, a circular inset. It's the three-ringed symbol."

"How do we know which ring fits which space?" asked Piper.

Perdita pointed again. Set below each indentation were small circles of glass: one was emerald green and the other sapphire blue. She took Anne of Cleves' ring, with its emerald clip and

Catherine Howard's ring, with its sapphire clip and placed them in the two higher carved beds. Then she placed the locket below them. There was a small, satisfying click as it slotted into place. The twins grinned at each other.

"The locket wouldn't stay in place before," Perdita said. "The diamond has made all the difference."

"Together?" asked Piper, her voice little more than a whisper.

"Yes, on three?"

Piper nodded. They clasped hands and Perdita whispered, "One, two, three…"

Perdita shut her eyes as she turned Catherine's ring. When she opened them again, she thought nothing had happened, then she looked more closely and realised the panel around the jewels had moved forward, causing the mermaids at its edge to join with those beside them, making it look as though they were swimming.

Dropping Piper's hand, she teased her fingers into the crack around the edges of the circular door and eased it forward. Behind her, she heard a click and the beam of Kit's torch illuminated the secret chamber within, making them all gasp. Bracing herself, Perdita lifted up the ornately carved wooden casket and brought it out into the light. The detail in the age-blackened oak wood was astonishing. There was the three-ringed symbol, the mermaid, various lilies and daisies, and in every corner there was a delicate variation on the Tudor rose.

Piper slid the three replica keys into the locks running along the front.

Perdita took a deep breath to steady her voice and repeated the words of Lady Katherine Newton: "You must turn the centre key first, then the remaining two will turn together and the lock will release."

Perdita saw her sister's fingers were trembling as she turned the keys. The lock clicked and, as the catch released, Marquess House gave up its final secret.

Pandora's Box was open at last.

CHAPTER TWO

Perdita carried the Tudor casket back to her suite and, after locking all the doors, cleared a space on the floor. The others gathered around her as she unpacked the stack of documents within.

The seals were intact on each one. When she opened a long document signed by Elizabeth I, Perdita was not sure whether to cry or cheer. Piper was equally ecstatic when she found intricate hand-drawn plans and designs for the mermaid cup.

In the casket was a lengthy confession written by Penelope Fitzalan. Perdita was staggered by the horrors Penelope had endured under her brother's reign and after Charles II's restoration to the throne. Tears coursed down her face as she read that Penelope, although in her mid-60s by the time Charles became king, had been arrested and thrown in the Bethlem Hospital in London, the notorious lunatic asylum known as Bedlam. It was Charles who had released her and explained her only other option was to do as he wished and rewrite history.

"Are you OK, Perds?" Kit asked.

Perdita wiped her eyes with the back of her hand. "Penelope's story is so sad," she said. "It's made me quite emotional." She steadied herself and told the others of her fate.

After they had all absorbed the information and looked through the other documents, Perdita said, "Now we know what's inside, I think we need to replace everything as it was, then tomorrow we can make a proper plan. These will need to be transcribed, authenticated and carbon dated. The last thing we want to do is to compromise them with accidental contamination which might leave their validity open to questioning."

It was 3am by the time they finished painstakingly replacing the ancient documents inside the chest. Piper handed the golden keys to Perdita. "Keep everything together," she said.

They returned the casket to its hiding place.

The next morning, they informed Alistair of their incredible discovery.

"The four of you were creeping around, opening secret doors…" he exploded, his voice cold with anger.

"We're not children, Alistair," Piper fired back. "We own Marquess House, and what we choose to do within it is no-one else's business. Somehow, I can't imagine you berating Granny in this manner."

The air crackled between them before Alistair, having taken a deep breath, said in the calmest tone he could muster, "My apologies."

"Apology accepted," Piper snapped in reply.

"Alistair, we need to protect this casket and its contents," Perdita interjected, trying to ease the tension. "When Deborah arrives from Andorra, she can assess it and advise us the best way to proceed."

"Where is it now?" Alistair asked.

"Back where we found it," Perdita replied. "It's been hidden there safely for over 300 years — we thought a few more days in the dark wouldn't do it any harm."

"Very well," said Alistair. "It would be safer if you didn't reveal the method of how you access it to anyone else, not even me."

"If you're sure," Perdita said, exchanging an uncomfortable look with Piper. "We can show you where it is and how to access it, Alistair. We don't mind."

"For once, Perdita, I feel it would be better if I didn't know. My dears, you didn't know us until last year, but I have known you all your lives and it's proving difficult for me to stop protecting you as though you are still children. My rule as Lord Chamberlain was with Mary as my monarch — it's Kit who has that privilege now."

"Dad, I don't want your job," Kit laughed.

"Maybe not, but it will be yours one day."

The next morning Deborah Black arrived, and Perdita showed her the cache of papers they had discovered.

"These are remarkable!" Deborah gasped.

"Even more astonishing is the list of people who have contributed to the casket," Perdita said. "Anne of Cleves, Thomas Howard, Lady Margaret Douglas, Lady Isabel Baynton, Queen Elizabeth I, Lettice Knollys, Arbella Stuart. I suspect when we've finished reading them, they'll corroborate our version of events and, hopefully, fill in some of the details we've missed."

"I concur," Deborah replied. "You do realise the vast amount of work we have ahead of us to transcribe, authenticate and catalogue this collection?"

"Yes," Perdita responded. "Mark, our chief conservator, has been putting together a dedicated team who can focus on this for as long as it takes. We have to choose carefully, because each person will have to be given the highest security clearance and will have to agree to signing a non-disclosure agreement. Alistair even considered The Official Secrets Act, but in order to obtain permission for that we would have to reveal our find to the Home Office, and we don't think it's appropriate at the moment."

Deborah frowned. "We will have to be very careful," she agreed. "These documents are a potential threat to national security. I think our first task should be to replicate them. It would be a disaster if anything were to happen to them before we could reveal their secrets."

Perdita felt a cold shiver run down her spine at the possibility. "I had the same thought," she said. "Mark will be here in a moment to help you with scanning and photography. They'll be stored in a database to which only you, me, Piper and Mark will have access. When we have our task force, they'll all work on individual sections but not entire documents, so no one will know the full extent of what we've discovered."

"It's quite a responsibility, isn't it?" said Deborah, but her eyes sparkled with excitement. "Perdita, this is the discovery of a lifetime."

"My emotions are veering between ecstasy and terror at the moment," Perdita admitted. "Last night I lay awake worrying that these could be forgeries."

"Working with Jerusalem, I've examined many forgeries," said Deborah with a reassuring smile, "but even with only a cursory glance at these, I'm certain they're genuine. Firstly, because there are so many of them — no forger would go to this much trouble, and, secondly, because of the detail on the seals, not to mention the varying ages of the parchment. These are genuine, Perdita; I'd stake my reputation on it. Anyway, have you seen this?"

Perdita leaned closer.

"There is a series of family trees here and they're fascinating," Deborah continued, "as well as being works of art. The detail within them suggests they're genuine — they give days, as well as dates, the weather at certain portentous births, and lists of christening gifts. If someone had forged these, I doubt they would have gone to such trouble. These were someone's passion, and the information in them is astonishing."

Perdita led Deborah to the corner of the room where a series of pages had been spread side by side. Images of mythical creatures edged each page and spread between these were detailed genealogies of Tudor families.

"Arbella constantly refers to the mingling of families and their family trees in her diaries," Perdita said. "There are fragments of genealogies throughout, as well as a few on the final pages."

"They must have been continued by someone else," said Deborah. "The final date on this one is Frances Marriotte Carey, who married Robert Williams in 1654. From the looks of the tree, they were second cousins."

Perdita leaned forward to examine the swirling handwriting. Her eyes travelled up the delicately inked link. "Frances Carey was the daughter of Alice Seymour and Eusebius Marriotte Carey — do you think he was part of the Carey family? The offspring of Mary Boleyn?"

"It's possible," said Deborah, "and Robert Williams was descended from…" She paused. "No, that can't be right."

"Yes," said Perdita, reading the names, "it is. I wanted to show you these so you could start planning the practical side of the archiving, but we've made some very startling discoveries concerning Oliver Cromwell."

Deborah turned to Perdita, her face wreathed in confusion. "This is correct," said Deborah, pointing to the names at the top. "Oliver Cromwell is recorded as marrying Elizabeth

Bourchier, but they had nine children and only one is recorded here, the eldest son, Richard, who did marry Dorothy Maijor, as this family tree states. Then his son, Robert, changes his surname to Williams and he marries Frances Carey, who according to this is the granddaughter of the mysterious Penelope Fitzalan."

"Who is the unknown daughter of Arbella Stuart," said Perdita.

Deborah looked startled. "I need to read my briefing notes before I begin trying to unravel this," she said. "We'll stick to copying and cataloguing first so we have records of every single document, then I'll get up to speed with your newest discoveries. I thought our revelation about Elizabeth I was the most unexpected thing we would find. Obviously, I was wrong."

Deborah moved away to retrieve her notes, leaving Perdita reading the names on the family tree. With a jolt, Perdita realised she was staring down at a family tree fragment featuring Penelope Fitzalan, and with her heart pounding, she bent down to read the tiny writing. Next to Penelope's name was written: *21 February 1595* — but, frustratingly, there was no record of her death — then her eyes moved to the name of Penelope's husband and she grinned in delight: William Seymour, 2nd Duke of Somerset and Marquess of Hertford. She had been correct — Seymour had been Penelope's husband, not Arbella's.

Searching for more information, Perdita was so engrossed in the family trees that the click of the door as Mark and Kit entered made her jump. The information about Penelope was fascinating, but Perdita had seen another name. "Murfyn," she murmured, her eyes roving over the twisted branches of the family trees. "Where have I read it?" Closing her eyes, she visualised the pages towards the end of Arbella's diaries. The surname, Murfyn, had been underlined. "Of course," she said aloud, drawing Kit's attention.

"I know that look," he said. "What have you found now?"

Perdita beckoned Kit to her side as she returned to the genealogies spread across the desk.

"Remember what I said about Arbella's son, Henry, and how as a child after his mother's death he was returned to Hinchingbrooke House under the care of the senior and real Oliver Cromwell?"

"Yes. We still haven't fathomed why The Scribe chose to eviscerate the Cromwell name through the pages of history."

"I wonder if some of the inspiration could have come from the connection between the Murfyn and Denys families. It was Sir Thomas Denys who was Arbella's executioner." Perdita pointed to the name. "His second wife was Elizabeth Donne, who was the widow of Sir Thomas Murfyn."

Kit followed Perdita's finger as it hovered above the ancient parchment. "With you so far, Perds."

"Sir Thomas Murfyn was the father of Lady Frances Murfyn, who was the grandmother of the Oliver Cromwell who was resident at Hinchingbrooke House and guardian of young Henry, Arbella's son."

Kit absorbed this information. "It's tenuous," he said.

"True," agreed Perdita, "but we only have this on paper — who knows what personalities these people had, what spite was handed out. Clearly something happened. Perhaps Ennie was enacting some private piece of revenge."

They stared down at the ancient document for a moment, then Kit said, "I'm actually here as a messenger. Olaf is leaping about your office in the research centre. Piper's trying to contain him, but your desk might be matchwood if you don't get over there soon. I've never seen him so ebullient."

Calling a farewell to Deborah, who was deeply engrossed in conversation with Mark, Perdita and Kit headed back to the main research centre.

"Perdita, at last!" Olaf exclaimed when they entered her office.

"Is there good news?" Perdita asked, sitting behind her desk.

"We should be able to raise the figurehead tomorrow!"

"How exciting!" she replied, catching his enthusiasm.

Olaf beamed. "I wondered if any of you would like to be there when she breasts the waves for the first time in four hundred years?"

There were general murmurs of agreement, then Olaf hurried over to his briefcase and pulled out some bound notes. "This is the further work we've been doing on the ship, following up on the information you provided a few months ago, Perds. I wasn't able to find a ship called *The Arbella* in this area, although the name of the ship owned by Peter Holland had been redacted and I wondered if it could be our wreck. But it wasn't. Holland was working out of Dale until 1605, so his tenure is far short of the year we think our ship set sail."

"What year do you estimate, Olaf?" asked Piper.

"It was sometime between 1662 and 1666. And we have located a ship operating around this time that was called *The Arbella*. During Charles I's reign, with the religious and political climate so unstable, many Puritans decided to emigrate and create a new world in the Americas where they could worship as they chose. *The Mayflower* is the most famous of the pilgrim ships but in 1630, another wave of Puritans left for the New World in the Winthrop Fleet. There were eleven vessels and they were led by the flagship, *The Arbella*."

Perdita gasped. "What happened to *The Arbella*? Is it our wreck?"

"This is the exciting part," said Olaf, bouncing up and down on the balls of his feet. "Migration continued steadily until Charles I was beheaded and life changed in Britain. As the Protectorate began, many pilgrims decided to return to help them fight and *The Arbella* is listed as returning to Southampton."

"Olaf, this is incredible," said Perdita. "What happened to her next?"

"She remained in British tidal waters for the next few years, then she changed hands a number of times. There is a document stating she was to be part of the first Bristol Virginian Fleet which was to set sail in 1662, two years after the restoration of Charles II as monarch, but there was a curious addendum in the shipping logs stating that *The Arbella* was to collect a passenger from Dale and would then meet the rest of the fleet en route. However, *The Arbella* was not at the rendezvous and despite waiting for an hour, there was no sign of the vessel, so the fleet sailed without her."

"So this must be our wreck?" said Piper in astonishment.

"We believe it is, but what we don't understand is why the ship looks as though it was deliberately sunk. There are three cannonball holes in the hull, but it clearly wasn't a pirate attack because there were a number of valuables on board and also there were no skeletons. *The Arbella* was sunk without hands but with all cargo. It's a conundrum."

"Do the records show who owned *The Arbella* when she was sunk?" asked Perdita.

"Yes." Olaf searched through the last few pages of the document. "Here it is. The ship is listed as being owned by Penelope Seymour, Marchioness of Hertford. Though we haven't been able to trace her. No doubt we'll find her eventually."

Perdita stared at Olaf. He had no idea of the bombshell he had dropped. She forced a smile to her face. "I'm sure you will, Olaf," she said. "What time would you like us tomorrow?"

"The tides are awkward, so it'll be an early start — 7am at Dale. Now, I must dash. There is much to organise."

Later that day, Perdita and Piper were in the Lady Isabel room, sitting either end of one of the wide window seats, watching out for the arrival of Lady Pamela Johnson. The morning after Izabel's disappearance, Alistair had asked if they felt it would be appropriate to invite Lady Pamela to stay so that she would be included in the protection of The Marquess House Treaty. Piper and Perdita had agreed. They had a tidal wave of questions about their mother and grandmother which they felt, as one of their grandmother's oldest friends, Pamela would be able to answer.

A throaty roar filled the air, and they looked outside to see a black Bentley Continental GT Coupé pulling up outside the house.

"Is that her?" said Piper, not bothering to hide the astonishment in her voice as the gleaming car sent up a spray of gravel.

"I hope so!" exclaimed Perdita. "Alistair did say she was quite remarkable."

They watched as a small woman of five foot climbed out of the enormous car. Her short, snow-white hair gleamed in the sunshine and Perdita was unsure whether the colour was natural or the result of an expensive and fashionable salon. She wore tailored black trousers, flat pointed shoes and a flowing red merino-wool bat-winged jumper. A black patent handbag hung from her arm and large sunglasses covered her face as she stood gazing at the façade of Marquess House.

Flinging open the vast double doors, Perdita and Piper paused on the threshold and Pamela turned to look at them. Removing her sunglasses, they saw she had brilliant blue eyes. Her smile was wide as she walked eagerly towards them.

"Oh, my dear girls," she said, and opened her arms. Perdita and Piper walked into Pamela's hug as though they had been doing it all their lives. "You are startling," she said, after she had released them and they had introduced themselves. "Perdita, you are the image of your mother, and you —" Pamela turned to Piper, taking her hand and squeezing it — "I thought for a moment you were Mary come back to life."

"Really?" croaked Piper.

"You have her hair, Piper. You're taller than Mary, but you are so like her when she was your age…"

"Pamela!" came Alistair's voice, and they were overwhelmed by people hurrying forward to greet their visitor.

Pamela stood in the Tudor Hall, staring around with such intensity Perdita felt it was as though she was taking a mental inventory, searching for changes, looking for unexpected additions. "You've moved the Rossetti," she said, pointing to a wall where a portrait of Mary by Lucien Freud now hung.

"It's on loan to the Victoria and Albert Museum," replied Piper, who now curated the art collection.

"As long as it hasn't been sold," she said, with a twinkle in her eye.

Once Pamela had been installed in her room, she asked Perdita and Piper if they would walk around the house and gardens with her.

"I'd like to give Mary some flowers," she said, indicating the large bunch of freesias Billy had carried in from the car.

384

"It would also be a wonderful opportunity for us to get to know one another properly," she said with a smile. "Do you have more questions about my archive, Perdita?"

"Not right at the moment," Perdita replied, "but I have some new documents to examine, and then you might be able to offer some guidance."

"I look forward to it!"

Perdita was in the library when Pamela entered.

"Hello, my dear," she said, as Perdita looked up from the long document she was poring over and smiled, "you're as dedicated as Mary. When she was on the hunt for something, she never stopped working either."

Perdita was examining her family tree in the library. Until now, she had never thought to check it, but with Arbella's continuous references to the sinuous links between families in the Tudor era, she had been intrigued to see how far back her own roots had been traced.

"It's not really research," she said to Pamela. "It's our family tree."

The family tree was in several rolls, and Perdita had chosen the long table down the centre of the square seating area in the entrance of the library to unravel it. Beginning with herself and Piper, she had been startled to see Piper's marriage to Jeremy had been noted, and also the date of Jeremy's death. She wondered if this was another task that came under the auspices of Jenny and her library team.

Pamela paused. "The family tree?"

"Yes, this is the first time I've thought to look at it — more for personal interest than anything to do with research."

Pamela joined Perdita and began reading the names. "Mary," she said, pointing to her friend's name, "and Cecily."

"Did you know Cecily Fitzroy?" asked Perdita.

"We were at school together," Pamela said. "I met Mary through Cecily and we were all friends. Then Cecily died." Her voice petered out as she became lost in her memories.

"I'm sorry," said Perdita. "This has upset you."

"Not at all, my dear," Pamela said, leaning over the extensive diagram. "Let's look at it together. There's your mother, Louisa, and Mary."

Perdita followed Pamela's finger and, to her surprise, saw the names of two other children were listed alongside her mother, neither of whom had lived for more than a day. Perdita felt tears spring to her eyes. "Mum had two brothers," she said.

Pamela squeezed Perdita's hand. "Mary had difficulty carrying a pregnancy to term," said Pamela. "The two little boys were both born prematurely and were too small to survive. After Louisa, your grandmother had complications and was forced to have a hysterectomy to save her life. It's why Louisa was so very precious."

"Oh, that's so sad," said Perdita. "Poor Granny and poor Mum."

The next few names were Perdita's great-grandparents, Eleanor Cecil and David Fitzroy, followed by Margaret Lakeby and Peter Cecil, then the familiar names from the tapestry: Laeticia and her twin sister, Seraphina, then their parents: Honora Fitzpatrick and John Hawkland. The last entry on the first roll was Arabella Talbot, who was born in 1716.

"Did you know Arabella Talbot wrote the first history of Marquess House?" said Pamela.

"I did. When I began my research here, I read it," said Perdita. "It's quite dated and it doesn't mention the tunnel…"

"You know about the tunnel?" exclaimed Pamela.

"Yes, Kit and I discovered it last year. Thank goodness we did — it saved our lives. Granny had left instructions for me to find."

For a moment, a look of petulance flashed across Pamela's face, then it was gone, replaced with a wry laugh. "You're the lucky one. She would never tell Cecily or me where the entrance was, although we suspected it was in the chapel."

"As the new owner of Marquess House and considering your long friendship with Granny, would you like me to show you the tunnel while you're staying?"

Pamela gave her a look of delight. "I would like that very much; we could take Piper too and have an adventure."

Perdita grinned.

"Is there any more of the family tree?" asked Pamela. "I'd like to see how you fit into the Tudor era."

Her excitement growing, Perdita returned to the leather case which housed the vast document, but as she reached for the final roll, she realised it was missing. Instead there was a note: *Scroll three: borrowed by Izabel Barnes*. The date was the day before she had vanished.

"Oh no!" Perdita exclaimed. She felt her fury towards Izabel rising again. This document was personal, and she suspected it was now in the possession of Randolph Connors.

"Perhaps there's another copy somewhere," suggested Pamela.

"I'll check with one of the library staff tomorrow," replied Perdita, but she was struggling to contain her irritation. After a few more minutes of staring at the document, she realised she would discover nothing else new this evening and carefully returned the family tree to its protective leather box.

Pamela had wandered away to peruse the bookshelves. Perdita turned to her and smiled, "It's late, I'm going to bed."

"When I've selected a book, I'll join you."

Perdita waited while Pamela chose from the selection on the bookcase near the armchairs. These were updated every week, ensuring the most recent publications were always on hand.

"A new biography of Aphra Behn," said Pamela, picking up the glossy new hardback. "I find her fascinating. Young Eaffrey Johnson. A woman born out of her time."

Perdita started when she heard the name. "Eaffrey Johnson?" she said. "It was Aphra Behn's birth name, wasn't it?"

"Yes, I've always secretly hoped she might be my many-times great grandmother."

"Maybe she was," replied Perdita, forcing a smile onto her face as her mind began to race. "Goodnight."

When Pamela had turned off towards her suite in the Victorian wing, Perdita ran up the stairs to her own apartment. Crashing through the door, she grabbed her laptop, knocking a book onto the floor with a thud. Ignoring it, she opened the Lady Pamela database and began checking the letter addressed to "My dear Eaffrey", reading it with care as she fitted in the final facts. The door joining to Mary's suite opened and Piper peered in.

"Are you OK, Perds?" she asked. "I heard a bang."

"What? Oh, yes, I dropped a book."

"What's up? Have you discovered something else?"

"I think I know what happened to Ennie," said Perdita, her voice full of excitement as Piper joined her on the sofa.

"How?"

"The family tree we discovered in the casket claims she married Edward Seymour, making her titles Lady Seymour, the Countess of Somerset and the Marchioness of Hertford, but we don't know how her story ended, only that she was planning to set sail on *The Arbella*."

"Even though the ship was deliberately sunk," said Piper.

"I know, but in the Lady Pamela collection, there is a letter signed by the Marchioness of Hertford — who I now realise is Ennie — addressed to 'My Dear Eaffrey' — who I think was Aphra Behn — and it states the Marchioness and her companion Anna had escaped after their race across the field and were in the 'Orange land', which I've checked, and it was a codeword from the Ladies of Melusine referring to the Netherlands. There's also a letter to Katherine Philips of Tenby stating that 'Lady Somerset and her companion, Anna, were due to leave on a vessel owned by her ladyship'…"

"*The Arbella?*"

Perdita nodded and continued, "This letter states Lady Somerset planned to meet Anastasia Howard, the daughter of Lady Alethea Howard in the Netherlands. Lady Alethea Howard was Arbella Stuart's cousin. I think this was the cousin Ennie was writing to in the letter about her brother's violent behaviour and how she hoped to stop him. It was dated March 1649, two months after Charles I was executed and Henry Fitzalan — who we know as Oliver Cromwell — was declaring himself king. Ennie didn't go at that point, but she did flee to her cousin's side some years later. Don't you see, Pipes? All these letters refer to Ennie; the titles and names are all Ennie's. She survived. After the Restoration, Charles II might have sent men to try and stop her, he may even have ordered the sinking of her ship, but Ennie escaped. It also explains how the locket came to be in the field. The 'Eaffrey' letter is confirmation that Ennie and her maid, Anna, survived."

Perdita beamed in delight and Piper, who Perdita could see was analysing the scenario she was placing before her, gave a slow nod of agreement and acknowledgement as excitement flared in her eyes.

"Ennie must have been trying to escape from her house-arrest once she had completed her task as The Scribe," said Piper, "particularly as, by then, it was probably clear that Charles didn't intend for anyone involved in the mass rewriting of history to survive."

"This must also be why the letters stop in 1662; *The Arbella* was meant to join the Bristol Virginia fleet that year, but she never arrived because Charles II's soldiers had destroyed her, while Ennie had fled to safety abroad."

"And the jewellery?" asked Piper. "We know why the locket was hidden, but the rings? Why was one left behind while the other one vanished?"

Perdita thought for a moment, trying to unravel this last mystery.

"I wonder if Penelope's intention had been to hide them all in the box in the tunnel," she said, "but then things went awry. She may have hidden the first one days before in preparation, but perhaps she was wearing one and in the rush of escape, had no time to place it with its twin. She said herself in the letter she was upset to have lost the locket; perhaps once this had gone, she kept the ruby ring as a reminder. After her death, it was probably sold or lost or even stolen, which was how it finally found its way to Hannah White and her family."

"It's all likely," said Piper.

"The important thing is that we know what happened to Ennie," said Perdita. "She may have been forced into being The Scribe, but she escaped and she survived. I bet it was her who updated the genealogies in the casket, adding her own daughter and granddaughter before she hid the casket for the last time. When they arrived in Amsterdam, she sent word to her old friend, the writer and notorious spy, Aphra Behn, using her real name."

"Is that how history continued to change after Penelope's death?" asked Piper.

"Yes, I bet Aphra did it on her behalf because the last change in history was after the removal of James II from the throne. William and Mary became joint monarchs on 11 December 1688. The following year, Aphra Behn died, and the changes in history stopped."

CHAPTER THREE

Early the next morning, the sky was shot through with pink and gold, the gentle breeze was warm and the sea glimmered like a magical mirror. Slicing through the waves on the launch heading for the salvage boat, which was moored further out to sea, Perdita was suffused with memories of all that had happened in this bay. It was over a year ago that Warren had arrived to tell of her Mary's death and the life-changing news that followed when she learned about their vast inheritance.

The sweeping bay had been the point where Stephen Haberfield and the MI1 Elite operatives had delivered them safely home, after saving them from the horrifying team of snipers sent by Randolph Connors to murder them. The innocent looking waters of Dale had borne witness to some of the most dramatic moments of her recent life.

Today, she thought, *will deliver another climatic event.*

"It's a shame we couldn't dive with them," shouted Piper over the roar of the engine. "The water looks beautiful."

"When I asked Olaf, he said Tommy won't even let him dive," replied Kit. "It's all to do with their insurance — only the registered crew can use the equipment."

"I can't say I'm all that fussed," added Callum, and the others laughed.

The launch drew alongside the large salvage boat belonging to Tommy Kamill and his team of experts.

"Welcome aboard," called Olaf as they scrambled up the ladder to the deck. "The rig they're using to raise the figurehead has been winched into place, so, with luck, our lady will soon be on her way to the surface."

"Does she look intact?" asked Perdita.

Olaf responded by crossing his fingers, then added, "There are bacon and egg sandwiches in the galley. It'll be an hour or so before there's any movement."

With breakfast in hand, Perdita led the others to a quiet corner where she and Piper brought Kit and Callum up to date with their discoveries the previous evening.

"The weird story about the woman escaping across the fields was Ennie?" gasped Kit. "Perds, this is crazy. The secret has been hidden in Marquess House the entire time."

"It's because Penelope planned it that way," replied Perdita. "If the ship she was supposed to catch — this ship — was last listed as being part of a fleet bound for Virginia, then we know Ennie fled in 1662. She may have been forced into rewriting her family history and obliterating herself into the bargain, but she left behind someone who could continue to do her work for her and ensure that the necessary clues were left behind. In the meantime, she hid as much of the past in Marquess House as she could find: the codex, her mother's diaries and, most secret of all, the casket. She also wrote her book of legends as a map to the casket, then littered the walls of the house and chapel with more visual clues. I'm sure when I've finished reading her confession from the casket it'll confirm everything."

"She left a lot to chance," said Callum.

"Often, when you know the answers, you think the clues you're leaving are obvious. She probably felt she was being as open as she dared."

"You said she had a daughter?" asked Kit.

"Yes, Alice Seymour, who married into the Carey family — whether it was the Carey family descended from Mary Boleyn,

I haven't had time to confirm — and she had a daughter, Frances, who married her cousin."

"So the bloodlines from Catherine Howard's twins combined and became one," confirmed Piper.

Perdita thought about this for a moment. "You're right, Pipes, they did. I hadn't realised."

"What's the significance?" asked Callum.

"It means that the offspring, if there were any of Frances Williams, were the direct descendants of both Catherine Howard's children. They were living Tudor heirs with a direct bloodline back to Henry VIII."

"And what happened to Frances?" asked Kit.

"I don't know yet," admitted Perdita. "We only discovered her yesterday. I intend to trace her though."

A shout from Olaf — "It's showtime, kids!" — brought the conversation to a halt as they hurried over to crowd around the monitor. "Our girl's free!" whooped Olaf.

"She's beautiful," exclaimed Piper, leaning forward. "Look at the scrollwork. Maybe we should commission a replica of her, too, Olaf, to sit beside the golden cup once the museum is open. I'd love to have a go at sculpting a figurehead."

It was several more hours before the mermaid was secure and the order was given to winch the cradle up to the surface. The ancient figurehead finally rose through the waves.

"She's enormous," gasped Perdita. "There are even hints of paint left on her."

Dusk was falling by the time they finally made their way to The Dairy and the vast storage facility that would house the mermaid. The enormous double-doors were open at one end as the truck that had transported the figurehead edged slowly backwards, bleeping a warning with every turn of its wheels.

Perdita wondered whether this magnificent object would hold any secrets to add to their story.

When the tank containing the figurehead was finally in place, Olaf called them all forward. Perdita looked around at the assembled crowd. Excitement was coursing through the air as the inhabitants of Marquess House and the divers began popping open the champagne bottles supplied by Sarah Eve and her catering team. Foaming glasses were passed around and an air of elated chaos reigned. Perdita saw Alistair and Susan with Pamela, who waved to Perdita, hurrying away from the noise to take a call on her mobile phone.

Scanning the enthusiastic faces, Perdita searched for Piper, Kit and Callum, who she spotted speaking to Olaf near the tank where the mermaid now resided in water to keep her safe. Grabbing a glass, she was hurrying towards them when there was another explosion. But this was too loud, too metallic to be a champagne cork, and as she spun around to face the doors, Perdita realised there was something terribly wrong.

"Nobody move!" shouted a harsh voice into the silence brought about by the gunshot.

Perdita stared in disbelief as her senses tried to catch up with events. A line of people, all dressed in black, carrying gleaming assault rifles were walking towards them in a slow deliberate manner. They spread around the perimeter of the room, blocking the few exits, until the inhabitants of Marquess House were surrounded. Then the silence was broken as Piper screamed, "You!"

A slim, dark-haired woman turned and gave a cruel smile. "Hey, Piper," Kirstin Chaplin said, her tone falsely light. "How's hubby?"

A scream of such fury erupted from her sister that Perdita felt it must have ripped her throat apart. As she spun around to grab her, she saw Callum and Kit had reached Piper first and were holding her back.

"Ah yes, I forgot, you two know each other, don't you?" said a drawling voice as a well-dressed man walked between the line of guards.

Although they had never met, Perdita recognised him. Randolph Connors. The man who had been haunting her every move as he tried to steal her and Piper's inheritance for his twin granddaughters, Ruby and Pearl. He was short, smaller than her, and had a prominent hawk-like nose which dominated his features. His eyes were narrow, the pale brown of milky coffee, and his skin was sallow.

"Well, Perdita and Piper, we meet at last," he said. "The nasty usurpers who stole my inheritance, my titles and my birthright. Though you have proved useful. If everything Izabel has told us is true, it seems you've solved the mystery my dear Aunt Mary had begun to unscramble before your mother was murdered. Thank you for doing that — it will make the next conference with my government so much more interesting."

"Your government?" came Alistair's scornful voice from behind Perdita. "I think the government belongs to Her Majesty."

Connors gave Alistair a withering look. "Let's not play silly games, Alistair, not now you're finally cornered. Your little Izabel has been most useful in keeping us informed. There you were, Alistair, thinking because she was distantly related to you, there was no way she would betray your trust. It's a shame you didn't pay a bit more attention to what was really going on."

"What are you talking about?" snapped Alistair.

"Didn't you wonder why she tried to frame your beloved son?"

Beside her, Perdita felt Kit stiffen.

"You're insane, Randolph," snarled Alistair with a brave attempt at icy disdain.

"She wanted him to be forced out so they could leave together," smiled Randolph. "She was in love with him, you see, had been for years. I told her I would arrange it all and they would live happily ever after. I'm an old softie at heart. In the meantime, my son entertained her."

"What do you mean, 'was'?" asked Perdita. "What have you done to her?"

Randolph turned to her but did not reply.

"What have you done to her?" shouted Kit.

"Are you worried, Kit?" sneered Randolph. "She's still alive, but for how much longer, well, that'll depend on how our evening entertainment pans out."

To her horror, Perdita watched as Izabel was dragged into view, her hands tied behind her back, gagged and with a black eye.

"Xavier can be awfully careless with his toys," said Randolph. He nodded to the man holding Izabel and she was pulled away again. "Izabel was very useful, particularly after Inigo was sacked by MI1 Elite." He nodded to the man standing beside him, and Perdita shuddered when she encountered his glacial grey eyes. "But when he came to work for me, he brought such good intel, it was possibly a good thing he no longer had to pretend to be doing everything for Queen and country."

"How dare you?" Perdita spat. "You have the temerity to call us 'usurpers' when you're the one who is trying to steal our lawful inheritance. Since the sixteenth century, this house has been passed down through the female line of the family and, as you are a man — an apology for one, I admit — you would never have been given Mary's house."

"But it should have gone to my mother, Cecily —"

"Who is dead," snarled Piper, appearing at Perdita's side and taking her hand.

"Enough of this," snapped Connors. "Inigo, Kirstin, sort this mess out. They —" he pointed to Perdita and Piper — "are to come with me. Apprehend the others and only use violence if necessary."

Two men appeared, and Perdita felt a gun jab into her back. She turned to Piper who was white-faced, although her usual defiance was radiating from her green eyes. A cry of protest came from Kit, Callum and other familiar voices, but they were hustled away, and the last she saw of Kit was him being forced back towards his parents by a burly armed man.

Connors led the way to the outer office, and Perdita felt her heart thudding with panic. Pamela had gone in there to take a phone call and she had not returned. Although she appeared young for her age, Pamela was approaching eighty and Perdita was worried the shock of seeing them being marched in at gunpoint would be too much for her.

But when Connors flung open the door, the room was empty.

"Wait outside," he ordered the two gunmen. Seating himself at the small desk in the corner, he offered them chairs.

"I think you'll find you're in our house," Piper snapped.

"Not for much longer," he smiled. "Now, we can do this one of two ways, the simple way, in which no one gets hurt, or the difficult way, in which I kill a hostage every time you refuse to capitulate to my demands."

Perdita sank into the chair, her legs giving way. "What do you want, Connors?"

"Marquess House, obviously —" he began, but Piper interrupted.

"Why? You're worth billions of pounds. What on earth do you want this house for when you have palatial homes across the globe?"

"It isn't the house, Piper," he said, and Perdita saw her sister shudder at the use of her name. It seemed intrusive and strangely menacing. "It's your status."

The twins exchanged a confused look.

"What? Our titles?" asked Perdita. "Marquess of Pembrokeshire and Viscountess Cleddau?"

Connors gave them a blank stare, his face registering first confusion, then a gleeful comprehension. "You don't know, do you?" he said.

"That you want the house and money, yes, we know that…" began Perdita, but she stopped when Connors began to laugh.

"Mackensie never told you, did he?"

"Told us what?"

"Maybe *he* doesn't know," mused Connors. "Perhaps this is one secret even the great Alistair Mackensie hasn't discovered."

"What are you talking about?" shouted Piper.

"Have you ever wondered about the date of the Milford Haven Treaty?"

Once again, Perdita and Piper shared a look of confusion.

"Not really, no," admitted Perdita.

"1886," said Connors. "How wonderful. I can give you a history lesson, Perdita." He gave another of his smooth but terrifying smiles. "It was a year when Queen Victoria's reign was at a bit of a low point," he continued. "There was trouble in Ireland, Prince Albert had been dead for five years, and the queen was still in mourning. There was a hard winter, there was rioting, there were many changes of Prime Minister in one year. You get the general idea; the populace was uneasy, and the queen wasn't helping by remaining at Osborne House. Then a rumour began that there was another potential heir to the throne."

"What?" Perdita was startled.

"You see, there was a resurgence for the love of all things Tudor, which became known as 'the cult of Mary, Queen of Scots'. Papers had been discovered, apparently, claiming there was another royal line: one that had a direct bloodline to the Tudors. It was rubbished by the press, suggested to be a flight of fancy created by society ladies with more interest in romance than fact, but despite the best efforts of the government, the rumour wouldn't go away. In the end, the Prime Minister, Robert Gascoyne-Cecil, needed to act. Under the guise of protecting a historic house for posterity and for the protection of a wealthy heiress, who was descended, distantly, from the Scottish queen, the government presented our ancestor Lettice Lakeby with The Milford Haven Treaty.

"She thought it was terribly quaint and romantic. Her pompous fool of a husband was flattered with a life peerage, and they were the toast of London society. It's where the bulk of the money came from; Lettice was wealthy, but nothing compared with how rich she and William Lakeby became once the government had made them various grants and payments to ensure their capitulation. What the government didn't tell her was that, although they were unable to prove it, because the jewellery and the documentation had been lost, the rumour was that our ancestor had a stronger claim to the throne than Queen Victoria. Even better, there was no taint of German blood in Lettice's veins. When you discovered the first ruby ring, I was mildly interested, but then you discovered the location of the second and it felt like a challenge."

Perdita's heart was racing. A memory flashed across her

mind; a name which at the time had seemed insignificant, passed by unnoticed, now added a new chill to her fear.

"C. Fitzroy Antiques," she said. "Your mother's name. It was you, the other letter Hannah White received about the ring, the one that spooked her so much she ran away to hide in a cottage in Cornwall."

Randolph grinned.

"I wondered if you would work that out," he laughed. "Although, you beat me to it; you reached Hannah White first and persuaded her to sell you the second ruby ring. You probably saved her life."

Perdita and Piper exchanged a horrified glance.

"What do you mean?"

"My team was supposed to apprehend you and secure the ring, by whatever means," he replied. "Haberfield's SWAT team got to you first. They also placed a secure perimeter around Hannah White's cottage."

Perdita felt sick but she had to know.

"And Hannah?"

"I believe she's gone travelling with the money you gave her," he replied. "I'm not a monster, cousin dear; once I realised she no longer had the ring, I called my team off and have left her in peace ever since."

Out of the corner of her eye, Perdita saw Piper briefly cover her face with her hands in relief.

"However, it did leave me in a very difficult position, which made me angry," continued Connors and despite his smile, his eyes flamed with fury. "You now had two of the jewels and being in ownership of Marquess House, I knew if it was still out there, you would find the locket, too. Then, Izabel informed me that you'd done exactly this: the mythical gems that were supposed to be the keys to the secret were reunited and were in your possession. Time was running out, and I knew I would have to act."

"What are you saying?" asked Piper, her face screwed up in revulsion.

"I thought you were supposed to be quite bright, dear," Connors mocked. "You really haven't a clue, have you?"

"Tell us then," snapped Perdita.

"The document Inigo found in the archives is an Act of Parliament that was created by Charles II in 1660 when he was restored to the throne. It's called the Act of Exclusion and, back then, was probably considered a watertight way to secure the throne for future Stuart generations. It claimed that the heirs of the body of Catherine Howard and Henry VIII could only inherit the crown through the female line. I assume Charles did this because he thought no one would ever give precedence to a female heir over a male heir. This Act has gone through several versions including the Second Act of Exclusion in 1668, banning Catholics from the throne after the debacle of James II's reign, and again in 1701, when it was consolidated and became known as the Act of Settlement.

"While the wording has changed over the years concerning the finer points of religion, the section concerning the passing of the crown through the female side of our family line has never been altered and is still law. Obviously, when I discovered this, it was something of a problem for me, especially as my only child was a son. Luckily though, I have two granddaughters now and I can claim my rights through them."

"You're insane," said Piper.

"No, I'm not," he replied. "We are descended from Penelope Fitzalan. The daughter of William Fitzalan, who was the grandson of Catherine Howard and Henry VIII. Penelope had a daughter, Alice…"

"Who had a daughter, Frances," interrupted Perdita.

"Who had a daughter, Elizabeth," continued Connors in a sing-song voice. "Have a look for yourselves." He opened a slim attaché case. "Here's a brief family tree, my dear cousins. Your family tree only went back as far as Penelope. With Izabel's help, I've been able to instruct the completion of the remainder of our ancestry. It connects Arabella Talbot to Frances Frankland to Elizabeth Russell to Frances Williams. You can probably work the rest of it out yourselves."

Perdita looked at the beautifully drawn family tree.

"This is ludicrous," said Piper.

"Yes, it is," agreed Connors. "However, thanks to all the hard work done by you and your sister, it's also possible to prove that it's true. What I need you two to do is to give me all the documentation that proves this claim, which I believe you've found, Perdita, in the legendary casket."

Perdita stared at him. They had discovered the casket after Izabel's disappearance. How could he know about it? "What casket?" she said.

"Don't try and play games, Perdita. I had a man in the diving crew. How else do you think we knew about tonight? Your friend Olaf is a real gossip, especially after a few whiskies, and while he might not have known exactly what you'd found, he gave us enough information for my team to make an educated guess. We knew that you must have recovered the casket from somewhere within Marquess House."

Perdita and Piper stared at each other in horror.

"All of which means, we, as a family —" he gave them a smile, which Perdita felt sure he thought was charming but was the most terrifying thing she had ever seen — "can now claim

403

our rightful place in society. But first, you two must agree to waive your rights to claiming the throne in favour of Ruby and Pearl, who will of course need their loving grandfather to rule for them."

"You want to be king?" Perdita said, incredulity dripping from every word. "Even if any of this was true, we would never agree to waive our rights."

"I suspected you might prove to be stubborn." Connors waved to the guards, and one put his head around the door. "Fetch the first hostage," he said.

Perdita felt bile rise in her throat as pure terror coursed through her. Kit had been forced to kneel on the ground with his head bowed. Kirstin Chaplin stood behind him with a gun to his head. "NO!" Perdita screamed.

"You bastard!" shrieked Piper, lunging at Connors, but before she could reach him, one of the guards slapped her around the face with such force she cannoned into the wall.

"You hold his life in your next decision…" began Connors, but then he broke off, all the colour draining from his face, as a stern female voice said, "Randolph, enough."

Lady Pamela stood in the doorway, her face wreathed in disappointment. Perdita dragged her eyes from Kit to look at Connors. He appeared cadaverous in the bright, overhead light.

"You?" he croaked. "No, you're in my imagination. You're dead."

"Stop this at once, Randolph," Pamela said, as though she were scolding a small boy.

"You drowned," Connors whispered. "You fell off the boat and you died. Daddy never found your body."

Unnerved by his strange turn of events, Perdita and Piper looked from Connors to Pamela.

"No, I didn't," Pamela snapped. "Your father was a bully who was trying to steal my inheritance. With the help of some friends, I faked my own death and bought myself a new identity and a new life. Cecily Connors did die that day, but Lady Pamela Johnson was born. It's surprising what money and the right connections can do. I watched over you from afar, but when it seemed clear you were your father in miniature, I stepped away. No one will die here tonight. Call your people off and send them away. Then we will discuss things as rational adults."

"You left me, you bitch," Connors snarled. "I was a child and you abandoned me. What makes you think anything you say now matters to me? In fact, just to show you how irrelevant I find you, the first murder can be on your conscience!"

With a swift upward movement, Connors issued an order and before Perdita had realised what was happening, she heard the violent crackle of a gunshot and a thud as a body hit the ground. With a scream of rage and fear, she fought her way past Connors, not caring that the two guards had guns, her only intention to get to Kit.

As she crashed out of the office, the room around her exploded into shouts, gunfire and a blaze of brilliant arc lights. At any moment she expected to feel the white-hot pain of a bullet, but none of it mattered. All she knew was that if she could get to Kit, he would be all right. People were being forced onto the ground and there he was, in front of her, motionless, his hands tied behind his back, his face against the concrete floor.

"Kit!" she screamed, throwing herself onto the ground beside him, dragging him into her arms, tears streaming down her face. "Kit, no," she moaned. "No, please, no."

She was incoherent with grief, staring down at his pale face, then through her panic she realised he was breathing. There was no blood. He was unconscious but he was alive.

Looking up in incomprehension, Perdita saw Kirstin Chaplin sprawled on the floor behind them, blood pouring from a wound in the back of her head. Then, the biggest shock of all, the tall man who was crouching over the body turned to look at her and Perdita nearly dropped Kit on the floor.

"Warren?" she gasped.

"You all right, Perds?" he asked.

"Yes, is she…" she hesitated over the word, "dead?"

"It was her or Kit. I thought you'd prefer me to aim at her," Warren replied. Perdita shuddered. "Don't feel sorry for her, Perds," said Warren. "She murdered Jeremy Davidson, and we're fairly certain she killed Mary too."

Tears sprang to Perdita's eyes, and Warren's expression softened.

"I'm sorry," he said. "Is he OK?" He nodded towards Kit.

"I think so," Perdita replied.

Warren stood for a moment, gazing down at them both. "I owed you a good turn, Perds, after all I put you through."

Kit stirred and Perdita whispered his name, pulling him into a tighter embrace. She did not see the look of sadness flit over Warren's face.

"Thank you for saving his life," she said, returning her gaze to Warren.

To her surprise, Warren saluted, as the other MI1 Elite operatives had done before, his stance becoming military and professional. "Just doing my duty. I'll send one of the medical teams over."

The next hour passed in a blur. Perdita remained on the floor, clutching Kit, who slowly regained consciousness. Piper and Callum joined them, the four of them huddled together, until Kit was stretchered away by a medical team to be kept in hospital for observation.

"I think she hit me over the head with the rifle butt," he murmured when Perdita finally let him go. "I'm OK, Perds, really."

When Perdita had tried to climb into the ambulance with him, Stephen Haberfield had emerged from the darkness and gently stopped her. "I'm sorry, ma'am," he said. "I need you to remain here where you're protected by The Milford Haven Treaty."

Susan climbed in beside her son. "I'll take care of him," she assured Perdita. "You're needed here. Everyone will want to see you."

Perdita had looked around at the chaos of the room, the number of people wrapped in foil blankets, others wide-eyed and white-faced with shock and, with great reluctance, she nodded her understanding to Susan.

Alistair and Piper were with Stephen Haberfield, waiting for her.

"I believe Connors revealed the contents of the Act of Exclusion," said Haberfield with no preamble.

"Yes, he seemed to think he was the rightful heir to the throne," Perdita replied. "He's obviously incorrect."

There was an awkward silence.

"Not completely," said Haberfield. "When the Act of Exclusion was first discovered during the Victorian era, the government did their best to neutralise any potential civil wars by suggesting to your ancestor, Lettice Lakeby, that it was a charming story and the treaty was merely a precaution. With no documentary evidence to prove this potential claim, there was no danger. The Queen's Men was formed to monitor the new academics and their discoveries; MI1 Elite is the modern-day equivalent. We have suppressed any documents that could suggest there might be an alternative royal family. Our job is to protect national security. Your family, even without knowing the truth, has always been a threat to that security."

Perdita stared at him. "We have all three pieces of jewellery," she said defiantly. "We've found the evidence to prove the real story."

"Do you think anyone would believe you?" Haberfield said. "We have powers to not only rubbish your hard-earned academic reputation, but also to arrest you for terrorism if you were to publish your findings."

"I think," said Alistair, stepping forward, "this is a discussion for another time. Perdita and Piper have now been apprised of the situation by Randolph Connors. Nothing will happen this evening. Perhaps tomorrow we could arrange a meeting with you, Haberfield, and hash out the details?"

Haberfield turned to Perdita and Piper, who nodded. He turned to leave.

"Wait," said Perdita. "How did you know to save us again?"

"Alistair had put us on alert," Haberfield replied. "The raising of the ship brought a number of unknown personnel within the vicinity of Marquess House and as an extra precaution, he quite rightly felt there should be additional security. We thought it would be prudent to have a discreet team nearby. An hour ago, we received news of a codeword which hasn't been used for over 40 years and we knew we would have to move quickly."

"A codeword?" asked Piper.

"Yes. It was first used by Cecily Connors before her 'death'. She knew her husband was selling arms to the Russians during the Cold War, and she wanted a way out of her marriage. We agreed to help in return for as much information as possible, and we gave her a codeword to use if she needed immediate assistance. This evening, she phoned the old number in London, and gave the word. We scrambled a task force immediately."

Perdita stared at him in shocked silence.

"Until tomorrow then, ma'am," he said, and saluted.

As he walked away, she called after him, "Mr Haberfield, what was the word?"

"Mermaid."

CHAPTER FOUR

The next morning, Perdita woke up to find Stephen Haberfield had insisted on posting armed guards around the perimeter of their land. It was still early when Alistair, Perdita and Piper met the head of MI1 Elite to discuss events.

"I suggest a revised update of The Milford Haven Treaty," Haberfield began when they were all assembled in the boardroom. "You are now aware of the Act of Exclusion and you are in possession of the means to prove your claim. However, should you choose to act upon the information you have discovered, we, Her Majesty's Government, will charge you under the Counter-Terrorism and Border Security Act of 2019…"

Alistair let out a bark of anger at his words, but Haberfield ignored him.

"I'm reading you the official line," he insisted. "It's a legal requirement. Then we can hash out what needs to happen in reality."

"What do you mean?" Perdita asked.

"There has to be official documentation in place," Haberfield explained. "More or less everything Connors said to you is true because his words came to him from my predecessor, Inigo Westbury. If it became common knowledge that Charles II had deliberately fabricated evidence in order to ensure his position on the throne and that the government has colluded with this command, we could watch 400 years of history unravel before our eyes."

"Would it matter?" Piper asked. "History changes all the time."

"On an academic level, no. But on a National Security level, yes, it would be a disaster."

"How though?" Perdita said.

"To suggest collusion and subterfuge by a government on such a scale would undermine our integrity in the eyes of the world. The pound would go into freefall causing huge financial, economic and social damage. Every crackpot and loon out there — and there are some dangerous people being monitored around the world — would try to avail themselves of this information in order to use it as a bargaining tool and, without wishing to sound overdramatic, this could be enough to light the touch paper on another World War. Plus, if word leaked out that you had this information, you would never be safe. We are trying to protect you as well as the country."

"So you want us to suppress the discovery?" Piper clarified.

"Unfortunately, yes," Haberfield responded.

"Why though? Why do you want to protect us?" Perdita asked Haberfield. "Wouldn't it be easier for you if we were eliminated?"

Haberfield looked horrified. "Your family is an important asset to this realm."

"In what way?"

"You must have heard the awful expression, 'the heir and the spare'?" he said. "It does no harm at all for us to know we have a very capable 'spare' waiting in the wings. When you're not being a threat to National Security, you and your sister are our greatest asset. Look back at what you've discovered, and you'll see there's always a spare royal family somewhere in the background. It happened with the Tudors when they took the throne from the Plantagenets, it happened with the Stuarts taking the line from the Tudors and then later, the Hanoverians took the line from the Stuarts. The government of the day always has an alternative version of royalty secreted somewhere in the shadows."

"And Izabel?" Perdita asked. "What have you done with her?"

"She's been very foolish," he replied. "An accessory to murder, theft, terrorism charges but, if we're able to do a deal and minimise her sentence, then we shall. Wiser people than Ms Barnes have been brainwashed in the way Connors and his son targeted her."

Over the next few hours, they discussed and argued the terms, finally agreeing on a new protective treaty, as well as the release of certain documents into the public domain with the agreement that all others would remain embargoed for another ten years when a review would be held. Depending on the result of this review, one would be held every subsequent ten years, to assess the political climate and the effect a release of some or all of the information would have on the world.

Later, Perdita and Piper sought out Lady Pamela, partly to check she was all right, but also because they were intrigued. When they knocked on the door to her suite, she opened it with trepidation and before they were even over the threshold, she begged their forgiveness.

"What for?" Perdita asked, taking her hands.

"For lying to you. When I married Albert Connors, it was for love, but I soon realised he was not the man I'd first thought. His money had been made by nefarious means of the worst kind: slavery, blood diamonds, gun running. When I discovered the truth, I was horrified. I tried to leave him on several occasions, but he made it impossible, threatening me, threatening Randolph, who was only a child, working out a way with his crooked lawyers to steal my inheritance.

"Eventually, through a man I met at one of the many parties Albert and I attended, I was able to arrange a way out. This man worked for the government, and it was through them I was able to stage my disappearance and create my new identity. It was dreadful watching Mary and my father on the news as they paid for search after search looking for my body, but part of my agreement was to hide even from them. It was heartbreaking.

"Strangely though, Mary found me. It was completely by accident. I was staying with a new friend in Cornwall for a few days. I walked out of a shop and bumped into my sister. She was there taking part on a dig. Despite the change in my appearance, she recognised me immediately. It was a relief because by then I was short of money and found it difficult to find work. We discussed the problem at length, and Mary came up with a scheme to be able to give me access to my inheritance — in my will, I had left it to her, not Randolph — by suggesting she 'buy' old documents from me. The letters that you have so wonderfully named *The Lady Pamela Collection* were never in my house in Norfolk, they were in the Marquess House archive. Mary gave them to me, then 'bought' them back.

"We did this many times, enabling me to buy the estate in Norfolk. She even helped to create the imaginary brother who had supposedly left me in such financial straits, forcing me to sell family documents. Alistair was the only one who ever became suspicious and, eventually, Mary told him the truth."

Perdita laughed. "Very little gets past Alistair Mackensie," she said. "And it explains why the letters compiled all those years ago by Penelope seemed to have wandered to the wrong house, only to miraculously find their way home."

Despite Pamela's fears that the twins would want to reveal the truth, they assured her the secret would remain, although they asked if she would mind if they referred to her as Aunt Pamela.

"Oh, my dears, that would be wonderful," Pamela enthused.

EPILOGUE

The ivory satin whispered against Perdita's skin as Piper helped her into her wedding dress. Her dark hair was piled on top of her head, and her dramatic eyes seemed wider and more ethereal than ever thanks to the subtle make-up. Stepping into the elegant matching shoes, she turned around to see her reflection in the full-length mirror.

"Oh my goodness," she gasped. "Are you sure it's me?"

Staring at the shimmering woman in the glass, she found it hard to believe all that had happened in the past two years and how here she was, about to follow in the footsteps of her mother and grandmother and walk up the aisle of the Marquess House chapel to marry Kit.

His proposal had come as a surprise while he lay in his hospital bed. "When I thought I was going to die, you were all I could think about," he had said. "I know this is fast but, Perdita, will you marry me?"

She had accepted without needing to think. The moment she had heard the gunshot, she had felt as though her heart had been ripped from her chest and that she could not bear to live if she were parted from Kit. Even now, as she stared at her reflection, she wondered when she had fallen so deeply in love with him, when her feelings had turned from friendship to love.

"Are you all right, Perds?"

Piper's voice brought her back from her reverie.

"Yes," Perdita said. "I was thinking about how our lives have changed since Granny died. It's a shame none of the rest of our family are here to spend this day with us."

"I know, it's been on my mind too." They smiled at each other's reflections. "Are you ready?" asked Piper.

"Yes," Perdita replied.

"And you're sure? We could always do a runner if you've changed your mind. I have excellent contacts in the Secret Service — no one would ever find us," Piper said with a grin.

"I'm sure."

"Let's do this then."

Perdita slipped her arm through Piper's, and together they walked to the top of the stairs that were lined with all the members of the Marquess House staff. Cheers accompanied their slow descent and their walk through the Tudor Hall and along the path to the chapel.

Through the open door, Perdita could see Kit waiting at the altar.

Several hours later, Perdita, still in her bridal gown, with Piper in her shimmering green bridesmaid dress, and Kit and Callum in their suits, ran back down the aisle of the chapel, heading for the hidden mermaid and the entrance to the tunnel.

Perdita pushed the brick that activated the secret door, causing Piper and Callum to grin in delight before they descended the stairs. The sun was setting as they emerged onto the island and headed for the beach. It was a cool evening, and the clear sky was streaked with magical brushstrokes of gold, purple and pink.

Perdita popped the cork from the bottle of champagne, while Piper, laughing, held up a glass to collect the gush of golden fizz. The water of Llyn Cel rippled softly in the spring breeze, lapping on the cool sand where Kit had thrown the blanket.

Perdita raised her glass towards the fiery glow in the sky. "To survival," she said, the red sky lighting up the pale liquid.

"To survival," the others echoed, tapping glasses.

"What will you do now, Perds?" asked Kit. "After our honeymoon, obviously."

Perdita looked down at the elegant golden band on her finger and felt a thrill of happiness at the matching ring on Kit's hand. "Keep going," she replied. "Historical research is my job; I may have finished with this story, but there is so much more out there waiting to be discovered."

"And Marquess House?" he asked.

"This is our home."

"It's a shame you can't publish the story, though," said Piper, moving closer to Callum, who slipped his arm around her shoulder.

"Not in the traditional way," said Perdita, "but discoveries don't always have to be entombed in the pages of academia."

"What do you mean?" asked Kit.

"There are plenty of other options available," Perdita replied. "Blogs, unexpected discoveries published in small journals, fiction. It's a big world, and Haberfield can't have it all his own way…" Her voice trailed off as she stared out to the lake where the rays were setting fire to the choppy waves.

A sudden gust of wind caused white horses to ripple across the surface, drawing their attention to the water. It happened in an instant. A figure emerged, black against the intensity of the gathering gloom, her arm raised as though in a salutation, before there was a splash and, with a shimmer of green, the image disappeared beneath the waves.

All four were on their feet, staring at the spot where she had vanished at the darkening centre of the lake.

"The Llyn Cel mermaid," said Perdita.

"But how…?" began Kit.

"Magic," responded Piper.

"And we all saw it?" confirmed Callum.

"What do you think it means?" asked Piper.

Perdita raised her glass, her smile lighting up her beautiful face and her unusual storm-coloured eyes. "*Spe et nereidum*," she said, taking Kit's hand, her eyes fixed on the water. "It means," she turned to face the others, "that no matter what happens, whatever life throws at us, we will always have each other, and, even when things seem impossible and terrifying, there will always be hope and mermaids."

A NOTE TO THE READER

Dear Reader,

Thank you for taking the time to read *The Arbella Stuart Conspiracy*. I hope you enjoyed joining Perdita as she revealed the final historical mysteries hidden within Marquess House and learned the truth about her and Piper's inheritance.

This is fiction but, once again, I have tried to use verifiable historical fact. During the planning stages of the trilogy, I always knew Oliver Cromwell would be the lost prince, especially when I discovered that as Lord Protector he had been through what amounted to a coronation. However, to use Cromwell as a main character would have broken with my intention to tell the story from the point of view of the women who were involved. Equally, it would also have broken with the structure if I had used the fictional Penelope Fitzalan as a main protagonist. I needed a real historical character to drive the action and when I began to look for potential candidates, Arbella Stuart came into view. By giving her real story a slight twist, she proved to be the perfect candidate.

Outside of historical circles, Arbella is relatively unknown. As explained in the book, Arbella was the granddaughter of Lady Margaret Douglas and it was through her that she inherited her claim to the English throne. Arbella's royal blood meant she was the link between the Tudors and the Stuarts, not only in my books, but in history, too.

Educated to be queen, she spent a life being thwarted and frustrated. Queen Elizabeth I used her a bargaining tool in many foreign treaties and Arbella's other grandmother, Bess of Hardwick, through fear of what might happen to her granddaughter, kept her a virtual prisoner in Hardwick Hall. A vibrant, intelligent woman with a mind of her own, Arbella fought back against these restrictions.

One of the most interesting discoveries was the network of people dedicated to helping her. She had a loyal entourage who risked their own liberty and lives for her on numerous occasions, yet, once again, she is usually presented as a rather sad and isolated figure. To redress the balance, I have included a number of real figures from Arbella's life: Bridget Sherland, Anne Bradshaw, Lady Anne Fitton, Margaret Byron, Lady Frances Kirton, William Markham and John Good.

The Bye and Main Plots were real and the characters I have used were the protagonists as listed in the primary sources. The strange thing is that the men who later went on to perpetrate the more famous Gunpowder Plot also had links to these two early plots, yet these connections are rarely discussed.

Throughout the book, Arbella refers to genealogies and the twisted connections of the families. Her comments are all based on real family trees. From the link between Lady Katherine Newton née Paston, who appeared in *The Elizabeth Tudor Conspiracy*, and her cousin, Gertrude Paston, there were ties to all the plotters in the Bye, Main and Gunpowder plots. These are names that have since faded from prominence, but in 1603 they were important people with a determined interest in the succession.

Arbella Stuart was never accused of being involved in either the Bye or the Main plot, even though the intention was to place her on throne. Until 1990, there were few remaining details about the trials as the court transcripts were sketchy, and there was no way to suggest Arbella even knew about the plot until its discovery. However, that year, a copy of the transcript taken during the interrogations in the Tower of

London of Rev Sir George Brooke came to light and in this, Arbella was incriminated as being at the heart of the plot (more details are online: Mark Nicholls' essay based on the 1990 document about The Bye and Main Plots. Also, in Sarah Gristwood, *Arbella, England's Lost Queen* (London, 2003), pg. 276). This document makes it clear she was writing and receiving letters from the main protagonists. Robert Cecil must have known this, yet Arbella was never arrested, questioned or charged. An anomaly in itself, and not one I can fathom, particularly when compared with the treatment of other women who were involved in or used as figureheads for treasonous plots.

Sources claim Arbella was a poet, but none of her work remains. However, this link to the creative side of the court allowed me to explore the burgeoning female writers of the age. Emilia Lanier was a real writer, and it has been suggested that she was the Dark Lady of William Shakespeare's sonnets. Edmund Shakespeare was the younger brother of Will. Whether Edmund was friends with Arbella or not, I have no idea, but I liked to think they could have been. All the dedications in the books to Arbella are real, as are the mentions of popular ballads.

The fact that all Arbella's letters from before 1603, the ascension of James I to the English throne, have been lost seems peculiar as she was a prolific letter writer. However, for me, it was ideal and I used this to suggest she had been married to my fictional character William Fitzalan, 2nd duke of Hereford and given birth to his heirs. Hence the reason it was all destroyed in order to hide the secret. The coup that cost the fictional William his life was based on the misguided attack on the palace by Robert Devereux, earl of Essex, the son of Lettice Knollys. It took place in 1601, and the most intriguing detail about this misadventure were the names of some of Devereux's companions: Robert Catesby, Francis Tresham, John Wright, Christopher Wright and John Grant — all men who went on to organise the Gunpowder Plot in 1605. Through marriages and extended families, these men all had links to Arbella and to the Bye and Main Plots.

Arbella is recorded as having eloped with William Seymour, Marquess of Hertford, 2nd duke of Somerset on 22 June 1610. Their dual blood-links to the throne resulted in their arrest and their imprisonment in the Tower of London. Arbella disguised herself as a page during her attempt to escape but she was captured. I have used as many real details as possible. Seymour did escape and remained abroad until after Arbella's tragic death in 1615. There are no records stating how she died, but there are rumours that she was poisoned. In Sarah Gristwood's biography of Arbella, she states there was a second escape attempt but one which was so secret no details remain. I have used this snippet to create Arbella's final desperate attempt to flee. The illness, porphyria, divides opinion. Some historians claim it was passed through the Stuart line from Margaret Tudor, others state the illness does not exist within the royal family. It has been suggested that Mary, Queen of Scots, James I, his son Prince Henry, Arbella and George III all suffered from this condition. We will never know the answer but as Arbella is widely considered to have lived with this illness, I felt it should be included.

The Lennox Jewel is a spectacular gem and was the inspiration for Arbella's sad ending. There is an excellent description in Alison Weir, *The Lost Tudor Princess, A Life of Margaret Douglas, Countess of Lennox* (London, 2015) pg. 238-242.

James I has become renowned for his obsession with witches

and witchcraft. He passed the Witchcraft Act in 1604 and was the instigator of the Berwick Witch Trials in 1590. Coupled with the strange interior of the Lennox Jewel, this seemed a predictable way in which James might dispose of a troublesome woman. The Denys and Murfyn connections are real. As is the unfortunate Thomas Benet, who was executed as a Protestant martyr in January 1531/2 outside the eastern city walls of Exeter. His burning at the stake was supervised by Sir Thomas Denys. The surname Benet tied in with one of Catherine Howard's ladies-in-waiting, Margaret Benet, who was said to be one of the women who gave evidence against the young queen consort. Whether these two Benets were related, I was not able to discover, but the coincidence was too great not to spin it into the story.

The ship, *The Arbella*, was a real vessel, as are the other ships mentioned. This information came to me during an impromptu visit to The Milford Haven Museum. Thank you to the unknown woman who handed an archive of Tudor shipping to museum staff approximately ten minutes after I had finished discussing my research with them. Thank you also to John Goldspink, who sent me scans of this amazing information and to all the staff at The Milford Haven Museum.

Using Oliver Cromwell as the missing Tudor was a risk. Many people consider him to be the saviour of the nation, others that he is devil incarnate. I have no strong opinions, but he was a figure who fitted the story I had created. My apologies if this causes any offence. It is fiction and any mistakes are mine. However, there were so many unexpected coincidences and parallels with my version of the story and the real events, it did become quite odd. Most of these anomalies have been woven through the narrative, but here are a few of the more interesting points.

Cromwell was brought up in Ely, Cambridgeshire by members of the Steward family who had distant links to the Stuart family. His uncle was the Oliver Cromwell who lived in Hinchingbrooke House and they were descended from Katherine Cromwell, the sister of Thomas Cromwell. The discussion about the family name being Williams is factually correct, as is the comment the real Cromwell made about going to America. In reality, he stayed, but it did surprise me when I found a Williams listed on one of the Puritan ships during the correct time period. The many mentions of Milford Haven in *Cymbeline* and throughout Oliver Cromwell's history are all accurate.

Thank you to everyone who has helped me create this trilogy, particularly Amy, Caoimhe, Richard and Natalie at Sapere Books and Sara Keane, my agent. It has been a huge and thoroughly enjoyable task. Once again, any mistakes throughout the text are mine. Please forgive me.

Arbella Stuart was a fascinating woman to research. For more information on her, I recommend Sarah Gristwood, *Arbella, England's Lost Queen* (London, 2003), also Ruth Norrington, *In the Shadow of the Throne, The Lady Arbella Stuart* (London, 2020) and Leanda de Lisle, *After Elizabeth* (London, 2004). She is another female figure who is a series of contradictions and, in these anomalies, I think lies the true Arbella. If you have enjoyed the novel and would like to leave a review on Amazon or Goodreads, I would be so grateful as reviews are very important to authors. I love hearing from readers, so if you would like to contact me, you can through Twitter. You can also follow my blog on my website.

Thanks again for reading *The Arbella Stuart Conspiracy*.

Alexandra Walsh

www.alexandrawalsh.com

Sapere Books is an exciting new publisher of brilliant fiction and popular history.

To find out more about our latest releases and our monthly bargain books visit our website:
saperebooks.com

Printed in Great Britain
by Amazon